THE FOUNDER OF THE HOUSE

THE FOUNDER OF
THE HOUSE

(First of the Gollantz Saga)

Naomi Jacob

PIATKUS
EDITIONS

DISCARDED

First published by Hutchinson & Co (Publishers) Ltd 1930

This new hardback edition published in Great Britain in
1983 by Judy Piatkus (Publishers) Limited of Loughton, Essex

ISBN 0 86188 271 7

Printed in Great Britain
by Mackays of Chatham Ltd

To
WINNIE AND HERBERT CORIN
with my love
MICKIE

Sirmione 1934
Merano 1935

BOOK ONE

1

I

FERNANDO MELDOLA shivered and drew his fur cloak more closely round his massive shoulders. He had lived in Paris for twenty years, and each year it seemed to him that he regretted the suns of his own country more acutely. He walked to the window, and drew back the heavy, gold brocade curtains, so that he could view the street more easily. Once more he shivered, for the outlook was grey and unfriendly. Worse, it was dull! The French might make great protestations of gaiety, but to Fernando they remained fundamentally serious, lacking that ability to smile at life which he had come to regard as the peculiar prerogative of his own countrymen.

He shrugged his shoulders under their covering of warm fur and turned impatiently from the window.

'Bah!' he ejaculated, addressing himself to no one in particular, for the room was empty, and his only possible listeners were two marble statues of Venus and Apollo, and a figure of the Madonna which stood under a carved golden canopy. 'Bah! These people! Always they must be fighting, breaking down and building up again. Perhaps I have lived in France too long, seen too many changes. It might be better if I left here and went back to Milan. There, at least, men can bargain without becoming hucksters and losing their tempers over the discussion.'

He moved to the figure of the Madonna, and touched the gold embroidery of her robe with an appreciative forefinger. 'You, they will never buy!' he chuckled. 'You would cost too much. They are amused because Meldola, the Jew, should like to have

7

you in his private room. They think because I am a Jew that I cannot be an artist. That is so like them.' Speaking in an assumed voice, he mocked one of his clients. 'But, Meldola, why should you—a Jew—value this statue so much? It can mean nothing to you!'

'*Per Bacco!* Can beauty mean nothing to me? Can the mellow loveliness of age say nothing to a Jew? Can form, colour, dignity find no place in his heart? No, no, my beautiful! You are not for them. For them I will find white marble statues, monuments of nakedness. The men will buy all the goddesses, and the women will get their lovers to buy the gods. He laid his hand almost affectionately on the outstretched foot of the figure. 'There is one word which the Catholics apply to you which will prevent any Frenchman taking a real interest in your loveliness. He would never be able to forget that you were—Immaculate.'

The door, over which hung a heavy curtain matching those at the window, opened slowly, and a girl of nineteen entered, carrying a little china tray upon which stood a tiny coffee-pot and a small cup and saucer. Meldola turned to greet her, smiling. He flung off his cloak, and sat down in a great arm-chair which stood close to a fine porcelain stove of the German type.

'My coffee!' he exclaimed. 'Miriam, it has arrived in the nick of time. In another moment I should have died of cold—and boredom.'

The girl looked at him, grave and sympathetic. 'Ah, this is one of your bad days, Uncle! This is one of the days when you forget how cold Italy can be, and only remember the blue skies. Exiles are often like that, I think. Their own country is always perfect—at a distance.'

Meldola nodded. 'It may be that you're right. Perhaps that is why Frenchmen have mistresses, so that they may love their wives —at a distance, eh? Yes, pour it out for me, Miriam. I like to have a pretty woman to pour out coffee for me. It enhances the flavour.' He laughed. 'You are rapidly becoming a very pretty woman, you know. Soon I shall have these corseted jackanapes clicking their heels and begging that they may pay their addresses to you. My answer will surprise them!'

'Mine might surprise them too!'

'I don't doubt it. Remember that you have two things, Miriam my dear, which few families can quarter on their coats of arms. Not that anyone has a coat of arms in these days. They are all busy forgetting them—they are all good citizens! *Per Bacco!*

Citizen This, Citizen That! How utterly silly it all is. You have an unbroken descent from the real aristocrats of the world, an aristocracy which is not national but international. More, you come of a family which is noted—I use that word advisedly—as having kept its integrity, its honesty unblemished not for two, three, four generations, but for centuries and centuries. And'—his gesture was wide, eloquent, and beautiful—'to what has it brought us. Look! Is there another room like this in Paris? Where else will you find such carpets, such furniture, such china as this from which I am drinking? We—you and I—what is left of the House of Meldola—are jewels, set in a unique setting.'

His words were boastful, but they were delivered with such conviction that they were robbed of pretence. Fernando Meldola, the dealer in antiques, in precious stones, in carpets, laces, ivories, old silver and gold, pictures and statuary, could make good all that he claimed. He was known to be honest, and the fact that this knowledge was public property was his chief pride.

He had lived in Paris for twenty years, and had watched changes, seen kings come and go, heard terrible things, listened to stories which made his warm blood run suddenly cold. He had been interrogated, pestered with questions, begged to declare himself as on this side or that, but he had remained aloof and untouched.

'I am neither Aristocrat nor Republican!' he declared. 'I have no political opinions. I have many acquaintances, and no intimate friends. I neither seek nor avoid confidences, but'—and his beautiful mouth would curve into a very kindly smile—'when confidences are bestowed upon me they remain confidences. I buy and sell, I give good prices and I expect prices, when I sell, to be a little better than when I buy. I name my price, and so it remains. To my friends, when they honour me by purchasing from me, I perhaps offer a little additional present; but when I do—that is my business, and when I do not—that is my business, too.'

His house was a store of wonderful things, for he felt no interest in anything which did not conform to his ideas of beauty or perfection. In his house nothing which was cheap, ordinary, or of the taste of the moment was to be found. He lived with dignity, eating well, drinking with taste, and spending his days in an atmosphere of luxury.

Two years before the afternoon when he sat sipping his coffee, with his lovely niece, Miriam Lousada, opposite to him, he had

decided that his life was lonely; and in the June of 1794 he had
sent to his brother-in-law, Lorenzo Lousada, to beg that Miriam
might join him in Paris. Lorenzo had died of fever six months
after his daughter came to Paris, and Fernando had formally
adopted her and declared that he intended to make her his heir-
ess. She conformed to all that he believed necessary in women—
she was beautiful, intelligent, possessed social charm, and was
able to manage his large staff of servants without permitting
those hitches and vibrations in the domestic machinery which are
so distressing to men who love comfort and perfect attention.

Fernando's generosity towards Miriam Lousada was unbounded, and it was his delight to give her jewels, old lace, and
perfect clothes in profusion. He possessed that content in giving
which is so typical of the Jew.

They sat talking, while Meldola sipped his coffee, watching
Miriam with dark, wide eyes full of affection. How well she understood him. How admirably she pandered a little to his weak-
nesses, and how gently she led his mind back from the melancholy
paths down which it wandered, to brighter and happier roads.

She, in her turn, loved her handsome uncle whole-heartedly.
She loved his fine figure, his magnificent head with its dark, close
curls, his beard and moustache which always smelt faintly of
some rare scent. She admired his clothes, which were always a
little more elaborate than fashion dictated, his rings, his seals,
and his gold-topped canes. Watching him now, she sighed in-
voluntarily.

Meldola set down his coffee-cup and looked at her, his eyebrows a little raised.

'Why?' he asked. 'What is it? You want something? A new
dress?'

She shook her head, so that the long ringlets swung against
her cheeks.

'No, indeed. I sighed because I was so happy.'

'Living alone with an old man!'

It was one of his small affectations to pretend to regard himself as old. She knew that if she disregarded the statement he
would enlarge upon it, and almost convince himself that he was
drawing near to the grave.

'Old!' She laughed softly. 'Old, you? The most handsome man
in Paris. What are you? Forty-two, and you look twenty-five.
People think that you are my brother!'

He pursed his lips, and began to protest that he felt very old, when the sound of a bell ringing in the distance made him sit upright, his eyes suddenly very bright.

'Listen! Is that Cambouchier returned for the picture? No, no, don't go ; you like him and, if I am not mistaken, he likes you.'

'I like him?' Miriam shrugged her shoulders. 'Sufficiently, nothing more. He is like all the officers of Bonaparte's new army, polished on the top, but underneath—oh, a *contadino*!'

A manservant in a plain but dignified livery entered ; he carried a letter on a silver salver.

'The gentleman waits below, monsieur.'

Meldola tore open the envelope, and a moment later sprang to his feet.

'This is marvellous!' he cried. 'Here is a letter from my oldest friend, and his father was the oldest friend of my father! It is from Nathaniel Gollantz of Rotterdam. He sends to me his son, Abraham. Oh where is he? François, go quickly and bring the gentleman here. No, no, I will go myself.'

The servant turned and was passing out of the door when Meldola pushed him aside and ran down the wide stairs, calling his greetings as he ran. Miriam rose, carried the little coffee-tray to a side-table, then turned to a great mirror which hung in a heavy, carved golden frame, to arrange the curls on either side of her face.

Her uncle entered, holding a young man by the hand.

'Miriam, here is the son of my dearest friend, Abraham Gollantz. My dear boy, this is my niece, Miriam Lousada—I say my niece, but in reality she is my daughter, if love counts for anything. Miriam, call for coffee and wine—or will you have brandy?'

Young Gollantz considered for a moment, then said: 'Perhaps—coffee and brandy, if you will be so kind.'

He was a tall young man, with fine dark eyes set a trifle too closely. His skin was clear and pale, his mouth a little too full and self-indulgent. His jaw and chin were firm and well cut, denoting firmness which might on occasion degenerate into obstinacy. His clothes were simple, well made, and elegant. His hands, long, slim, and well kept. Meldola decided that he was distinctly personable.

'Now, tell me. Your father—how is he?'

'When I left him he was tolerably well,' the young man replied. 'I admit, Fernando Meldola, I had expected to find you older.

Surely you are much younger than my father. He was fifty last birthday.'

Meldola's opinion of the young man mounted. Nothing pleased him more than to be complimented upon his youthful appearance. 'Your father is eight years my senior. I was always a little old for my years, and he young for his. But tell me more about him. He prospers?'

Abraham nodded. 'Yes, he prospers—moderately. He wished that I should enter his business, but'—he wrinkled his fine nose—'hides and skins do not appeal to me. Art, furniture, pictures—do. So I persuaded him to let me come to you and beg that you would, if possible, find a niche for me in your business which has so great a reputation. I shall do my best to learn ; all I ask is that you will tell me of a place where I may lodge ; somewhere simple, for I have not a great deal of money. My father did what he could for me, but I am afraid that I have been extravagant.' He spread his hands as if begging forgiveness for his former follies. 'And there were debts to be paid.'

'And those debts *are* paid!' Meldola cried. 'I know your family. I know that their outlook on life is at one with my own. They are paid, and you are willing to live simply, with strict economy, until you can begin to earn money, eh?'

For a second Abraham hesitated, his bright eyes on his host's eager face ; then he said with some emphasis: 'Paid, of course! I am content to live on bread and cheese if need be—until, as you say, I begin to earn money.'

'Splendid! Miriam!'—to his niece who had entered the room a moment before, 'Miriam, tell me that this house is too big for you and one old man. Tell me that we can find an attic, some place with a hard bed, a straw mattress, perhaps a chair and table, and a few nails on which he may hang his clothes, for an honest young man!'

Miriam, busy pouring out more coffee, smiled without raising her eyes.

'If we had such a room he could have it.' She looked up, met Abraham's eyes, and her smile widened. 'But as we have not, he will have to make do with one slightly more comfortable.'

So it came about that Abraham Gollantz was installed in one of the rooms of Fernando Meldola's big house in the rue Castiglione, a room which satisfied even the luxury-loving nature of its occupant. The two large windows were draped in blue brocade shot with gold thread, the bed was of carved wood picked out

12

with gold, the carpet was Aubusson, and the rest of the furniture was in keeping with the general magnificence.

Fernando's house was not only his domicile, it was also his place of business, and from time to time various pieces of furniture were sold, but they were immediately replaced by something else which was in harmony with the scheme of decoration.

Abraham Gollantz made a tentative offer to pay for his board and lodging. These offers were greeted with roars of laughter; they were refused but remained in Fernando's memory as additional proofs that young Gollantz resembled his father in honesty and straight dealing.

He was quick and intelligent, there seemed nothing that he could not remember with ease, and his flair for furniture and *objets d'art* of real value was astonishing. After a very short time he was able to report to Fernando where some fine picture was for sale, or where a particularly beautiful specimen of furniture might be bought cheaply. The goods he mentioned were always worth consideration, and gradually Fernando grew to rely on Abraham to make all the discoveries for the business.

His attitude towards Miriam pleased Fernando. It was friendly without being familiar. It was attentive without becoming fulsome, and he was so delightfully grateful for all the small things which she did for him.

Clients liked him, and it seemed that wherever he went in Paris he made friends. Gradually he began to bring in clients, men he had come to know while he was out on business. Elderly politicians came to look over the cases of jewels, to choose bracelets or rings for their mistresses. Gollantz was the soul of discretion. While he allowed it to be obvious that he realized for whom the gift was intended, he never permitted the fact to make him less decorous in his behaviour towards the customer. Young officers, in the gorgeous uniforms which Napoleon was already having made to attract the younger generation of soldiers, came, laughed and joked, paid Miriam extravagant compliments, and wasted a great deal of time in the house, but never went away without some trifle in their pockets for which they had paid an appreciable amount of money.

Meldola rubbed his hands, smiled, showing his splendid teeth, and twisted the end of his dark, silky beard in his fingers. Business was good; it had always been good, but now it seemed that his sales were not confined to bankers, diplomats, and the higher

13

ranks of the army, but they were also made to the younger—and it must be admitted slightly gayer—generation.

February ended, March passed, and April came in with sunshine and blue skies, with showers when the sun suddenly burst through the clouds and the rain ceased as quickly as it had begun. Flowers were for sale in the streets, and Miriam sang as she arranged blossoms in the tall vases which Fernando liked to see all over the house.

II

Fernando entered the big room, with its four long windows which overlooked the rue Castiglione one afternoon. The light was growing a little dim, but the thick wax candles in their sconces had not yet been lit. He walked over to the fire-place where a small wood fire burned, for he hated the cold as much as he loathed the intense heat. He stood there, one foot resting on the polished steel fender, the light catching his brilliant shoes and throwing up a gleam of silk in his stockings and the small buckles of his knee-breeches.

He heard the murmur of voices and, turning his head, saw that Abraham was in deep conversation with a man who stood together with him in the bay of the long window. Abraham's voice reached Fernando, mellow and cultivated, while the voice of his companion grated a little on his sensitive ear; it was rough and heavy, incapable it seemed of modulation—the voice, Fernando decided, of a person lacking in any but a superficial refinement.

'. . . and you say that you speak Italian?'

'I do,' Gollantz replied. 'We Jews are good linguists, and I have had opportunity to perfect my pronunciation since I came to Paris.'

'You damned Jews are too clever! You know everything. And Italian art—you understand that, too?'

Gollantz made a gesture which included the room and its contents.

'Here is Italian art in plenty! Ask me questions and see if I can reply.'

'Pooh! How should I know if you told the truth or lied?'

The young man laughed. The sound reached Fernando—impertinent, and carrying a certain arrogance. Surely Gollantz was getting ready to rebuke this impudent client! Fernando waited,

14

and the heavy voice began again. Gollantz had allowed his opportunity to escape.

The polished shoe was removed from the fender and Fernando Meldola moved towards the window. His own soft Italian voice, speaking French with entire correctness, checked the words of the client he could see only dimly.

'Pardon, monsieur—I entered the room and did not realize that it was occupied. I heard you ask a question a moment ago, and I hasten—at the risk of appearing intrusive—to supply the answer. You asked how you might know if Abraham Gollantz told you the truth or lies concerning any articles offered for sale here. The answer is this: first, because this is the house of Fernando Meldola; and secondly, because he is my friend and the son of my friend. Monsieur, we deal in many things here—but never lies.'

Turning to Abraham, he said: 'Ring, if you please, for the servant to light the candles.'

The owner of the heavy voice moved forward, so that he stood without the shadow of the heavy curtains. Meldola saw him clearly, and saw too that he wore the brilliant uniform of a marshal of France, that his breast was plastered with gold braid, and that he carried under his arm a flat cocked hat fringed with a little rim of feathers. The handsome, common face was decorated with curling black whiskers, the eyes stared, the head was carried a little on one side.

'*Nom de Dieu!*' the man said, showing his moist red lips parted in a smile. 'What a fuss about nothing. You Jews are confoundedly touchy. I only joked. Eh, Gollantz?'

'Some jokes remain always in bad taste, Marshal Lannes.'

'Oh, you recognize me! Well, well, there's nothing to be annoyed over. I take back what I said if it offended you. I want to borrow this young partner of yours, Monsieur Meldola.'

Abraham came forward and began to speak very rapidly.

'The Marshal wishes to know if I can be spared to go with the army to Italy. I speak Italian better—thanks to you—than I did when I first came to Paris. It would be an opportunity——'

'For what?' Meldola asked.

Lannes answered, smiling and showing his white, strong teeth. 'To see something of the world, monsieur. Surely part of every young man's education?'

Meldola stood, impassive, watching them both. There was something in his bearing, in his plain dignified clothes, his air of subdued magnificence, which made the Marshal in his gold-faced uniform and the young man, despite his youthful and colourful good looks, seem cheap and unworthy. When he spoke the words came slowly and gravely.

'It is a little difficult for me to listen to this—request, unmoved. I take, as you know, no part in things political. I am a Jew, and I live in Paris ; that is sufficient for me. But I was born in Mantua, and though a Jew has no nationality—except that of being a Jew —I have a warm feeling for this country against which General Bonaparte intends to proceed. I ask for what purpose you wish this young man to accompany you, for what reason will he be of value, and for what do you wish to make use of him? Until I hear these things, I cannot make any reply.' He made his little Jewish gesture with his fine, large hands, as if excusing himself for an overstatement. 'Naturally, I have no control over Monsieur Abraham Gollantz, but I have some say over the movements and actions of my . . .' He paused for a moment, then continued: 'my junior partner.'

The Marshal held up one square hand with its stubby fingers, and ticked off his replies with the forefinger of the other hand.

'First, he speaks Italian. As you know, the army is not made up of linguists. We have had no time for study,' he laughed, 'and might not have taken it if we had. Secondly, he speaks French, and some German, Dutch as well. All assets. Thirdly, he wants to see the world, and I want to oblige him if I can. Fourthly, he comes from the house of Fernando Meldola, and that is a sufficient guarantee of his integrity! You say that you feel kindly towards Italy, Monsieur Meldola. Very well—here is your opportunity to do a kindness to that country. Send a man trained under your auspices to accompany the army, and know that he will— well, he will—do what he can for Italy.'

He stopped, rather breathless, puffing his scarlet lips, his dark, protruding eyes staring at Meldola.

Meldola nodded gravely, fingering his beard. 'I see. Very well. I shall release him. I take it that he goes with you as a clerk in some section of the army's organization?'

'Exactly!'

Meldola smiled. 'Hardly "exactly", Marshal. My question was sufficiently vague. However, he is released. My good wishes go with him.'

Abraham Gollantz left Paris four days later with the army for Italy. Meldola spoke to him before he left, spoke kindly and

16

seriously. He repeated that he had nothing but affection for that country where, whilst all Europe had persecuted his race, protection had been offered to them. He spoke of Riva, Trento, Verona, Mantua, and Venice, stressing the fact that in these places his race had been allowed and even encouraged to work and ply their trades.

'Remember that Shylock was invented by an Englishman. *The Merchant of Venice* is not history ; it is merely a good play.'

Young Gollantz protested that he had no personal animus against the Italians, that he merely wished to see the world, and that he longed for adventure.

'Adventure is good,' Meldola said, 'if it is good adventure. Too many men in these days are only adventurers, and base adventurers at that. Keep two things, Abraham—your head and your honour—and I shall be satisfied.'

Gollantz left Paris early in April, and with him seemed to go all Miriam Lousada's smiles, laughter, and content. She was restless, her eyes were shadowed, and she rarely smiled at Fernando's rallies. Her uncle watched her, silent, and concerned. She had always been so happy with him ; she had taken such an interest in his work, his purchases, and his sales. Now, she was listless, and appeared bored with everything. He suggested that she needed a holiday, that the house in Paris was too dull for her, that she should go out more. He took her to the opera, to the theatre, and bought a new carriage so that she might get fresh air without the exertion of actual bodily exercise. Finally, he spoke to her frankly, trying to hide his anxiety.

'Miriam, you are not very happy, I think?'

'Not very, Uncle Fernando.'

'What can I do? You know that I would do anything—anything.'

For the first time the flicker of a smile touched her lips ; she leant forward and laid her hand on his. 'I know—oh, I know that so well. Believe me, there is nothing, except to be patient with me.'

Meldola rose, and walked to the long window. He spoke without turning back to watch the effect of his words upon her. His natural fineness forbade that he should voluntarily witness the distress of others.

'Perhaps,' he said slowly, 'you miss Abraham Gollantz, Miriam?'

He heard the sudden catch of her breath, and waited for her reply.

'Yes, Uncle Fernando.'

'Does he love you?'

'He told me that he loved me devotedly. I love him terribly.'

There was a long pause, and Meldola stood rigid at the window. His heart cried, suddenly panic-stricken: 'Now, it is coming! Now she will tell me! God of my fathers, help me to be wise, and just.'

'Uncle Fernando, I am dreadfully afraid that—I have loved Abraham too much.'

He needed time to rally from the blow, a blow which wounded not only his heart but that overwhelming pride of race which filled him. For a brief moment he shook from head to foot; then the spasm passed and he turned and walked back to her, laying his hand on her shoulder. When he spoke, his voice was like that of a mother speaking to her child.

'I understand. Please believe, Miriam, that in saying that I say everything. It is dreadful however one looks at it. It may be that it is not so far-reaching in its effects as you believe at this moment. I have heard—I have read—that anxiety, fear, loneliness, may all lead women to imagine that things are worse than they are. Forgive me if I speak too plainly. To me the most terrible thing is that he should have betrayed the trust I placed in him, that he should have treated the person I love best in the world so ill. . . . No, no!' as she made a sudden movement of protest. 'I cannot listen to you when you speak in defence of him. You—you are young; you have lived a very sheltered life; whatever you have done I can find no harsher word for than foolishness. Very often foolishness is the child of love in a woman. Women want always to give and give and give.

'My poor Miriam. Why have you kept this to yourself for six long weeks? Why didn't you come and share your trouble with me? However, that is over, and we shall see. Have no fears. You wish to marry him? By that I mean—apart from everything else—you love him sufficiently to wish to spend the remainder of your life with him?'

'Yes—I do! I can't help it. He may be unworthy; he may have betrayed your confidence, but—I love him.'

'Very well, you shall marry him, I swear it.' He stooped and placed his hand under her chin, lifting her face so that their eyes met. 'Never be afraid of me, Miriam,' Mendola said. 'From now

I am still your uncle, but I am also your father and mother and sister.'

That night he sat at his desk and wrote to Abraham Gollantz and to Marshal Lannes. His letter to Gollantz was cold and formal ; it contained neither threats nor recriminations, merely demanding that he should return to Paris immediately. To Lannes he wrote with great care, weighing every word, and stating that business demanded the return of young Gollantz. He hinted that should this necessitate loss or disorganization of the official work of any particular person, that sufferer would be not only amply, but generously, compensated.

'Lannes loves gold on his uniform,' Fernando Meldola mused, 'but he likes the chink of it in his pocket even better. He may put the price of a king's ransom on the services of Abraham Gollantz —well, king's ransoms have been paid before and can be paid again.'

2

I

DURING the days which followed the despatch of his two letters to Italy, Fernando Meldola was restless and preoccupied. He found it impossible to remain at home, and wandered about the streets of Paris in a vain endeavour to find something of interest which might distract his mind from his own worries. He had liked Gollantz, and had believed that he had in his character all those qualities by which Fernando set such store. Now, he recalled incident after incident which he felt should have warned him of the real mentality of the young man. There had been the affair of the vase, which Gollantz had repaired so cunningly that only an expert could have discovered the places where it had been broken. That vase, Gollantz had been on the point of selling to the stupid and half-educated wife of one of Bonaparte's generals as a perfect piece. Fernando had entered the room in the nick of time, and had explained that the vase was a restored piece.

'Restored so beautifully, by my clever partner here, that he cannot detect the marks of breakage himself, eh, Abraham?'

Gollantz had laughed, protested that he was a great fool, and that for the moment the fact that the vase was imperfect had entirely escaped his memory. 'Not clever, madame, but a great fool who cannot remember the most simple things. I wonder every day why Monsieur Meldola puts up with me!'

There had been the occasion when the age of a piece of silver had been under discussion. Meldola had agreed that, in his opinion, it was of a certain date, but that he could only offer it for sale as a 'speculative' piece, because it lacked the silver stamp. Gollantz had tentatively suggested that the silver mark, removed from a less expensive piece, might be grafted on to the piece under discussion.

'It could be done so neatly that it would defy detection,' he said.

Fernando had stared, amazed and almost unable to believe his ears.

'Graft?' he exclaimed. 'Me—Fernando Meldola—to graft a silver mark!'

Like lightning, Gollantz had burst into a shout of laughter.

'How easily I can make you believe a joke,' he laughed. 'I was only in fun. Don't I know you well enough to realize that such a thing would be as impossible for you as it would be for me. I joked with you.'

Fernando wondered if these small things ought not to have warned him of the young man's true character? He blamed himself, because he felt that he was responsible for this disaster which had overtaken the niece he loved so dearly. He continued his peregrinations round the streets of Paris, a tall, dignified figure, notable for his dark beard and moustache and his splendid carriage. Men and women turned to stare after him, whispering of his money, his success, and his beautiful house; he neither heard nor saw them, but walked on with care and disappointment as his companions.

It was on one of these days that he met his old friend Comparetti, who knew more concerning ancient manuscripts than any man living. He was a strange old man, shabby and still retaining the long side curls of his race.

'Greeting, Fernando!' he said. 'It is a long time since we met. Let us go and drink coffee together.'

Fernando looked into his kind, shrewd old eyes, and decided that he would be glad to talk to one of his own people and that this friend might be able to drive away, for a time at least, the depression which sat so heavily on him.

'I shall be glad to, Dominico. Here, in this little place. We shall be able to talk in peace.'

Comparetti laughed. 'Peace! That's a word we have almost forgotten in this country, Fernando. For the last forty years I have never known any peace except that which I carried about with me under my own hat. It would seem that the French have banished peace from their country. It may be that they fear her as other nations have feared the Jews, and they have driven her out to become a wanderer on the face of the earth, eh?'

'Perhaps. Your country and my adopted home is suffering at the moment.'

Comparetti lifted his thin hands. 'Poor Italy. This is not war—this is a great commercial campaign, Fernando. Presently you will see the walls of the Paris galleries, the homes of the marshals, the bedroom of the Creole, hung with spoils from Italy! The bronze horses from the Piazza San Marco used as mascots for one of the regiments. The statue of Cangrande side by side with that of Henri Quatre.'

'Pooh! My dear friend, what do the marshals of Franch know of the value of these things?' Fernando demanded. 'They will never be able to distinguish the wheat from the chaff.'

'Where have you been, Fernando?' Comparetti asked. 'Have you been living in your cellars for the last few months?' He leant forward and sank his voice to a whisper, speaking in rapid Italian. 'There is a commercial spoliation going on there in Italy. Nothing is left to chance. The whole thing is done on business lines ; the advice of experts is taken. Why do I tell you these things? You know them already, of course ; I had forgotten.'

His fine old face changed, his eyes lost their kindly twinkle and met Fernando's coldly. He drew back a little, as if he wished to increase the distance between them.

'I know?' Fernando said. 'I know? What do you mean, Dominico? Why do you look at me so coldly? How should I know of this?'

'You provided one of the experts.'

'I did? Expert in what? Explain yourself.'

Comparetti frowned, then began to speak with some irritation.

'Did you not know that Monge and Berthollet were taken with the Army to Italy in the position of advisers on matters of art?'

'No—and I question of how much value either of them will be.'

'Did you not allow Lannes to take your partner, Gollantz, with him as an unofficial expert?'

'Gollantz? He went to Italy as a clerk, because he wished to see the country and spoke the language. Lannes himself told me that was to be his position—a clerk who spoke the language.'

Comparetti gazed earnestly at the face before him, as if he endeavoured to see into the soul of his friend. At last he spoke.

'Fernando, you have been made a fool of by Lannes and this young man. I know, Monge and Berthollet know, all Paris knows that he has gone to Italy to assist in the work of spoliation. He is a valuer, an assessor, an assistant thief! Legalized theft, perhaps, but theft none the less.'

'Why should they approach him? An unknown young man. It is fantastic.'

'The whole army is that, my friend. Napoleon loves fantasy. He sees himself as king of the world, his marshals, kings under him, his whole court a gorgeous, perpetual carnival. Why did they choose this young man? Because they dare not ask Fernando Meldola, and yet they relied on the tuition which Fernando Meldola had given this fellow. That is why.'

Fernando pushed away his empty coffee-cup, and sighed.

'Dominico, I ask you to believe that I knew nothing of this. Believe that, please, and believe too that Gollantz shall return to Paris immediately. I pledge my word.'

'Which has always been the best guarantee in the world to the man who know you, Fernando. *Shalom!*'

Fernando walked back to his house, his head bent, his hands clasped behind him. Dominico had said: '*Shalom!*' Peace! He felt that peace had left his house for ever, that it must have taken flight when Abraham Gollantz entered it.

That night he wrote again to Lannes, stating that Gollantz must return immediately, and offering, quite frankly, a large sum of money, which should be paid into the Marshal's private banking account on the same day that Gollantz arrived in Paris. The sum was considerable, and Meldola was too good a man of business not to resent losing such an amount.

'It is fantastic!' he said softly. 'Dominico was right—the whole affair is fantastic. To think that this man's child may one day be my heir!'

Gollantz returned to Paris in August, when the dusty streets and hot days, heavy suns and suffocating nights had begun to rob Miriam of some of her beauty. Meldola watched her pale face and her general air of lassitude with anxiety. He knew that she suffered intensely, and that her days were filled with a nervous dread that Gollantz might refuse to return. She knew nothing of the money which her uncle was prepared to pay for that return.

He arrived, tired and dusty, bringing with him several large boxes, and far more bags than had comprised his original luggage. His manner was untinged by nervousness; he held his head high, and greeted Meldola with respectful affection.

'You look well in spite of the heat,' Gollantz cried. 'It is hot in Paris, but in Italy it was like living in an inferno. How is your niece? I have brought her some little trinkets from her own country. They will please her, I hope.'

Meldola looked at the slim young figure, noted the well-shaped head set so admirably on the broad shoulders. For the first time he realized that he hated Abraham Gollantz, and that he could have seen him lying dead at his feet without a pang of regret.

'Sit down,' he ordered. 'Before you see my niece there are many things which I have to say to you. First, you are a seducer, a liar, a cheat, and a common adventurer. You hear that? Good! Please remember that always in my mind those epithets are used silently when I mention your name. Secondly, you will prepare immediately to marry my niece whom you have wronged so cruelly. Tomorrow we shall make arrangements. You understand?'

The young man's face reddened under its tan. 'I had no idea —I did not know. Miriam never wrote to tell me of this. I can understand that you feel angry with me, despise me. I despise myself for having brought a moment's anxiety on either her or you. I am speaking honestly now, sincerely.'

'Pah! You have never been sincere in your life! You will tell me next that you love Miriam!'

'But I do. I love her devotedly. You tell me that I *must* marry her. There is nothing which will make me happier. I was wrong, foolish, to make it possible for her to—to suffer. I admit it. I was tempted, I yielded to temptation. She's young, beautiful; I am young, and young blood is hot. Can't you understand?'

Meldola's fine lips curved into a sneer. 'My business has taught me to differentiate between fine shades of colour. I admit no shades of behaviour. Right is right, decency is decency—and lying is always lying.'

'Then there is no good purpose in my trying to defend myself.'

'None! You cannot defend yourself in this matter or the question of going to Italy—as a clerk. You—you *gonoph*! Thief in the pay of other thieves. Robbing churches, palaces, defacing history! I know, Abraham Gollantz, you realized that to admit your reason for going with Lannes would be sufficient for me to disown you. So you lied, you poor, pitiful fool—and I found you out! What have you brought home as a result of your private robberies? How much has your master allowed you to purloin from a nation which extended hospitality and tolerance to your own race? Those boxes will be opened tomorrow, and everything —mark that, everything—will be returned in due time to the place where it belongs. Not yet—or it might again fall into the hands of the Corsican and his hordes, but later, when it is safe to return it. Now, go and tell Miriam that you are home. Tell her that you love her, and will try to make her a good husband.'

Young Gollantz stood for a moment, uncertain. He was ashamed, not only of what he had done, but because he had allowed his plans to miscarry. His quick brain already tried to think of some way in which he might save the treasures of gold, silver, and ivory which he had brought back with him.

He believed that abasement was the best method of obtaining forgiveness.

'Very well,' he said gravely; then stretching out his hands with a gesture which was admirably impulsive, he cried: 'Oh, forgive me! I've been foolish, stupid, nothing more. Criminally stupid, I admit it. I will make amends. Will you try to forget the past and let me begin again?'

Meldola drew his beard through his fingers. His eyes were hard and unmoved. 'No,' he said. 'You ask the impossible. You should know that Jews do not forget. Go to Miriam.'

However his reception by Fernando might have surprised and dismayed Gollantz, Miriam's greeting atoned for it. She was pathetically happy to see him, offered no reproaches, only repeated again and again: 'Oh, to have you home! I have missed you so. Never leave me again, my beloved.'

They were married a week later, and Meldola gave them a suite of rooms in his house. His manner towards Abraham was coldly civil. He never again allowed him any say in the management of the business. He might sell goods, but only at the sum which Meldola put upon them. He was paid a substantial salary, which—to give Gollantz his due—he tried to earn honestly.

Only on one occasion did Meldola hold a conversation of any length with him: that was when the boxes which he had brought from Italy were opened, and the contents marked with the information as to where they had originally belonged. The boxes were sealed again and not opened until eighteen years later, when various parish priests, impoverished noblemen, and people of lesser aristocratic pretensions in Italy received packages containing their long-lost property. No letter was enclosed, all charges were paid, and in some cases the goods were delivered by special messengers, who made no statement except that the goods had been 'taken away in error, and are now returned by a gentleman who lives in Paris'.

Meldola never accustomed himself to the fact that Miriam had married a man he despised and hated, but his affection for her was sufficiently strong to make him refrain from adding to her worries. He was as generous as ever to her and, when the child was born in the November of 1796, he insisted that she must be attended by the finest and most expensive doctors and nurses, and that the boy must be clothed and treated like a prince.

It was a real grief to him when the child's life ended during an attack of croup in the following December, on the very day upon which Napoleon returned, laden with the spoils he had gathered, and entered Paris with all the pomp of a conqueror.

For seven years the strange household existed: Meldola, aloof and growing more and more reserved, Gollantz holding no official position, being little better than an assistant, and Miriam becoming every year more beautiful, utterly content with her husband, and scarcely noticing that her uncle lived a life of almost complete loneliness.

Gollantz, once full of ambition, had grown to lack all initiative. Once he had planned to create a great business, to make a fortune, and become a rich and successful man. He was chilled by Meldola's treatment; gradually his initiative died, and he was content with the position allotted to him by Fernando. To his wife he was always kind and considerate, and never ceased to love her with every appearance of devotion. Once or twice he embarked on small trading exploits on his own account, and carried them through to a successful issue, but the heart had gone out of him, and he grew less and less inclined to venture from the security he knew into the insecurity of adventure which had once fascinated him.

It became obvious in the early part of 1804 that he was very ill. His lips had lost their brilliant red and had become tinged with a dullish purple ; he often pressed his hand to his side and complained that a sudden pain stabbed him there. Miriam worried and besought him to see a doctor, who pronounced his heart to be gravely affected, and ordered that he should live a life of complete quiet. Frantic with anxiety, Miriam told Fernando of the verdict, and he immediately decided that they should retire to the country, away from the noise and bustle of Paris. Gollantz protested, but Fernando was firm. He provided everything, paid for everything, and behaved with his customary generosity, without abating in the slightest his attitude towards Gollantz. However Abraham Gollantz resented his position, he was obliged to accept it. His father in Amsterdam was dead, his brothers and sisters scattered, married with families of their own to support.

Miriam and her husband left the big house in the rue Castiglione in April 1805 ; and when the leaves were changing to gold, and the brilliant sunsets told of the approach of winter, Abraham Gollantz died in the little house on the edge of the forest, leaving his inconsolable wife expecting her second child.

She refused to remain away from Paris ; she turned to Meldola for comfort, and never again did he speak of Abraham harshly or unkindly. She went back to Paris, took up her old position in the house, and Meldola realized that he was less lonely, that his life seemed fuller and happier. He looked forward, with an intensity which was almost painful, to the birth of the child, and would talk gently and with great tenderness of it, making plans for its youth, its education, and its care.

In an atmosphere of expansive generosity, of magnificence, and the utmost comfort, Miriam Gollantz throve and blossomed. At twenty-seven she was growing a little heavy, full-bosomed and wide-hipped. Her skin and hair, her eyes and the rich colour of her lips, were as vivid as ever. She looked what she was, a lovely matron, a woman whose destiny was to bear children as physically splendid as herself.

Her son was born on May 18, 1805. Fernando Meldola held his grand-nephew in his arms and smiled his gentle, secret, Jewish smile.

The boy was strong, he made himself heard almost the moment

after he arrived in the world. His small wrinkled face and closed eyes, between the lids of which could be seen a faint glimmer of blue, his clenched fists and his shrill protesting voice delighted Meldola.

'He resents that so much attention should be paid to the Emperor!' he said to the nurse. 'I like his self-assertiveness. We shall make a man of him.'

The boy was named Hermann, and on the day when he was formally received into the Jewish religion, Meldola gathered to his house all the best known and most distinguished Jews of Paris. He provided the finest wines, the most elaborate cakes, and presented every one of his guests with a costly souvenir of the occasion. Hermann Gollantz lifted up his voice and wept; then sank into a profound sleep apparently unmoved by the liberties which had been taken with him.

As he lay in his decorated cot by his mother's bed, she turned and looked at his sleeping face. Her eyes smarted, and her throat stung with unshed tears. She stretched out her hand and gently touched the cheeks of the child.

'My son, my baby,' she whispered, 'you will grow like your beloved father. I shall be so proud of you. You shall never forget that your father was chosen as adviser by the Emperor himself— no matter what people may say. Oh, Abraham, Abraham, why are you not here to rejoice with me!'

III

Few children in Paris during that time could have received as much care and attention as the small Hermann Gollantz. His mother adored him, his expensive *bonne* treated him like a small prince, and his great-uncle watched over him with an anxious care which was almost pathetic. It was a miracle that the boy was not hopelessly spoilt. He developed into a sturdy fellow, fair-haired and blue-eyed, as unlike the typical Jew as could well be imagined.

Meldola admitted frankly to Dominico Comparetti that he had centred all his hopes in the child, and that he intended to make him his heir. Meldola's strongest characteristic was pride, a pride which forbade him to associate himself with any project which was not strictly honest. His love for his race, his knowledge that he was a stranger within the gates of Paris, and as such a marked man, made him live a life which was almost fanatically upright and rigid. He felt himself to be regarded as a type of his whole race, and determined that through him his people should be raised to a place of high esteem in men's minds.

'They watch us always,' he said to Dominico one day, as they sat sipping their coffee. 'They look at us sideways, when they think we do not observe them, hoping to catch us slipping. They would derive great satisfaction if they could say: "Dirty Jew", "Defrauding Jew", "Mercenary Hebrew dog". I refuse to give them that satisfaction, and, moreover, I regard the man who does so as a traitor to his people, to his whole race.'

Dominico shrugged his narrow shoulders. 'Pah! What does it matter? These stupidities are shibboleths. There is a sort of legend that Jews are dirty, mean, avaricious, untrustworthy, cheats, and liars. I know that they are old, time-worn imaginings; what do I care for them! I live my life, go my own way, that is sufficient for me.'

'But not for me!' Meldola cried. 'For me I must lift the banner which has been trailed in the dust. Oh, in many ways it has been our own fault. The world has been hard for our race, and sometimes they have taken the easier, less admirable course. They have made golden calves and worshipped them; they have amassed money and lent it at high interest; they have allowed themselves to become drunk with money, to be ostentatious and vulgar. Some of them have been ashamed of their race, of their names, of their physical characteristics. There may have been reasons for all these things, excuses even, but that does not make them less regrettable.

'I have had a very bitter experience of the type of Jew who betrays his race—I need not, indeed I shall not, enlarge upon the circumstances. Now, I have under my care a little boy, and every day I congratulate myself upon my good fortune. He is young, plastic, and impressionable as are all little children. He shall grow up in an atmosphere where pride of, and for, the Jewish race shall predominate. He shall hold up his head and say: "It is quite impossible for me to be dishonest, because I am a Jew". That is how he shall live his life, and if only a hundred men in all the world recognize his high character, his integrity—well, that will be a hundred Gentiles less to believe and chuckle and grin over those horrible old *canards*.'

With this determination fixed in his mind, Fernando Meldola brought up little Hermann Gollantz. The boy was indulged, petted and loved, but he was encouraged to regard that strict honesty, that meticulous truthfulness, and that pride of race in which Meldola believed so fiercely, as the first duty of a Jew.

The training was easy, for Hermann loved his great-uncle dearly, and looked upon him as the world's greatest man. He liked his smooth, sweet-smelling hair and beard; he admired his beautiful, dignified clothes, his knowledge of china, pictures, and old books. His mind seemed to Hermann to be a great storehouse of rich things, a storehouse which was always thrown open to him, and from which treasure after treasure would be drawn for his pleasure and enlightenment.

Certain precepts were instilled into his young mind, precepts which were delivered in Meldola's soft and beautifully modulated voice, without passion but with a grave sincerity. It appeared that no matter what Hermann might hear of the debts incurred by the great ones of the earth, that gentlemen did not have debts, and particularly debts to people who were poorer than themselves.

'But I heard my mother talking to Madame Comparetti the other day,' Hermann protested. 'She said that the Empress had many debts: to dressmakers, jewellers, and goldsmiths.'

'It is possible.' Meldola's tone implied that Josephine Beauharnais held little interest for him.

'And the sisters of the Emperor too.'

'That, too, is possible. Women are apt to buy what takes their fancy without considering the cost. The Emperor—as the head of their house—will be responsible to these tradesmen.'

'Is the head of the house always responsible, Uncle?'

'The head of the house ought to be proud to consider himself so.'

'Shall I ever be head of a house?'

'It may be; and when you are, you will remember that the honour of your house rests in your hands, and see that it rests safely.'

Hermann nodded. 'It would never do to drop it in the mud, would it?'

'It would be unthinkable.'

Slowly and carefully, Meldola instructed the boy in more material matters. At ten years old he could be trusted to judge the age of a piece of silver with reasonable exactness, he could recognize the marks on many kinds of china, and he had a small but precise knowledge of fine woods. It was evident that he lacked the flair of either Meldola or his dead father. Hermann would always work slowly, carefully, and rely on his head and his knowledge, never on his imagination.

On the festivities instituted for his *Bar Mitzvah*, he conducted himself with grave dignity, reading in the synagogue with painstaking correctness, his young voice clear and calm. Meldola was full of pride, and once again filled the big house with all his Jewish friends, and made the occasion an opportunity to give largely and generously to many charities. He watched the boy move among his friends, smiling and modest, answering their questions with good sense and understanding. His heart was filled with gratitude, and his eyes smarted suddenly when he heard Lindo, the picture dealer, say:

'And how did you obtain all this knowledge? It is commendable in a boy of thirteen.'

'I obtained it, Monsieur Lindo, from the same source that I have obtained everything except those things which my mother gave me—from my great-uncle, Fernando Meldola.'

Though Hermann was a serious youth, he was in no way priggish, and he enjoyed his hours of recreation as much as those which were devoted to study. He was popular with his schoolfellows and his masters, who found him carefully studious, though never intellectually brilliant. He loved music, and hailed with delight those occasions when Meldola took him and his handsome mother to the opera. Like most of his race he had a passion for the theatre, and his critical faculty was, even at an early age, quite admirable.

His mother made no attempt to conceal her intense love for him, and when he was still very young would tell him long, tender stories of his dead father, in which Abraham was depicted as a kind of astonishing paladin, a compound of all the virtues, possessed of every physical and mental gift.

Where Meldola said: 'Never forget that you are a Jew, or forget the debt which you owe to your race,' Miriam begged: 'Never forget that your father was a great man. Though he was so young he was chosen as artistic adviser over the heads of men older than himself, chosen by the Emperor. He was the most handsome man in Paris, the most amusing, and the most wonderful husband in all the world.'

3

I

HERMANN GOLLANTZ saw many changes from the big house.
Fernando insisted that no political discussions should take place
within its walls, and the various changes were accepted and commented on without heat or partisanship. The Emperor ceased to
be the Emperor: a great battle was fought because the Emperor
had become head of the State once more. He had escaped from
his prison and the army rallied round him. He was defeated, and
Hermann asked if once again he had ceased to be Emperor.

'It seems probable,' Meldola replied, and made no further
comment. Other kings entered Paris, people said that a little boy
was to be Emperor ; then they decided that he was not going to
hold that position after all. A king ruled in France again, and
Meldola said that the taste of the monarchy was very bad and ran
to too much gilt.

Hermann seemed quite suddenly to find himself twenty years
old. It appeared to him that one day he had been a small boy,
carrying a parcel of books, held together by a strap, to school
every morning ; in an instant, he had changed, it seemed, to a very
big boy, who read heavier books, and began to really understand
something concerning the values of pictures and furniture. Then,
one morning, Fernando Meldola sent for him, and began to talk.

'Today,' he said, 'is your twentieth birthday, Hermann.'

That was how Hermann felt that the years had passed. Quickly,
almost unobserved, only marked by sudden and inexplicable
changes in himself and his surroundings. The uncle he had known
when he was at school, had been tall and upright, with beautiful
black hair and a beard which looked like silk ; the uncle who
spoke to him on the morning of his twentieth birthday was not
quite so tall, because he stooped a little, and his hair and beard
were like snow. His hands were as fine as ever, but they seemed
frail, and the veins stood out like pale-blue cords on them. His
mother too, had changed, though he did not know when or how.
Once she had been young, had laughed a great deal, and at other
times wept and dried her eyes on a very small, lace-edged handkerchief. Her eyes had been very large and brilliant. She had

sometimes danced with him, crying as she did so: 'One, two, three —there, that's right!' Now, with this strange suddenness, she had grey hair, her eyes were smaller, and she had grown very stout. She moved slowly, and when she climbed the stairs would hold on to the wide hand-rail and say: 'Oh dear, oh dear, these cruel stairs!' She never wept now; only said sometimes, with a note of regret in her voice: 'Ah, your poor father!'

That morning Hermann had looked at himself in the glass when he had finished dressing. He saw a young man of average height, with broad shoulders and a reasonably good figure. His tight coat and tighter pantaloons made him appear taller than he really was. His elaborate stock pushed up his chin and made his chest protrude like that of a pouter pigeon. His hair was fair and meticulously neat, rather shorter than was fashionable, for Hermann dreaded to be taken for an actor, poet, or painter. The blue eyes, set well apart, stared back at him from the mirror, honestly and fearlessly; the nose was short and rather blunt, the mouth well cut and firm.

This was the young man who stood before Fernando Meldola's desk one spring morning. Meldola held out his hand and took Hermann's for a moment.

'Today is your twentieth birthday,' he said. 'Sit down and let us talk together.'

Hermann sat down and, while Meldola's fine hands busied themselves with some papers on the famous desk which had a history almost as long and intricate as that of the French kings themselves, he looked at the room in which they sat. What a beautiful room it was! How wise Uncle Fernando was never to crowd it with furniture, however beautiful. The other dealers: Berthollet, young Monge, and the rest, filled their rooms to over-flowing; period jostled period, china and glass littered the same table; ivories, gold trinkets, pieces of old silver reposed in the same case, and the effect was one of distraction and mental discomfort. Meldola arranged his rooms with care, not only selecting pieces for their own value, but seeing them in relation to the rest of the furniture in the room.

Fernando's voice broke the thread of his thoughts. 'What are you thinking of so seriously, Hermann?'

'I was thinking how wise you were, Uncle.'

Meldola leaned back in his chair and laid the tips of his fingers together.

'That pleases me very much,' he said. 'I hope so earnestly that

I have been wise for you, my dear boy. I have had you under my care for twenty years—twenty years ago I held you in my arms and said that we should make a man of you. I wonder if I have given a good account of my stewardship?'

'I know that I owe everything to you, to your generosity and kindness.'

'Pooh! That is nothing. I only hope that I have equipped you well with knowledge, taste, ability, and principles. Those are the things which money can't buy. Those are the only real gifts an elder man can give a younger.'

Hermann flushed. He was a modest fellow, but not such a fool as to be unable to assess his own worth.

'Knowledge—they tell me that my judgment is second only to your own ; taste—I don't often make mistakes——'

Meldola chuckled. 'True, it is several years since you sent me running into the town to see a piece of Gobelins which you had found. You remember? What reds, what blues, what terrible greens!'

'I was only fourteen then,' Hermann expostulated. 'I don't make those mistakes now, do I? As for ability, I have some of that commodity, I think, and principles—if I can live up to the standard which you have set me, I shall be satisfied.'

Meldola nodded. 'Very well said,' he commented. 'Now, I have plans for you. I am going to send you away to travel. Every young man ought to travel, and you must do so. There are places and people I wish you to visit. I have letters prepared for you. There is your father's family in Amsterdam. I do not know them —I only knew your grandfather—but it is right that you should. Simeon Gollantz of Amsterdam. There are the Lousadas in Italy —at Mantua and again in Milan. There are the Jaffes in Budapest, the Salamans in Bucharest. There is my good friend, Marcus Moise in Brussels, Francis Leon who lives at some place called Igat near London, Isadore Breal in Vienna—many more, but you must meet them, know them. They are your people, and it is right. Tomorrow we shall begin to seek for suitable gifts for you to take with you. You shall have money, drafts which you will be able to cash, and you may buy, up to a certain amount, whatever you think worth buying. You will make the grand tour as the final stage of your education. Now, tell me, does that please you?'

'If only it were possible to take you and my mother with me— it would be quite perfect,' Hermann said.

33

A fortnight later, Hermann Gollantz left for England, which he found less cold than Paris in winter, very neat and tidy, rather compressed, and where his uncle's old friend Francis Leon gave him a greeting which was sufficiently warm to dispel his slight attack of homesickness. He decided that the English had worse taste than the French, but warmer hearts, and at the end of a month's stay the number of friends which he had made surprised him. He left for Holland with real regret, which not even the pleasurable expectancy of meeting his father's family could dull. Holland was even more tidy than England, even smaller. The exquisite cleanliness delighted him, and he wandered through endless picture galleries almost prepared to declare that the Dutch were the only real painters in the world.

His father's family were not particularly sympathetic. His uncle was hard-working but unimaginative, and seemed to resent a little the obviously easy circumstances in which his nephew found himself. Hermann disliked his perpetual questions as to the price of this and that. It appeared to him that his stay was an endless catechism. 'That is a beautiful watch, Hermann. One would fancy that it cost a great deal of money—yes?' or, 'That overcoat is very fine. Perhaps it was made in England. Would it be permitted to ask what price English tailors charge for such a coat?'

Brussels appeared to be the very antithesis of Amsterdam. Hermann fell in love with the place, loved its gaiety, and the crowd of well-dressed women. He had not seen such clothes since he left Paris, and he almost lost his heart to the youngest daughter of Marcus Moise, who was the last word in elegance and distinction. The fact that she was betrothed to an elderly and immensely rich lace-merchant only served to make her more romantic, more deliciously unattainable in Hermann's eyes. He bought her a great many bouquets of expensive flowers, contrived to wrap himself in a cloak of delicate melancholy for several days, then decided that he was wasting his time, that she really loved her stout merchant—and promptly forgot all about her.

He reached Italy by easy stages, buying a good deal here and there—goods which he had despatched to Paris to await his return. He had been told that Italy would entrance him, and was disappointed to discover that it had no attraction for him. He found the inns filthy, the food poor, and the people lacking in finer intelligence. The country was beautiful, he decided, but even that did not compensate for the discomfort in which almost everyone lived as a matter of course. To him, after the luxury of Fernando's house, his mother's family seemed little better than peasants, and he turned with relief to begin his journey to Budapest and Bucharest.

He arrived at Budapest in time for the wedding of Artom Jaffe and a beautiful young girl with strange slanting eyes and a mouth which was impossibly red. The whole of his stay was a whirl of excitement and entertainment. He danced, rode, played cards, attended operatic performances and theatrical entertainments. He flirted a little, he gave presents, and spent long hours in intellectual discussions with Menassah Jaffe, which would begin in grave seriousness and end in wild bursts of laughter the moment the elder man began to feel bored with the subject on hand.

'I have never had such a splendid time in all my life!' Hermann assured Menassah when he was leaving. 'I didn't know that such laughter, such wonderful times existed. I have never known people who were so kind, so generous, and so gay.'

'Gay!' Menassah laughed. 'Wait until you get to Vienna, my boy. That is where all the gaiety of the world meets, lives, and circulates. All roads they say lead to Rome ; well, believe me, that all laughter has its source in Vienna.'

Hermann found that he was right. Budapest had been gay, but Vienna made it seem like the gaiety of an untutored village. He looked at the town in astonishment. Had there ever been so many beautiful shops, so many luxurious restaurants, so many brilliant theatres gathered in one city before? Withal, there was a dignity about it which pleased him. Paris had grown noisy ; there was too much gilt furniture, too many heavy, gilded mirrors in Paris. The stamp of the plebeian court still remained printed there. These people were aristocrats, and Hermann Gollantz, with all the intolerance of the Jew for the second-rate or mentally inferior, felt that somehow he must contrive to spend the rest of his life in Vienna.

He returned to Paris, leaving his heart in the city by the Danube.

He found Fernando older, more shrunken, less able to move quickly, and inclined to grow irritable on the smallest provocation. It seemed to the young man that some of the keenness of his intelligence had been dimmed, like a bright mirror dulled by a passing breath. His mother, who was overjoyed to see him, was stouter and heavier, it seemed not only in body but in mind.

For a year Hermann forced himself to consider no one except these two people who depended upon him so much for their happiness. He was a dutiful son, full of real devotion and affection, always ready to accompany his mother wherever she wished to go. To Fernando he was obedient, ready to listen to his advice, anxious to soothe his nerves, and always eager to prevent him realizing that he no longer could hold the reins of the great business. His judgment was no longer as sound as it had been, and he lacked the ability to seize opportunities as he had once done. Many of his friends were dead, and he had sunk into a kind of melancholy seclusion, which he at once resented and yet found impossible to break.

It was difficult for a young man, possessed of plenty of money, reasonably good looks and a liking for amusements of the less vivid kinds, to be content. Hermann's only companions were an old man of seventy-two and a woman of fifty who had aged prematurely. He was growing stale and he knew it.

I am losing the capacity for enjoyment [he wrote to Menassah Jaffe]. *I love both my mother and my uncle dearly—I would gladly devote my life to either of them—but I cannot exclude every form of amusement which pertains to my age. Advise me, I beg of you.*

Menassah Jaffe, worldly, pleasure-loving, and as devoted to his wife as he was to his mistress, replied that Hermann was behaving like a fool.

The wine of youth [he wrote, with that flamboyance which was characteristic of him], *is not suitable for laying down as vintage. It goes sour too soon, loses its flavour. Drink it at twenty-four and it is delicious, keep it until you are forty and your stomach will turn at the very sight of it. I never recommend loose living. I always prescribe light living! Let me be your doctor.*

Hermann, reading the letter after a stormy interview with Meldola, who had grumbled that he wished to make too many modern innovations, stating that it was worth while buying heavy antiques even though the present taste might favour lighter furniture ; after an equally trying conversation with his mother, who declared that it was her firm conviction that she had not long to live, and that her heart was affected, even though the doctor might ascribe her shortness of breath to her weight, decided that Menassah was right.

He visited his tailor, bought a great many new clothes, ordered a very handsome cabriolet and pair of horses, engaged a box at the opera, and spent a considerable amount of money. He declared his intention of going out more, and to his surprise it was greeted with warm approval by his uncle and his mother.

'How right you are!' Meldola said. 'I have always given it as my opinion that you stayed at home far too much. Youth is the time to enjoy yourself. Only go to the best places and always do me credit—and I am satisfied.'

Miriam nodded her head energetically. 'I am so happy. Has Paris so many good-looking young men that she can afford to dispense with the best looking of them all? Assuredly not! Do not break too many hearts, and whatever you do, don't get your own broken, that is all, my Hermann.'

III

For the first time in his life—except during his grand tour—Hermann knew what it was to taste the sweets of popularity. He found that doors opened readily to him, that men liked him, and women were willing to be kind to him. He was never at any time a libertine, always retaining a regard for women which almost amounted to reverence, but he enjoyed their company, and nothing delighted him more than to offer small and exquisite gifts, so open-handedly and generally, that it was impossible for any one woman to consider herself selected for special attention.

For nearly three years Hermann led the life of a discreet young man about town. His days were devoted to his work, but much of that work was done out and about Paris. The business flourished, and since he had declared his intention of enjoying himself, he found Meldola much more amenable. He was allowed to make small innovations, to introduce some of the modern, luxurious trifles which Vienna was manufacturing so rapidly and which made an instant appeal to the fashionable women of Paris.

He had made friends with a young Polish nobleman, who was willing to send him splendid furs from his estate, furs which brought large prices, and benefited not only the Pole, but the House of Meldola. Fernando, it seemed almost as if in imitation

37

of his young partner, had emerged from his seclusion and had begun to go out more. Miriam, though she continued to grow stouter and stouter, followed his example, and delighted to give select luncheon- and dinner-parties at every new restaurant which opened, over-eating from any dish which particularly took her fancy. The old house in the rue Castiglione had taken on a new lease of life.

Hermann was content. He was rich, young, and able to hold his own in society. His life was distinctly pleasant, and he might have been described as a young man without a care in the world.

'When are you going to bring home a wife, Hermann?' his mother asked him, and Fernando looked up from his book, his eyes twinkling, and added: 'Provided she is sufficiently good-looking and good-tempered, we shall welcome her.'

Hermann laughed. 'I don't know. I like them all so much, these young women. Besides, I want so much. Looks, intelligence, pride, humour—oh I shall be difficult to please, believe me.' He picked up a small painting, framed in mother-of-pearl cut in geometrical patterns which had come from Vienna that morning—modern, but very attractive and terribly expensive. 'Perhaps someone like the subject of this picture,' Hermann said, handing the painting to his mother.

'Lovely!' Miriam exclaimed. 'Who is she?'

'A lady who is causing a good deal of excitement,' Hermann said. 'Not only, I gather, because of her beauty, but—for other reasons.'

Fernando held out his hand. 'Show me! Ah, Lola Montez! Impossibly beautiful and unbelievably dangerous, if all I hear is true. So that's your idea, eh, Hermann? Well, you're in reasonably good company.'

To say that the face haunted Hermann Gollantz would be to imply that he was an ultra-romantic young man; but it certainly remained in his mind's eye, and for days he found himself comparing the women he met with the portrait of the extraordinary adventuress who was already setting half Bavaria by the ears.

'Hermann, you have the air of a man who is seeking something,' his friend, Louis Caveau, said to him one evening as they sat in the Rocher, dining admirably and with discretion. Although Meldola held his race in such respect, he had never observed or caused his niece and her son to observe the dietary laws of the Jews, and Hermann was something of a gourmet.

Hermann nodded. 'I am. I am young. It is spring-time; and I

want to find someone upon whom I can lavish my affections.'

Caveau yawned. He had just emerged from a tempestuous love affair, and found the attitude of cynic very much to his taste. 'As your friend,' he said, 'I hope you may never find what you seek. Believe me, you are happier as you are. I, Louis Caveau, speak of what I—unfortunately—know.'

Hermann was a little bored with Caveau's eternal cynicism; such very artificial cynicism it was too. He glanced round to find some object which might turn the conversation.

'Look!' he said, relief in his voice. 'There is Rodolphe—and what a lovely girl with him!'

Caveau craned his neck to catch a glimpse of the couple. Rodolphe was an actor of some repute as a comedian, a tall, thin fellow, with a long upper lip and a wide gash of a mouth. The girl—Hermann knew that his heart beat suddenly very fast, that his memory stirred and woke—the girl was like Lola Montez. There were the same wide-apart eyes, the hair falling in graceful ringlets on the shoulders, a fine sensitive mouth, and a skin which was as white as snow.

Forgetting his rôle for a moment, Caveau whistled softly. 'Lovely's a poor word, my friend! She is . . .' Then with an effort he remembered that he was Louis Caveau, suffering from a disastrous love affair, and added quickly: 'Probably as false as she is beautiful.'

Hermann caught Rodolphe's eye and greeted him, then continued his own dinner, finding it more and more difficult to prevent himself staring in the direction of the girl.

He made an excuse to wander over to where they sat and, offering his apology for the interruption, asked Rodolphe when he was going to appear again.

Rodolphe shook his head. 'How can I tell? They're jealous of me, these beautiful young men, because I get laughs and spoil the public for their sugar-and-water love scenes. Presently—presently, they will have to send for me! Meanwhile'—he turned to his companion—'may I present Monsieur Hermann Gollantz to you ? Monsieur Gollantz—Mademoiselle Lorette.'

Hermann clicked his heels, bowed, and bent over the narrow white hand which was offered to him. Then, excusing himself, returned to his own table.

'An obvious ruse if ever I saw one!' Caveau murmured, passing his hand over his smooth and well-greased hair. 'I wonder at you, my friend.'

'Never wonder at anything,' Hermann said. 'Fate was on my side. I have been looking for her for days. I always follow my luck.'

A few moments later it seemed that fate indeed smiled upon him. The door of the restaurant opened, and a messenger entered, glancing round until he saw Rodolphe, to whom he delivered a letter. The actor tore it open, read it, and immediately began to talk rapidly and excitedly to his companion. In another moment the actor had left his table and strode over to where Hermann sat.

'Monsieur Gollantz, I am going to ask a great favour of you, and at the same time confer a great favour upon you. This letter is from the theatre—tomorrow is the dress rehearsal of the new play: *L' Indifférent*. Heros Barye who was to play the comedian —not that he could ever have played it, or, rather, he could only have played at playing it—is ill. They have sent for me! Pride would dictate that I refuse, but my love for my art is greater than my pride. I must fly.'

'My congratulations!' Hermann said. 'Be certain that I shall be there. There will be no necessity for the *claque* to attend. I shall make sufficient applause myself. But—the favour?'

'I come to that now. Mademoiselle Lorette—here for the first time—a woman of taste who understands the finer shades and delights of good food, has only this moment begun to eat her fish. Is she to be robbed of the excellent dinner which Rocher provides? Never! Is she to be left alone in a public restaurant? The very thought is an insult! Will you give yourself the honour to have her at your table, or yourself the pleasure to dine at hers —naturally with your friend, Monsieur Gollantz?'

Hermann rose. 'For myself I shall be delighted to join Mademoiselle. And you, Louis?'

For an instant, a struggle could be seen on Caveau's good-looking face. He, the cynic, the disappointed man of the world —was he to change his table to spend an hour in the company of one of the false sex? Yet he liked women, he liked Gollantz. . . . The struggle ended. 'I shall be proud if I may join you, Hermann.'

The change was effected quickly. Rodolphe rushed away to his rehearsal, and Hermann found himself forgetting to eat, staring into the dark-blue eyes of Marie Lorette. She was delightful. She spoke well and with intelligence ; she listened with an even greater intelligence. Her laugh was ready, but never tedious. Her smile was gay without being affectedly so. She had come to Paris recently, from Rouen, in company with her mother's elderly step-sister. She was an orphan, bereft of father and mother when she was a small child. She had, she admitted modestly, a tiny income, which she hoped to augment by singing at concerts and receptions. Oh no, not the opera! Her voice was too small, too undistinguished. She had known Rodolphe when he had toured France and come to Rouen. She liked him; he was kind and amusing. Yes, she loved to be amused.

The dinner ended. Both Hermann and Louis declared themselves to be entirely at her service whenever she cared to summon them. Louis railed again at the fact which made it necessary to leave to join some business friends; Hermann begged that he might be allowed to escort her home.

He drove her to a tall old house divided into apartments, where an old concierge hobbled out of her little hutch to open the door. The house, an old palace, still retained its dignity and beauty; to Hermann it seemed a fit place to shelter this girl to whom he had lost his heart.

'Is it too late to ask you to come and meet my aunt?' she asked.

Hermann, who dreaded the moment when he must leave her, protested that it was still quite early. He mounted to the first floor, and was duly presented to a slightly over-blown woman, fashionably attired, with a florid complexion and hair which was palpably false. He was offered wine and small cakes. He listened to Madame Pilon's opinion of Paris, and heard of the various engagements which had already been secured by her niece. He heard the names of her employers with some dismay, for they were all people mixing in society which was too exclusive to permit Hermann Gollantz, the rich Hebrew antique dealer, to enter their doors. It had become sufficiently safe in Paris for families to remember their aristocratic lineage, and there was a certain section who made the most of the fact that they possessed ancestors of distinction.

Madame Pilon not only imparted knowledge, she asked questions. She wanted to know his opinion of this piece of silver, of that little picture, and showed a very sound commercial understanding of values. The girl spoke very little, and to Hermann it was sufficient to watch her as she sat, with her long red-gold ringlets falling on either side of her heart-shaped face, while her aunt conducted the conversation.

'Come again, Monsieur Gollantz,' Madame Pilon ordered.

'Yes, please come again,' Marie begged. 'It is sometimes rather lonely in a strange city.'

Her aunt smiled. 'Poor child! But I am stern. I cannot have your work interrupted. There is a time for study, a time for work, a time for rest—and a time when you can see your friends, Marie. Today is Friday. Monsieur, will you take coffee with us on Sunday at five o'clock?'

'I shall count the hours until five o'clock on Sunday,' Hermann said. He walked home, because the thought of riding seemed impossible. He wanted to be alone to collect his thoughts. He had fallen in love for the first time, and he felt that he had been translated into a new earth which closely resembled Paradise.

He went out early the following morning and bought flowers. Not one bunch, but masses of the most beautiful blooms he could find. It seemed to Hermann that morning, that money had only been made so that it might be spent on flowers for Marie Lorette.

Sunday came, and he went to the tall old house armed with gifts of more flowers, fruit, and expensive sweets. He was greeted warmly. Madame Pilon praised his taste, nibbled his sweets between strong white teeth, and declared that the fruit was the best she had eaten since she came to Paris. Marie spoke very little ; she smiled at him, listened to his stories of Paris, and here and there interjected a few words upon which Hermann hung as if they had been the sayings of a sybil. Later she sang, while Madame Pilon accompanied her, and Hermann was entranced with the delicate beauty of her voice. It was not strong, but beautiful in tone, and she used it with considerable artistry. Her songs were what might have been termed of the provocative type, which lent themselves to a certain variation of expression ; it might almost have been said that Marie acted as well as sang. Hermann found himself laughing at the clever innuendoes, which never degenerated into *double entendre*, and at the same time admiring the real loveliness of the voice.

Nature had not only made Marie Lorette the present of an excellent voice, an ear which was perfectly true, but had endowed her with all the gifts of comedy. In addition she possessed a sense of fun and knew precisely how to deliver her songs with perfect diction, and no unnecessary labouring of their points or exaggeration of their high lights.

Hermann, almost delirious with happiness, ventured to offer an invitation to dinner. With hesitation he begged that he might

42

be allowed to take them to Vérys, and dwelt for a moment on the
excellence of the truffles. Madame Pilon's eyes became almost
melting at the word. She bowed her acceptance. 'My niece and I
will be charmed, Monsieur.'

4

I

WEEKS passed, and Hermann Gollantz still found himself in
love with the girl who was like Lola Montez. Indeed, his devotion
for her had grown, until now, when the autumn was beginning to
change to winter, he felt that she was his whole life. His mind was
constantly turning to her ; she occupied his thoughts during the
hours when they were apart, and his time was filled with discovering what things she wanted most and obtaining them at all costs.

He did not neglect his work, because that work was part of
the man. His innate honesty prevented him accepting money
from Fernando which he did not earn. Very often it was a struggle
when Marie said that she could see him at such and such a time,
on such and such a day, to reply that he must attend an important
sale, interview an important customer, or that he had promised
to escort his mother to some picture gallery or concert.

'The trouble is that we are both busy people,' Marie said. 'I
must study new songs, find new songs, rest, do my exercises,
and many other things which sound trivial, but in a singer's life
are important. You are a man of affairs, and your time is not
entirely your own. So—shall we say four o'clock on Thursday,
you will come and take coffee?'

For weeks she was elusive, and seemed determined to accept
him as nothing more than a good friend, as she accepted
Rodolphe, who had made such a success of his part in L' Indifférent. Hermann, with native caution outweighing natural impulse, delayed declaring himself for what seemed to him an age.
Then one afternoon, while Madame Pilon interviewed her dressmaker, his passion was too strong for him.

He caught her slim hand in his, and tried to tell her what she
meant to him. 'I loved you the moment I saw you,' he said. 'To
me you are the whole world ; you are everything that is beautiful,

wonderful, and good. I live for you, because of you. Your coming changed my whole life, and all I ask is that I may devote my life to you. Marie, tell me that you love me half as well as I love you—I shall be utterly content.'

She drew back a little, whilst allowing him to retain her hand.

'Oh, I had no idea of your feelings,' she faltered. 'I thought—I thought that you just—well, just liked us, my aunt and me. I didn't think.'

'But now,' Hermann begged, 'now you will think, beloved, and think very hard and seriously, if you could love me sufficiently to promise to marry me?'

Her lovely face lost some of its radiance. 'Marriage! It is impossible. Listen, let me tell you. We are poor people—you will never know how poor. My aunt has made sacrifices for me ; great, great sacrifices. She had money, not very much it is true, but what she had was spent on my musical training. I promised her—for she is ambitious for me, my kind aunt—that I would repay her everything. How can I do that unless I make a success in my career? Already I begin to make headway. People like my work ; I amuse them ; I am engaged at the finest houses—oh, such wonderful houses!—and my fees are mounting steadily. To relinquish it all now would be not only foolish but unfair to her. You see that, Hermann?'

'I realize that what you say is typical of you. You have that truth and honesty in which I have been taught to believe. But—oh, my dearest, I love you so. I have a certain amount of money. . . . If you married me, might I not make it my pride, my privilege, to repay your aunt for all she has done for you? It would make me so happy.'

Marie shook her head, so that the long curls which seemed to Hermann to have caught his heart in their twists and twirls, swung backwards and forwards.

'No, that is impossible. I have told you that my aunt is ambitious. It is not only money she wishes for ; she wishes to see me famous, well known, sought after as an artist. That is her dream, and I must not shatter it. It would be too cruel when I owe her so much.'

'Tell me, then, that you love me.' He tried to hide his disappointment, because he loved her for her honesty and uprightness, for her consideration for the woman who had been good to her. 'Say—Hermann, I love you.'

Very softly she repeated : 'Hermann, I love you.'

44

'One day you will marry me? If I am patient? I would be so very patient. I would wait seven years, and a further seven years for my lovely Marie.'

Her blue eyes lit up with sudden laughter. 'Could you wait so long? My dear, patient Jew!'

'For you I could wait for ever and ever.'

She lifted her hands and laid them on either side of his face. 'I promise that you shall not wait too long, my dear. Only let me work. When I say that I cannot see you, cannot dine here or drive there, call on that patience of yours, and understand that I must work—must make a success—if we are one day to be happy together. Promise me!'

He caught her hands and kissed them. 'I promise, I promise. God bless you, my splendid Marie.'

He gathered that Madame Pilon understood the love which they felt for each other. She was considerate, and often allowed them to sit alone together. Hermann in his gratitude showered gifts upon her, and never came to see Marie without bringing with him some tribute for her aunt. The old concierge at the gate seemed to understand too. She smiled at him, and very often the well-dressed young man, with his beautiful clothes, and his fair hair parted so meticulously down the back of his head and brushed forward over his ears, would stand, cane in hand, and chat with the wrinkled old woman.

'How is your rheumatism today, Madame Lepic?' Hermann would ask, ready to stand and talk because he knew that he was five minutes too early for his appointment with Marie.

'Bad, Monsieur. Very bad. The cold will kill me.'

'You must wrap up more. You ought to wear warmer clothes.'

'That is very well!' Madame Lepic snapped. 'It is very well for you to talk. Why, the cost of that cane would keep me for a year.'

'Scarcely—scarcely. However, today I have sent a big woollen shawl for you. Wear it to please me.'

Or he would come with his parcels of sweets and fruit, and hand one containing good red meat, a bottle of wine, or, perhaps a capon, to the old woman, always begging her acceptance of his gifts as if she did him an honour in taking them.

He was so happy himself, that it seemed a small thing to Hermann Gollantz to carry meat or wine or chicken to an old woman who was old and rather tired of a life in which she had always been poor.

45

He never knew how often Madame Lepic commented upon his charity when she pointed him out to her neighbours.

'There goes a Jew,' she would say. 'He tries his best to atone for the fact that his ancestors crucified the Lord! What a good young man! Yes, a Jew, but give me that kind of Jew before the aristocrats who come here, who speak to me as if I were a dog, and keep their hands on their purses, trembling that they might have to give away the smallest coin to the poor. That's a man, I tell you, that Monsieur Gollantz.'

As the winter drew on, Hermann persuaded Miriam to give a great entertainment, and to engage Mademoiselle Lorette to sing for her. It was not a great success. The Jews who came to the gathering did not care for light music, and Marie's exquisite comedy seemed to jar on them a little. They preferred their own German music, played with passionate affection and complete mastery, by a great pianist. Fernando listened with attention while Marie sang, and summed up her performance in one word 'Trivial'.

Miriam, splendid in velvet and pearls, immense and a little heavy in mind as well as in body, said: 'Amusing perhaps, but when I want amusement I prefer to pay for a seat at the theatre. In my own house I prefer to set a standard, not lower my present one.'

True, the mother of Louis Caveau, the grandson of old Comparetti, and the young wife of Hermann's friend, Manuel Lara, gave Marie engagements. Hermann was able to be present, and note with some amusement that most of the younger women disliked his beloved, the older women appeared to distrust her, old men glanced at her under heavy-lidded eyes, and young ones opened theirs very wide and stared with unconcealed admiration.

He decided that women believed comedy to be a male prerogative, and they would have admired Marie more if she had sung the ultra-sentimental and slightly sickly Italian songs which were so common at that time.

Nothing shook his own admiration and devotion for her. She absorbed him, became—apart from his work—his only real interest. He dreamed, he planned, he imagined; and knew that his love grew stronger and more steadfast every day. It seemed that nothing could be good enough for her, and each week his gifts increased in value. He begged to be allowed to buy her clothes. She must look well dressed at her entertainments, and he swore

46

that she must regard it as his investment—an investment in the art of a great comedienne.

Marie blushed, even cried a little, protesting that it was terrible to think that he had evidently found her clothes old and shabby. Hermann, half demented at the idea that he had hurt her, pleaded, and finally appealed to Madame Pilon. Madame Pilon considered the matter gravely, and admitted that, while she sympathized with Marie—'the poor little one'—she thought, since they were virtually betrothed, it might be permitted.

The rest was easy. Hermann protested that if clothes were permissible, then why not shoes, stockings, gloves, and hats? Madam Pilon, laughing at his practical outlook, agreed that if one had a logical mind—and it appeared that hers was supremely logical—these things might indeed be permitted.

Marie Lorette was dressed by the best dressmakers in Paris, wore shoes which were the envy of all right-thinking women, and carried above her wonderful curls hats which were the most delicious creations imaginable.

Fernando increased Hermann's salary, and noticed that the fellow never by any chance bought new clothes. He was becoming positively shabby. Hermann, who had been perilously nearly a dandy!

'You don't play very high, do you?' Fernando asked one morning when they were inspecting some of the new playing cards which were one of Hermann's innovations into the stock.

'I rarely play at all—and then very moderately, sir.'

'Or speculate, perhaps?'

Hermann, his face flushing suddenly, shook his head. 'No, sir.'

Meldola made his little gesture of demanding forgiveness with those fine thin hands of his. 'Believe me, I never wish to pry into your affairs. The only thing which concerns me is your happiness, Hermann. I should find it difficult to forgive anyone who hurt you.'

Hermann, his face still flushed, met the kindly, shrewd old eyes with a glance of genuine affection. 'I am very happy, Uncle Fernando,' he said.

II

There was no mistake about it, old Madame Lepic detested her clients on the first floor. She scowled at the straight, soldierly back of Madame Pilon, and found herself unable to join in the chorus of admiration which followed Mademoiselle Lorette when she took her walks abroad.

'That one is hard as nails,' she said to her daughter one morning when Madame Pilon crossed the courtyard on her way to do the morning shopping. 'She does her own marketing—and why? Because she is too mean to pay the extra few centimes which I should demand—and with justice—to do it for her!'

Annette, who was a dressmaker, turned forty, disappointed, and losing both her teeth and her figure very rapidly, bent over her stitching. 'That may be, but the girl is beautiful.' She sighed. 'I wish she would sometimes let me make clothes for her. I should take such a pride in the work.'

'Pah! Better make clothes for honest people!' her mother returned acidly. 'Beauty is nothing; what matters are the honest hearts which beat beneath coarse clothing.' She made the assertion with pride, fingering the rough cloth of her own bodice, though Madame Lepic's heart had never been overburdened with that quality of honesty which she extolled. 'Let me tell you, Annette, that there are things which I know, and which it might be well for the young Jew if he knew also.'

Annette lifted her tired eyes, blinked, and said with sudden interest:

'Oh, Mama, what things? Tell me!'

Her mother shook her untidy grey head. 'I tell nothing! One day, however, I shall be paid for all the insults offered to me by that stiff-necked old horror, and all the impertinences handed to me by the young—ah, well, I shall not soil my lips!'

The spring had burst on Paris suddenly. The streets seemed to bloom with flowers, the trees showed buds of brilliant green, fat, sticky buds which swelled and expanded in the soft air and gentle sunshine. Paris was gay, and the Parisians were gay and in accord with the mood of their beloved city. Hermann surveyed the clothes which he had worn through the winter and decided that he must buy new ones. Only last night Marie had laid her hand on the cuff of his blue coat and said that it was growing shabby, adding that the clear spring sunshine made new clothes necessary for everyone.

'The spring is unkind to poor people,' she said, half laughing, half wistful. 'The sunlight shows up the worn places, makes the seams shine a little. In spring when all the flowers wear such beautiful new clothes, one feels shabby, and a little disheartened.'

He had thought how beautiful her mind was, wondered at her

48

imagination, and been touched by the fact that she longed for new clothes. Mentally he added up the balance which stood to his credit in the bank and decided that he could, he must, afford to make her happy.

'If the flowers wear beautiful new clothes, then it is only right that the queen of all the flowers should do the same. Marie, go and get a new gown tomorrow. Let it be my spring-time present to you.'

'My dear, you are so good to me!' she cried. 'What have I ever done to deserve your thoughtfulness and love? Hermann! Dear, dear Hermann, what can I do to show my love for you?'

He held out his arms. 'Come and kiss me, and tell me that you love me.'

She lay in his arms, her beautiful head on his shoulder, silent and content. Presently she spoke to him, softly and tenderly. 'Things are coming right for us so soon, my dear. My engagements increase every month, and my fee grows larger. Look at the flowers which are sent to me. . . .'

He glanced round the room, and saw that there were many flowers which he had not sent to her. It was not in Hermann Gollantz's character to feel jealousy ; he would have regarded any such feeling as an insult to Marie.

'I see! And who sent all those, pray?'

She nestled closer in his arms. 'I don't even know their names. There were cards on the flowers ; I tore them off and threw them in the basket there by the desk. Who cares? I only want you. The rest—let them send me flowers ; why should I want to know their stupid names? There is only one name I wish to see—yours.'

She would let him listen to her new songs, and delight him by asking his opinion, and admitting very often that she relied upon his judgment. Once he found a little song for her—which his friend Caveau set to music—and brought it to her to try over. She liked it, though she found it lacking in comedy. Hermann, leaning over her shoulder as she read it, repeated some lines which delighted him.

> *Jusqu'à ce que les mers soient à sec, ma chère,*
> *Et que les rochers fondent au soleil:*
> *Je continuerai de t' aimer, ma chère. . . .*

49

'That is how I feel,' he said. 'That is true of me. I shall always love you, my dear. Remember that, won't you?'

There were times when he grew a little impatient that he could not see her more frequently, when he felt that to be limited to an hour here and an hour there was unnecessary and almost unworthy. He begged that he might sometimes call when he was in the town on business, explaining that he could often snatch an hour between appointments, and declaring that these unexpected moments were so precious, so lovely.

Marie listened, then shook her head.

'Hermann, if only I could say yes. What pleasure it would give me. To have you slip in at eleven to take a cup of chocolate with me ; to know that any moment of the day might bring you and—sunshine for your Marie. But it is not possible. My aunt would never allow it. My day is planned—every hour. I bath, I do exercises, I walk quickly for half an hour. I return and run over my songs and work at new ones. I lunch lightly. I rest. I work again. Oh, my life is not easy, and when I think that you are not satisfied —I am utterly miserable.'

Immediately at the sight of her distress, he was penitent. He declared that he was thoughtless, unkind, and begged her forgiveness. She cried a little, dried her tears on his handkerchief, and finally smiled at him a little mistily, and assured him that there was nothing for her to forgive. He was always the dearest, kindest, and most considerate of lovers.

Then, one afternoon in April, when the streets were flooded with the bright thin sunshine of spring, and Hermann was conscious that his heart was very full, that his love enveloped him and seemed to wrap him round in a golden haze, he was seized with an irresistible impulse to see her. What did it matter for once? Surely, if he disturbed her at her work for one half-hour it would not be such a great disaster? They had parted the night before with difficulty. Hermann knew that his passion for her had almost got the better of him, he had caught her to him and begged and pleaded with her to allow him to stay with her. Marie had been distressed, she had cried, and blamed herself, had asked if they should part, and if their life was too difficult? She had been gentle, kind, and had assured him that she loved him too much to give herself to him without the sanction of the Church.

'Now, you think it would make you happy,' she said between her sobs, 'but later, when we are married, you would look back with regret. You would remember that your wife was unable to bring with her that complete purity which all good men—and you are so really good, my Hermann—long for so passionately in their wives.'

He had agreed. He had been a little ashamed of himself, and begged for her forgiveness, but the scene had left him shaken and wretched ; and today he longed to see her, hold her hand, and assure her again and again that he understood how right she had been. His arms were full of daffodils, great bunches of other spring flowers, and as many bouquets of violets, each bound with clean yellow bass, as he could carry.

He felt very young and amazingly excited. Never before had he ventured to call upon Marie without her express permission ; he was daring greatly, and he felt that he was instituting a new order of precious intimacy. He arrived at the gate of the house and greeted Madame Lepic with a smile. A smile which held all the expectancy of youth, all the joy of a lover.

'Hello, Monsieur! This is an unusual hour for you to call.'

Hermann laughed. 'It is spring, and many strange things happen in spring. Is Mademoiselle Marie at home?'

The old woman looked at him curiously, her thin lips set tightly.

Finally she nodded. 'Mademoiselle is at home, but her aunt— her good aunt—is out.' She grinned, showing her discoloured and broken teeth. 'Think you that it is *convenable* that you visit Mademoiselle alone, Monsieur Hermann?'

Hermann looked at her appealingly. 'For once, and for only a few minutes. I have brought all these flowers—because it is a lovely day and the winter is over.' He spoke almost confidentially. 'There could be no possible harm—it is only a little surprise for Mademoiselle Marie.'

Her grim face broke into a smile, and under all her ugliness Hermann seemed to see something almost tender in her gaze. He wondered suddenly if she had ever had a son, and if she realized how high the hearts of young men beat in April ; if she remembered her own youth, when some young Parisian had come bringing her flowers in his hands, his eyes full of love.

'A little surprise, Monsieur Hermann! Ah, I understand. See, I will play the good fairy for you. Here is the key of the apartment, which Madame Pilon dropped only this afternoon as she left the house. I found it, and now it would seem that the fates arranged it for you. Open the door softly and you will find made-

51

moiselle singing one of her beautiful songs; you can give her your flowers as a—a—tribute! Eh?'

His face was alight with mischief; he looked to old Madame Lepic like a schoolboy. For a moment she hesitated, then took the key from a nail and gave it to him.

'There! Be quick!' she said, and as he almost snatched the key from her and ran quickly up the stairs, the old woman turned and went back into her little hutch-like office, shrugging her shoulders.

'Poor boy,' she murmured. 'Poor, good boy—but it is better. I shall be the loser; but why should they make a fool of him between them? Such women!'

Hermann opened the door softly, entered the apartment and, turning to the right, found himself in the salon. It was empty, and he stood for a moment, a smile on his lips, listening. Where was Marie? Perhaps in her bedroom which led out of the salon, the door of which was open a little. He listened and a faint sound reached him. It was as if Marie had whispered. . . . His smile widened—perhaps she was carrying on an imaginary conversation with himself. The thought delighted him, and he stood listening.

'My dear—oh, my beloved! How I worship you!'

He could bear it no longer. She was lonely, thinking of him. He called softly: 'Marie—Marie.'

For a moment there was dead silence; then another voice, quick and imperious, ejaculated: 'My God, what's that?'

A second later Marie's voice, shrill and hard, demanded: 'Who is there?'

Hermann felt the blood rush to his head, it beat against his temples like iron hammers, his heart suffocated him, hammering against his ribs, his throat was constricted. He could not reply. He stood, his face deathly white, the pulses in his forehead showing as they beat out their terrible percussions, his lips pale, drawn back, showing his white, even teeth.

The door of the bedroom was flung open, and a young man, his dress disordered, his hair rough, and his eyes flaming, burst into the salon.

'What the devil are you doing here? What are you? A thief? My God, you shall answer for this, my man, whoever you are.'

Still Hermann could not reply. His voice was dead, his throat paralysed. He clutched his flowers—those flowers which were to have surprised and delighted Marie. Where was Marie? What had she to do with this young man? He shivered suddenly, as

52

Marie appeared standing in the doorway—Marie in a peignoir of lacy, filmy material, and ribbons, her hair falling about her like a red-gold cloud.

'Hermann! Oh, my God!'

The sound of his name galvanized him into life. He drew himself up, stiffly, and almost like a soldier facing the enemy's guns.

'I ask your pardon, Mademoiselle,' he said, and his voice sounded strange in his own ears. 'I committed a grave breach of etiquette in entering the apartment. Pray believe that it was—a mistake.' Then, taking a step forward to draw nearer to the young man, lifted the flowers which he still held and struck him across the face with the blossoms.

The young man, tall and handsome, with curled dark hair and beautiful little side-whiskers, instinctively raised his hand to his cheek where the flowers had touched him. His rather sallow face was suffused, his eyes met Hermann's, hot and angry.

'You shall answer to me for that!' the young man said furiously.

'Whenever you wish, monsieur.'

'Your name?'

Hermann's fingers went to his waistcoat pocket. He took out a card and offered it. The other took it as if its touch contaminated his hand. He looked at it, then tore it in pieces and flung it on the ground.

'You damned swine!' he stammered with rage. 'You infernal scoundrel! How dared you! A Jew—a Jew tradesman.' He half turned to Marie, who still stood in the doorway. 'Imagine it. This —this common shopkeeper dares to strike me! The insufferable coward. Now he will go round Paris boasting that he struck Lucien Marcel Savonnier de Loménie—and lived! What a position!'

Hermann watched his furious face, twisted with rage ; listened to his stammering speech, for he was almost inarticulate, and knew that his own anger had changed from hot fury to a cold calculating hate. This exquisite young man, curled and scented, dressed in the height of fashion, had been granted the favours for which he himself had scarcely dared ask. He had lain in her arms, felt her lips against his, listened to the murmured words of love for which Hermann had hungered.

His voice was entirely under control as he said: 'It is unnecessary to insult me further, Monsieur. I will meet you when and where you wish ; the sooner the better.'

The other lifted his hands above his head. His rage had reached its climax. He was almost speechless. 'Hell and damnation!' he shouted. 'Don't you realize that it's impossible? How can I—the Duc de Loménie—meet a Jew, a little shopkeeper? France has seen some strange sights during these last years, but she has yet to see the members of her old nobility fighting—meeting as equals —Jew traders!'

'You mean,' Hermann said slowly, 'that you refuse to meet me?'

'Refuse! What else is there for me to do?'

'Very well. One excuse will serve as well as another. I warn you that all Paris shall hear of it ; Paris shall judge who is the coward.'

Marie rushed forward, her hands outstretched. 'Hermann— you cannot mention this! It would ruin me. Oh, I trusted you.'

'As I did you, apparently,' he said coldly. 'What does it matter to me what people think or say of you? Can't you understand that—now, you don't *matter* to me? You are of no account whatever.'

'Then you will spread this scandal—you will ruin me, Hermann?'

He stared at her, wondering how he could bear to lose her. Words meant nothing ; he might speak coldly, might adopt an attitude of indifference, but he knew that his love for this woman would not die easily. He must face days and nights of pain, lone-liness, and bitter regret, when his one thought would be how he might see her again. Even now, he knew that he could not bear to hurt her in any way. His lips were sealed, his hands tied.

'No,' he said. 'I shall do—nothing. You are quite safe.'

She made a movement to catch his hand, but he drew back quickly, saying as he did so, in a tone which was almost fearful: 'No, no, don't touch me.'

He turned and walked out of the room, closing the door behind him. He felt chilled, numb with pain, scarcely conscious of what he did. He stumbled out into the courtyard, where old Madame Lepic sat in her hutch, knitting. Hermann paused and stood, swaying a little, before her.

'You knew?' he said.

She raised her eyes from her work. 'Yes, I knew.'

'And you let me go in—knowing what I should find?'

'You found what I hoped you would find,' she said. 'You found what you might have found a hundred times, only'—she gave a

54

grim chuckle—'you would not always have found the same man.'

'It was terribly cruel. . . .'

She rose and came close to him, laying her dirty, wrinkled hand on his arm. 'See here,' she said, 'I did this for one reason— because I liked you. You'd been good to me. You're honest. Too good to be tricked and used by those two women. You think that you hate me now, but you won't always feel that—and even if you did, it wouldn't matter to me. I don't suppose that I shall ever see you again. Good-bye, Monsieur Gollantz.'

Mechanically he said: 'Good-bye, Madame Lepic.' Then, from force of habit, his hand went to his pocket. He took out a handful of money, looked at it as if the coins meant nothing to him, and with painful care selected a gold piece and handed it to her.

'You're too kind, Monsieur,' she said, as she had said a hundred times before, and Hermann answered as he invariably answered: 'Not at all, Madame Lepic.'

He walked out into the quiet street, where the afternoon light was soft and kindly. He saw nothing, heard nothing, only walked, his hands deep in his pockets, his head bowed, on and on without sense of direction, or feeling of fatigue. Later he found himself seated in a little café which he did not recognize ; he was drinking black coffee, tasting the crude bitterness of it against his lips. He wondered how long he had been sitting there ; then the sound of the great clock of St. Germain struck twelve, and Hermann listened to the heavy, booming strokes. He stood up, called to the shabby waiter and paid his bill. He thought: 'I must have been there a long time, and drunk a great many cups of coffee.'

The night was cool, calm, and the sky bright with stars. He was in a little cobbled square, there were a few trees, and as he stood there a white cat scurried past as if she realized how late it was. Before him narrow streets led down, and in the distance he saw the lights of the heart of Paris. Hermann straightened his shoulders, then began to walk slowly down the hill, making his way back to the big house in the rue Castiglione.

5

'MARK what I say,' Fernando Meldola said to his stout, magnificently gowned niece. 'The boy is unhappy.'

'I could see that with both my eyes shut,' she returned.

'More—he is unhappy because of some woman.'

'That, too, is obvious to me, and I can tell you something, Uncle Fernando, I know who the woman is! She is that little singer who came to my conversazione and sang those stupid songs. I know!'

'That creature!' Meldola's fine face expressed acute disgust. 'Surely you are wrong. What attraction could Hermann, of all people, find in her?'

Miriam wagged her handsome head with its crown of grey hair, so that her multitude of chins swung from side to side. 'Why ask me? I am only a woman, and to me she was—revolting. Men are strange things.'

They talked long of Hermann, sympathizing with him, regretting that the poor boy should have been hurt and disappointed, that he should have spent his money—for it was evident that he had spent a great deal of money—on a woman who was worthless. That she must have been worthless seemed palpable to them both, otherwise how could she have treated their beloved Hermann badly?

'He has grown so thin!' Miriam said mournfully.

'So serious, and his clothes are terrible. He takes no care.' They agreed that Hermann was in a bad way, and discussed how they might best soothe his heart and make him take an interest in life again.

Hermann himself cared very little for anything in those days. He found that, in spite of himself, his mind turned back again and again to his last meeting with Marie. Again and again he saw her, standing in the doorway between her bedroom and the salon, with her peignoir of lace and silk falling round her like a cloud. He saw her wide, startled eyes, her parted lips, and heard her voice begging him not to betray her to the world at large. He visualized her dark-haired lover, whose insults to himself and his race stung afresh whenever he remembered them. Paris had seen many strange things, but nothing so fantastic, so impossible and wildly improbable as the sight of an aristocrat defending his honour against a Jew! The House of Meldola, noted for its honesty and strict integrity, was still to the nobility nothing more important than a shop kept by a huckstering Jew.

Hermann, seated in his own room, with tightly compressed lips, with new lines on his pleasant face traced there by misery and loneliness, would clench his fists and try to conquer his indignation.

'I did wrong,' he would decide. 'I should have forced him to fight me then and there. Our fists would have been sufficient. I should have thrown convention to the winds and defended myself against the insults of a member of a worn-out aristocracy. For years they were afraid to raise their heads; they begged to be designated Citizen This and Citizen the Other—now they remember with belated pride that they are dukes, counts, and all the rest of it!'

His pride—that indomitable pride nurtured by Fernando, encouraged by the fact that Jews were occupying the topmost rungs of the ladder in most of the arts, recollecting the fine taste, the good manners, and the culture of his uncle's friends, had suffered terribly. Again and again he knew that his face flushed suddenly when he remembered the epithets which had been bestowed upon him by Marie's lover.

To be born a Jew had been held by Fernando and by Miriam Gollantz to be a just cause for congratulation. It had permeated the whole life of the house in the rue Castiglione. One must not do this and one must do that because being a Jew laid rules and regulations of conduct upon one.

Now, a dark-haired young man, who had helped Marie to deceive him, had dealt a blow at this pride, this satisfaction. It would have been sufficient to have lost her, but that was not enough; in addition fate must wound his pride, and leave him insulted and without opportunity of revenge. His life seemed so empty, so utterly purposeless. What did his work matter? Why buy and sell? Why congratulate himself that he and his uncle possessed the finest store of antique and beautiful things in all Paris? What was the use of working, of amassing money when there was no Marie on whom to spend what he earned?

For months Hermann had lived in an atmosphere of romance, and now, when he found himself living in bitter and lonely reality, his life was desolate. He had a nature which was as sensitive as it was kindly, and the thought of his betrayal almost broke his heart. The whole thing had been so utterly cruel, and had been charged with a certain mercenary vulgarity which made his fine nature shrink.

He would not allow himself to speculate as to whether the Duc de Loménie was Marie's only lover, or whether he shared her favours with others. The thought had obtruded once, and Hermann had recoiled from it, feeling that he wronged himself to allow such ideas a place in his consciousness. What did it matter to him if he had been betrayed by her with one man or with a dozen? That was beside the point; nothing could either increase or diminish his pain and grief at that betrayal.

Miriam watched him with large dark eyes full of sympathy. She hesitated to intrude upon his obvious unhappiness; all that she could do was to take great care that the table bore the dishes he loved best, that his room was kept even better than it had been formerly, if that were possible. She was intelligent, but the thought of trying to make Hermann confide in her seemed impossible. So she spent money on her son, buying him those small luxuries which he had once loved. The finest lawn handkerchiefs, socks and stockings of the richest and heaviest silk, cravats of the latest shape and shade, newly published books in magnificent bindings, and canes with heads of ivory, jade, even of gold.

Hermann thanked her gravely: his lips smiled, but the smile never reached his eyes.

Miriam sighed, bought exquisite foods, chickens cooked in rare wine and stuffed with the truffles Hermann liked so much, a bottle of wonderful sherry from Grignon, who only consented to sell it to her because she was a valued client, and ordered her cook to prepare *vol-au-vents* which were miracles of lightness and rich flavours.

Hermann ate very little; he no longer savoured the food with appreciation or tasted the wine which she offered with the almost beatific expression of a connoisseur.

Fernando did his best to rouse him. He would invent arguments over the articles in their store.

'This, in my opinion, is a fine example of Caravage at his best,' he would declare, standing before a palpable and recently bought Ribera.

Where once such a statement would have called for arguments, reasons, and comparisons from Hermann, he now barely glanced at the picture, and said: 'Do you think so? I should have believed it to be a Ribera,' and relapsed into silence. It was the same with china, glass, furniture, and silver. He no longer cared, and he did not pretend to show an interest which he did not feel.

Meldola watched him during the hot summer, and was still trying to arouse his interests when the leaves began to fall in the Bois, and people shivered a little as they sat outside the cafés, turning their eyes towards the warmer interiors.

'Something must be done,' he said to Miriam. 'The boy is allowing himself to grow old, bitter. He finds no interest in anything; he becomes self-centred in his grief. May the devil fly away with that—that——'

'Hush!' Miriam ordered. 'Do not soil your lips with either her name or description.'

'You are right. I shall speak frankly to Hermann.'

The next day he ordered Hermann to sit down near him at the big desk. He was growing old, and he dreaded the interview more keenly than he would have cared to admit. At over seventy such interviews were apt to be a little exhausting; the sight of pain on Hermann's face was disturbing. Meldola shivered. How he loathed pain, either for himself or for those he loved.

'I have to speak to you, Hermann,' he said. 'It is time. For nearly six months your beloved mother and I have tried to make your life pleasant, and—you have not responded. I do not ask for your confidence, though if you offered it I should be glad; it might make my task easier. What I must insist upon is that you make an effort to recover yourself. You are slipping, at twenty-seven, into the habit of life only suitable to a man of my own advanced years. More, you are making your mother unhappy—that dear sweet woman—and you are robbing my last years of their brightness. In other words, my dear boy, you are being infernally selfish.'

Hermann raised his haggard eyes and met the dark, kindly ones of the old man. 'I am sorry,' he said.

'That is not enough,' Meldola said sternly. 'I want more than a mere expression of regret. I want a promise to mend your ways, to realize that one has a duty to others as well as to oneself. I may tell you that you pay this—woman too great a compliment.'

Hermann raised his eyes; his pale face flushed suddenly and painfully.

'I should prefer not to speak of her,' he said.

Meldola nodded. 'Possibly, and I only mention her because I am forced by the position in which I find myself. I repeat, you

59

pay her too high a compliment in allowing her to ruin your life. What is over—is over. What was to be—was to be. It is better to discover that you have taken the wrong path early in the morning than late at night, for you have still time to retrace your steps and find the path which leads to content and peace.'

He sighed, and looked at Hermann with grave eyes filled with affection. 'Youth is very cruel,' he said. 'You are typical of youth. You have been hurt—and in your pain you forget that neither your wonderful mother nor myself have lived lives which were free from pain. You believe that no one has ever suffered as you suffer. Pah! How youthful that is! Wrapped in a cloak of selfish misery—a cloak in which secretly you glory a little, for there is something romantic in unrequited love to men of your age—you forget that of necessity we who love you share your every joy and every sorrow. I appeal to you. For six months you have made us suffer with you, through you, and for you. Have we not suffered enough? I am old; your mother is a woman who has known many sorrows. Hermann, are you not sufficiently brave, sufficiently kindly, sufficiently affectionate, to put an end to the pain of an old man and a woman who both love you?'

The sight of his handsome old face, with its crown of white hair, the kindly eyes, the sensitive, mobile mouth, and the voice which, however hard the words might seem, was so musically gentle, touched Hermann profoundly. He moved towards Fernando impulsively, and held out his hands.

'I am sorry,' he said. 'Perhaps I did not understand how unselfish your love for me was. I have been self-centred. I have proved myself unworthy of all the consideration and affection which you give me. It is over. I shall begin again, and you shall see a new Hermann who will really be the old Hermann you loved.'

With a resolution which held some element of fierceness, Hermann flung himself into his work again with his old wholeheartedness. He forced himself to smile, and realized that each day the smiles came more easily. He praised the elaborate food which Miriam offered him, he admired her gifts and wore them with pride, he went with her to the theatre and the opera; and six months later the memory of Marie Lorette had become vague and just a little dim. He thought of her with a half-romantic, half-grieving tenderness. She emerged from his dreams as a creature who had possibly been the victim of circumstances, more sinned against than sinning, driven to deceits and follies by the lack of money and the ambition of that hard-featured old woman, her aunt.

That change of feeling was typical of Hermann Gollantz throughout his life. He could never at any time harbour resentment for very long, and would always find reasons and excuses for everyone except himself.

Though he took up his life again, though his business prospered, Paris had lost her attraction for him. The streets, the boulevards, the cafés and restaurants which he once loved now bored him. He saw the Parisians as a race which made no real appeal to him, neither physically nor intellectually. Again and again his mind turned to the city where he had been so entirely happy, the City of the Winds, with the wide Danube flowing round it.

Alone, he dreamed dreams, and always those dreams were staged in Vienna. The only time he listened with real attention to the talk of his acquaintances was when they talked to him of Vienna, of the life there, and of the splendid opportunities for business and building fine positions in the life of that city.

Miriam, who despite her luxury-loving nature and her indolence, had an eye which was very keen and a sensibility which was remarkably astute, noticed the change in his attitude.

'I think you don't like Paris so much these days, my Hermann.'

Hermann started. It came as a complete surprise to him that his mother realized his feelings. 'Like it? Oh, well enough, Mama. I am not enamoured with it—as I once was.'

'I believe that a change might be good for all of us,' she said. 'Your uncle talks of retiring from business, of leaving it to you.' She shrugged her massive shoulders. 'I do not like the idea of your wearing the shoes of other men, however well made they may be. I had rather you made a pair for yourself. Well, why make them in Paris? There are other places.'

'Yes.' Hermann's voice was suddenly eager. 'Indeed, yes.'

'London, for example.'

'Yes, possibly London.' His voice was not so eager.

'Brussels. . . .'

'Very like a small Paris.'

'How right you are! Your business must not begin in a provincial city. Perhaps Berlin?'

Hermann shook his head. 'Art in Berlin—I doubt it.'

'Milan.' Then, catching sight of his expression: 'Ah, no. I remember Italy made no appeal to you. There is Vienna. . . .' Her heart leapt as she noted the sudden light in his eyes. It was almost

61

as if she had mentioned the name of a beloved mistress. 'Yes, I have always felt that Vienna was a fine place. I should like to see it myself.'

For an hour he talked to her of Vienna and she listened, delighted at the enthusiasm with which he spoke. He was years younger, it seemed to her, and her great heart swelled with affection as she listened. What a fine fellow he was! How deeply he appreciated beauty, how he loved life and music, art and culture. How she loved and admired him, and how determined she was that he should make a life for himself where he could be happy.

That evening she talked with Fernando. She sat sipping her over-sweet coffee, taking bon-bon after bon-bon from a decorated box and nibbling them with her strong white teeth.

She yawned suddenly, noisily. 'O-oh! Forgive me, that is liver! I find in these days I am always liverish. I should not wonder if I died of some liver complaint.'

'No, no,' Fernando expostulated. 'I can tell you that it is only you take so little exercise, Miriam.'

'Exercise! How can I take exercise when I never enjoy it? Paris has changed. It has become vulgar, ordinary. I no longer find Paris amusing.'

Her uncle, with the melancholy retrospection of the old, agreed. 'Paris is no longer the centre of the world. Paris has become—commercial. I notice it in business—not that I do very much now. I leave it all to our good boy. And who could do it better!'

Miriam leant forward and with grave care selected another and rather larger bon-bon. 'I wonder you do not retire, Uncle Fernando. Hermann is young and active, and it is always better for a young man to work—for himself. He ought to be his own master.'

'I agree, I agree. I have thought it over. I long to leave this work and take my ease, reading all the books I have always longed to read, hearing all the music I have longed to hear, listening to all the arguments which I have never had time to talk to a finish. The place is ready for him to step into. It is time that the old man was laid by, waiting for the time when he will be gathered to his fathers.'

Miriam swallowed the last pieces of bon-bon, rose and walked over to where he sat. She put her arms round him and drew him to her bosom, as if he had been a much-loved child.

'Never, never!' she cried. 'Do not speak of such things. I could not bear it. It would kill me if I lost you, you have been everything to me for so long. But'—and her voice became less charged with emotion—'I agree that it is time you rested a little, played a little, enjoyed life. Moreover, it would be good for Hermann— but not here, not in Paris.'

Meldola sat suddenly erect, and pushed her gently from him. Her words startled him. 'Not in Paris! Leave the business which I have founded! My Miriam, have you gone *meshugge*?'

'You think me a foolish woman—a little mad,' Miriam said. 'It is not so. Since that horrible woman treated Hermann badly he has never been the same; that is one reason why he should leave Paris. Again, I wish him to make his own way in the world, not to climb to prosperity on your shoulders. In addition, as I have said before, Paris does not suit me. I shall probably die soon if I stay here. And you, are you ever well in Paris? No, you suffer from cold, rheumatism, many things of which you say nothing because you have such a brave heart—but because I love you, I notice a great deal.'

Fernando Meldola who, at over seventy, was healthier than many men of half his age, who had never suffered from anything worse than a cold in the head, and a slight palpitation which his doctor knew very well to be stomachic and not organic, immediately saw himself as a silently suffering old man, drawing rapidly to his end.

'My Miriam is too clever,' he said tenderly and with some emotion. 'I agree that Paris has changed. After all, I have sufficient money to allow Hermann to begin again somewhere else, and my reputation—well, it goes beyond Paris! Where might we go? To London?'

Miriam lifted her fine, beringed hands in horror.

'London! And you hate the cold! For six months of the year it rains, and for the other six it is wrapped in fog.'

'Milano?'

She pursed her lips. 'Too hot for you after this climate.'

'Berlin?'

She shrugged her shoulders. 'The Germans know and care less for art than even the new French. You would die with horror at their vulgarity.'

'You think too much for me, and what will suit me,' Fernando protested.

'Impossible,' she laughed.

'Budapest? No—too far away. Madrid? No, you are right, they

have no money for pictures in Spain.' He frowned. 'It is difficult. I wonder if Vienna would suit you?'

'Would it suit *you*?' she asked. 'For me, I have always longed to go there. There is gaiety, culture, music—I believe that their opera is delightful, and the food, I am told, is superb.'

Meldola rose, set down his coffee-cup and smiled. 'I shall think it over. It was a lucky thought. Vienna! Who knows—I may develop into one of the typical old men who hum waltzes and ogle all the pretty girls.'

II

So it came about that, a month later, Fernando announced to Hermann that he was going to give up his business, and that he believed they had all been in Paris too long. He explained at great length that, after all, the French had treated Italy anything but well, and he stressed the fact that at heart he was, and would always remain, an Italian.

'France has changed,' Fernando said. 'I believe that you have noticed it. There was a time when all that was exquisite in art, in furniture, in thought, emanated from France. Then she sold her soul to a man who believed that decoration could be expressed by a scattering of bees and his own initial. Since then—well, you and I have seen. So if you like the idea we might break new ground, and take our taste, our knowledge, and our treasures to a country where people still admire the beautiful.'

Hermann, his heart suddenly beating very fast, said: 'You mean——'

'I mean that we shall transport Meldola and Partner to Vienna.'

Miriam was delighted; Hermann smiled again. He was almost boyish in his expectancy. Meldola moved among his treasures, deciding which Hermann must take to Vienna, and which might be sold in Paris.

'We shall need new clothes,' he laughed. 'No Paris tailor has ever been able to cut properly. We will go shabby until we can place our orders with tradesmen who know what is implied by the word "style".'

All the resentment which had lain in his heart since the years when Napoleon descended upon Italy, robbing her of her treasures, flamed and was voiced by the old Italian Jew. Perhaps under it all lay the old grief that through Napoleon and his adventure into the realms of piracy, the man he had trusted and admired had fallen. Though he had never spoken of Gollantz since his death, though he had never referred to his bitter disappointment, Fernando had never forgotten, and his sudden denunciation of France and French manners may have sprung from that old grief.

It was decided that Miriam and Hermann should leave Paris in the early days of 1833. Hermann should attend to the safe delivery of the small but exquisite stock which they were transporting; then Miriam and he were to find a suitable apartment, and make it ready for Fernando.

The arrangement was Miriam's. She was a masterful and capable woman, and wished to have the selection of her future home in her own hands. She knew what she wanted, knew, too, that nothing was impossible for the woman who had two men and an ample bank balance behind her. She realized that neither her uncle nor her son would deny her anything on which she set her heart, and she determined that the life of Miriam Gollantz, with her distinguished old uncle and her good-looking son, should be a very different and much gayer affair than it had been in Paris.

She had loved Abraham passionately, but she had mourned him for many years, and now, middle-aged and immensely stout, she knew that her heart remained young and ready for adventure.

As they sat at dinner on their last night in Paris, Fernando handed a folded paper to Hermann, saying as he did so: 'From this moment the House of Meldola ceases to exist. I am merely a sleeping partner in the House of Gollantz. Take this with my blessings—peace be to you.'

Hermann took the paper, and unfolding it found that Fernando had transferred the whole of the stock to him together with a substantial sum, merely reserving for himself a small percentage of the profits on each year. His eyes filled with tears, and he stammered his thanks and gratitude.

Fernando lifted his hand, smiling.

'Please do not thank me. Ever since I sent to Italy for the beloved daughter of my sister—peace be to her—ever since that daughter became in effect my own child, she and her son have brought me all the happiness I have known, and'—he bowed to Miriam, still smiling—'I count myself to have been a very happy man indeed. I am the patriarch, and I am sending you out, Hermann, to open up new ways for us. It may be forgiven me if I say one or two things to you before you go, things which are very

65

near my heart. I shall join you presently. I shall, if the God of my Fathers wills it, be with you for some years more; but you are going to be master. Remember that a good master makes good servants. Remember that all the gold in the world cannot buy honour. Remember that to you the honour of your race must remain always a personal thing, a thing which you are ready to guard with your life. Act as a *shomer*—a guard—on behalf of your fellow Jews. Make your name so respected, keep it so spotless, that when you are gathered to your fathers, men may say: "Hermann Gollantz—an honest man." And others will object, saying: "It is sufficient to say that he was a good Jew."

'I have cared very little for forms and ceremonies, Hermann. I have been called *link,* and perhaps rightly, but I have kept my name clean, and I have made it impossible for any man to say that he was robbed of one penny by me, or because of me. One more thing and I am done. Never shirk responsibilities, and never evade them. That is all. Miriam, my dear, you must forgive me if I have become garrulous. It is the privilege of the aged. It is the duty of the young to be tolerant with them.'

They sat late that night, talking of their plans. Hermann's eyes shone, and his voice was quick with excitement. Words, ideas, plans, poured from his lips. Miriam, sipping her late cup of chocolate, nibbling sweets, and smiling with complete content, listened to him. This was her son as she had known him before that wretched woman robbed him of his youth.

Meldola watched them both. The two people he loved best in the world. Miriam to him was still his beautiful young niece; he scarcely noticed how stout and heavy she had become; it never occurred to him that she ate too much and took too great an interest in the seasoning of her food. Hermann was all that he had wished Abraham to be, but Hermann was better material, he had the blood of the Lousadas and the Meldolas in him, which counteracted the hated streak which Fernando believed to have come as a heritage from the Gollantzes.

When at last Miriam put down her empty cup and brushed the last grains of sugar from her skirt, and, rising, declared that she was going to bed, he stood up, and in the language of his fathers blessed them both. Then, embracing them very tenderly, he bade them good night.

The next morning the coach left the house with Miriam Gollantz and her maid, while Hermann rode beside them. The heavier baggage was to leave later in the day. Meldola stood at the door of the old house and watched them go. Miriam leant from the window, tears streaming from her eyes, kissing her hand to him, begging him to take the greatest possible care of himself, and adding as a last injunction:

'Uncle Fernando—if you *must* eat oysters, eat them uncooked!'

Hermann waved many times before the party turned the corner, and Fernando Meldola walked slowly back into the house, which felt suddenly strangely desolate.

Miriam dried her tears, opened an elaborate box of sweetmeats, and ate them contentedly. Hermann rode on ahead; his horse was young and fresh and cantered gaily. His heart was filled with excitement. He was going to forget all that had been sad, and begin a new life in his dream-city by the Danube.

BOOK TWO

1

I

MIRIAM GOLLANTZ in Vienna and Miriam Gollantz in Paris were, it seemed to Hermann, two different people. His mother, in Paris, had been indolent, inclined to grumble at the changes in the weather, finding fault if there was too much or too little seasoning in her food, always ready to stress the fact that she was growing old, and found life difficult in consequence. In Vienna, installed in the finest hotel, within easy reach of the Stadt, she blossomed and flourished. She wore her elegant clothes with an air, and, wrapped in her splendid furs, made a tour of the crowded streets little less than a royal progress.

Women turned to stare at her clothes, to admire her sables, to comment upon her headgear, and congratulate themselves that her bulk prevented her becoming a possible rival in the affections of the men. Men, noting her size, prepared to turn away, but were caught and held by the gallantry of her carriage, the thick, matt whiteness of her skin, and her dark, compelling eyes. Young men might only notice her as a magnificently dressed, over-stout Jewess; their elders, with eyes that were more understanding, looked and wondered, and even sighed regretfully that Miriam Gollantz had not come to Vienna twenty years earlier.

Hermann attracted less attention. He was merely a suitably elegant young man accompanying a splendid woman. His figure was good, his clothes admirable, and his general bearing that of a man of breeding and position. Both of them spoke German fluently, and their French was exceptional. They were received by the families to whom Fernando had sent letters of introduction, with open arms.

Within a month, Miriam had found and signed the lease for a fine house in the Bargerspital, a building which it was said had at one time been a religious house, but which now, possessing hundreds of rooms, had been divided into at least ten splendid dwelling-houses, each with its internal courtyard inside the main building. The rent was high, and Miriam spent several delightful days arguing with the agent. She laughed at his demands; she cast ridicule upon the prices which he asked; she protested that the rooms might be well proportioned, but that the stairs were mean and without distinction, the porters' liveries were threadbare, and the decorations of the apartments were out of date.

'Twenty rooms, a kitchen which will make any reasonable cook contemplate suicide, and—only one insignificant bathroom! Is this how Vienna lives?'

The little agent protested that in the king's palace there was only one bathroom. He seemed to regard it as slightly treasonable that mere Jews should ask for more.

Five times Miriam rose, declared that nothing would induce her to take the place; five times the agent reduced his price, and promised new concessions. Finally, with a burst of rhetoric which surpassed anything she had uttered previously, Miriam agreed to take the apartment on condition that two new bathrooms were installed, the porters provided with new liveries, and the whole place redecorated according to her own taste.

'That is to say,' she added hastily, 'according to the taste of my son, who is acknowledged to be the master of decoration throughout France. And,' confidentially—for since she had gained her points her affability had increased considerably—'I need hardly remind you that Paris is the very centre of the world of elegance and exquisite taste.'

The agent was impressed; he mentioned the arrival of rich new tenants to his son, who was employed as major-domo to Prince Metternich himself. The major-domo, when ordered to issue instructions for the redecoration of the palace of the prince some months later, advanced the name of Hermann Gollantz and quoted him as the finest exponent of the art of interior decoration in the whole of Europe.

The winter months passed pleasantly for Hermann and his mother. They were not only accepted but welcomed by their fellow Jews; they found the hospitality unbounded, the amusements delightful, and the whole outlook of their friends cultured in the extreme. They were busy with the house, and both sent frequent letters urging Fernando only to wait for the warmer weather and then to join them at once.

Early in March they returned from an evening party given by Emmanuel Breal, the banker, to find a letter awaiting them from Paris. Miriam, loosening her furs, sat down and tore open the letter. Hermann busied himself with lighting the little stove to heat her evening chocolate. A sudden cry of anguish made him turn to his mother. Her face was white, her hands shaking.

'Mama, what is it?' Hermann cried.

With a determination which was startling, she recovered herself.

'Uncle Fernando is ill. We must go at once to Paris. Hermann, call the servants. I want the coach ready in ten minutes. Quick!'

'But, dearest,' Hermann protested, 'I don't need the coach. I can ride. They shall get my horse out immediately. I will go and change.'

Miriam rose ; she towered huge and magnificent in her evening-gown, with its festoons of lace and points of light where the rays from the candles caught her jewels.

'You! Certainly you can ride, but I need the coach. And change —there is no time to change. We leave in ten minutes—as we are. He is ill, dangerously ill, don't you understand?'

Hermann never forgot that journey to Paris. He felt that he travelled with a woman he had never known before, a woman who was tireless, who never uttered a complaint at the cold, who would scarcely have waited for food had it not been that they must change horses very often. Again and again she would lean from the window of the coach and urge the driver to make the pace quicker.

'They are doing all they can, madame. It's heavy going for them.'

'I know, I know. Poor beasts, I understand. They will understand too. It shall be made up to them when we change horses next. This is life and death. Faster, faster!'

They got to Paris early one morning, when the milk carts were clattering over the cobbled streets and the city was scarcely awake. Hermann sat his horse wearily, swaying a little in the saddle. He felt that he had been riding for years, felt that he had never known any life but this eternal going on and on, punctuated by the orders of his mother to go faster.

Miriam sat upright in the coach, her face deathly pale with fatigue, her eyes heavy and tired. Her beautiful hair was disarranged, her hands lay on her ample lap, dirty and stained with travel. The coach swung into the rue Castiglione and slackened speed. Like a flash she was on her feet, and the vehicle had barely stopped when she flung herself out of it and sped through the gate, through the courtyard into the old house where Fernando lay. A nursing sister coming down the stairs stood aghast at the sight of a dishevelled, elderly woman in a travel-stained, torn, and once magnificent dinner-dress, with unbound hair, and eyes which were sunk deeply into their sockets.

'My uncle! He lives?'

'You are Madame Gollantz? Come softly, if you please. Since the stroke, Monsieur Meldola has not spoken.'

With Hermann following closely, Miriam entered the huge bedroom. The air was heavy, and to Hermann it felt charged with death. A wood fire burnt sluggishly, as fires do when they have burnt for many days. By the bed, with its almost regal hangings, its swinging golden cupid supporting a finely wrought lamp, another nursing sister was seated. As they entered, she rose and came towards them.

'He is still unconscious, but once or twice I have thought that he felt the return of consciousness.'

Miriam pushed her gently aside and went to the bed. She stood looking down on the fine face of the man who had been a father to her. As she watched, all his thousand kindnesses came back to her ; she remembered his gentleness, his consideration, and his unfailing affection.

'I have come back,' she said. 'I ought never to have left you. Oh, speak to me, say that you forgive me for ever leaving you, dearest.'

The eyelids flickered, the hand which lay on the embroidered coverlet quivered. Miriam caught it and pressed it to her lips. Fernando opened his eyes, stared vacantly into space for a moment, then turned and met her imploring gaze. His lips moved.

'Miriam—my beloved Miriam.'

'Uncle—Father . . .' Leaning down she saw that a change had come over his face, and realized that he was leaving them.

She turned and caught her son's hand, drawing him to her side, then cried passionately: 'Bless me also, O my Father.'

For the last time Fernando Meldola's keen, beauty loving eyes opened and met hers. With difficulty his lips moved.

'*Shalom Alichem* . . .' he whispered.

Miriam, with a cry which went to Hermann's heart, sank on

her knees by the bed, and the room echoed with the sound of a Jewish woman mourning for her dead.

II

Hermann did not return to Vienna until the summer. There was much business to be transacted, stock to be disposed of, lawyers had to be interviewed, and finally the old house had to be given up. Fernando had died a wealthy man, and the whole of his fortune was divided between his niece and his grand-nephew.

Miriam remained for weeks inconsolable. She felt that Fernando's death was due to her leaving him, and repeated again and again that she had neglected her first duty in going with Hermann to Vienna. She refused to return alone, and wandered about the big old house, suffering deeply as each room recalled a thousand incidents.

Hermann, sorrowing sincerely and acutely, went about his business, doing his best to expedite matters so that they might return to happier surroundings. It was with a feeling of thankfulness and relief that he mounted his horse and for the second time rode out of Paris beside his mother's coach.

Back in Vienna, Miriam recovered much of her old gaiety and enthusiasm. The new house delighted her, and she planned and arranged tirelessly. At the beginning of September everything was in order and Hermann was free to begin his business on the lines which had served Fernando so well.

The Jews came to inspect his stock. It was not large, but it was excellent. It was set out among his own personal belongings, and displayed to the best possible advantage. Hermann himself, with his tight, dark coat, high black-satin cravat, with its two black-pearl pins united by a tiny golden chain, his embroidered waistcoat and heavy bunch of seals hanging from his wide fob, his tight trousers strapped under highly polished, well-fitting boots, and his general air of quiet distinction, was a figure which found favour in the eyes of both men and women. Old men found him deferential, without a trace of subservience; elderly women felt that he realized they had once been young and lovely, and hinted that he still found it easy to imagine them both. With younger men he was pleasant, amusing, and friendly; with younger women he allowed his admiration to be apparent, but never permitted it to degenerate into familiarity. He was never an Adonis, but

73

he was the possessor of considerable charm of manner, and his good looks were of the type which goes hand in hand with youth and a life lived decently and without excesses.

He was thirty, and his mother lived in a perpetual state of hope and fear regarding him. Fear that he might marry a woman who would prove unsuitable, and hope that he might marry one who was entirely satisfactory. Since the disastrous affair in Paris he had shown little interest in women; he liked their companionship, he danced with them, escorted them to the theatre and opera, but showed no particular wish to make any of them his wife. Despite the fact that Jews were not admitted into the highest grades of society, they were welcomed in financial and political circles, and Hermann's money and successful career opened many doors to him.

Sometimes when he had accompanied his mother to the opera, where she had listened to Rettich as 'Desdemona' or watched Anschirtz tearing passion to tatters as 'Othello', Miriam would glance at him under her heavy lashes, trying to discover if he watched any woman with particular interest. It was at once a relief and a disappointment when she discovered his eyes fixed on the stage.

'When are you going to marry, Hermann?' Miriam asked.

He would smile back at her contentedly. 'When I find a woman as beautiful, as intelligent, and as kind as you, Mama.'

Once, when he returned from a great dinner given to mark some public occasion, she asked if he had found his perfect woman there. He hesitated, laughed with some embarrassment, then replied: 'I have at least met the woman who possesses fascination, such fascination that it might be very difficult for a man to forget her.' Then he added quickly: 'Mama, I talk nonsense. I have become a boy again tonight, ready to play at knights and ladies. In that huge company there was one woman tonight—she was not even very handsome. Someone presented me and'—he laughed—'I believe it was intended to be a compliment to me, as a Jew, that I *was* presented.'

He sat down, clasping his hands round his knees. 'What is it, Mama, that makes it possible for someone to utter the most ordinary words and charge them with something new and utterly delightful?'

Miriam said: 'That is charm, Hermann. Nothing else matters so much.'

'Charm,' he repeated. 'Marvellous! Small talk, ordinary things

74

—the weather, the theatre, the newest plays—and suddenly—like a flash—a word which fills everything with a new interest. Thalberg playing softly, the lingering remembrance of an excellent dinner, the savour of good wine still clinging to one's palate—you see, even when I am romantic, I remain a materialist—and talk. Real talk, it might even be small talk, but it was exquisite.'

His mother leant forward, and tapped him lightly on the arm with her fan.

'Her name? I am impatient!'

Hermann threw back his head and laughed. 'Her name—Sophia.'

'What a *chen*!' Miriam ejaculated. 'You're *meshugge*, Hermann. Sophia Lieven, the ugliest woman in Europe.'

'Is she? I didn't know,' Hermann said, his lips still touched with a smile. 'I only know that she returns to Paris in three days—and she will take my whole-hearted admiration with her.'

The next day she came—ugly, elegant, and indisputably attractive—to his house. She wanted beautiful things, and knew beauty when she saw it. She liked his honesty, too, and liked most of all his implication that he regretted having to be so honest.

'That,' she said, pointing to a little painting in the classical style, 'is surely a Lorrain.'

'Alas! Your Highness, it is only a little painting by a clever young man in the style of Lorrain. I am imploring him to adopt no style, but to father a style of his own. Then Monsieur Delacroix will be able to ask high prices—and I shall make large profits.'

She nodded. 'Adopted children are almost always ungrateful.'

She bought a great many things, and Hermann handed them to his assistant, who piled them high on a fine marble-topped table. She finished her tour of the rooms and came back to her purchases.

'So much? I must have been here hours!'

'Hours by those lying inventions called clocks, Your Highness.'

Her ugly face broke into a smile. 'I know nothing about time,' she said; 'I only know that I am dreadfully hungry.'

'When one is hungry,' Hermann said, 'there is only one thing to do—eat.'

'What—here?'

His eyes were shining, the light caught his brown hair, making it look very bright and soft. He was personable, this young Jew.

'If you would honour me,' he said, 'I might even suggest a meal which would be sufficient, and scarcely a meal at all. For example, a very small cup of *bouillon*, served in a cup which once belonged to Napoleon ; a little—very little—*paté* with a great many truffles, served on toast so thin that it will be like a wafer—but hot! A glass—oh, I have a glass which is a poem, it was cut for one of the English Hanoverians—the second, I think—of wine, and last of all a cup of coffee, made as only my mother can make it. The cup, painted by Watteau. Your Highness—does my poor hospitality make any appeal to you?'

'Indeed it does. And you?'

'I shall write—when you have gone—something for my children, and grandchildren, to read with pride. In my diary will be the words: "Today I served at table the most wonderful princess in the world." '

'They won't know my name—you will have to add my name.'

'Your Highness!' His tone was indignant. 'My family will not be altogether ignorant, my description will be sufficient to give them the name. Will you sit here, in a chair which was made for Charles the Second of England. See, carved with roses and thistles. Here is a little book of prayers—the illuminations may interest you—do not attend to the prayers, I am saying them all at the moment.'

As he hurried from the room, she called after him: 'Herr Gollantz, what of my coachman and footman?'

Hermann paused, his hand on the door. 'I believed that what I had to show might interest Your Highness, might even delay you some little time ; the horses are well covered, the coachman and footman are both eating the dinner which was prepared for them.'

Later, as he stood beside her, ready with an embroidered napkin on his arm to play the part of waiter, she said: 'You think of everything.'

'No, Your Highness, of one thing only.'

He amused her with his rather elaborate and diplomatic compliments. His manner was easy, his behaviour perfect. Only once, when she met his eyes, did she find a light in them which startled her. Almost uneasily she wondered if this suave young Jew was taking the incident seriously, if his lightness of conversation went no deeper than his lips. What did it matter? He was pleasant, well-mannered ; his knowledge was comprehensive and complete ; he was a change from elderly diplomats and swaggering soldiers, and the day after tomorrow she returned to Paris. She sipped her coffee and assured Hermann that it was delicious.

When she rose to go, she decided to take some of her purchases with her ; the remainder might be sent. Hermann picked up a gold and enamelled pomander which she had chosen, and pointed out that one of the little catches was loose.

'I will have it repaired, and, with your permission, deliver it at Your Highness's house tomorrow.'

'Tomorrow is my last day in Vienna,' she sighed. 'I love Vienna —Vienna likes me too, I think.'

'Tonight,' he said, 'you are going to *Don Giovanni*?'

She nodded. 'I hope they will sing better than usual. I dislike to hear any music sung badly, but when it is Mozart's music—it is murder!'

Hermann escorted her to her carriage, deposited her various small packages, bowed from the waist, clicking his heels as he did so. He was the young antique dealer again ; the light had gone from his eyes.

That night he sat in the ugly, rather shabby opera-house, and heard not one note of Mozart's music. Instead he kept his eyes on the box where the princess sat, her ugly, intelligent face intent on the stage. Once or twice she turned and whispered behind her fan to the old dandy, Prince Metternich, who at sixty-five still contrived to retain his good figure and a certain air of youth.

That night, Hermann was invited to an evening-party at the house of the financier, Drach. He left the opera-house, and stood for a moment uncertain whether to return home or accept the invitation. He flung his cloak round him, and frowned. Why go anywhere? The party was certain to be dull. The parties given by Drach always were—too much to eat, too little to drink, and the music was always atrocious. As he stood there, he heard a stir among the people behind him, and turned to find himself almost face to face with the princess. She was talking with animation to a tall soldier with auburn side-whiskers and a drooping moustache. His uniform glittered, his sword clattered, and the spurs on his brilliantly polished boots seemed to scatter sparks of light as he moved. On her other side walked some member of the Diplomatic Corps, in his grave, dignified uniform, his breast covered with medals and orders, while a wide red ribbon crossed his shirt-front.

Hermann remained perfectly still, his heart beating unbearably. The soldier, bending towards the princess, whispered something which made her laugh, and as she threw back her head her eyes met Hermann's. For a second he held her eyes, then, with the smallest possible acknowledgement, a movement which was almost imperceptible, she passed on.

He walked away, his cloak wrapped round him, swinging his hat in his hand, scarcely aware of where he was going. On and on through the narrow, well-kept streets he went, his lips compressed, his eyes hard. Alternately, he laughed at himself and offered himself commiseration. He had been a fool, and yet only a few hours ago she had laughed with him ; he had imagined foolish things.

She had admitted that he interested her, and that in an hour she had learnt more of antiques than she had ever known before. He had held his head a little higher because he had realized that Hermann Gollantz, the Jew, could entertain this fascinating princess. She had been more than Sophia Lieven ; she had been a symbol that, if he were patient, all roads, all doors, all positions might be open to him and his descendants. Now, that imperceptible acknowledgment, that meeting of their eyes which had shown recognition and nothing more, had broken all his dreams. A soldier, an overdressed puppet, a diplomat, dry as dust, might accompany her, while he could never hope to meet her as anything except a tradesman.

It was the old story of Marie's lover again. The Jew had his uses, but he must be kept in his place. He might have taste, erudition, education, perfect manners—but he remained with all these qualities something less in the scheme of things than a swashbuckling cavalryman, or a diplomat with no imagination beyond the signing of official documents.

'Even here in Vienna,' Hermann mused, as he walked rapidly towards the walls of the city, 'where we are superficially accepted, there is always a barrier. Metternich is lauded for working for peace—and men forget that Rothschild has done as much, and more, for its attainment. We may be bankers, we may dominate the world of finance, but we are never allowed really to enter the world of politics—except by the back door. Our money is good, our wine is good, our food is good—our manners may be better than theirs, but no self-respecting Austrian aristocrat would give his daughter to a rich, honest, cultivated Jew, when she might marry an impoverished soldier, with his sixteen quarterings and a mistress in every *corps-de-ballet*.'

It was a bitter young man who returned to his house that night, and went immediately to his room, to pace the floor and meditate upon the injustice of life in general. Hermann Gollantz suffered, as do most of his race, from tremendous fluctuation of spirit. This tendency, only that morning, had made him feel that the world was his for the taking, that all doors were open to him, and had almost convinced him that the world was becoming more tolerant, more broad-minded. That morning every man had been his friend ; that night every man's hand was against him.

He rose the following morning, shaved meticulously, assured himself that his hair was parted with precision down the back of his head, and brought forward in the correct sweep over his ears. He dressed with extreme care, choosing a shirt of the finest linen, a collar which kept his determined chin at an almost defiant angle, a cravat which was the last word in elegance. His waistcoat, double-breasted with flapped pockets, was embroidered with minute sprigs of cornflower blue, and his high-collared coat had been pronounced a perfect fit by the most expensive tailor in Vienna.

He ordered his cabriolet, and when his mother, eyeing him with pride, asked where he was going, he replied with calmness: 'I am going out to deliver goods to a customer, Mama. I like sometimes to be my own errand boy.'

Miriam said nothing. She noticed his appearance ; from the window she saw the cabriolet waiting in the inner courtyard, and she watched Hermann wrap himself in his cloak of fine cloth with a collar of astrakhan before he climbd into it. As she turned from the window, she sighed gustily. 'It is time he was married. He grows too romantic. In a boy of twenty romance is very well ; in a man of thirty it is dangerous ; it may easily become a habit of mind. Marriage will cure him.'

He drew up at the palace of the princess, gave the reins to his groom, and carried the tiny parcel to the door. The footman who opened it hesitated a moment. He wondered who this young man might be. Ought he to be admitted? Was he an emissary from some foreign state? Was he a young aristocrat demanding audience with the princess?

Hermann watched his puzzled face, his lips twisted a little.

'This parcel is to be taken to Her Highness,' he said.

The footman stared, took the little packet, and still hesitated.

'I will wait to hear that it has reached Her Highness safely.'

'Very well, sir. . . .' Again that hesitation, then: 'Would you be good enough to wait in the entrance-hall?'

Hermann entered, stood erect and aloof, swinging his hat in his hand, until the footman returning told him that Her Highness wished to speak to him. 'That is, if you are Herr Gollantz?'

'I am. Take me to the princess.'

For some reason the man flushed. Curse these Jews, they looked so like aristocrats one never knew where one had them! The fellow wore his clothes like a Viennese, spoke like one—damn, he even smelt like one of them. Jews ought not to be allowed to use the same hair-oil as gentlemen!

Hermann was ushered into a small room with polished walls and a ceiling beautifully decorated in stucco, from the centre of which hung a chandelier of coloured Venetian glass. He glanced round him, admiring the furniture in its chintz covers, and noted with some satisfaction that the two pictures on the walls were inferior to others by the same painters which he had in his own house.

The door opened and the princess entered. Hermann saw that she was dressed for travelling. Her ugly face looked yellow in the morning light, but her eyes—those queer eyes which varied in colour from gold to dark brown, from green to hazel—were as brilliant as ever. In her long fur-trimmed travelling-coat, she looked unbelievably tall and elegant. As she came towards him she dropped her huge sable muff on a couch.

'Herr Gollantz—good morning.'

Hermann bowed. 'Your Highness's most obedient servant.'

'The pomander is beautifully restored.'

'I am happy that it gives satisfaction, Highness.'

She laughed suddenly. 'When you Jews adopt the role of humility you are the most arrogant creatures on earth! I liked you better yesterday.'

'Yesterday is over,' he said. 'Perhaps through Your Highness's kindness I presumed—yesterday. Today, I am twenty-four hours older and wiser.'

She shrugged her shoulders. What an attractive young man he was. She thought of the long journey to Paris, and for a moment wished that she need not undertake it solely in the company of a bored and boring lady-in-waiting.

'I go back to Paris today.'

'I hope Your Highness enjoyed the opera, that they did not murder Mozart.'

Inconsequently, she said: 'I saw you.'

'And I—Your Highness.'

Something in his tone reached her. She remembered that their eyes had met, and that for one brief instant she had been tempted to call him to her, to order him to accompany her, because young

80

Liechtenstein and the midle-aged Harrach had bored her so with their inanities. Then she had realized that she was in Vienna, and that Jews were not admitted to the highest social circles; that to have spoken to him in front of Liechtenstein would have been a positive insult to Viennese aristocracy. She came a little nearer.

'And you were hurt because I greeted you so—so coldly?'

'Highness! What right have I to be hurt?'

She smiled. 'All the same, admit that you were.'

'I admit that I was—a fool.'

'Listen,' she said, and it seemed to Hermann that, miraculously, her hand lay on his arm. 'Listen, I understand. You are proud. You have a right to be. Only the minds of other people move slowly, and sometimes they are afraid. It may be that they are wise to be afraid of you. You have too much of too many things. Let me give you advice. Don't try to enter a society which is almost worn out, which at the best—or worst—can only hold out against time for a few more years—fifty, a hundred—who knows? It totters already. Make a society of your own; be sufficient unto yourself. What do you want with invitations to listen to the inanities of a Harrach? You wrong yourself by feeling more than a tolerant amusement that you are barred from the houses of people who have nothing to offer except an ability to waltz divinely, to choose the best wine and the most exquisite women, and—their eternal sixteen quarterings.'

He felt his face burn suddenly. He realized that he had been petty, childish, unworthy.

'I only hated it—because it came from you,' he said.

'Me,' she laughed. 'Can't you see that I'm caught in it all? I can't get away now—at least not in Vienna. I'm part of it. I find myself wishing you had not left Paris.'

'If I had even seen you when I lived there,' Hermann said, 'I never should have left Paris.'

'My dear! The ugliest woman in Paris. That's what they say, and it's the truth.'

'They say!' He snapped his fingers.

'Yesterday we play-acted and laughed,' she said. 'Today we are serious, because we are wiser. Hermann Gollantz, come back to Paris.'

He shook his head. 'Your Highness, you force me to disobey you. Paris would spoil it all.'

'You would be happy.'

' "More happy, but less wise".'

'Oh wisdom.' Her face was very near to his, the scent from her hair reached him, a scent which was provocative and exciting. He made a sudden movement, caught her in his arms and kissed her passionately.

She made no effort to repulse him, but as she lay in his arms her queer eyes met his.

'Now, will you come to Paris?'

He let her go, very gently. 'No, and no, and no. I am too old, and too wise. Yesterday I was young, too young to understand your munificence ; now I understand—everything.'

She was herself again, light, defiant, astonishing. 'It's good-bye, then.'

'Good-bye, Your Highness.'

'I don't think I shall come to Vienna again. . . .' She watched him as she spoke.

'I will turn my eyes towards Paris, as the Arabs turn towards Mecca.'

'One word of advice, Herr Gollantz—marry, marry soon.'

'Your word is law, Highness. Poor woman, whoever she is.'

Once again her face broke into a smile. 'Do you want me to ask why she will be poor?'

'Your Highness knows why. . . .'

'Good-bye, Hermann Gollantz.'

He bent and kissed her hand. 'Your Highness's devoted servant always.'

The young footman who swung open the great door to him, said to his fellow:

'He came in looking white about the mouth, he went out looking like a ghost. I shouldn't wonder if he'd been brought to book over some fault in the foods he delivered. They can't do as they like with our Sophia, eh?'

2

I

THE brief episode was over, and Hermann went back to his work again. The affair—if it could be given so important a name—left no sting behind it ; rather, it was, in retrospect, a beautiful dream, which for one moment had become unbearably painful and in the next regained all its original delight. He never heard from her, never even saw her again, and gradually the outline of their meeting became softened and a little blurred, a tender recollection which he shut away in his heart and only allowed himself to gaze upon at long intervals.

The meeting, short though it had been, had accomplished a great deal. He no longer looked with envy and dislike upon the gorgeous soldiers, the uniformed diplomats, and sighed with some bitterness because he could never be admitted into the circles which were theirs. He watched his own race and found that among the best of them there was culture, breeding, and a deep love of beauty. He discovered that artistic circles were open to him, and that there—as a Jew—he was credited with taste and discrimination. He met Strauss and Lanner ; he became friendly with Thalberg and young Vieuxtems ; he knew the most successful of the artists at the opera and the theatre. The stage doors at the Bourg and the lesser theatres were open to him, and gradually he found that life was a full and pleasant business.

There were times when Miriam railed against the fact that her people were not recognized in the highest society ; and when Hermann laughed at her, she stared at him in surprise.

'What has happened to you?' she demanded. 'Once you were so bitter.'

His smile widened, and in it and in his voice when he answered there was, Miriam felt, a half-hidden tenderness.

'I know—but I have reconsidered my verdict. Why should we wish to force our way into a society which may be rigorously select, rigidly exclusive, but where we can gain nothing that is worth having? I'd rather think that Jews made a society of their own, where the card of admission was mental attainment.'

Miriam watched him narrowly. 'I wonder where these ideas came from?'

'They are mine by adoption—a legacy,' Hermann said, still smiling.

II

He met Adolfus Hirsch in the spring of 1838. Adolfus was a stout, handsome old man, interested in money in whatever form he encountered it. He was reputed to be rich, and lived in a fine house in the Hohen Markt. Hermann liked the stout, elderly Jew, who made no pretence at culture, but who loved life and all the good things which money could buy. He had the reputation of being essentially mean in business and essentially generous in his hospitality.

Miriam had first taken Hermann to the house in the Hohen Markt, and old Hirsch had taken an instant liking to the young man. Miriam herself looked with favour on Rachel Hirsch, who at that time was slender, dark-haired, with bright eyes and a good skin. She noted how well the house was run, the excellence of the food, and the well-drilled servants. Rachel was a good hostess, and could contrive to listen to the longest story with every appearance of interest.

Hermann paid her his usual deferential attention, but when Miriam hinted that Rachel might make him an excellent wife, he pursed his lips and murmured something about 'uninteresting wives mean an uninteresting life'.

'Nonsense,' Miriam said sharply. 'The girl was shy.'

'I don't like shy women.'

'Perhaps,' acidly, 'you prefer bold ones?'

Hermann shrugged his shoulders. 'Maybe. I certainly don't find women who stare alternately at me and their finger-tips attractive.'

Again and again Miriam sang the praises of Rachel Hirsch, again and again she gave evening parties to which the whole family—Adolfus, Rachel, and the son, Ishmael—were invited. As always, Hermann was polite, even amusing—but unmoved. Miriam was at her wit's end. Here was her good-looking son, at over thirty, still unmarried. It was unthinkable.

Then, as if in answer to her prayers, Arbarbanel Jurnett arrived in Vienna. She met him at the house of a friend, and he made it patent immediately that he was attracted by her. He scarcely left her side all the evening, and insisted on escorting her home ; true, the escorting consisted in riding beside her in her own carriage, and being driven on to his own home afterwards—but his intention was palpable.

He was a tall, thin Jew with a parchment-coloured face, which had fallen into folds rather than lines with the increasing years. His clothes were not in the best taste ; the material was bad, and the cut lacked that excellence to which Miriam had become accustomed. His manner was heavy, plastered thickly with over-sweet compliments ; he never missed an opportunity of kissing hands, bowing, or raising his hat with a flourish.

Miriam Gollantz, casting longing eyes at Rachel Hirsch as a wife for her son, watched Jurnett and deliberately encouraged him. She made inquiries. The man had come from Greece and was a merchant of some kind—fruits and spices, Miriam believed. He was not well off, and his private life only bore close investigation because he was, in addition to being a reasonably clever man, a very careful one. His age she guessed was sixty or a little more.

Hermann grew a little tired of perpetually finding Jurnett in the house. The man was there for luncheon, for coffee in the afternoon, and for dinner. He was for ever taking Miriam to the opera, the theatre, and to smart restaurants. His mother seemed to like the fellow, and was always quoting him. 'Jurnett said this,' or, 'Jurnett told me that.' Then one day she prefaced a remark with: 'Arbarbanel told me——'

Hermann set down his morning cup of coffee with a clatter.

'*Who* told you?'

'Arbarbanel told me,' Miriam began, her beautiful dark eyes wide with innocence.

Hermann's temper was a little short. He had dined with Mademoiselle Löwe, Anschritz, the Rettich, and some other members of the theatrical profession. The party had broken up very late, and he had awakened with a slight but determined headache.

'Ar—bar—ban—el,' he repeated, giving each syllable its full value. 'My dearest Mama, you surely don't call that man by that impossible name? It's not a name, it's a joke!'

Miriam lowered her eyes and twisted her fringed napkin in her fingers.

'Really, Hermann,' she expostulated in a low voice, 'you're very unkind.'

'Unkind, Mama! What is there unkind in saying that? It's a preposterous name—as its owner is a preposterous person.'

This time she raised her eyes. 'Really, Hermann! How—how dare you!'

Hermann stared at her, his eyes wide, his mouth half open. The idea had never occurred to him. Could it be possible that his beautiful, clever, and entirely charming mother was in love with that yellow-faced, flamboyant creature, Jurnett?

'My dear—you don't mean—I mean you are not trying to tell me—oh, it's impossible!' He rose in his agitation, flinging down his napkin and overturning his coffee-cup.

Miriam turned and rang the bell at her side. 'I don't think we will discuss it,' she said with dignity. Then, turning to the servant who entered: 'Bring Herr Gollantz a clean cup and napkin.'

'Thank you, Mama, I don't want more coffee. If you'll excuse me I'll get to work. I have a great deal on hand.'

Alone, Miriam poured out another cup of coffee, stirred into it a very ample allowance of thick cream, added a good deal of sugar and, buttering another small hot roll, leant back in her chair, sighing.

'Poor boy. Still, it will be all for the best—in the end.'

That evening Hermann dined with Adolfus Hirsch and his daughter. After dinner Rachel played, not without distinction, though her music lacked great feeling. Hermann stood by her side, watching her fine, small hands moving over the keys. Once or twice, remembering Jurnett, he sighed.

'You're sad tonight, Herr Gollantz,' Rachel said.

'A little, perhaps. I have worries ; to me—serious worries.'

Her pretty face expressed sympathy. 'Oh, I am so truly sorry. Can I help you in any way? I—I should be so happy if it were possible.'

He looked at her attentively ; perhaps for the first time he saw her as she really was. Pretty, kind, and essentially warm-hearted. He wondered if it would be permissible to confide in her, to explain how terrible it seemed to him that his mother, whom he admired so whole-heartedly and loved so dearly, should encourage a man who lacked every endearing quality. Rachel did not press for his confidence, but returned to her playing, and Hermann, watching her steady, capable little hands, felt a new interest in her. How few women could have resisted the opportunity to force the conversation into a more personal and private channel!

Later that evening, when he sat beside her on a sofa upholstered in two shades of green satin, he began to explain his difficulties to her. He was in the middle of his explanation before he actually realized what he was saying.

Rachel, her dark hair parted in the middle, falling in ringlets on either side of her serious, heart-shaped face, listened without comment.

'So, you will understand, Fräulein Hirsch, how deeply this affects me. I cannot feel that this man—that fellow with an impossible name!—can be in any sense worthy of my mother. To me it seems incredible.'

Rachel lifted her dark eyes to him. 'Indeed, Herr Gollantz, I do feel for you. Your mother is so—so splendid, and I too dislike Herr Jurnett. He is so—so inferior in every way.'

Hermann noticed that she had a little trick of hesitation in her speech, something less than a stammer, and rather charming, he thought. It was some comfort that she agreed with him! Somehow the outlook seemed less dreary, less cold and grey.

He returned home feeling more hopeful. Rachel Hirsch had felt, with him, that it was impossible for his mother to consider Jurnett as a husband; his own opinions had been backed and stabilized. He entered the hall of his own home, whistling Strauss's latest waltz softly. Then his eyes fell on Jurnett's hat and long, dark-green cloak with its collar of slightly moth-eaten fur, and the gay tune died on his lips. He squared his shoulders and entered the drawing-room.

His mother was seated in a low chair, her skirts spreading round her like billowing waves, her hands clasped, the bracelets on her fine arms glinting in the light from the wax candles in their gilded wood sconces. Jurnett stood before her, looking down at her with an expression which struck Hermann as being particularly inane. Both of them turned as he entered. Jurnett's face lost its expression of fatuous sentimentality, and Miriam, holding out her hands, smiled a welcome.

,'Ah, my dear. I would not allow them to bring my chocolate until you came. Ring for it, will you? Herr Jurnett, thank you for escorting me home.'

Jurnett looked suddenly dismayed. Hermann chuckled inwardly. It was evident the fellow had expected refreshment!

Hermann, who had restricted his greeting to a curt nod, stood swinging impatiently on his heels whilst Jurnett bowed over Miriam's hand.

'Good night, Frau Gollantz. And tomorrow . . . ?'

'Tomorrow?' Miriam queried.

'You promised to dine with me tomorrow, at the new restaurant in the Joseph Platz.' His voice was reproachful.

'I will send my servant with a note tomorrow morning.'

Again he bowed. Hermann thought what a fool he looked, too long and too thin—'A long drink of cold water'.

'Then, good night.'

Hermann opened the door for him, closed it behind him, and returned to his mother.

Miriam glanced at him. 'You don't like Herr Jurnett?'

'Does anyone like him?' Hermann knew that his tone, if not his words, was discourteous.

'Many people like him exceedingly. The Hirsch family, for example.'

'I think you are misinformed, Mama. One member of the family at least dislikes him as much as I do.'

She said with dignity, 'I am sorry that you dislike him, Hermann. It makes matters very difficult for me.'

Hermann looked at her gravely. How handsome she was ; how well she wore her clothes ; how beautifully her hair fell, how meticulously kept! Her skin, unwrinkled and soft as ever. Her voice smooth, liquid and delightfully modulated. He loved her so dearly, wanted to make her so content, and here she was becoming entangled with a third-rate Greek merchant. He detested Greeks, they were as bad as Armenians.

'I never wish to make anything difficult for you, Mama dear,' he said. 'We won't discuss Herr Jurnett. Surely for you and me there are other and more interesting topics. Here is your chocolate. Franz, bring me a glass of lemonade.'

As the weeks passed, Hermann became more and more oppressed with the thought of Arbarbanel Jurnett and his mother. It seemed that the man was never out of the house, that Hermann never arrived at the front door without finding Jurnett's rather shabby manservant there with a note to deliver, or he met his mother's servant going out, carrying a note which Hermann always felt sure was destined for the Greek. In his unhappiness—and it was very real indeed—he went more and more to the house in the Hohen Markt. Rachel was so kind, so gentle ; she understood his feelings so well, and admired his mother so tremendously. Hermann never left there without feeling that he had been soothed and rested. Scarcely a day passed but he went round to talk to Rachel Hirsch, and never in all those weeks did she fail him.

Then the blow which he had dreaded fell. He sat talking after luncheon one day with his mother. Miriam was looking particularly well ; her dress was of sprigged lilac silk, with long loops of violet velvet ribbon on the bodice and skirt. Her curled hair was arranged at the back of her head, one curl only falling over her left shoulder. Hermann, watching her, thought that he had never seen her look so handsome.

'I believe that you grow younger, Mama,' he said.

Miriam smiled, and something in her smile warned Hermann

that others—at least, one other—had made the same remark. He felt suddenly chilled, as if the shadow of Jurnett had fallen on their table.

'I don't think I change a great deal,' Miriam said. 'I don't seem to. Perhaps the most marked changes are those which do not show physically. I mean mental changes.'

Trying to keep his voice light, Hermann said: 'Have you changed mentally, then?'

'I think I may have done. Things which at one time would have seemed impossible, are not so any longer. They are not only possible but desirable.'

'Such as . . . ?'

She shrugged her lilac-clad shoulders, so that the silk made a little shivering sound. 'Oh many things. Life in other places apart from Vienna, new interests, new affections—even marriage.'

He lifted his glass, and making her a cold little bow, said: 'My most loving wishes for your happiness always, Mama dear. Now, if you will excuse me, I will leave you.'

'Always busy?' She smiled at him.

His face was set and hard, the lips were closed in a thin line. She realized how terribly hurt he was and her heart ached for him.

'I try to keep occupied. Good-bye, Mama.'

'Good-bye, Hermann.'

Half an hour later he was shown into Rachel Hirsch's salon. She was seated at an embroidery frame, but at the sight of his pale face she rose and came towards him.

'Hermann—Herr Gollantz—what is it? You are ill?'

He shook his head. 'No, not ill. Rachel, she has told me. Admitted that she is thinking of marriage with that horrible Greek. I realize that I cannot bear it. I shall go away until it is over. To think of it—my beautiful mother! Oh, it is impossible!'

She took his hand and led him unresisting to a chair, making him sit quietly while she rang for coffee, and then came back to him, laying her hand on his shoulder.

At last he raised his eyes to hers. 'No one understands except you, Rachel,' he said. Then, taking her hand in his, he added: 'Dear, kind Rachel.'

Her eyes were brimming with tears as she answered: 'I have tried to understand. My poor, poor Hermann. If only I could help you.'

Suddenly it struck him that she might help him, help to make

89

life tolerable if Miriam left him for her unspeakable Greek. She was young, charming ; their tastes were alike in many things. She loved books, had some knowledge of music, and her conversation, if not brilliant, was at least intelligent. How pretty she looked now! Standing with her hand in his, her dark eyes filled with tears, her little face grave and intent with sympathy. Dear Rachel!

As the servant entered with coffee, she withdrew her hand and moved to pour it out for him. Hermann watched her silently. Her movements were graceful, her hands were deft and capable. It would be very pleasant to always have her to pour out coffee for him. She would look delightful in the morning, adorable at the luncheon-table, charming in the light of many candles at the dinner-table, and at other times . . . Hermann's mind seemed to falter. To hold in one's arms, to caress, to recount small successes to, to share confidences with. Oh, she was wonderful—so satisfactory, his Rachel!

She brought back the cup of coffee to him, smiling softly.

'I have not put in very much cream, and remembered that you like very little sugar.'

Hermann took the cup from her and set it down on a little table at his elbow. 'Rachel, dear,' he said, 'will you marry me, please, because I love you very much?'

She made no protestations of surprise. Rachel Hirsch was never surprised. She gave him her hand and answered softly: 'And I love you, Hermann.'

III

He walked home, his heart singing. Rachel was his ; they were to be married and live happy ever afterwards, like the prince and princess in the fairy tales. Then, because he was a Jew, in his moment of happiness he allowed a faint melancholy to intrude, a grey shadow which slanted across his bright vision. He thought that he heard a voice saying: 'Marry—and marry soon.' The vision became clearer. He saw a woman in a long, fur-trimmed travelling-coat, a woman with a delightful, ugly face. Then his own voice: 'I am your Highness's obedient servant.' Hermann paused in his rapid walk. The sudden sweep down into melancholy was half painful, half pleasant.

He sighed. 'Well, I have kept my promise—wonderful Sophia.'

He turned into the Volks Garten ; he was glad to be alone for a

90

little. His mind went back to Rachel, and his momentary unhappiness disappeared into thin air. That was the Past ; Rachel was the Future. How delightful to have so charming a future. Underneath all his delight in her there lurked a satisfaction that he would be able to announce to his mother his approaching marriage. He wondered how best he could make the announcement. He would be dignified, and a little aloof. Restrained. That was the note which he meant to strike—restraint.

And now! What would his mother do? Would she marry Jurnett? The idea came back to Hermann, bringing pain with it. Two hours ago the thought of her marriage had sent him flying to Rachel for comfort. How far had his mother's hints influenced him? Had he asked Rachel to marry him only because he was afraid that he might lose his mother? He tried to see himself and his real motives clearly.

'No, no, I love Rachel. I have loved her for weeks. Only this— this threatening calamity forced me to see clearly. It made me realize what Rachel means to me.' Somehow all his assurances were a little unsatisfactory. 'At all events I shall be very, very good to her,' he whispered. 'I swear to make her happy in every possible way.' Then, as a turn in the path brought him face to face with the huge marble group by Canova, he paused and stared at it. 'Of course I should come upon that monstrosity today of all days! How I hate your horrible stark whiteness, you—you impossible bit of materialized sensuality and sentimentality! Old Joseph the Second in his bronze decency is worth twenty of you.'

He went to his mother's boudoir when he got home. She was reading a novel and nibbling sweets from a purple velvet box as he entered. She laid the book aside and greeted him.

'Mama, I have something to tell you,' he said. His voice was emotionless and his pleasant face serious. 'Something important.'

'My darling, you look terribly grave. What is it?'

'Today you spoke of changes, hinted that many things might be possible for you—change of residence, new modes of life, even —marriage. I have come to tell you that if you felt it was difficult to leave me alone, that difficulty is now at an end. I am going to be married. I asked Rachel Hirsch to be my wife this afternoon.'

Miriam Gollantz hurled herself to her feet ; the purple velvet box fell to the floor, scattering expensive sweets all over the carpet. She flung her arms round her son and drew him to her.

'My boy, my boy, how happy I am! This is wonderful! That sweet girl. You love her, tell me that you love her.'

'Very dearly, Mama. She is perfect.'

She kissed him passionately. 'Ah, how right I was. The very wife for you, as you are the very husband for her. I have always loved her. So gentle, so pretty, so beautifully behaved. Oh, Hermann, I am so happy. I must send her a note and a present. What present? I have it!' She dragged a fine pearl ring from her fat finger and hurried to the little inlaid desk which stood by the long window. Seizing a sheet of her own thick, mauve note-paper, she began to scrawl a letter in her characteristic hand.

'My beloved new daughter' [she read as she wrote], *'Hermann has told me, and I am faint with happiness.* What am I standing on? One of those horrible sweets! Pick it up, Hermann, or it will tread into the carpet. *I send you this ring as a little proof of my love. Come and see me tomorrow. My arms are aching to hold you. I sign myself, your devoted Mother.*

'There! Now tell me all about it, tell me——'

The door opened to admit Franz. Miriam said irritably: 'What is it, what is it?'

'Herr Jurnett is waiting to know if you will see him, madame.'

Miriam frowned. 'Certainly not. Tell Herr Jurnett that I am engaged. You might infer, Franz, that I am not accustomed to receive visitors who come uninvited. And—wait one moment—when he calls again, I am engaged.'

'Always, madame?'

'Always!' And as the door closed, she said to Hermann: 'The man bores me to extinction. I refuse to make a martyr of myself any longer!'

'But I thought . . .' Hermann stammered. 'I thought that you and he——'

'My precious son! How you make a success of your business is a mystery to me. Such a child you are! It was evident to me that Rachel liked you; it was almost as evident that—if you allowed yourself—you would like Rachel. I knew that you would confide in someone, because you loathed Jurnett as much as I did. The day you told me—or didn't tell me, but I understood—that you had confided your dislike of him to Rachel I knew that all was well. Conversations, confidences, sympathy, and—love.

'Oh, but how weary I have grown of that idiotic Greek! He smelt of oil! Olive oil! It was like talking to a salad, and as insipid. I only blame you for one thing, Hermann, that you should

92

have so doubted my good taste—how would it have been possible to even consider a man like Jurnett? However, it is over, and we must plan the wedding. It shall be soon, Hermann; there is no need to wait. I shall take two rooms and a bath-room—perhaps three rooms and a bath-room, and have my own apartments. No, no, I do not believe, like so many Jews, in living together with my son and his wife. The same roof, yes; but apart. You may invite me, I may invite you, but—together always, no!'

She was vitalized, full of energy, an energy which never flagged until she saw Hermann stand with Rachel Hirsch under the *chuppa*, held by four young Jews, of whom the bride's brother, Ishmael, was one.

Miriam watched Hermann, her eyes full of admiration. She felt that no other man in Vienna could wear his clothes with such unobtrusive distinction. His coat with its swinging tails and tight sleeves, which allowed a considerable amount of equally tight cuff to be shown, his peg-topped trousers, tapering to the ankle, strapped under varnished boots, combined with his high, narrow silk hat, all combined to show off his height and figure. He had never grown the fashionable whiskers, and he had preferred to leave the admired drooping moustache to the military, but his brown hair was worn rather long and brushed into well-ordered curls over his ears.

His bride was all that Miriam could have wished, lovely, capable, and deeply in love with her bridegroom.

She sighed with happiness. At the conclusion of the service, as she watched Hermann, gravely, but with a faint smile touching his lips, break the wineglass, Miriam felt that her cup of happiness was filled to overflowing.

She turned and whispered to the aunt of Rachel who had travelled from Munich: 'How beautiful they are! How splendid that they are both still young!'

Frau Benscher returned with some acidity, for she had five un-married daughters of her own, all older than Rachel: 'Not so young. Your son is over thirty and Rachel is already twenty-four.'

Miriam made a gesture which swept away all years. 'It is their hearts which must be considered—those are young and clean, praise be to God!'

To Hermann, the reception afterwards seemed like a gathering of all the tribes of Judah. There were Lousadas and Meldolas from Italy; Jaffes from Budapest; Salamans from Bucharest; Marcus Moise came from Brussels; a young, dark Gollantz came from Amsterdam, and a tall, thin man with burning eyes, who was Francis Leon, came all the way from England. They were all well dressed, they appeared to speak every language in Europe fluently, and they all paid court to Rachel as if she had been a newly crowned queen.

The bride's family were more localized—few of them came farther than from Germany. They were heavier in build, slower in speech, and Miriam, watching them, felt that they had every reason to congratulate themselves that Rachel had married into the family of Gollantz.

Old Breal, the banker, whose son, Marcus, had been one of the bearers of the canopy, whispered to Miriam that the girl was a beauty. 'Where did she get those ankles, and wrists, tell me, please, Frau Gollantz?'

Miriam, not displeased, tapped his shoulder with her fan. 'Shame on you, Herr Breal! How should I know. But you are right ; the others—worthy, but, oh, so dull. That old woman from Munich has nearly killed me. She talks of nothing but the way to make *paté*! They are good, I am sure, but they are not—of us.'

Breal drew his long fine beard through his fingers. 'Worthy,' he repeated. 'I do not doubt it, in every case but one.' Behind his hand he whispered to Miriam: 'I should assess the worth of young Ishmael—very low indeed.'

Francis Leon, who spoke German as well as he spoke English, overheard him. Miriam's smile gathered him into their conversation. Francis nodded.

'We have at the moment the same type in England,' he said. 'It is called—a gent. Believe me, it has nothing to do with gentleman.'

Breal smiled. 'And, if they would be wise,' he said, 'gentlemen would have nothing to do with—a gent.'

3

I

RACHEL GOLLANTZ found life very pleasant in the house in the Bargerspital. Miriam had kept her word and retired with her personal belongings to three large rooms, and a kitchen and bathroom. From there she emerged only when invited by Hermann and his wife, and never attempted to interfere or dictate in the running of the rest of the house. She had satisfied herself months ago that Rachel was a good housekeeper, that was sufficient. She spent her time visiting, and assisting her own cook to prepare such meals that Miriam's invitations were things to be sought after by those people who appreciated good food.

Rachel was deeply in love with her husband; she regarded him as the kindest, cleverest and handsomest of men. Her eyes would follow him about when he moved in the rooms in a way which made Miriam's lips curve into a smile as she watched her.

'And what a fine thing,' Miriam reflected. 'My boy is not one who will run after other women. If he was, then she'd lose him with that wide-eyed admiration. As Hermann is what he is—I doubt if he'll ever notice it.'

She was right. All that Hermann noticed was that his wife ran his home smoothly, that she always looked adorable, and that he had never been so happy. He came back to her with stories of his business, he recounted his successes and told her of the times when he had made mistakes. True, these were rare, for Hermann had an excellent instinct for business and his reputation was growing by leaps and bounds. Not only was he a connoisseur, but his taste in decoration was unimpeachable, whilst possessing originality. In the year 1841, Hermann Gollantz made more money in the decorating side of his business than on the antique.

Their first child was born in May 1842. He was named Marcus, after the son of Herr Breal who had attended Hermann's wedding and helped to hold the canopy. The boy was well made, with his mother's heart-shaped face and his father's brown hair. Hermann was delighted, he saw himself as the Head of the House of Gollantz, and together he and Miriam hung over the boy's cot and whispered plans for his future.

It was while Rachel was still delicate after her confinement, and obliged to rest a good deal every day, that a little cloud appeared on the horizon of Hermann's life. He had never found his brother-in-law, Ishmael Hirsch, an attractive personality. Ishmael was too smartly dressed, his clothes clamoured for attention, but Hermann noted that the material of which they were made was as inferior as the cut. He appeared to work very little, and whenever Hermann went into the busier parts of the town, round the Stadt, the Neue Markt, and the narrow, busy streets around the Stephansplatz, he was almost certain to encounter his brother-in-law. Ishmael was always on the point of 'making a pot of money', but he never seemed to achieve his aim, and it was evident to Hermann that the young man was fast journeying to that place in life where, unless he was forced to work, he would slip into the profession of living by his wits.

Hermann spoke to his father-in-law about the young man.

Adolfus pursed his lips and shook his head. It was difficult. The boy had no mother ; he was attractive to women, popular with men. He was too clever, and that was a fact. There was nothing he could not do. What he needed was an opportunity to give rein to his imagination. Business, an office stool, buying and selling, were too dull for Ishmael. Adolfus repeated: 'It is very difficult indeed.'

Hermann spoke to Rachel. She, too, spoke highly of Ishmael's capabilities.

'All he needs is opportunity, Hermann. Poor boy, commerce —work such as my father offers him—is no use to him. His brain is too bright, too colour-loving. He has great artistic sense. Poor Ishmael.'

That night, when Rachel had retired, Hermann walked down the corridor to his mother's apartments. He found her sipping chocolate, reading a novel, with the inevitable box of sweets at her elbow.

'How nice this is! Rachel is well? Good! And that lovely boy? What a prince among children! Sit down. Let me order more chocolate? No? Very well, smoke if you wish. I don't mind.'

'I wanted to talk to you, Mama, very seriously. I feel that something ought to be done about Ishmael Hirsch.'

'I have felt that for a long time,' Miriam returned acidly. 'There are many things I could suggest. Why have you to bother about Ishmael Hirsch?'

Hermann looked at her, his clear eyes grave and troubled. 'I must do what I can,' he said. 'I have married his sister ; his family and mine are joined. I must assume responsibility—to some extent—for him. It seems that he is very clever, that he only needs a chance to make a good citizen. I wanted to consult you about giving him such an opportunity, Mama.'

Miriam nodded. 'Ah, these are the principles instilled into you by my Uncle Fernando, peace be to him. Hermann, those principles are good, fine, noble, but I don't know that the world is suited for the demonstration of them. If everyone were good, direct, and honest—well and good. They aren't, and unless I am

96

very mistaken, young Hirsch is one of the least good, least direct, and possibly the least honest. Leave him alone.'

Hermann moved impatiently. He had that streak of obstinacy found in many essentially honest people. His mind was straight and when he saw the path which he felt was the right one, it was almost impossible for him to deviate from it.

'It is only fair to give him an opportunity,' he persisted. 'His sister is my wife, the mother of my son. I'm sorry, Mama ; I must do what I feel to be right.'

'Very well. Only, if your mind is made up, why ask me?'

'I wanted you to know what I proposed to do. I shall offer him the management of the outside work. There is the yard, the store where we keep paint, glass, and so forth. Materials for building, for decorating. He can take that over.'

'Does he know a ladder from a plank?'

'He will learn. His father tells me that he is brilliant.'

The following day he interviewed Ishmael. Instinctively he disliked the young man, with his thick curly hair, his hard, dark eyes, and his gleaming white teeth which showed so often between his moistly red lips. His clothes were terrible, Hermann decided. Who ever had seen such check trousers and such a velvet coat, cut like a sack! He mastered his dislike, despising himself for feeling it so acutely. After all, the fellow had a right to dress as he pleased. He made his offer, and waited to hear Ishmael's expression of delight and pleasure.

The young man smoothed his dark whiskers, then said: 'Does that mean a very early start in the morning?'

'I have been going down to the yard every morning at half past seven.'

'Yes? Ah, but then you had the—the shop to get back to.'

Hermann tightened his lips with annoyance.

'As you say—I had the shop to get back to. Shall we say that you would have to be there by eight.'

Ishmael laughed. 'I shall probably arrive there in my trousers pulled over my night-shirt. Eight! It's the middle of the night. What do I start with? Counting the buckets and the ladders, and mixing a little paint, eh?'

Hermann flushed. He loved his business, he was proud of everything concerning it. It gave him a thrill of pleasure when he passed his own workmen in the streets and noted how different the buckets, ladders, and other tackle looked from those of other firms. Gollantz' men with their blue-and-white buckets, their ladders painted in the same colours, and their general air of smart competence were, Hermann often said, the best advertisement he could have devised. Now, to have this young man laughing at him was too much. He rose, his kindly face scarlet with annoyance.

'I don't think there is any more to be said.' Hermann spoke coldly. 'I sent for you to make you an offer. It is evident that it makes no appeal to you. I am sorry for having wasted your time.'

Ishmael laughed. 'Don't get angry, keep cool. I didn't say that it didn't appeal to me. Of course I'll take it. I don't say that it's my line, but I'll take it—temporarily at all events. I'm cn the point of pulling off a very big thing, as a matter of fact, but until I do, thanks very much.'

Hermann in his heart knew at that moment that he should have refused to accept such a half-hearted arrangement. He knew that this attitude was no guarantee for good and steady work; he knew that Ishmael would only keep this job until something better turned up. He hesitated, and lost his opportunity.

Ishmael held out his hand and said: 'Thanks very much, Hermann. I shouldn't wonder if I slip into it like one o'clock.'

For a few months he did fairly well. True, old Hans Broder grumbled that Herr Hirsch never issued material methodically, complained that half the time he allowed the men to go into the store and take what they wanted. He said that the men themselves were growing slack; that their materials, plant, and gear were no longer kept in that meticulous order which had been Hermann's pride. Hermann tried to listen with tolerance, and the following morning went down to the yard himself. Old Broder was there, pottering about, clicking his tongue at various things which annoyed him.

'Where are the others?' Hermann demanded.

Old Broder cocked an eye at him, and replied with more than a streak of malice in his voice: 'It's only five minutes past eight, Herr Gollantz. We like the chill off the morning before we start work these days.'

A moment later Gustave, Fritz, Murden, and Joseph entered the yard. Broder chuckled as he watched the dismay on their faces. Hermann spoke crisply, told them to get their materials together, and to come to him for any issues from the store.

Murden came forward. 'Sash-cords and pulleys, please, Herr Gollantz.'

'Where's your order form?'

'Couldn't say. Herr Hirsch doesn't bother with 'em.'

Gustave and Fritz were hauling out long ladders. Hermann stared at the worn paint, and noted two rungs which were cracked and bound with thin rope.

'Where are the new ladders? Those need repairing.'

'These are the newest we have, Herr Gollantz. There are no newer ones.' Last week he had given Ishmael the money for new ladders, to be painted in the regulation blue and white. In the store he stood aghast. The stock had never been so low; the paucity of material made him gasp. A few paint-pots, a few pieces of rope, sacks of powder for whitewash and colouring stood limply against the walls, half empty. This was the store of which he had boasted: 'Our stock is always kept up to the mark. As we take out, we fill up again.' And this change in a few months!

The men were sent off to their work, Broder was ordered to make out a full list of materials required. The clock in the nearby church struck nine and Ishmael Hirsch entered. He hesitated for a moment; then came forward, smiling.

'Hello, Hermann. I'm a bit late this morning. I went round to see why the devil the man hadn't delivered the new ladders. I ordered them weeks ago. Slack as they can be, these chaps, if you don't keep 'em up to the mark.'

Hermann said: 'Come into my office a moment.'

'Your office!' Hirsch laughed. 'It's my office, my friend.'

'It was until eight this morning. It's yours no longer.'

The young man swung round and stared at him. 'Oh, I understand. Your anxiety to do your best for Rachel's brother didn't last long, did it? Well, I don't doubt that I can manage without you as I did before.'

Six months later old Hirsch died. Hermann had never believed that he was rich, but even he was surprised at the small amount which he left. The will was a magnificent affair; there were legacies to his dear son, his beloved daughter, his respected son-in-law, his affectionate brothers, and even to his faithful servants. The only flaw was that when Hermann investigated, there was nothing to be divided among these people. Hermann paid the legacies to the old servants out of his own pocket; he even bought some of the silver and furniture at the price which Ishmael placed upon it, though he knew that he was paying too highly.

The house in the Hohen Markt was given up, and Rachel tentatively suggested that Ishmael might come and live with Hermann and herself. Hermann hesitated. He disliked outsiders in his house; even his mother never entered without a more or less formal invitation.

Rachel looked pathetic, murmured something about 'poor papa' and 'my dear brother', and his heart softened. Ishmael Hirsch was installed in one of the large, well-furnished rooms in his brother-in-law's house, and on the night he arrived expressed his pleasure that the room had such a pleasant outlook.

For the first month or six weeks he behaved tolerably. He was kept busy disposing of the few things which Hermann had advised him to keep out from the general sale. His ideas of their value were inflated, and he spent a good deal of time running round Vienna trying to find someone who would pay the price he demanded. Once this business was concluded, Ishmael began to make life in the house unbearable. Hermann lived a life of routine; he rose early, worked hard all day, and unless he had some definite invitation to attend the theatre, opera, or some private entertainment, he liked to retire early. Rachel ran her house like clockwork, and it was a severe strain on her order-loving mind to have her brother lying in bed until midday, demanding coffee, hot water, and ordering the servants to carry notes to various ladies for him.

Ishmael rose late, dressed, and swaggered out to return in time to dress for the evening, when he disappeared again and did not come back until the early hours of the morning, slamming doors, flinging his boots on to the floor with a bang, and frequently knocking into the furniture in a way which spoke ill for his sobriety.

One morning Hermann opened his heart to Rachel. He had been down at the yard early, and had returned for his coffee and hot rolls. As he turned into the courtyard he saw Ishmael Hirsch climb the steps and ring the door bell. Hermann frowned, hurried forward and spoke to him.

'You're late coming home, Ishmael.'

'I should call it early, brother Hermann.'

'Call it what you wish, I dislike people entering my house at this time. More—I won't permit it.'

'Perhaps if you choose to ask what detained me you might be less harsh. I have been sitting with a sick friend.'

Hermann didn't believe him, indeed he wondered—as he met Ishmael's hard, bright eyes—if the fellow even expected him to do so. The door opened and they entered, Hermann giving his hat and cloak to the servant, Ishmael walking off to his own room, calling back over his shoulder to the servant:

'Heinrich, get a hot bath ready for me, will you, and see that it really *is* hot.'

Hermann, biting his lips with annoyance, entered the dining-room. Rachel, looking charming in a morning gown of pale-grey muslin, smiled as he bent down to kiss her affectionately. His ill temper vanished. He loved his wife, and it was very pleasant to come home from the bustle and dust of the yard to find her ready with hot coffee, and delicious rolls, still warm and crisp.

'I thought I heard you bring someone in with you, Hermann.'

Hermann smiled a trifle grimly. 'Your brother, returning— he tells me that he has been sitting up all night with a sick friend.'

'Oh, poor Ishmael. Did he say who the friend was?'

'I don't think I should inquire too closely.'

Rachel lifted her eyes and stared at him blankly. 'Why not, Hermann? It might be a friend of mine, too.'

Hermann's smile deepened. 'If that is so, I recommend that you terminate the friendship without delay.' He broke a roll and began to spread it with butter and honey. 'Rachel, one of us must speak to your brother. It is impossible that he can continue to disorganize the household, and quite impossible that he should return at such hours. I cannot allow it.'

Rachel pushed away her coffee-cup, her pretty face flushed, and Hermann saw with dismay that her eyes filled with tears.

'I have said that he must alter!' she said. 'I have talked to him. He—he only laughs at me.'

'He laughs, eh? Splendid! We'll see if he laughs at me!'

Rachel suddenly burst into tears, and, dabbing her eyes with a tiny, lace-edged handkerchief, became inarticulate with emotion and sobs.

Hermann rose and went to where she sat.

'My dearest, don't! Rachel, my loved one, don't cry like this. What is it? Tell your Hermann, who adores you. Rachel—don't —I beg you.'

Rachel sobbed that she could not bear quarrels, that Ishmael was not really bad, only thoughtless. She added: 'I'm sorry that I gave way, Hermann. I—I don't think that I feel very well just now. I think—I think'—she buried her face in his arm and sobbed again—'that I am going to have another baby.'

Hermann comforted her; he promised to take her to the theatre that evening. She must see the family doctor and talk to him. If they were to have another child—well, he for one, Hermann told her, would be very proud and happy. Marcus was fifteen months old and a fine, strapping fellow. It would be wonderful for him to have a companion. Meanwhile, he would speak tactfully to Ishmael and try to make him understand that he must mend his ways.

'I won't be harsh, I promise you,' he added hastily, as he saw Rachel's eyes fill again with tears.

Later he interviewed Ishmael. The young man sauntered into one of the show-rooms, wearing a magnificent dressing-gown with collar and cuffs of tartan silk and a smoking cap of purple velvet, with a long gold tassel hanging down at one side. He was smoking a particularly good cigar, and looked at peace with the world.

'Sorry that I annoyed you this morning, Manny.'

Hermann disliked nothing more than the abbreviated version of his name. He looked up frowning, then remembered his promise to Rachel.

'I think we must have an understanding, Ishmael,' he said. 'Your sister has apparently spoken to you about these late hours, and tells me that you treat the matter as a joke.'

'Oh, Rachel's been carrying tales, has she? Damme, you can't expect a man to live like a cloistered nun!'

'While you live in your sister's house and mine, I expect you to conform to the rules of the house.'

Ishmael took his cigar from his lips, stared at the glowing end of it; then said, with apparent irrelevance: 'I'm in a devil of a hole, Hermann.'

With a queer, half-swaggering, half-cringing tone, he told Hermann of what he termed his 'bad luck'. He had lent money to a man who had promised to pay. He had left Vienna, and taken Ishmael's money with him. He produced various crumpled and grimy pieces of paper which purported to be receipts for money advanced.

'You want me to reimburse you?' Hermann asked.

' 'Pon my soul, no!' Ishmael exclaimed. 'I want you to give me a chance to earn money for myself. Oh, I know I didn't do so well in that disgusting yard—not my line. Take me on here, in the show-rooms, or whatever you call 'em. I shall soon learn the jargon—and I've got a persuasive way with the ladies.'

Hermann's teeth were set on edge. Learn the jargon! Persuasive way with the ladies! For twopence he would have thrown the fellow out neck and crop. Then he remembered that Ishmael was his brother by marriage and he owed something to his wife's family. He sighed. It would never answer, he knew that, but he felt it his duty to give him another chance. 'The stars in their courses fight against me!' Hermann thought.

'I'll give you a trial,' he said, 'only'—and he smiled suddenly— 'you can't come into my show-rooms dressed in a velvet coat and checked trousers.'

II

Ishmael didn't do badly, Hermann decided. He was interested and amused by the people who came in and out of the rooms. Soldiers in their splendid uniforms; gentlemen of Vienna, tall, elegant, with beautiful, insolent manners; attractive women who never seemed to know exactly what they wanted; even stout, well-fed priests of the higher orders came to the House of Gollantz, either to sell or to buy. Ishmael learnt quickly, and what he lacked in actual knowledge he made up for in fluent inexactitudes. Hermann disliked inexactitudes, but he was worried about Rachel, young Marcus had developed whooping cough, Miriam was suffering from some sort of liver complaint, and his mind was too occupied to bother very much about his brother-in-law.

Rachel began to get stronger; her apprehension at the prospect of another child died down, Marcus threw off his cough, and Miriam decided that her doctor was a fool, that she was bored to death with a strict diet, and ate again, as she had always done, the choicest and richest foods. Hermann was able to devote his time to his business once again.

'You've a lot of broken stuff here, Hermann,' Ishmael said one morning.

'It's inevitable,' Hermann replied. 'People break stuff. I buy things in lots, perhaps at a sale; some of it is smashed in transit— oh, in a dozen ways. It might be mended, but mended china has precious little value.'

Ishmael stroked his chin. 'It might be worth while mending it all,' he said. 'Open another shop, further in the town, sell fakes.'

Hermann frowned at the word. 'Not fakes! No, no, I don't like anything that's a fake. But there is something in the idea. We might have the stuff repaired and sell it as that—repaired stuff. I'll think it over.'

The idea interested him. His expenses were heavy, the house was costly, his mother took quite a considerable percentage of the profits, Rachel spent money well, but she spent freely, and young Marcus was an expensive luxury. The decorating side of the business paid—on paper, but aristocrats expected tradesmen to wait for their money, and whilst he waited he had his own staff of workmen to pay. It seemed that another, smaller shop might add something to his income, and might at the same time clear off stock which in its present state was dead.

For once Ishmael was really helpful. It appeared that he knew of a man who could mend china, of another who would carve wood to perfection, and yet a third who had some knowledge of restoring prints and engravings. Hermann listened, and decided that at last they had found the right niche for Ishmael. There was no doubt that when he gave his mind to anything he was as clever as paint.

The smaller and less ambitious shop was opened. Hermann himself spent a good deal of time there for the first week or two, assuring every customer that although the goods were genuine enough, they were repaired, and that he sold them at a lower price for that reason.

'This, Baroness, is Capo di Monte. Beautiful—why yes. But, look, if you please, here and here. It had been cracked, and this piece broken. It is repaired, and so, instead of its price being one hundred gulden, it is only forty. You are satisfied? Very good, then it shall be sent home immediately.'

People came, admired the goods, listened to Hermann's little lecture, to his demonstration concerning the rivets, joinings, and chips, and went away saying, as people had said so often before, that Hermann Gollantz was that admirable thing—an honest Jew.

Ishmael returned home one evening carrying a small flat parcel under his arm, a parcel which he unwrapped with some excitement, and showed Hermann a number of small and exquisite pictures.

'What d'you think of them?' he demanded, his very nonchalance betraying his satisfaction.

Hermann carried them to the window, examined them closely, then brought them back to the big centre table. 'Engravings, eh?' Ishmael nodded. 'Modern, of course, and very attractive. You might introduce them into your stock. Where did you get them?'

'A young artist I know—one Anton Mulcher. He engraves

them on thin metal plates—but, of course, you know that. I had
never seen it done before. He can print a great many from one
single plate, which makes the cost comparatively small. His only
difficulty is that he knows nothing of where to buy the plates, and
can only get them in small quantities at considerable cost.'

'I can help him. I will see Boaz Hulme, who supplies these
things. Only keep the idea to yourself, Ishmael, or we shall have
half Vienna making these pretty pictures. Let Charles frame them
—in black and gold, or maple ; nothing ostentatious, keep it simple, and sell them for seven and ten gulden apiece. We will draw
up a small agreement with Mulcher, and give him seventy-five per
cent on the sales of unframed pictures, and fifty on the framed
ones.'

The little engravings, each bearing the scrawled signature—
Anton Mulcher—which came to be so well known twenty years
later, sold well. The profits of the little shop were growing each
week, and Hermann encouraged Mulcher to try his hand at larger
and more ambitious subjects. His set of twenty 'Types of the
Viennese Streets' was eagerly sought after, and later he produced a second series of 'Beauty Spots around Vienna'.

'I have some very clever fellows working for me,' Hermann
told his mother one evening when she dined with Rachel and
himself. 'There is Mulcher, Charles the wood worker, and that
young Greek whose name is utterly beyond me, so we call him
Franck. Only yesterday he showed me a set of dessert dishes which
he had painted, and which I am sending to the ovens to be fired.
They are beautiful. Oh, I am very content!' He sent a smile across
the table to Rachel. 'And as for Ishmael—he is a different man.
So energetic, so keen—it is a pleasure to have him about the
place.'

Miriam shook her head. 'You are an antique dealer,' she reminded him. 'Not a dealer in modern bric-à-brac. I don't like it.
It's undignified.'

The next morning Hermann had been to inspect some work
which his men were doing at a huge house in the Faubourg. He
was pleased with their progress and when he left sauntered along
whistling softly from sheer light-heartedness. He was stopped
by a tall man in a long, light overcoat, who swung a cane with an
amber top, and whose hat was worn on the back of his head.

'Ah, Herr Gollantz, the very man I hoped to meet.'

Hermann bowed with dignity and not the slightest trace of
servility, but this was Baron Kinsky, one of the richest men in

Vienna, a generous patron of the arts and a great collector.

'What can I do for you, Herr Baron?'

The baron smiled. 'Accompany me to my house and give me your opinion on some china which I have bought, if you will be so good.'

'I shall be delighted.'

As they walked they discussed a number of topics. The baron spoke of music, the theatre, and an exhibition of pictures. He was surprised to find how deep, how appreciative was Herr Gollantz' understanding of all these things. 'Confound it!' Kinsky thought. 'The man has taste, he doesn't confine his knowledge merely to prices!'

They entered the splendid house where the pictures, statues, and cabinets of glass and china made Hermann long to linger. The baron hurried him on to a long room at the back of the house. He led Hermann to a table on which were displayed some pieces of china. His face was suddenly grim and unfriendly.

'This is what you want me to give an opinion upon?'

'If you will be so good.'

Hermann picked up a dish, elaborately decorated with figures and flowers. His sensitive fingers moved over the surface, his keen eyes examined the piece closely. Finally he laid it down. 'Ostensibly,' Hermann said, 'this is Capo di Monte, with the pale-blue mark of 1736 ; in reality, I am sorry to tell you, it is a modern and fairly clever—fake. And what else? This ? Again, an imitation of what is known as "T'jungue Moriaans Hofft", date about 1764.' He put down the dish. 'I am sorry, Herr Baron, you have been sold two—only moderately clever fakes.'

The grim face did not change ; Kinsky made a little gesture of impatience.

'I paid a hundred gulden for the di Monte—so called—and ninety-five for the Delft. I bought them both at your shop in the little street—near the Stadt two days ago.'

For a moment he felt a sensation of pity for Hermann Gollantz. His face was ghastly, his eyes stared in something like horror. The hand which rested on the table trembled. When he spoke his voice was hard and controlled. 'Unfortunately I know you too well, Herr Baron, to be able to doubt any statement you make. To anyone else I should have replied, "Impossible". As it is, I can only suppose that there has been some terrible mistake. For the first time in my life—I am ashamed. I beg that you will allow me to return to you the hundred and seventy-five gulden—and take these—these abominations away with me.'

He took out his wallet, extracted the money and laid it on the table.

The baron, watching him, again felt genuine pity for him. It was obvious that the man was suffering acutely.

'Don't take it so hardly,' he said. 'I was tricked—even the marks are right, you see for yourself. I am certain of one thing, Herr Gollantz, that I was tricked by someone who is deceiving you as they deceived me. I can assure you that this unfortunate matter will go no farther, on my word of honour.'

'I am very grateful. I shall try to prove my gratitude. I will take these pieces with me. Baron, I wish you a very good morning.'

As he watched the upright, broad-shouldered figure walk away, Baron Kinsky frowned. 'Curious people, these Jews. Damme, the man's a tradesman, and he has the manners and address of a gentleman. He looked as if someone had given him a blow over the heart when he discovered that the china was imitation.'

4

I

HERMANN walked rapidly, looking neither to the right nor the left, he was only conscious that he was more angry than he had ever been in his life. He felt shamed, disgraced, almost unclean. He, Hermann Gollantz, credited with selling fakes, accused of taking advantage of men with less knowledge than his own. God only knew how many others had been imposed upon! Kinsky had promised to let the matter rest, to keep silent, but all clients were not of the calibre of Baron Kinsky. Others might have discovered the frauds perpetrated upon them, they might talk, his reputation would suffer, and he would no longer be able to voice his proud boast that the House of Gollantz was only willing to sell the best.

Only a few days before a stout cleric had bought a set of fine glass from him, asking, when the bargain was concluded: 'And you will give me a guarantee that this is genuine Venetian?'

Hermann's pale face flushed when he remembered how he had answered.

'Your Eminence, I have given you a guarantee. I have sold this glass to you as Venetian. That is my guarantee—my word.'

He entered the shop, and unobtrusively placed the two pieces of china on a side table. Ishmael was speaking to a customer. His eyes danced: he was laughing and protesting a little too much, Hermann thought. What a fool he had been to believe in the fellow. His manner was bad, cheap, like some huckster at a fair.

'You will not find its equal in all Vienna, Madame. It is—like all things found at the House of Gollantz—unique.'

The lady—Hermann suspected that she was the mistress of some rich man—smiled back archly. 'And does that apply even to the salesman?'

Ishmael bowed. 'Assuredly, Madame. Regard me! I am unique among salesmen.'

Hermann stepped forward briskly. 'What does Madame desire, Herr Hirsch?'

Ishmael's start was unmistakable. 'This mirror Madame finds very attractive. White Dresden.'

Hermann glanced at the pretty little looking-glass. 'Not White Dresden,' he said coldly. 'This, Madame, is Meissen. You will observe that it is a restored piece, that is why the price is so low. Thirty gulden.'

The lady stared at him. 'But he said eighty-five gulden. He did not say that it was restored. I don't want broken stuff!'

Hermann's bow was beautifully calculated. 'I regret that my assistant made a mistake, Madame. The price is as I have said.'

'Oh well, I might as well take it——'

'I will give you a receipt, stating that it is not perfect.'

When she left the shop Hermann turned to Ishmael. 'How long has this been going on?'

'I don't know what you mean. If you're referring to the price for the damn' mirror, that was a mistake on my part.'

'A most unfortunate mistake. Now, I will see the books, if you please.'

Ishmael Hirsch blustered a little. What was the game? Did Hermann suspect him? Who had been telling lies?

'I don't know—as yet,' Hermann answered coolly. He went through the books. Many of the prices struck him as slightly lower than they might have been; the fact reassured him a little.

Then he found the entry for which he sought—Baron Kinsky. 'Capo di Monte restored dish, sixty gulden. One Delft dish, thirty gulden.'

He turned and ordered another assistant to put up the shutters. Then, when the candles were lit, the storm broke. It seemed to Ishmael and his fellow assistant that they had never heard any man so much a master of cold, searing invective. He appeared to know everything. He knew the name of the wretched, almost bankrupt factory where the china had been made, he knew that Franck had painted in marks, and carefully chipped bits of the decoration here and there. He stared at them with cold, fierce eyes ; with lips that were hard and tight he flayed them alive, his face livid with rage.

'Thieves, liars, cheats! Filthy hucksters! Scum who have robbed me of my good name. Renegade Jews. . . . God of my Fathers, what a crime that you should belong to the Jewish race! *Gonophs* —that you are!'

Suddenly he spoke calmly, as if his anger were past.

'For many years I have worked to build up a name which men should respect. That is how honest Jews live, working for that end. I have boasted that my word was my bond, I have stated that to buy in the House of Gollantz was to buy only what was real and honest and good. Austrians have grown to believe in me ; it has been left to two of my own race—you, Ishmael bar Adolfus, and you, Simon bar Cohen—to drag that name down, and make me a byword in this city! Go, both of you. Leave me. I will not give you the joy of watching my misery. How you both must have hated me to be willing to give me such pain.'

Young Cohen's face was scarlet with shame, his eyes brimmed with tears, and he fell on his knees, sobbing out his regret at Hermann's feet. Ishmael scowled, shuffled his feet, muttered that it was 'all a great fuss about nothing', and turned away.

Hermann looked down at the sobbing boy—he was only nineteen—and his face softened a little. He laid his hand on Simon's shoulder.

'Get up!' he said. 'Tell me, why did you do this?'

'I wanted money, Herr Gollantz. My mother is a widow, she is poor. My sister was ill. The doctor ordered her wine and the finest fruit. He said that she must go away for other air or she will die. I was frantic.'

Simon Cohen never forgot the expression on Hermann's face as he spoke. Years afterwards it came back to him as one of the most tender and beautiful things he had ever seen.

'Please forgive me, Simon,' he said. 'I must have seemed to you a hard man, or you would have come and confided in me. The fault has been mine that I hid my friendship for you. That is over. Tell me, how much have you saved—how you obtained the money does not matter at the moment.'

'Two hundred gulden, Herr Gollantz.'

Hermann's expression was tinged with a sort of bitter amusement. Two hundred gulden was a poor price to obtain for selling one's honour!

'Tomorrow we will talk this matter over. Be very certain that your sister shall have all that is necessary for her, and you—well, there is work waiting for you with me, when this shop is closed, as it will be this very evening. I am done with selling second-rate stuff!'

Young Cohen caught his employer's hand and pressed it to his lips. It seemed to him that this man was something removed from ordinary mortals, that he was finer, cleaner, more upright.

Hermann drew his hand away. 'Get up, my boy. That is over. I am satisfied.'

'Never again!' Cohen protested, his voice still thick with sobs. 'I promise you, Herr Gollantz, I promise you. From now I shall try to live as you live——'

'Hush! I have said it is over. I have no need to extract promises from you.' He turned to Ishmael. The gentleness had vanished from his face, his eyes were hard and cold. 'And you—you must go. I cannot afford to go on for ever giving chances to you.'

Ishmael smiled. 'That's all right,' he said. 'I began to think it was time for me to launch out on my own. You've no initiative, Manny. You don't see openings when they're offered to you. I do.'

Hermann bowed. 'I am satisfied to remain as I am. Cohen, please call Mulcher and Charles and the Greek.'

The three men came and stood before him. Hermann noticed that while Charles and the Greek looked puzzled, Mulcher shot uneasy glances in the direction of Ishmael. Very briefly, Hermann told them that he was closing the shop, and added that he could provide work for them if they cared to take it. Again he saw a quick glance pass from Mulcher to Ishmael and saw Ishmael shake his head. Charles and the Greek agreed to work for him at his other establishment. Mulcher shrugged his shoulders and spread his hands in deprecation. There was nothing he would have liked better, it would have been a pleasure to work for Herr Gollantz, but he felt that, perhaps, it would be well for him to— Hermann cut short his protestations.

'Very well, there is no more to be said. It only remains for me to wish you all a very good day and lock up the shop.'

When he told his mother of what had happened she shrugged her massive shoulders. 'What did I tell you? Cheap goods breed cheap customers, and cheap customers breed cheap salesmen. You are well quit of it. I always felt that it was undignified.' To Rachel he told no more than was necessary. She loved her brother, and Hermann could not bear to hurt her by telling the whole story. He said that he was giving up the shop, that Ishmael was going to strike out on his own, and he hoped that he would do well.

Ishmael came and collected his clothes, packing them in a large leather bag of Hermann's which he found in one of the attics and did not think worth while mentioning to anyone. He took a tender farewell of his sister, told her that he was leaving Vienna with Anton Mulcher; that they were going to work in other towns, selling the engravings which were so popular.

'I shall write, my dear little sister,' Ishmael assured her. 'I may not write very often, but you shall hear from me and you will hear good news. I am going to make a fortune.'

II

Rachel had two letters from him, one which was sent from Budapest and the other from Munich. In neither of them did he appear to have made a fortune, but he seemed contented, well, and happy, and Rachel folded the letters and laid them away, smiling as she did so.

Ishmael was young, handsome, and he liked change. Later he would come back to Vienna and settle down, become Hermann's trusted partner.

Her second son was born in the winter of 1844. She was very ill, and for hours Hermann paced up and down the long show-room, biting his lips and shaking with anxiety. Young Cohen watched him, his eyes full of mute affection. It was agony for him to watch Hermann Gollantz suffer.

At intervals the door would open to admit the magnificent figure of Miriam Gollantz. She would walk over to where Cohen

111

sat, and in a loud whisper demand if Hermann had eaten anything.

'Nothing, Madame. He is too anxious to eat.'

'He must eat! Simon, go to the kitchen and tell them to give
you a small basin of strong soup, carry it to him, and make him
drink it.'

Hermann, hearing, would turn and stare at his mother as if
he scarcely recognized her. 'I want nothing—nothing—nothing.'
Then, 'How is Rachel?'

'She is very brave, my son. She sends you her love. She says you
must not worry. She commands you not to worry.'

The thought of his gentle Rachel commanding him to do anything was incredible. Hermann knew that the story was his
mother's invention, and that Rachel could never have evolved
such a phrase. He smiled.

'Mama, you think I am a fool,' he said, with kindly intolerance. 'I know you made that up as you walked from Rachel's
room to this one.'

The day was dying. Simon lit the candles and brought in a
painted porcelain lamp. A nurse brought little Marcus to bid his
father good night. Hermann caught the child in his arms and held
him closely; the warm contact of the small human body comforted him, made him feel more hopeful.

'God bless you and take care of you—of us all,' Hermann said.

As he gave the boy back to his nurse, the door was flung open,
and Miriam stood there, her beautiful eyes shining, her lips
parted.

'Hermann—it is over. Rachel is safe—tired, poor darling, but
doing well. Oh, so brave! So splendid! I am proud of my daughter.
And the child! Never have I seen anything so beautiful. Raphael
might have painted him. Come and see them for one moment.'
She turned and caught Marcus in her arms. 'My little one, you
have a brother with whom you shall play very soon. When you
sleep tonight, dream of the wonderful games which you and he
shall play. Sleep well, little angel.'

The baby was, as she had said, quite remarkably beautiful.
From the first his tiny features were formed and definite. His
skin was fair, and his cheeks touched with rose. His fine, silky
hair curled round a beautifully shaped head. His body was long,
and there was no blemish on him anywhere. He was the world's
most beautiful baby. Moreover he was good. He rarely cried,
and when he did, his sobs died almost as they were born. His

112

large, dark eyes with their thick fringe of lashes appeared to notice objects while he was still very young. He smiled, and though Miriam and the nurse might protest that his smiles were the outcome of wind, neither Hermann nor Rachel could ever quite bring themselves to believe it.

He was called Emmanuel, and upon the day when he was formally accepted as a professed Jew, his behaviour was so admirable as to call praises from the dignified rabbi who performed the ceremony.

Hermann went about his work in utter content. Rachel was better, his two sons were all that could be desired, his business prospered, his employees were steady, Simon Cohen was learning rapidly, and Miriam was better than she had been for years.

Marcus was six years old and Emmanuel two years younger when Ishmael Hirsch returned to Vienna. He called at the house in the Bargerspital. Hermann greeted him, but did not offer his hand. It seemed to him that Ishmael had not improved. True, his black velvet jacket was heavily braided, his black-and-white trousers and white waistcoat might be the latest mode, but to Hermann they were not the mode for a gentleman. The fellow was too conscious of his smart clothes, too proud of his long, black whiskers, and the moustache which covered his upper lip. He wore too many rings and reeked of scent. He was pleasant enough, but—Hermann sought for words which should describe his manner.

'Damme, the fellow's too affable and condescending!' he decided with some annoyance.

Rachel was delighted to see him. 'Looking so well and handsome, eh, Hermann? I believe that you've grown, Ishmael. You're certainly broader.'

Ishmael pulled his black, scented whiskers, and smiled. 'And you! You're a picture. And what about these two wonderful children? When am I going to see them?'

Rachel rose, and went to find the little boys. As she entered, her wide crinoline skirts billowing round her, her curls falling over her shoulder, her tight-fitting brown velvet bodice showing off her figure, leading her two children by their tiny hands, Hermann thought that he had never seen a more charming sight. The two little boys, in dark-blue frocks with wide, shining leather belts, with white socks and strapped shoes, were tall for their age. They had no fear, but ran into the room, pulling their hands from their mother's and rushing to embrace their father, whom they both adored.

'Gently, gently,' Rachel said. 'Look, Marcus, Emmanuel, here is your uncle come to see you.'

Marcus planted his legs wide, and stared up at Ishmael. Emmanuel clung to his father and, after a glance in his uncle's direction, continued to whisper some important secret in his father's ear. Hermann chuckled inwardly. The two little boys didn't like their new uncle—they had taste even at this early age.

Ishmael dived his hand into the pocket of the black-and-white trousers.

'Let's see if I can find something for you.' He produced a handful of small silver, and began to turn it over in the palm of his hand. Marcus watched him for a moment, then turned and walked back to Hermann, saying as he did so:

'I don't know this man. Need we keep him here?'

Emmanuel twisted round to make a closer inspection of the stranger who did not appeal to his brother. His large dark eyes stared, he frowned a babyish frown. 'No, we don't want him, do we, Papa? He smells bad.'

'I was ashamed of them both,' Rachel said later, when she and Hermann recounted the meeting to Miriam, but she laughed as she spoke, and it was evident that she regarded both her sons as marvels of intelligence.

Ishmael came very little to the house of Hermann Gollantz. He was always to be seen in the town, seated in a fashionable café, walking along the smartest streets, talking to the smartest —if not the most aristocratic—women. He appeared to be well off, and wore a tremendous number of new clothes. Hermann tried to discover what he had done, what he did for a living. Ishmael talked vaguely of 'my business' or 'my partner, Mulcher', but he gave no details.

He would wander into Hermann's show-rooms in the morning, pick up an article here and there, stroll round asking the price of this or that, dropping cigar-ash on the Aubusson carpet to Simon Cohen's annoyance. Sometimes he would pull out a beautiful red-leather case and take from it a wad of notes, examining them and swearing under his breath because they were all for large amounts. Then, stripping one from the roll he would offer it to Cohen or Hermann, saying as he did so: 'Oblige me with change, will you? Must have some small stuff—chicken food.' Then, the change jingling in his pocket, he would wander off again, leaving vague messages for Rachel.

He came one evening, ready to go to the opera. His white bow was the largest Hermann had ever seen, and the shirt he wore elaborately frilled. He seemed annoyed as he entered.

'I'm furious!' he said. 'Furious! The town is full of bad money. These sneak thieves of Austrians! Nothing better than a mob of comers.'

Hermann held up his hand. 'Please,' he said. 'I don't like it. They've given me an excellent living, and apparently they're doing the same for you.'

'Very well for you to talk. Wait until you find yourself with a fistful of bad notes. See here!' He put his hand in his pocket and took out a crumpled note, spreading it flat on a marble-topped table. 'Look at that! An impudent forgery if ever there was one.'

Hermann picked up the note and examined it. 'Yes, it's not good. Still, one swallow doesn't make a summer. You can't condemn all Austria on the evidence of one small forgery.'

'I had a bad gold piece the other day. Half the gulden in Vienna are counterfeit. Damned disgraceful. I shall be glad to be out of the place.'

Still muttering and cursing the Austrians, he went away.

Three days later he came in again. He was in high spirits, or, Hermann wondered, was he nervous? His hands twitched, he laughed very often and very loudly. He congratulated Hermann on the sale of a valuable picture which had been bought by Prince Harraps.

'Strange old fellow, isn't he?' Ishmael demanded. 'Is it true that he always pays in cash for everything?'

Hermann nodded. 'In my case he did. Notes and gold coins. Which reminds me, someone must take it to the bank. I dislike keeping money—large sums—in the house. Simon, you might take it down this morning.'

'Herr Gollantz, you promised the baroness that I should go there this morning with patterns of brocade——'

Hermann snapped his fingers impatiently: 'And I have to see General Volkesburger!'

Ishmael said: 'Get Rachel to take it down for you.'

Hermann smiled. 'Rachel loathes banks. She says that she always feels they suspect her of trying to deceive them when she enters one. No, it must wait.'

With an air of making a concession, Ishmael said: 'Then let me take it for you. I don't mind. Only someone must get me a coach. I can't walk through the streets carrying the family money bags—flaunting the ill-gotten Hebrew gains before the whole of Vienna.'

Hermann concealed his momentary irritation. He disliked jokes about his race, but he wanted the money out of the way and Ishmael was the only person free to take it. The money was produced, counted out, checked, and a slip for the bank filled in. Five thousand, seven hundred and fifty gulden—in notes and gold.

Ishmael whistled. 'By Jove, I wish it was mine!' He drove off.

Hermann laid out the small collection of old coins which the General had expressed a wish to see, Simon went off with his patterns of brocade, and for a few moments the long show-room was very still.

It was then that the door handle turned carefully and the two boys entered. Hermann smiled, and allowed them to climb on to his knees, and examine his big gold watch. Marcus was content, but Emmanuel soon scrambled down and began to walk down the room, looking first at one thing, then at another, asking an endless stream of questions in his piping little voice.

'Father, what is this?' or 'Tell me, Father, has this a name?' He loved beauty, colour, and fine textures. Shown a piece of old embroidery, he would stare at it as another child would stare at a picture-book, and touch the surface of china with the tips of his fingers as if he derived real pleasure from the smoothness and quality.

Rachel, coming in, found them both standing beside a table on which was a great Dresden bowl, with clusters of flowers and fruit, and here and there a cherub holding a streamer of blue china ribbon.

'I thought that I should find them here. Quick, children, go to nurse and be dressed to come out for a walk.'

'A mere walk!' Hermann said, as the boys trotted away. 'You look far too magnificent for a walk with the children! That bonnet is a thing of real beauty. I have never seen you in anything more becoming.'

She twisted before an old gilt-framed mirror. 'This spoon shape is becoming, I agree. I only wondered if it was a trifle— well, young for me.'

He caught her in his arms. 'Untruthful creature! You thought nothing of the kind. You only say these things in front of me because you like to hear me deny them. I always fall into the trap, and so you always get what you want. Too young! What nonsense! Only, such a bonnet demands a new coat. When you are in the town, look in the window of the new French shop. There is one which I saw yesterday. I thought: "If Prince Harraps buys the picture, that shall be my Rachel's before the day is out." He did buy the picture! . . . The coat? It is grey, with wide sleeves and some kind of white under-sleeve, made of cambric perhaps. There, the boys are ready. Go and buy your coat.'

She went off, smiling, her charming face a little flushed with pleasure and excitement. Hermann stood at the window, and Rachel made the two boys look up and wave to him. Hermann's heart was very full. How pretty she was, and the boys—what fine little fellows. Marcus sturdy and straight, Emmanuel tall for his age, walking already with an air of distinction that made people turn to look after him. The old General found Gollantz particularly pleasant that morning, talking with knowledge concerning the antique coins, asking a price which was slightly lower than he had either hoped or expected.

The old man, his white hands folded on the heavy, silver head of his stick, nodded and smiled. 'Always a great delight to come here, Herr Gollantz. I never feel that I am coming to a shop— I feel rather that I drop in to have a talk with a friend!'

'I am very happy to hear you say so, General.'

'You—pardon me—do well here?'

'Sufficiently, thank you. Naturally I wish to do even better. I have a family, and I intend that they shall have every advantage. An attractive wife, two fine sons, and my beloved mother—these are not only joys, but luxuries.' He turned to take a note from a servant who had entered. 'Will you pardon me?' He ripped it open and read it slowly, the colour draining from his face as he read.

Hermann, my friend, will you come down to the bank as soon as possible. There is something very wrong here, and you must know of it immediately. Don't delay, every minute is precious. Marcus Breal.

He turned to his client, made his excuses, and in a few minutes was driving towards the centre of the town to the bank which belonged to Marcus Breal. As he walked through the outer office

117

he noticed that the clerks eyed him curiously. Breal, stout, hand-some, and kindly, rose to greet him.

'Sit down, Hermann. First, I want you to allow me to send a messenger to the lodgings of your brother-in-law. You know where he lives?'

'Yes, in one of the houses which look out on to the Bastei. The number is seven. He lodges with a widow woman on the first floor.'

'Good, give me a moment to tell someone to bring him here.'

A few seconds later he was back. 'Here is the story. Hirsch drove up this morning, and came in carrying a canvas bag and a slip signed by you stating the amount to be paid in to your account. The clerk who took it is young and inexperienced. He began to count it, but Hirsch expostulated that he could not wait. There was the slip, signed by you, surely that was sufficient? He refused to listen, and left the bank while this clerk, Carl Rosher, was still counting the money. My cashier, noticing that Rosher was disturbed, came over to him and asked what was wrong. Rosher explained, and the cashier told him to count the money quickly, and send the acceptance slip back to you immediately. One of the gold pieces fell to the floor. It did not ring! It fell flat, dead, lifeless. The cashier examined it. He examined others—false. The notes—forgeries. In all we found only five gulden which were genuine.'

He pulled a slip of paper towards him. 'In short, Hermann, my dear friend, unless we can find this scamp of an Ishmael Hirsch, you have been robbed of five thousand seven hundred and forty-five gulden.'

Hermann sat staring before him, his face white, his fingers twitching. How could he have been such a fool? What had made him trust Hirsch? He ought to have known—this was not the first time. A knock on the door made him start to his feet. The messenger entered.

'Herr Hirsch is not there, Herr Breal. The woman tells me that he left an hour ago, taking his bags with him. He drove away in a private coach with another gentleman.'

Marcus Breal nodded. 'Very well, you may go.'

'Now, Hermann, we must take this to people who can deal—officially—with thieves. Come, let us go to the Prefecture.'

Hermann did not move. 'No, Marcus,' he said slowly. 'I cannot do that. Hirsch is my wife's brother. The law is no use to me. It would break her heart. Ask your clerk and your cashier, as a personal favour to you, to say nothing. You see—as Rachel's brother, he is one of my responsibilities. I could never lower her pride—never, never.'

Breal nodded. 'I expected this,' he said. 'You're a fool, but a fool I am proud to call my friend. Did you know anything of this —suspect him?'

'Never! Now—now I can see how he pulled wool over my eyes, talking to me of the amount of bad money in Vienna. Only a few days ago, he showed me a counterfeit note, given to him, he said, by a Viennese trader. I can see it now. He works hand in hand with one Anton Mulcher, an engraver. Think of it, Marcus, I have continually changed money for him. Do you suppose it was all counterfeit? Have I helped to spread bad money throughout Vienna? It's horrible! Horrible!'

'And yet, horrible though it is—because I am afraid that is just what you have done—you refuse to accept the help of the law?'

'No, I cannot go to the law! But, Marcus, if people come to you with counterfeit money—poor people, it may be—make it up to them, for me. I can do that at least.'

5

I

ONCE again Ishmael Hirsch disappeared from Vienna, and his sister neither saw nor heard anything of him for years, when he returned with an exceedingly pretty and well-dressed wife. There had been changes in Vienna ; the old Metternich régime had gone, and with it that 'grandmotherly' government which encouraged the Austrian people to think as little as possible, to enjoy themselves, and behave like obedient and well-conducted children. The old axiom that if two people stood talking for more than a few minutes in the street they were better moved on because they might be talking of some serious matter, was gone.

The young Emperor—who had signed over two thousand death warrants before he was twenty-five—and his beautiful young wife had ascended the throne. Vienna was a town of magnificent gaiety, of waltzes, of operas, and expensive shops. The court was dignified, exclusive, and discreet. The Emperor was much admired, and was ready to admire in return. True, his wife was a strange, wild creature, but if—as it was said—she was miserable at the court of Vienna, it was judged to be very much her own fault, because she had such astonishing ideas of what was enjoyable.

The Emperor ruled Austria, and his mother ruled him. People smiled and said that 'Sophie was the best man at court.' They might not love her, but they admired her strength, her capability. When Hermann Gollantz saw her driving, at the opera, or in the royal box at the theatre, he noted her narrowed eyes, fine masterful nose, and full sensual mouth pinched in at the corners, and shivered.

'Thank God,' he whispered to Rachel, 'I was not born her son!' The past six years had been very happy for him. Business prospered, and he had made good, many times over, the loss he had sustained at the hands of Ishmael Hirsch. It was not in Hermann's nature to nurse revengeful feelings, and once he had recovered from the shock of his loss he did his best to forget the whole business.

The years passed, his business grew, his sons were strong and healthy, they were both intelligent, and his life was full of interest. Simon Cohen was his right hand; there was nothing which Hermann might not safely entrust to him and know that it would be done as well as he could have done it himself.

Hermann was growing a little stout; his face had become rather heavy, and his fair skin had deepened in tone. His eyes retained all their old kindliness and his nature was as sunny as ever. His two boys adored him, regarding him as the finest man in the world.

Marcus was twelve, and Emmanuel ten. Both were well-grown, both were clever, but Marcus promised to be brilliant. At ten he had played the piano exceedingly well, and at twelve studied it seriously, with a view to becoming a professional pianist. Emmanuel, who was less intellectual, had a brain which was sufficiently good to earn him the upper places in his school classes. He had fulfilled his early promise of extreme beauty, and no one admired him more than his elder brother, whilst no one rated his good looks lower than Emmanuel himself. The two brothers were devoted to each other, and were never so happy as when they were together. At the time when Hirsch returned to Vienna it would have been difficult to have found a more united family than that of the Gollantz.

Ishmael arrived unexpectedly one evening shortly before the evening meal. Dinner was at six, and Rachel prided herself upon the excellence of the food which was provided. On this particular evening Miriam was dining with them, and Rachel had ordered a dinner with even more care than usual. The old lady, who was well over seventy, frequently spoke with feeling and gratitude for the fact that neither her taste nor her appetite had ever deserted her.

The family sat, waiting for the clock to strike six, in the large and dignified drawing-room. From the ceiling hung two large chandeliers of fine cut-glass, each holding thirty candles; a large lamp of painted china stood on a side table, and the room shimmered with soft radiance. The lights caught the satin stripes of the sofa coverings and shone on the touches of gilt on the legs of the chairs. Miriam—immense, and looking almost impossibly massive—sat on a low chair, a huge crinoline of blue silk draped with festoons of lace caught up here and there with tiny bunches of pink roses, billowing round her. Her heavy white shoulders emerged from the low bodice, and her thick and beautifully dressed hair fell on to her shoulders in ringlets. She still retained her beauty, and her dark eyes were as fine as ever; it was her boast that she could still pick caraway seeds out of cake without glasses.

Rachel sat nearer to the lamp, embroidering a very large, fine linen handkerchief for Hermann. She had kept her figure at a time when most Jewish women lost theirs in the late twenties. She had never dared to dress as modishly as her mother-in-law, but in her more subdued colours and less flamboyant styles she contrived to look distinguished and distinctly attractive.

Hermann, in a frilled shirt, with a high white collar and a broad white linen bow tie, with a double-breasted white waistcoat and tail coat of very smooth, fine cloth, stood with one arm on the mantelpiece listening to his younger son recounting the beauties of a picture which he had seen that afternoon. Marcus leant against the arm of his grandmother's chair. Both boys wore their hair rather long, had short, dark-blue cloth coats with velvet collars, and white frilled shirts which turned over the jackets in a wide sweep of linen, and were finished off with large black silk bows. Their trousers were of very light fawn cloth, strapped under their polished shoes.

Into this peaceful group entered Ishmael Hirsch and his wife. They were announced and had entered before Hermann had realized what had happened. Rachel sprang to her feet, and with a cry of delight flung herself into her brother's arms.

'Ishmael, my dear brother! How delightful! When did you arrive? Oh, and this is your wife—I am so glad to see you, so very glad.'

Hermann forced himself to greet his brother-in-law with some show of cordiality. He had hidden everything from Rachel ; there could be no turning back now. He must behave as if he were reasonably glad to meet the fellow. Ishmael had grown very stout, with a stoutness which spoke of too much drink and too little exercise. His face was florid, his clothes unpleasantly smart. Hermann summed him up briefly : 'Second-rate.'

Ishmael bowed to Miriam Gollantz, who returned his greeting coldly.

'You come back as unexpectedly as you leave,' she said. 'Present your wife to me, please.'

The pretty, fair-haired little Frenchwoman chattered easily enough. She was delighted with Vienna—she called it a 'toy Paris'.

Miriam sniffed. 'Rather—an exquisite reproduction, Madame Hirsch,' she suggested.

Rachel begged them to stay to dinner ; they accepted, and she hurried away to make the necessary arrangements. Hermann felt a thrill of satisfaction that Hirsch should see his home under such pleasant conditions. He knew Rachel's capabilities as a housekeeper, she looked well, his mother was dressed splendidly, his two sons looked charming. He saw Hirsch eyeing them both.

During dinner Ishmael spoke with some pomposity of his plans. They were living in an age of progress, he said. Change was everywhere. Now was the time for men of ability to take their rightful place in the world. Trade was growing, international relations demanded international trading. There was money to be made in organization, to be made out of goods which one need never handle, merely making arrangements for their delivery.

'My partner and I have found fine offices near the Burgtheater——'

Miriam leant forward. 'Your partner?' she said. 'Mulcher?'

For a second Ishmael's eyes faltered as they met hers. 'Mulcher? No, no. He is in Paris, poor fellow, very hard up indeed, I believe. No, my partner is the brother of my wife—Louis Sousa. He, too, with his wife and family, have come to Vienna with us. Tomorrow we begin our work. We shall be quite a large family.

Rachel. I have brought you back sisters and brothers.'

Hermann listened with apprehension. Ishmael was bad enough, but to have a whole colony of French people introduced was too much. Everything had been so delightful, so prosperous in the past. He sighed and turned to listen to Marcus and Emmanuel.

'Papa, if I go with Marcus to hear Herr Thalberg, will you tell him that he must come with me to see the exhibition of pictures which opened today?'

He forgot Ishmael, and listened to the two boys talking.

II

It seemed to Hermann that Ishmael's advent was the end of his peace. He was in and out, asking for an introduction here, some advice there. He begged pieces of furniture for his office, he begged that the carpenter might make a crate for some goods which had to be repacked, he begged for a small loan until some firm paid their bill; and in less than a month Hermann felt that the peace of his house was ruined.

His wife, Henrietta, was constantly running in and out to see Rachel—to borrow a dish in which to make jam, to ask for a recipe for *paté* or pastry, to know if she might beg a little of Rachel's preserve which Ishmael had liked so much. Her two children were always hanging on to her skirts—Marie and Jean. Unpleasant little things, with sallow skins and dirty noses. Madame Sousa came with her, drank coffee noisily, and ate a great many sweet cakes, scattering crumbs all over Rachel's fine carpets. Her fat husband dropped in and sniffed the aroma of Hermann's cigar, lamenting that he could not afford to smoke anything so good. He accepted one with a bow which Hermann felt was overdone, implying that he expected a boxful.

'The house is always filled with people,' Miriam grumbled. 'I never come out of my rooms but my ears are offended by Madame Hirsch and Madame Sousa's cackling voices, or my eyes offended by their dirty children, or my sense of good taste offended by that gross Frenchman with his waistcoat spotted with grease. Pah! One might as well live in the back streets of Paris.'

Marcus, sitting down at the piano, would lift his hands from the keys with an expression of disgust. 'Mama, these keys are covered with jam! Those horrible little children have been thump-

123

ing on my piano. Oh, Mama, *must* they be allowed to do that? I do hate it so.'

Or Emmanuel would open one of his precious books on art and find large crumbs squashed flat between the pages. His face would be eloquent of disgust and distaste and, as he carefully removed it, Hermann would see in him old Meldola living again. He never spoke of it—Emmanuel never lost his temper—but the books were never left lying about again.

For eighteen months the peace of the house was destroyed for Hermann. Then rumours began to reach him that Hirsch and Sousa were in a bad way. More, there had been shady transactions: goods paid for and never delivered; goods which had not been up to sample; goods which had been imported without payment to the sellers. It appeared that the firm was looked on with grave suspicion. Hermann, fear gripping him, sought out Marcus Breal.

'If you had not come to me,' Breal said, 'I was coming to you. The two of them are swindlers, Hermann. The whole business— no, no, not the whole, let us say all of their business except possibly five per cent—is shady.'

'I felt certain of it,' Hermann said. 'And see, Marcus, it begins to reflect on me. Only yesterday a client came to me, an Englishman, a man I like and respect very much. A lord, he is—Sir Harley. He knows Vienna very well indeed; he is in the diplomatic. He wanted some china and pictures sent over to England. Then, quite suddenly, he looked at me very queerly. "You don't belong to Hirsch and Sousa, do you?" I said that I had nothing to do with them. "I thought someone told me that Hirsch was your brother-in-law?" I admitted it, but said that I had no business dealings with him. Sir Harley said it was good that I did not deal through him. Then he cleared his throat and said: "They are bad 'uns, Gollantz. Give them a wide berth." Many people have hinted at—things. Marcus, it will reflect on my business. What am I to do?'

Breal thought for a moment. 'You're not a rich man, Hermann.'

'No, indeed. We live very well, we like to live well. I am afraid that there is very little actually saved—except for the boys' education. I want Marcus to have the very best musical training, and Emmanuel to travel all over Europe. He will be as great an expert as my father—you remember he was employed by the Emperor Napoleon, Marcus.'

'Could you raise money? If I advanced half of ten thousand

124

gulden, could you raise the other half?' He leaned forward and spoke confidingly. 'I want you to realize the gravity of the position. Your business is so much a personal business—you have built it, and you cannot afford to run risks with clients such as yours. One breath and they would go elsewhere.'

'I know.' Hermann agreed. 'I know—but ten thousand gulden!'

That evening Hermann sat in his study and tried to reckon how much he could afford to buy out his brother-in-law's business. Would he sell? Might he not suspect that Hermann feared him and decide to remain to extract money? Already he owed Hermann several hundred gulden, and Sousa owed as many more. It was so difficult; nothing seemed to shake Rachel's love for her brother.

It was then that Ishmael Hirsch was announced. He entered, his face white, his hands shaking.

'Hermann, Hermann!' He stammered in his fright. 'I've come to beg for your help.'

Hermann stared at him, then said coldly: 'Not for the first time.'

'This is serious,' Ishmael protested. 'This is beyond me. I'm—we're in a mess. It's Sousa's fault, not mine—the damned fool! He'd pulled it off before and swore that he could again. Goods do go astray, they do get lost, and if one has part payment before despatching—well, it's not bad.' He was actually regaining his composure, almost swaggering about his cleverness.

Hermann watched him, disgust on every line of his face. What scum these people were! Was it to be wondered that Austrians—that all the world—looked with disfavour on his race, when these men were of it.

'Go on,' Hermann said. 'Let me hear the whole abominable story.'

Ishmael shot a glance of hate at him. 'Oh, you've never been tempted. Things have always been easy for you. You had a rich uncle, a rich mother. I had none of these things. I've always had to struggle to keep my head above water——'

'And only succeeded in keeping it in the mud, eh? Well, I suppose it's the old story. Goods ordered, paid for—and neither you nor anyone else had more than a faked sample, eh? And now you and your precious partner are found out.'

'How was I to know that Feluca of Verona had a brother living here? How was I to know that a greasy Italian would come round making inquiries, asking under another name to see the samples of Smyrna figs! One can't know everything. . . .' There he was, blustering again!

'And the upshot of it?'

'The upshot? That Feluca demands the money paid for his brother's goods—fifty per cent of the consignment——'

'Which was never consigned,' Hermann interpolated dryly. 'And . . . ?'

'He had carried his tale to Boccio of Milano, who has a cousin living here, and they have made it their business to interview Fernandez, whose warehouse in Madrid we—well, whose Madrid house ordered goods from us. They are threatening to go to the law, demanding payment. Not only they, but everyone else to whom we owe money. It seems that all Vienna has heard of it.'

Hermann had been standing by his desk, his fingers resting on its polished top. He felt that his knees had suddenly lost their strength, that they could not support him. He drew a deep breath and sat down.

'If the money is paid, are they willing not to call in the service of the law? In other words, if someone will pay for you, will they promise not to have you punished for—swindling?'

Ishmael licked his lips. 'Yes, they promise that. I asked them.'

Hermann pushed his head forward, his eyes suddenly blood-shot, his lips drawn back over his white teeth. At that moment he looked fiendish, a creature possessed by terrible hate. Ishmael shrank back.

'And they, knowing that you had a Jew for a brother-in-law,' Hermann said, 'knew that the money would be paid, and promised to let you go!' He sprang to his feet and caught Ishmael by the shoulders, shaking him furiously. 'How much is it in all? Tell me, you dog! If I did right I should allow you to go to prison, I should allow your wife and children to be outcasts, allow your fat, dirty partner to beg in the gutter before I would give one gulden to save you. I can't! I can't, and you know it! Each time I help you I am tying a millstone more securely round my neck! Because of your sister, my wife, I dare not denounce you. How much is it in all? Quick, before I kill you!'

'Nine thousand eight hundred gulden—in all.'

The cold fury who stood before him twisted its lips in a sneer.

'You lie! No swindler ever told the right amount of his obligations. I want the truth, the full amount ; and add to it suffi-cient to carry you, your family, and your disgusting partner away from Vienna. I shall come with you and pay these debts myself, so that everyone shall know that I—Hermann Gollantz—have not been a party in any way to your swindles. Now, tell me—and honestly if you can—what will cover them all. All!'

'Twelve thousand gulden.'

'And take you all away from Vienna?'

'Scarcely—add another two thousand gulden perhaps.'

Hermann nodded. His anger had passed, leaving him cold and numb.

'Fourteen thousand gulden. A fortune! The last time was nothing compared with this. How you have caught me, Ishmael bar Adolfus! Because you know what your sister means to me, because you know that I could not bear to lower her pride, because you know that, having married her, I regard her family as my own, and assume—rightly or wrongly—responsibilities, you watch and wait, and at last rub your hands, saying: "No matter how deep we sink, Hermann, the poor fool, will drag us out!" The poorest *schnorrer* is richer than you, because he has at least kept his decency, his honesty. Now go—and tell your creditors that tomorrow they will be paid by me.'

That night Hermann sat late with Marcus Breal and Simon Cohen. Together they planned how the fourteen thousand gulden might be raised. Breal advanced seven thousand, and Hermann—with something almost like despair in his heart—decided that he could raise the other seven. True, the effort would cripple him for years, it would leave him with scarcely a gulden to call his own. His business would suffer, but he would be rid of Ishmael.

'It is well worth it,' he said 'Vienna will be a sweeter place without him.'

'It's a grave mistake,' Marcus Breal objected. 'He will come back and call on you again. The law might safeguard you, and give him a little of the punishment he deserves. For the last time, Hermann, I beg you to consider this.'

Hermann, white-faced and heavy-eyed, shook his head. 'It is quite impossible. To have him branded as a swindler, to saddle my sons with the knowledge that their mother's brother was a criminal, to break my wife's heart and lower her pride—no, no, Marcus, it is impossible.'

The following day, with Simon at his side, Hermann sat in the dirty office of Hirsch and Sousa, paying out money and receiving receipts from angry and cheated traders. To everyone he made the same set speech:

'Please believe that this was unknown to me—this man is the

127

brother of my wife, and neither she nor I tolerate injustice nor trickery. Please sign this paper—and assure me that all the obligations have been discharged in full.'

Rachel never knew anything of the affair, but Miriam Gollantz heard of it. She had many friends among the elderly Jews of the city, and they came very often to take coffee with her and bring her the news of the day. It may have been that she heard of Hermann's action from Samuel Mocatta, the tall, dignified financier ; or from Sebag Rosengard, the Professor of Ancient History in the university. Again, it is possible that the stout little merchant in precious stones and fine amber, Woolf Berditzev, told her. Perhaps Maurice Strauss—a distant cousin of the musician, and himself a brilliant performer on the piano—imparted it to her when he sat letting his lovely melodies slip away under his fingers at her piano. She never told Hermann from what source she had obtained her information, she merely asked him if it were true.

Hermann, feeling suddenly like a small boy again, said: 'Yes, Mama.'

Miriam wagged her head. 'Fourteen thousand gulden!' Then, drawing a deep breath, she demanded: 'Hermann, with two sons —how dared you?'

'Mama!' He was startled. 'You think that there was any other course open to me?'

'I think that there was only one course open to you,' she returned. 'You married Rachel, not that *gonoph* and his objectionable wife and dirty-nosed children! It is over, and you will have to bear the brunt of it, for I warn you now, my son, at my age I do not intend to cut down my expenses and my comforts! But let this creature—this worm, this thing that calls itself a man, ever return here, and I—Miriam Gollantz—will denounce him before his own sister for what he is!'

'I should be very sorry if you did that, Mama.'

She turned away, opened a box of *marrons glacé*, and said, as if she were merely making a comment upon the state of the weather: 'I have taken an oath to do so ; nothing shall make me break it. These *marrons* are excellent, Hermann—pray take some to Rachel.'

For two years nothing was heard of Ishmael, and then he wrote to Hermann stating that he and his family were in Warsaw, and demanding money. Times had been hard, and they were on the point of starvation. Hermann worried, pondered, and finally sent the money for which Ishmael asked. It was impossible to allow a woman and her children to be either cold or hungry. From that time letters came at regular intervals, always asking for money and, partly because he could not bear to think of children—even unpleasant children—living in want, and partly because he wished to keep his brother-in-law out of Vienna, Hermann always complied with the requests.

Only Simon Cohen knew of his generosity. 'I have so much,' Hermann would say, after a further gift of money had been despatched. 'I have two beautiful sons, my mother has been spared to me, my wife grows dearer to me every day, and—after all, Simon, we don't do so badly in the business, do we?'

'Not badly, dear Herr Gollantz, in fact very well—but, forgive me, now is the time when your capital should be growing. Instead, though your takings increase, your expenses always increase with them. Your capital—well, only you and I and Herr Breal know how small it is.'

Hermann laid his hand on the younger man's shoulder; his lips were touched with a very pleasant smile. 'And only you and I and Marcus Breal need ever know how small it is, Simon, eh? Don't worry—one day we shall discover a Rembrandt in a back attic, buy it for ten gulden and sell it at a fabulous price to the nation.'

Simon still looked grave. 'I should like so much to see you with a great many good investments, Herr Gollantz——'

'But I have them! You were an investment, and what a good one! My sons are investments—don't they pay magnificently? Everything round me is an investment. Do you know, Simon, in my really sane moments I realize what a very wealthy fellow I am!'

The winter of 1859 was very severe, and both Hermann and Rachel tried to persuade Miriam to remain in the house and guard against colds and chills. She replied indignantly that she had never taken a cold in her life and was not likely to do so at considerably over seventy. Her two grandsons were growing up; Marcus was seventeen and Emmanuel two years younger. They were devoted to their grandmother, finding her amusing and stimulating. She, for her part, delighted to take them about with her. Marcus had a love and understanding of music which was a great bond between them, while even at fifteen Emmanuel's striking looks made him an object of interest wherever he went.

Nothing delighted Miriam more than to visit the opera or the play with her grandsons in attendance. She spared no expense to make herself look handsome, and lavished new clothes upon them to such an extent that Hermann objected she would turn them both into dandies.

One evening in November Miriam planned a *festa*. Emmanuel, when he wished to tease her, always said that *festa* was the one Italian word she remembered. 'And a very good word too!' she returned. 'I have made my life a perpetual line of *festas*—and don't I look well on it?'

Marcus, playing one of the new waltzes which delighted her, turned from the piano. 'The best-looking woman in Vienna!' he said.

'Tonight,' she announced, having leant forward in her chair to tap him on the shoulder with the fan which she always carried, 'the best-looking woman in Vienna goes to the play with her grandsons—Grillparzer's comedy. That should be interesting, for until now he has plunged us all in gloom—magnificent, splendid, but so deep!'

'Yes, I know!' Emmanuel exclaimed excitedly. '*Weh' dem, der lügt* . . . Grandmama, how wonderful. They say that the play turns on the hero always speaking the truth, gaining everything by doing so. . . .' He laughed suddenly. 'Mark my words, it won't be a success! The idea will be too fantastic for Vienna to credit its possibility.'

'We shall dine here,' Miriam continued, oblivious of his fifteen-year-old cynicism. 'I have had special dishes sent in from Dehmels. It shall be a real *festa*. Marcus, you are not to mock me!'

They dined—the old woman and the two boys—at a quarter to six, on a menu consisting of carp stewed in cream with onions and pepper, fried chicken and lettuce, followed by almost impossibly thin pancakes, and wonderful ices and creams. They drank the pinkish champagne which Miriam loved because it was very sweet, and took her back, so she said, to the wines of Italy which she had drunk as a girl. All the way to the Burgtheater she laughed and talked, and only during the second act did Emmanuel notice that she drew herself up stiffly and pressed her hand to her side.

'You're not in pain, Grandmama?' he asked.

She turned and looked at him in silence for a moment, then smiled and said: 'It is nothing. That carp was too heavy.'

When the curtain fell, Emmanuel asked if she felt better. Marcus, leaning forward, noticed a change in her face which filled him with alarm. He sprang to his feet. 'I will get some brandy—stay here, Emmanuel.'

Miriam laid her hand on his arm. 'Help me out—this box is stuffy. I can't breathe.' Emmanuel gave her his arm, and she walked steadily into the foyer, where he brought her a chair.

'You're better?' He bent his handsome head, his eyes full of anxiety.

'Better? Of course! We'll sup at Sacher's—the new place. You're right, Emmanuel, this play won't run—it's too—fantastic for them.'

She held out her hand and took his, then gave a little cough and slipped back in her chair, dead.

6

I

MIRIAM'S death affected them all. Rachel had feared her a little, but at the same time loved and respected her. To her grandsons she had been a delightful companion and friend, able to understand their interests, to share their pleasures, and always ready to listen to their plans and hopes. To Hermann the loss was terrible. All his life he had turned to her for advice, affection, and consolation, and every year had taught him more clearly what a great heart and clear head she had possessed.

'I have always been so proud of her,' he said brokenly to Emmanuel. 'She was my ideal woman, I think—proud, loyal, and generous. Only through her did I know and understand my father —your grandfather—who died before I was born. She taught me what manner of man he must have been. A great judge of art— chosen by the Emperor Napoleon to go on the Italian campaign, hard-working, and the best husband in the world. I once said to her that he must have been almost worthy of her—being all those things. "No," she said. "Never say that he was worthy of me; only hope that I was almost worthy of him."'

Hermann sighed. 'It is a great thing for a man to have had both parents so wonderful in every way.'

'A piece of good fortune, Papa,' Emmanuel said, 'that Marcus and I share with you.'

He had begged to leave school at Christmas, and declared that nothing interested him so much as his father's business. For years he had studied woods, materials, china marks, paste, and colour. Quietly and unobtrusively he had entered the show-rooms and wandered about, asking questions of either his father or Simon Cohen. He was passionate about old things, possessed a great faculty for correct judgment, and had a love of beauty which was demonstrated twenty times a day. He was not content to remain in the show-rooms, but spent a great deal of time with the workmen, trying to understand the practical side of interior and exterior decoration.

Hermann, broken by the death of his mother, welcomed Emmanuel's young presence and watched his progress with real pleasure.

Marcus, at eighteen, it was evident, had a brilliant career before him. Strauss was interested in him, and declared that the waltzes which Marcus composed were as good as his own. Life in Vienna was a long series of waltzes ; they were played everywhere, danced everywhere. The composer who could find melodies which appealed to the public taste was certain of success. So young Marcus Gollantz, good-looking, well-spoken, and with his head filled with tunes which he felt he must write, and write quickly, was forging his way to the front rank of composers of dance music. He had his own small and very admirable orchestra which, though it was less noted than that of Johannes Strauss, held a position of distinction in the city.

'I once dreamt that I might be a Thalberg or a Vieuxtems, then that I might be a Mozart or a Handel. Now I shall be content if I can be a follower, at not too great a distance, of Johannes Strauss.'

'You write the waltzes,' Emmanuel replied, 'and I will dance them and make every woman in Vienna want to dance them too.' He added, 'I dance very well. The other night I was at a dance— just a small affair at the Hauptmanns—and there was some dreadful old baroness there. They were very proud to have her! How funny people are—to want a fat, stupid old woman because she was a baroness! She danced with me—it was terrible. Then she asked me if I would be her gigolo, and dance with no one else.'

Marcus grinned. 'And you said?'

'I said that it would make me very happy, though the life would

132

be terribly dangerous because all the other young men would be so furiously jealous of me. She laughed and said: "I would make it worth your while. I would pay you seven gulden a night." For a moment I felt quite sick.'

'I believe many of them do that,' Marcus said. 'I see them at dances where we are playing. I heard the other day that a cook demanded higher wages because she had to pay her—dancing man so much!'

'It's a mad world,' Emmanuel said. 'They're queer, these Austrians. They seem to live only for dancing and fêtes, and eating and drinking. And they think—or say they think—that we live only to make money.'

Emmanuel did everything well. He rode, he danced, he even sang a little, and he was the best skater in Vienna. There was nothing he loved more than to feel himself skimming over the ice like a bird, then with a sudden twist to swirl round and execute some elaborate figure.

'It is the nearest sensation, I am certain,' he said, 'to flying.'

'And as you'll never be able to fly,' Marcus said, 'you don't know how like or unlike it is.'

Early in February the whole city was skating. They danced on skates, and Marcus, with his little orchestra in fur-trimmed coats, himself wearing a round astrakhan cap and a collar of the same skin to his coat, conducted on the edge of the various lakes which were as popular at the moment as ball-rooms.

'It's thawing,' he said to Emmanuel, as they walked home together. 'By tomorrow the skating season will be over for another year.'

'I don't think so. I don't want to think so. I hoped that you and I might go off tomorrow early and have a great time together.'

The morning dawned bright and clear; Emmanuel was delighted. They must hurry off; he knew of a place just outside the town where the ice was good.

Marcus was like a schoolboy on holiday, calling for a dozen things at once. 'My cap—my short fur coat—my skates! Mama, are the sandwiches ready? And what is this? A flask of cherry brandy! Oh, splendid! Come on, Emmanuel! Good-bye, Mama, we won't be too late coming back.'

Rachel watched them go from the window, smiling, thinking what fine boys they were and how little trouble they had ever given anyone. They looked a picture, swinging down the wide road, their shining skates in their hands.

'This is good!' Marcus said, with real satisfaction, as hand-in-hand they sped over the ice together. 'It's nice to be alone sometimes.'

'You don't mean alone,' Emmanuel said; 'you mean together.'

'It's like being alone—you and I are so much at one with each other.'

'You see, apart from affection, we like each other so much.' He laughed. 'I expect that we should hate each other's wives, don't you?'

Marcus glanced at him. 'I should never think that any woman was good enough for you.'

'And I should know that no woman could be good enough for you. Let's make a compact to stay as we are now—the Gollantz brothers—shall we?'

'I wonder who would want to break it first?'

They scrambled to the bank and sat on a fallen tree to rest. People could be seen coming through the bare woods to the little lake. Emmanuel watched them, half vexed. 'They'll come and swarm all over the place, and spoil it all.'

'Let's make the most of it then!' Marcus got to his feet and called over his shoulder, 'Come on, catch me! You can't!'

Emmanuel, with long swinging strokes, skated in his wake. Marcus was making for the farther shore, when Emmanuel heard a noise like rapid pistol shots. He felt his heart miss a beat, then shouted: 'Marcus! Back—back! The ice is giving! Look!'

He checked his flying forward, and saw to his horror that the ice was cracking badly and that the dark water was showing through. Marcus did not stop sufficiently quickly, he skated less well than his brother. In a second he was on the treacherous ice, his hands were flung over his head, and he disappeared into the blackness below. Emmanuel stayed for a moment to shout to the people coming through the woods, ordering them to bring logs, rails—anything; then, tearing off his jacket and fumbling with his skates, he flung himself down and began to wriggle his way along the ice.

A quarter of an hour later two men struggled with a slim boy, who fought and cursed like a madman because they would not allow him to try again to dive under the ice to find his brother. His hands were cut and bleeding, his clothes hung on him, dripping with icy water, and there was a cut on his forehead which bled profusely.

'He's there, I tell you!' he shouted. 'I can hear him calling, he's

134

calling to me. Murderers, let me go! Marcus, Marcus, I'm coming!' Twice he wrenched himself free, and they only dragged him back at great danger to themselves. It was quite hopeless—the body of Marcus Gollantz had been swept by the spring which had melted the ice, far out of reach, and now lay under the thicker ice quite beyond chance of recovery. Half delirious with grief, Emmanuel was led away and taken home.

The body was found two days later, and brought back to the house of Gollantz, where Rachel wept for her children and would not be comforted. Marcus, her first-born, was dead, and Emmanuel lay tossing on his bed, sobbing and screaming that Marcus still called to him, and that whoever tried to hold him back was worse than a murderer.

Hermann, silent and white-faced, went about like a man in a dream, while Simon Cohen, watching him, wondered a little why Fate allowed these things to happen and what Hermann Gollantz had ever done to merit such treatment.

II

Marcus had been buried a fortnight when Emmanuel woke one morning with his senses clear. The pain of reality was almost too much for him. Previously he had known nothing, his cries and screams had been unconscious; now he was sane again, and he had to face the fact that Marcus was gone for ever. For hours at a time he lay in his bed, thinking, wondering, trying to understand what life would be without the brother he had loved so dearly. Marcus was dead, dead when life was just beginning for him, when people were beginning to talk about him as a promising young musician, when he was beginning to make real headway, and had been enjoying life in his own simple and decent fashion.

One moment they had been laughing and talking, making a pact that neither of them would ever marry but remain close companions always—the next . . . Emmanuel shivered and pressed his hands over his mouth to keep back a scream of terror, as once again he seemed to see the ice crack, divide, and his brother disappear beneath its surface.

He had scarcely realized until now what a shock his grandmother's death had been to him. Now he went over those last few moments of her life again and again, finding new horrors in the fact that she had had no warning of death's approach, but like Marcus had been struck down almost instantly.

He saw Death as something sinister, evil, revengeful, something which waited until people were happy, rejoicing in their content, or their wealth, their health, or their youth, and then, when they had reached the pinnacle of happiness, struck quickly and ruthlessly.

He wondered if they saw Death coming nearer. Had his grandmother, as she sank back in her chair, seen the dread figure coming towards her? Had she shrunk back, watching the weapon come closer, knowing that the instant had come when the blow would fall? Had Marcus, caught in the ice, seen Death leer at him, grinning because he had caught a young victim? Might it not be that those last few seconds, packed tightly with horror and the knowledge that escape was impossible, wiped out a lifetime of content?

Eternity—what, where was eternity? Had Marcus carried with him nothing but the terror of those last few seconds? Were they perhaps so strong, so vivid, that he had forgotten everything else which had made his life pleasant? Did he remember the applause when he had played his waltz, *Der Erde Paradies*? Did he remember the rough draft which he had shown to Strauss of his newest waltz? Did he remember how Strauss had hummed it over and smiled, saying: 'I shall have to look to my laurels, young Marcus'?

Most of all, did he remember his brother, and how dearly that brother had loved him? Did he understand how Emmanuel had fought to try to save him, how he had torn at the ice with his hands, and plunged into the water again and again, shouting: 'Marcus, I'm coming to you! Hold on'? Did he, if he thought at all—if he could still think—fancy that Emmanuel had not tried sufficiently hard? Was it possible that thoughts of him were tinged with reproach? 'If you had tried just a little harder I might have been still with you.'

Days passed. He was stronger, he was able to get up and walk about again. His mother looked old, his father seemed to have left his youth behind him. Emmanuel wondered if they hated him because he lived while Marcus, the first-born, was dead? He sometimes fancied that they glanced at him coldly.

He said to his mother: 'I did try to save him!' speaking abruptly, almost brutally.

Her eyes filled with tears, and she held out her hands to him.

136

'My dear—I know—I know—everyone told us. You were so brave.'

He turned away, feeling that perhaps she was only trying to be kind, and that in her heart she regretted that he lived instead of Marcus. His father spoke very little. He stooped more than he had done, he scarcely ever smiled. His eyes looked like the eyes of a faithful dog, hurt beyond bearing. Simon Cohen watched him, wretched, dumb with misery.

The whole house had been robbed of its joy with the going of Marcus. The piano stood silent, very few people came to see them. Rachel still ordered wonderful food—it had become a habit—but she scarcely ate, and Hermann sat and stared at his plate as if food was something he could not understand.

'Eat, Hermann,' Rachel begged.

He would start, pick up his knife and fork and say hastily: 'Yes, yes, of course.' He would eat a few mouthfuls, and then forget and sit silent, staring at his plate again, while the good food grew cold.

Emmanuel dreaded these meals. He would try to talk, then relapse into silence, and when that silence oppressed him so that he felt he might either burst into tears or scream, he would push back his chair and walk from the room.

One evening he walked into the show-room and found his father there alone. The lamps had not been lit and Hermann was seated at his desk, his head bowed in his hands. Emmanuel, tall and slim in his mourning, came closer. He stood silent, watching the pathetic figure ; then something stirred in him.

'Father,' he said, 'I'm your son as well as he was.'

Hermann lifted his head and looked at his son. His face wore that look of inexpressible tenderness which Simon Cohen had once seen upon it. He stretched out his hand and laid it on Emmanuel's.

'My son . . .' he said. 'Do you think that I don't thank God for you?'

'I don't know—I thought . . .'

Hermann rose and laid his hands on Emmanuel's shoulders. He felt the bones under the fine cloth, and realized how thin the boy had grown.

'I am afraid I have been selfish,' he said, 'but I have never forgotten that we are blessed in still having one son, and a son who shows himself so full of courage and self-sacrifice. Because I have mourned, I never forgot you, Emmanuel. I can only ask you to

137

help. The time of mourning ends, as the winter ends when the spring begins. You must help to remind us that spring is here again, because in remembering that there is a future, we shall not forget him who belongs to the past.'

But the old wound still smarted. Emmanuel said, his voice harsh with emotion which he tried hard to suppress: 'I loved him better than anyone in the world!'

His father nodded. 'It may be—though I think we all imagine that. When my dear mother died—on her be peace—I felt that my loss was the greatest because I had known and loved her for so long. It may be that I only knew one aspect of her—that to you, to your mother, she was as much as she was to me. Let us try from now to live without outward signs of mourning. I am glad that you spoke to me. You are my dearly loved son—always remember that. A good father—and I have tried to be a good father —does not love one son more than another. They are all his sons, and so are infinitely precious to him.

'I have never been *froom*, I have never been orthodox, and I do not intend to alter my scheme of life. I do not wish you to observe all the conventional rules of mourning. How can one say: for a wife, so many days; for a brother, so many? Mourning is in the heart, not in the clothes, or the voice, or the unshaven chin. So when your friends come and ask you to go here and there—go, and know that your mother and I shall be glad. You hear that? Glad! You are young, you have a right to happiness; exercise your right, and know always that we love you more than any poor words can tell you.'

'Happiness!' Emmanuel said harshly. 'I begin to think that happiness is dangerous. My grandmother was happy—death came; Marcus was happy—no one will ever know how happy he was that morning.'

'It's all too near to us,' Hermann said gently. 'When you stand too near to a picture, you cannot see it. You must stand back, move away from it, then it is clear; you see beautiful colours, form, lovely brush-work. One day you will stand back from this tragedy, and see that even death cannot kill the beauty of a life. That is something you have had—the beauty of your love for him and his for you. That is the best of non-material things, spiritual things—once you have had them, no one, nothing can take them from you.'

Emmanuel listened, he even appeared to acknowledge the truth of what his father said, but in his heart there remained a

138

profound distrust of life. He saw it as a thing which might be cut short to gratify the whim of some power who held the threads.

For a year he scarcely left the business. He spent his time either in the show-room, in the work-rooms, or down at the yard. When there was nothing more to be done there, he went off to some gallery or museum where he worked for hours, making notes, sketches, and using the pictures and cases of exhibits as text-books. In six months he had amassed a tremendous amount of knowledge, and often Hermann and Simon consulted him on some difficult point ; they were astonished at the depths of his understanding, at his keen perception, and his perfect taste.

'He was born with taste,' Hermann said ; 'to that he has added sound knowledge and understanding. Nothing is too great for him to grasp, nothing is too small for him to give it his undivided attention. My father was an acknowledged expert. I have not been quite unsuccessful, but Emmanuel will be a master where we were pupils.'

Emmanuel, tall, and growing every day more beautiful, saw everything, noticed everything, remembered everything. He realized that however well his father might appear to do in business, there was obviously a lack of capital in the firm. When he came home and reported that he had heard of some masterpiece which was for sale and begged his father to buy it, he noticed the sudden look of embarrassment on his face. He would temporize. 'We will go to the sale and see what it runs to. It may be that we can buy it—but perhaps it may be too expensive for us. We shall see. Be patient, Emmanuel.'

Emmanuel hated to exercise patience. He liked to act quickly, and he believed that in rapid and definite action success was to be found. He went through the stock and discovered many pieces which were out of date, pictures which had outlasted their popu-larity, furniture which had ceased to make an appeal, *objets d'art* which no longer caused clients to exclaim: 'How charming.'

'They take up room,' he grumbled to Cohen. 'They have to be dusted and polished, repaired and cleaned—they do nothing for their keep.'

'Yet they are stock,' Cohen objected. 'All stock has a certain value.'

'Not here,' Emmanuel persisted. 'Here in Vienna we are too up-to-date. We must keep our finger on the pulse of the times. No one wants the furniture of 1830 and 1851. It is too old and too new. Give me time and I will think of a plan.'

139

Some days later he met at a café a young playwright called Gustave. He was laughing and talking at the top of his voice; it was evident that he was very excited and happy. Emmanuel watched him from where he sat, and gathered that he had sold his play that morning. Emmanuel rose and walked over to where the little fair-haired man, with his round rosy face, sat drinking ice-cold beer and laughing immoderately.

'Herr Gustave, will you forgive this intrusion?' Emmanuel said, his hand outstretched. 'I have heard of your good fortune. I felt that I must offer my congratulations.'

Gustave was delighted. Emmanuel Gollantz was a remarkable figure. Women looked at him and sighed if they were elderly because they had left their youth behind; young women sighed because they were young and he never seemed to notice them; and men sighed because they realized that in a few years this good-looking young Jew would be a serious rival. Gustave begged Emmanuel to join him, offered him beer, and began to talk about his play. Emmanuel, in five minutes, had discovered that it was to be produced by an elderly man named Calish, but that Gustave had insisted on retaining the right to have a voice in the setting, casting, and even at rehearsals.

'How right you were,' Emmanuel said softly. 'Calish is admirable, but he is—just a little out of date. I imagine that your play is essentially modern, Herr Gustave?'

Gustave's merry little eyes twinkled. 'The title would infer that it is profound,' he said. 'It is—profoundly modern. The title is: "*Die Hochste Weisheit*", but, believe me, that Highest Wisdom proves to be something very far from the recognized form.'

'In short,' said Lipmann, who prefaced everything with those two words, 'it is a farce.'

Gustave looked suddenly indignant. 'Please, Lipmann! It is a comedy.'

'A comedy—a farce—not much difference.'

'Indeed, a great deal,' Emmanuel said. 'Tragedy is something more than life; farce is something which pretends to be life with a *motif* of laughter at itself; comedy is something less than life set to a waltz tune.'

Gustave was interested. He looked at the young Jew and wondered why, with that figure and profile, he was not an actor. His voice was good too, easy and full without being noisy; his speech was cultured and distinct. Slowly Lipmann, Crackav, and the rest drifted away and Gustave was left with Emmanuel.

They discussed the play. Emmanuel was interested and enthusiastic. The date of its setting was 1830 and 1831, with a last act—very modern and up to date—set in the present year.

Emmanuel clasped his hands. 'Oh, what a pity that the *décor* is always so bad, so unimaginative. Always the same tables, the same chairs, the same dreadful hangings. Because the Burg is a state theatre—because an Emperor once shrugged his shoulders and said: "They will come", nothing is ever done to make them come!'

Gustave leant back in his chair and watched Emmanuel, his dancing blue eyes half closed. 'Then do the *décor* yourself,' he said. 'Why not? You know what furniture is correct, you have taste—everyone tells me so. Tomorrow we will go to see Calish, and I will raise my voice and declare that Emmanuel Gollantz, and no one else, shall provide and arrange the furniture for my scenes. It is done!'

And done it was! The play, with its attention to detail, was the talk of Vienna. People watched the scenes, commented on the furniture, decided that the tables and chairs of 1830 had charm and a certain distinction. It would not be possible to have a house furnished entirely in that style, but one room—perhaps, as a sort of freak room. How amusing! Everything correct, even to the wall coverings, pictures and ornaments! The last act, a scene in a bedroom—and dreadfully modern and very *risqué*—was gorgeous, but the first two scenes had a charm entirely their own.

Ladies of fashion flocked to Hermann Gollantz. Emmanuel worked out schemes, and the smart thing in Vienna that summer was to have an 1830 room like the first or second act of *The Highest Wisdom*.

The old stock was cleared; it melted away like snow in the sun. Emmanuel was forced to hunt round the town for ornaments of the date, for odd chairs and old carpets.

'But, Herr Gollantz,' one lady objected, 'the Baroness von Bihar had two china castles on her mantelpiece—you have given me spotted dogs.'

Emmanuel bowed his head so that his mouth almost touched the small ear of the lady. 'Madame, you have found me out. I was experimenting with your room. The date of the room which I did for the baroness is 1830; yours is a slightly earlier and more interesting period—it is 1829.'

Gustave's play was a success. His second, written a year later, was considered too modern for the Burgtheater, and was produced at a theatre which was not state controlled. Once again Emmanuel designed, planned, and produced two scenes in the style of the first Empire—and once again women of fashion sent for him to redecorate and furnish their boudoirs.

'It would seem that the work of Gollantz becomes fashionable,' Calish said to Gustave.

Gustave laughed—he was always laughing these days, with his pockets full of gulden and managers clamouring for his plays —he couldn't write them fast enough. 'His work may be fashionable today,' he said, 'but tomorrow it will be Gollantz and not his work! He is very young, but women are crazy about him.'

Emmanuel, going through the books, was satisfied. Here was capital and, what was almost as good, all the old stock cleared, and cleared at a good price. Now he could buy the pictures he wanted, pictures which he felt were speculations, which in twenty years' time would be worth their weight in gold. There was a young man called Millet, a painter whose flesh tints were superb, with a queer name—Ingres. He had found in an obscure art dealer's a small picture of a woman seated on a brocade-covered sofa, her dress of a strange, illusive blue, her skin deliciously pink-and-white. It was signed carelessly in one corner with a name beginning with a B— ; he knew that it was good.

There were two others he had seen, and seeing had hated, but he felt certain that they would sell. 'Sentimental realism', he called them—a massacre, with every detail marvellously done ; an overladen boat, with Don Juan aboard. Stupid, over-done stuff, but stuff which would sell and sell quickly. Emmanuel felt that Byron would have liked the boat and the dying Don Juan.

He showed the result of his work to Hermann. 'Look, Father. The old stock cleared, and we have made—this is clear profit— twenty thousand gulden.'

Hermann, older and stooping more, his eyes still as kind as ever, nodded. 'Magnificent, Emmanuel. You're a clever fellow.'

'But I want some of it!' Emmanuel cried, his lips smiling. 'I am the daughter of the horse-leech, crying, "Give, give!" I want ten thousand gulden, please, Papa.'

He saw his father's face change, watched the light fade from his eyes and the smile disappear from his lips. 'I'm sorry, very sorry, Emmanuel. It won't be possible to let you have so much— I owe the bank'—he stammered and looked terribly old, shaken and pathetic—'a great deal of money.'

'But we need to invest, Papa,' Emmanuel persisted. 'There are new artists coming on; I can buy their work cheaply, and sell again in a few years at a huge profit. I'm prepared to back my opinion. There is no chance of losing.'

Hermann shook his head. When he spoke his voice sounded dull and lifeless. 'I am very sorry, Emmanuel. I owe the bank ten thousand gulden. I will let you have three thousand to spend on pictures. I—I can't do more.'

'Very well. I will do the best I can.'

Hermann watched him turn and walk to the farther end of the long room. The boy was disappointed. It was hard on him, such a good boy, working so hard, seeking new channels for their activities, and succeeding. Hermann sighed heavily. If only Ishmael wasn't continually demanding money, always in some trouble and needing money to extricate him. A couple of months ago had come an appeal. His wife was ill, the little boy had developed a weak chest, the little girl promised to play wonderfully if they could find the money for lessons. That last fact had touched Hermann, reminded him of his dead son, recalled the brilliance of Marcus, made his heart ache.

Now, two days ago, had come another letter. The story of some woman who, Ishmael said, had 'led him on' and finally proved to be an adventuress with a blackmailing husband. The husband demanded eight thousand gulden as a salve for his honour. Hermann's face had flushed as he read the letter. Honour! What did these people know of honour! The word on their lips was a mockery.

He had sent the money, because he was afraid that otherwise Ishmael might return to Vienna. He had written to Rachel saying how he longed to be back in his 'beloved Wien'. Had that been a hint that he might come back? Marcus Breal had shaken his head, and protested that it was sheer folly. Hermann had repeated his old formula: 'I cannot do anything else. I must meet my responsibilities—he is my wife's brother.'

He sighed. 'I grow old,' he said to Simon Cohen. 'My courage has died. I feel useless, worn out.' Then, with that smile which never failed to touch Cohen's heart, he added: 'Thank God we have Emmanuel.'

BOOK THREE

1

EMMANUEL was the real head of the firm of Gollantz. He knew it, Cohen knew it, Hermann knew it, but none of them ever put the fact into words. Hermann, at fifty-eight, looked ten years older. His hair was white, his shoulders stooped, and his thin hands had lost their grip on matters of business. Everyone turned to Emmanuel, and it was only by the exercise of exquisite tact that he contrived to make his father believe that the world of Vienna still believed him to be the head of the firm.

The firm prospered—on paper. That was the puzzle which Emmanuel never solved. He worked from morning until night, he planned and arranged, managed and ordered; he invested in what new stock he could, and always found that he could sell again at a profit. And yet—and when he thought of it he would draw his fine brows together in a frown of perplexity—when he came to ask for money it was never forthcoming.

His father still attended to the financial side of the business. It seemed sometimes to Emmanuel that he guarded that last bit of authority jealously. He allowed no one to inspect the firm's private ledgers, he paid the bills himself, and paid over the salaries of both Cohen and Emmanuel. When a good sale had been effected it was evident that he was pleased, and yet whenever Emmanuel asked for money for the business he always received less than he demanded. It was always the same.

'Father, may I have five thousand gulden? There is some furniture to be sold at the house of Baron Marchand; it is exactly what the princess told me she needed for her new salon.'

Hermann would stare miserably at his son, shake his head and say: 'I am sorry, Emmanuel. I can only let you have three thousand. I am very sorry indeed.'

So it continued. Emmanuel, too devoted, too proud to ask for reasons; Hermann only reiterating that he was sorry, looking wretched, stooping a little more as the days passed. Sometimes Emmanuel wondered, debated whether his father gambled, speculated—and always lost, Or—and he blushed as he pushed the thought from him—was there a woman somewhere, an early indiscretion, perhaps children who must be provided for? No, it wasn't possible. Nothing seemed in the least probable, and finally Emmanuel shrugged his shoulders and decided firmly that it was, after all, his father's business and he must run it in his own way. His father paid him a salary which was generous and declared that he was worth every penny of it; that was all he needed to remember.

Then, in the July of 1863, when Vienna lay basking in the sunshine which continued day after day, his mother announced with joy that they were to have a visitor. She laughed and smiled, saying that it would be fine for Emmanuel to have a real friend— almost a brother. Rachel Gollantz was a simple soul and accepted everything at its face value. To her it was delightful that Ishmael should have sent his sixteen-year-old son to stay with them. It seemed to her that Jean and Emmanuel might become dear friends, and, after all, the same blood ran in their veins; and blood, as everyone knew, was thicker than water.

Emmanuel, suddenly, unbelievably tall and erect, met her eyes coldly.

Rachel's smile died. 'My darling boy, what is it?'

'Mama!' His voice was passionate in its intensity. 'How can you say that—almost a brother! I had one brother; I lost him. No one ever could, ever should, replace him.'

His father said to him later, speaking half nervously: 'I hope that you will get on well with your cousin. You don't remember him. He came here when you were quite a little boy.'

'I remember him,' Emmanuel said grimly. 'He looked at my books and left crumbs and currants, the marks of sticky fingers, and daubs of cream in them. I disliked him very much.'

Jean Hirsch came. He was tall for his age, and sophisticated. His hair was black and very curly, his skin was dark, and his eyes heavily lidded. He spoke with a lisp, and dressed like a man of twenty. Emmanuel disliked him on sight.

'He is what Christians call a typical Jew—when they want to insult us,' he said to Simon Cohen. 'He reeks of the ghetto. His finger-nails are very long and unbelievably filthy.'

Rachel loved him dearly. She said that he reminded her of her brother Ishmael, and did not notice how Hermann's lips twisted as he heard her. She looked over his clothes, wrung her hands and protested that it was dreadful that he had only three sets of underclothes, and those patched and darned. Jean was attentive to her, always lavishing caresses and kisses on her, always asking if he might go shopping with her, if he might carry her parcels, and learning very quickly that if he admired anything in the shop windows sufficiently he was certain to get it before long.

He spoke French, as did Emmanuel; he also spoke Polish and possessed a smattering of English. Emmanuel knew neither, and it was a source of irritation that his cousin continually greeted him with English phrases to which he could not reply.

' 'Ow do you do, plez, goot night?' Jean would say at the breakfast-table when Emmanuel entered. He was never early for breakfast, because his splendid, sombre cravats took such a long time to tie correctly.

'You have the advantage of me,' Emmanuel would say, trying to keep his temper.

Jean would grin, showing teeth which were already slightly discoloured.

'I wished you a very good morning, and said that it was a pleasant day.'

'Indeed! Thank you, Mama, I will have coffee, not chocolate.'

Indirectly, it was owing to Jean Hirsch that Emmanuel Gollantz learned to speak English. Emmanuel possessed all the pride which had existed in Fernando Meldola, all the arrogance which had existed in his grandmother, and the conviction which had, and still permeated the whole being of his father—that to be a Jew was a source of pride, a fine thing, a thing on which to congratulate oneself. It irked Emmanuel that this whipper-snapper should speak a language—however badly—which he could not speak himself. He looked round for someone who could teach him.

Some days later he walked into a café in the Stock-im-Eisen; he had sauntered past the magnificent shops, his eyes always open for articles which should indicate the latest trend of modern taste. People turned to look after him, and women's eyes followed him with something more than kindness in their gaze. His height, his splendid figure shown to advantage by the tightly buttoned coat, his white starched collar which kept his handsome head very erect, the perfectly tied silk cravat of real English silk, dark and glistening as its folds caught the light, all served to make him a notable figure.

His face had already lost its boyishness. It was oval, and his skin lacked colour. It was not the unhealthy pallor of illness, but the clear, pure whiteness of a magnolia, the texture thick and matt. His nose was the typical long, straight nose of the well-bred Jew; his eyes, dark, large, and intelligent, met the gaze of his fellows directly and with an evident honesty. His mouth, unspoiled by the moustache which Viennese youths considered fashionable and wore in imitation of the military, was wide, full, and turned up a little at the corners.

Swinging his gold-topped cane he entered the fashionable café and made his way to the table where Gustave sat. The little playwright smiled and nodded.

'This is delightful. I began to think that you were not coming. I was growing melancholy, thinking that things were too easy for me, that one day Vienna might treat me badly as she has treated other men of genius.'

Emmanuel looked at his round, rosy face with affection. He knew that his friend was no genius, he knew that Gustave understood it too, but it was a little affectation which amused them both, to pretend that Gustave was the world's greatest dramatist.

'I think that I shall write a play on Mozart,' Gustave said. 'I shall leave comedy for tragedy.'

Emmanuel shook his head. 'No, Gustave, no. Think of it—the life of Mozart with musical interpolations, and the curtain falling to half a dozen bars carefully selected from the *Requiem*. Mozart butchered to make a Roman holiday. No, he suffered sufficiently.'

'Perhaps you are right. I was only seeking for a subject worthy of my art. . . .' He broke off suddenly, staring at a man and woman who sat at a table some distance from them. 'God in heaven! There is Stanislaus Lukoes and his English wife. Then he is back. Forgive me, Emmanuel, I must speak to them.'

Emmanuel nodded, and his eyes followed his friend's progress down the brilliantly lighted café. He stopped at a table where sat a man and woman—the man tremendous in build, with huge shoulders and heavy, bushy whiskers. He had with him a woman dressed in the height of fashion—that style which had been created to suit the Empress of the French, and which every other woman had adopted.

Emmanuel looked and shuddered. How ugly they were, those tight bodices and puffed sleeves, those immense skirts festooned and draped, embroidered and decorated. The style hid all the real beauty of a woman's shape ; even her feet were invisible. The wearer of the dress scarcely interested him. She was no longer very young ; her face was long and narrow, her nose was not quite straight, her brown hair, though carefully dressed, was of an uninteresting shade. He turned away and sought among the occupants of the other tables for acquaintances. What a long time Gustave was, talking to that plain woman. Half unwillingly he turned back, and it was evident that Gustave had been speaking of him, for he found the woman's eyes directed towards him.

'Strange eyes,' Emmanuel thought. 'They're—what colour are they?—not brown, but golden. Rather wonderful eyes.'

Gustave was beckoning to him. Emmanuel rose and made his way to the table.

'May I present my friend, Emmanuel Gollantz, Baroness Lukoes?'

Emmanuel clicked his heels together, bowed from the waist and, taking the hand which she offered him, kissed it respectfully. What a fool he had been to think that she was plain! She was devastatingly attractive. He turned and greeted Baron Lukoes. Gustave was immediately engrossed in a conversation with the huge Pole ; the baroness turned to Emmanuel.

'We are just back from Paris—we returned yesterday with the Empress.'

'Ah, the Empress has returned?'

The baroness nodded. 'More beautiful than ever. You admire her, Herr Gollantz, of course.'

Emmanuel looked into her queer golden eyes ; he felt that he would never be able to forget them. 'I used to admire Her Majesty —I thought that she was the most beautiful woman in the world. As a little boy I used to dream of her.'

'And now of whom, of what, do you dream?'

He sighed. The sigh was a little overdone, but it was considered smart for young men to be slightly fantastic in their mannerisms. 'Now—until last night—of my work. Tonight ... Forgive me, you have finished your coffee, may I order some more for you?'

'What is your work, Herr Gollantz?'

'I am an art dealer. I work with my father.'

The baron glanced up from his conversation with Gustave. 'Oh, Gollantz the Jew. I thought for a moment you were a soldier. You don't look like a Jew.'

'On the contrary, Baron, I am a very typical Jew.'

The red-faced man threw back his head and gave a yelp of laughter.

'What, with that narrow, straight nose! All the Jews I have known had beaks like hawks—it is the nose that gives them away.'

Caroline Lukoes saw Emmanuel's pale face flush, saw the full lips tighten suddenly, then relax. It struck her that the smile was dangerously pleasant.

'How curious the preconceived ideas of what constitutes a physical type are!' Emmanuel said. 'The type you describe is the type which I should regard as the lowest of my race—the ghetto Jew. Carpet-dealers in back streets, money-lenders of the baser kind, petty tradesmen——'

The gusty voice of the Pole changed to a growl. 'Are you insinuating that these are the people I have known?'

Emmanuel's face was devoid of expression. 'I, Baron? I insinuate nothing, I was merely trying to explain to you a fact concerning my race.'

Caroline watched her husband's florid face. She knew his temper, knew how easily it changed from rowdy good-humour to flaming anger.

'I suppose we all have ideas concerning the physical aspects of other nationalities. I found that all Frenchwomen believed their English sisters to have feet as long as from here to Saint Stephan's, and teeth like old horses.' She spoke quickly.

Emmanuel said lightly: 'The French are fundamentally an ignorant race.'

'Have you known many English people, Herr Gollantz?'

'None, Baroness, until I had that honour conferred upon me this afternoon.'

He sat and listened to her conversation, convinced that never before had he encountered such poise, such dignity, and such charm. Lukoes talked well, but to Emmanuel his words were like a bludgeon striking on iron, whilst hers were like a rapier flashing backwards and forwards. He remembered now that Lukoes was said to be much liked by the Emperor, and he smiled a little at the thought. If the conversation of Stanislaus Lukoes was regarded as amusing at court, no wonder the unfortunate Empress preferred her yacht.

As they were leaving, the baron turned to him. 'You might come and look at some pictures of mine. Give me an opinion on them, will you? I bought them as a speculation in Paris. I suppose you charge a fee?'

Emmanuel replied, his voice expressionless. 'Invariably, Baron.'

'It will be paid.'

'I am certain of that.'

Caroline frowned. Why was Stanislaus such a boor? Couldn't he see that this young man was resenting his attitude, that he was making another enemy when a little tact might have made a friend? She glanced at Emmanuel, and thought: 'And a very good friend. Under all his affectation he's honest.'

'Perhaps,' she said, as he bowed over her hand, 'I might come and see your galleries. Old things, beautiful things interest me immensely.'

'At any hour of the day or night they will be open for you.'

They were gone and he was left alone with Gustave, Gustave who for almost the first time seemed to chatter terribly. He was full of the importance of Baron Stanislaus Lukoes, of his friendship with the Emperor, of his wealth, his influence, of his love of women, cards, and amusement of every kind. 'What a client for you! I am so glad that we were able to be seen with them, it was a great honour.' Gustave was childishly pleased, as pleased for Emmanuel as for himself.

Emmanuel yawned behind his lemon-coloured kid glove. 'And the Baroness?'

'The daughter of an English lord—earl, do they call them? They are belted, I believe, always. Very poor, and—oh, how plain she is! How could he bear to marry her?'

'How could she bear to marry him!' Emmanuel exclaimed.

II

Emmanuel, calm, suave, and utterly unmoved by the grandeur of Baron Stanislaus Lukoes' palace on the outskirts of Vienna, examined the pictures which had been brought from Paris. With his magnifying glass in his hand, he peered and judged. He gave his opinions crisply and with certainty.

'You seem to know a good deal about it,' Lukoes said grudgingly.

'I am recognized as an expert,' Emmanuel said. 'You have been fortunate. The pictures which you have here are nearly all very good. They may have no great value at the moment, but later— they will represent a fortune. This, and this, are doubtful. They are possibly of value. I think this may be a Mazzuoli—a painter who died young and, to my mind, his death was not a matter for any great regret. This is Dutch, but the painter is unknown to me.'

He handed the baron a sheet which he had torn from his note-book.

'There are the estimated values. I will send the information, properly assembled and written out, to you this afternoon. You may regard it as reliable should you ever wish to sell the pictures.'

The baron watched him from under his shaggy brows. 'You're very certain of yourself, aren't you?' he said.

'Perfectly,' Emmanuel returned calmly.

In his heart he wondered if he were quite certain of himself, wondered if the queer golden eyes which had haunted him for the past few days had not shaken him more than he cared to admit even to himself? Now he was standing in her house, the palace which was her home, the home which she shared with this scarlet-faced Pole, in his white tunic and tight blue trousers with their their wide red stripe. Standing there, he wondered what he would do if she entered the room, wondered if he should continue to play the part of art expert and bow to her, book in hand, so that she might realize that he was in the employ, for the time being, of her husband?

As if fate knew his thoughts, the door opened and Caroline Lukoes entered.

Lukoes turned. 'Oh, Caroline! He's just finished. Thinks they're good. I've had my usual luck. It's becoming a proverb, that luck of mine.'

'I'm delighted. Herr Gollantz, good morning.'

Lukoes said: 'Well, if you've finished—that's all. Send back the report, and state the amount you want for a fee with it.'

He swung on his heel and with a word to his wife, which Em-manuel did not catch, walked out. Emmanuel put away his papers and magnifying-glass in the leather case which he always carried, straightened his tall figure, and bowed.

Caroline Lukoes stopped him as he turned to go. 'Herr Gol-lantz, please, one moment.' She noticed his flushed face, the tight line of his lips, and realized that this good-looking young man was wounded, that his pride smarted and stung.

'Yes, Baroness?'

'My husband doesn't mean—to hurt you. He doesn't understand.'

His eyes met hers. 'But why should he behave differently? That is the proper and accepted way to treat—tradesmen, particularly when they are Jews. I understand perfectly.'

'And how bitterly you resent it!' She spoke impetuously, scarcely thinking what she said.

Emmanuel stared at her, his eyes sombre and brooding. He ceased to be a very hurt young man, he seemed to her to be the incarnation of all Jews down the ages. When he spoke his voice was very gentle ; she fancied that she caught the faint lisp of his race speaking a language which is not their own.

'Don't you think that anyone would hate it?' he asked, speaking softly. 'Are we so different? Had I been an officer in the Imperial Army, who did not know one great master from another, who lacked every idea, whose outlook was dictated by convention, and whose conversation was a series of *clichés*—my uniform would have demanded respect.' He stopped, and laughed quietly, almost soundlessly. 'How utterly foolish I am! What does it matter to me? I have allowed my pride to get out of hand, like a runaway horse. I ought to be grateful—I am grateful. The baron has shown me a new form of amusement in life—the diversion of allowing oneself to be baited by the Gentile! It amuses them and cannot hurt me.'

She thought : 'He is like one of Disraeli's heroes, handsome and bitter. He'll suffer and batter himself to pieces over slights and insults because he is so proud. How beautiful he is!' And with the thought of Benjamin Disraeli, another thought came to her.

'Listen, Herr Gollantz,' she said. 'In England there is a Jew—he is even a little like you in appearance—he entered the House of Commons, which is the most exclusive club in Europe, where the laws are made for the country, some years ago—in '32 or '33, I forget which. My countrymen were not used to admitting Jews to the House ; they neither understood him, nor did they particularly wish to. He was young and very colourful, his clothes were more elaborate than those to which we are accustomed. His hair was curled, he wore a good deal of jewellery. The first time he rose to speak they laughed at him. They refused to listen to what he had to say. He looked at them in silence, and his only comment was, "One day they *shall* listen to me". Herr Gollantz, already they are listening to him, one day he will be the Prime Minister. He has forced society to accept him.'

'Thank you for telling me that story,' Emmanuel said. His eyes were alight, his lips parted in a smile. 'I shall always remember it. How I wish that I could speak English!'

'How I wish that you could! No one knows how I long to speak my own language with someone. If it were possible I would teach you.'

Two days later she came to his show-rooms. In the meantime, Emmanuel had scoured Vienna, and had found an elderly and retired valet, who had been in England many times with his late master. He spoke English with a fair accent and considerable fluency. He was willing to give lessons for a few gulden an hour; but when Emmanuel Gollantz demanded that each lesson was to be of two hours' duration and that he wanted no grammar, but only words and conversation, the old man was staggered.

'Two hours is a long time. You'll be sick to death of it.'

'Every evening from nine until eleven,' Emmanuel persisted. 'I shall speak English in a fortnight.'

He greeted Caroline Lukoes with a carefully prepared sentence in her own language. 'I veesh you a good morning, Baroness. Theese ees a grr-eat h-onour.'

Her strange eyes danced with amusement. 'You don't sound the first letter in honour,' she said. 'Now show me your beautiful things.'

He talked well, his manner was easy but never familiar. Mentally she contrasted him with the young aristocrats at court, to their disadvantage. She watched his hands as they touched old ivories, trinket boxes, jewel cases, exquisite china figures. They were so sure, and yet so gentle. She found that her eyes went back again and again to those hands. She was allowing herself to speculate too much about this young man. She wondered what books he read, what music he loved—if there were some girl in his life, and how much she meant to him? She rebuked herself impatiently.

'Don't be a fool, my dear. He's a handsome young Jew, and you are the wife of the Emperor's friend.'

Her easy, friendly manner changed. She spoke formally, said briefly that she would have this and that. 'Please send them, Herr Gollantz.' Then, meeting his eyes, she saw that he was smiling.

'And lace?' she asked, still coldly. 'I need some old lace, but it must be good.'

'I regret, Baroness, that at the moment I have no lace which

154

could interest you. Would it be possible to make another appointment? I will find the most lovely lace in Vienna in two days.'

For a moment she decided to refuse, then changed her mind. 'Very well. In two days' time—or three days. I am very busy. I cannot promise.'

'Very good, Baroness.'

He watched her carriage drive away, then returned to the show-room and carefully went through the drawers full of old lace, selecting the finest pieces with great care, his lips still smiling. Brussels, English point, old Italian handworked lace, petit point, pillow lace made in little out-of-the-way villages by old women with gnarled fingers, lace which had decorated the cottas of priests, and one beautiful fichu that had belonged to Marie Louise.

She came again ; he showed her the beautiful work.

'You must have worked very hard to find all this in three days.'

'Very hard indeed,' he answered. 'Hard work has rarely given me so much pleasure.'

'Lace is fashionable,' Caroline said. 'Her Imperial Majesty is very fond of it. I think that these galleries of yours would interest her.'

'I should be very grateful if you would be so gracious as to interest Her Imperial Majesty in my poor things.'

His humility was so obviously overdone that she laughed suddenly. 'How utterly ridiculous you are! How do the English lessons progress?'

'Very well, thank you. I am learning to conjugate the verbs. How simple they are. Have, hath, has, love, lovest, loves—a child could learn them.'

'Yes . . .' she said and turned back to the old lace. 'This is a very beautiful piece—oh, it is caught! Be careful.' He freed the lace which had caught on the fastening of her bracelet ; their hands touched, she saw his face flush scarlet. 'There! I will take that, and this.'

Without raising his eyes from the lace as he folded it, he said : 'You will come again? Tell me to find you a roc's egg, a white elephant, the dodo, and I will find them—if only you will come back. I am mad, I know that I am risking everything—I cannot help myself. I shall die, I think, if I cannot hear your voice, cannot see those wonderful, miraculous eyes again.'

'Herr Gollantz. . . .' Then, as he raised his face, she saw how white he had grown, how brilliantly his eyes shone, as though he had a fever. Those long, delicate hands shook as they held the lace. 'I—I scarcely know what to say.'

'Say nothing—only come back.'

'I should like to—come back,' Caroline said slowly. 'I have been almost afraid because I wanted to come back so much. We are being very foolish.'

'Oh, leave wisdom for old, tired, ugly people!' he cried.

'I am one of the plainest women in Vienna!'

He laughed. 'They used to say that of Princess Metternich. But they said also: *"Das ist unser Wien, Es gibt nur eine Prinzessin. Das ist du Pauline"*. There is one other name which could be substituted for Pauline—you know what name that is. This is the only place in Vienna where I can see you, where I can meet you as someone who is not inferior, someone whose presence is not almost an insult to you. Listen, I have been learning my lessons very hard. I will speak to you in English.' He frowned, making a great effort to remember what he had learnt, then said slowly: 'Von tay you shell listen to me! Is that good?'

'Too good,' Caroline said. 'I repeat that we are being very foolish. I must go. Herr Gollantz, will you try to find me a chicken-skin fan, decorated in the style of Watteau—as soon as possible?'

'Baroness, I shall search all Vienna. It shall be found.' He smiled because he remembered that such a fan lay in one of the cases in his show-room at that moment. He opened the door of her carriage, bowed, and then took a step towards her in obedience to the sign she gave.

'I shall not mention your galleries to the Empress,' she said very softly.

2

'I AM afraid that you do not find your cousin sympathetic, Emmanuel.' Hermann Gollantz put the question in a tentative tone, his tired, mobile face showing clearly how much the fact worried him. Emmanuel watched him, his heart filled with a great tenderness for this worried, lonely man, who carried all his burdens alone, neither asking for nor expecting help. He longed to pull up a chair, sit with his father in close and private conversation, ask for explanations and assure him that no matter how difficult things were, he, Emmanuel Gollantz, would overcome them.

'And I am afraid,' he said, smiling, 'that this obvious fact worries you, Father. Admit now, that you like Jean Hirsch no better than I do. The only person who does like him is Mama, and that is only because he reminds her of my Uncle Ishmael.'

Hermann temporized. 'Oh, I don't know that I dislike the boy —he is, perhaps, precocious, but many children who have travelled a good deal are that.'

'I should like him to travel even farther—anywhere, so long as he went away from Vienna. Father, why keep him here? He is seventeen, he has been here for nearly a year—eight months at least. How long is he going to stay?'

Hermann shook his head. 'I don't know,' he said, his voice suddenly weak and ineffectual. 'Your mother likes to have him here—and he is learning the carpet trade with Paul Boad. Boad tells me that he is very clever.'

Emmanuel shrugged his shoulders. 'I am sure he is—too clever,' he said coldly.

At the moment he was living in a feverish state of excitement and expectancy. Caroline Lukoes had come again for her chicken-skin fan, but her black-whiskered husband had accompanied her, and Emmanuel had been cast into the depths of misery by the occurrence. For once his composure had almost deserted him, and he had found the insolence of the baron terribly difficult to bear. Once or twice he had caught her strange eyes watching him, trying, he felt, to ease the sting of her husband's words and tone. He had escorted them to their carriage, and as he offered Caroline his hand to assist her to enter the vehicle he fancied that she pressed his fingers for one brief instant. Her face had betrayed nothing, and now, after three days, he was wondering miserably if he had been mistaken.

He had never fallen in love before. While Marcus lived they had been sufficient for each other. After his death Emmanuel had been too wretched to take any interest in anything except his work. Now Caroline Lukoes and her strange, beautiful eyes had taken complete possession of him. He thought of her all day, and at night resented the hours which sleep claimed, because

157

he would have preferred to lie awake and hold imaginary conversations with her.

Emmanuel knew that his nerves were strung up to breaking point, and knew too, that this was not the moment to discuss his cousin Jean with his father. He disliked Jean, and in his present state of mind realized that the additional irritation of a conversation concerning him was assuming vast proportions. He would be wise to change the subject and leave Jean alone for the time being.

'Don't be too hard on him,' Hermann Gollantz said, and, stretching out his hand, laid it on Emmanuel's arm. There was something very appealing in the gesture, and Emmanuel, watching his father's face, thought with tender certainty: 'He likes him as little as I do—but for some reason he feels that he can't send him away. Poor Father!'

Aloud he said: 'Very well, Father. We will make the best of it —you and I—shall we?'

He saw his father's face twisted suddenly by a spasm of emotion, and heard his voice shake a little as he replied: 'You are a good son, Emmanuel. I couldn't do without you. I know—I know that to you I must often seem to grudge you many things—I don't. I can't explain. I am the victim of circumstances. Only let me say this—I do nothing, have done nothing, which need make you ashamed of your father. I have tried to live always in accordance with the precepts of my wonderful great-uncle and friend, Fernando Meldola.'

Emmanuel listened; he was deeply touched. 'My dear, dear Father. . . .'

'And,' Hermann continued, his voice still very gentle and affectionate, 'I don't want you to devote your time to nothing except business. Find pleasure, enjoyment. Work is good, but there are other things that are good too. I look forward to the time when you will come and tell me that you have found a woman you can love, and who loves you.'

'That time is so far distant, Father, that you will have to wait a long time.' Emmanuel laughed softly; the serious moment was over and they both turned with something like relief to the business of the day.

As Emmanuel went back to his room to find some papers he ran into his cousin Jean who, with his eyes still heavy with sleep, his hair unbrushed, was wandering down the corridor clad in a gorgeous dressing-gown. Emmanuel eyed him with some distaste.

'Got any tobacco, Emmanuel?' Jean asked. 'I've run out.'

'I think I have. Come to my room and I'll see. I thought that you were working?'

Jean's dark, sallow face wrinkled into a grin. 'I ought to be, but I was late last night. I went to a ball with a girl—my word, she was a high-stepper and no mistake. I didn't get in until half past three.'

Emmanuel opened the door of his room, half bedroom, half study, and unscrewing the lid of a tobacco-jar, offered it to his cousin.

'If you don't mind my saying so, Jean, you're too young for pipes.'

Jean, packing the porcelain pipe which he held, looked up, scowling.

'Is that how I have to pay for a pipeful?' he asked. 'A sermon from you.'

'Please forgive me. I apologize.'

'You're too damned superior, Emmanuel. You give yourself infernal airs. Because women stare after you in the street, you think you're an aristocrat.'

Emmanuel with great care replaced the lid of the jar. 'There is no more to be said. Please go, I am busy.' He turned to his desk and began to search there for the papers he wanted.

Jean stared at him in silence for a moment, and then turned and, as he walked out of the room, contrived to take two fine linen handkerchiefs which lay on the top of a pile of clean clothes. As he stuffed them into the pocket of his dressing-gown, he turned to make certain that Emmanuel had not noticed. 'Thanks for the tobacco,' he said.

Emmanuel did not turn. 'It is nothing,' he said, still absorbed in his papers.

A moment later he gathered them together and left the room, to find his cousin still in the corridor, talking and laughing with one of the maids. There was something so impudently familiar in his attitude, and in the tones of his voice, that Emmanuel flushed with annoyance. The girl had evidently been carrying a note, and Jean had snatched it from her, and was holding it behind him, refusing to give it back to her. The girl, a fair, pink-faced wench from Tirol, was giggling and stammering.

'Please, Herr Hirsch, give it back to me.'

'You'll have to pay for it! Come on, what will you give me for it?'

'Herr Hirsch, please. . . .' The girl was between mirth and distress. 'Give it to me. It's for Herr Emmanuel.'

'What if it is? Only from some old hag who wants him to sell her a picture, and hold her skinny hand while he does it! Come on now, Gerta, give me a kiss and you can have it. It's no use——'

Emmanuel halted immediately behind his cousin. 'Might I have my letter, please?' His voice was quiet and even pleasant.

Jean started and met the cold eyes which stared into his.

'Here it is!' He offered the letter, all his assurance gone.

'Thank you. Gerta, get on with your own work.' The girl turned and fled down the corridor. 'Jean, will you kindly keep your charming comments on my business and manner of transacting it to yourself? I don't know what is customary in your own home, but here we don't snatch letters from the servants and demand kisses as payment.'

Jean scowled. 'Oh, more preaching! Go to hell, and take your letters with you!' He went off, entering his own room and slamming the door behind him.

Emmanuel glanced at the letter, then instinctively took out his handkerchief and dusted the envelope as if to remove something unpleasant which clung to its surface. He took out a little pocket-knife, for he disliked opening letters with his fingers, and cut the covering. The paper pleased him, it was smooth, and very thick. He lifted it to his nose and sniffed it delicately. His frown disappeared. He loved delicate and delicious scents, and this was perfect. As he walked down the corridor he read the letter.

Herr Gollantz, the Princess Maria Dietrich is here, and has been admiring the lace which I bought some days ago. She is interested in embroidery. Would it be possible to bring some very good pieces here for her to see? Nothing very large, and with a good deal of colour if possible. The bearer will wait for a reply.
Caroline Lukoes.

The change in Emmanuel was extraordinary. He crammed the letter into his breast-pocket and rushed down the corridor and into the long gallery.

'Where is the messenger, Simon?' he demanded. 'The messenger who brought a letter for me some time ago? I have only this moment received it.'

'Waiting in the ante-room, Emmanuel. He hasn't been here

160

long: he is one of the footmen of Baron Lukoes. What a livery! You can scarcely see the cloth and velvet for gold lace.'

Half an hour later, Emmanuel entered the palace of the baron. His heart thundered, the blood beat at his temples, his pulses felt like sledge-hammers. His face was pale but composed. He was shown into a small drawing-room, and stood face to face with the woman who had occupied his thoughts for the past days. As he bowed before her, he wondered if he detected a faint expression of amusement on her face ; certainly those golden eyes were very bright.

The Princess Maria, small, fair, and exquisitely dressed, sat on a wide sofa, her little feet resting on a footstool covered with satin. She looked to Emmanuel like a painting by Boucher.

'You have brought the embroideries?' Caroline asked.

'I left them in the hall, Baroness.'

She rang and ordered a footman to bring them. The man, Emmanuel thought, stared at him superciliously, resenting that he should be made to fetch and carry for a tradesman, no matter how well dressed he might be.

The Princess, speaking in a delightfully high, clear voice, with the delicious lisp of the Viennese, said: 'Are they brightly coloured? I refuse to even look at dull old things. My house is sufficiently dull already.'

'They were chosen for their brightness, Highness.'

He displayed his materials, he stated their age, style and particular beauties, crisply and with interest. The two women listened and watched. Caroline found that she experienced a peculiar pleasure in listening to his easy, well-modulated voice, that she derived a certain satisfaction from the assurance of his hands as he unwrapped and flung materials over chair-backs to display them to their best advantage. How strong his hands were, and yet utterly lacking in the brutal clumsiness of her husband's. He was polite and attentive, without servility. She looked at his clothes, admired the care with which they were worn and the air of distinction which clung to them.

'There is another parcel!' Emmanuel glanced round the room in search of it. 'No, pray do not ring, Baroness. I will bring it in a moment.'

As the door closed behind him, Maria Dietrich leant forward and said ecstatically: 'Caro—what a beautiful young man! Is he really only a tradesman? How dreadful! He ought to be at court! Then one could afford to be indiscreet!'

161

'If he were at court, someone else would probably be indiscreet first.'

'My dear—he's ravishing! Like one of Byron's heroes. I'm certain that he lives a terrible life, gambles, and breaks women's hearts.'

'Are you?' Caroline's voice was full of amusement. 'I doubt it. Maria.'

'These are the best of all,' Emmanuel said as he entered. 'These are old church embroideries—it is better not to ask their history perhaps. Here is a stole—look at the flowers: roses, violets, and poppies. After three hundred years they bloom as brightly as ever. And this, a cope—see the amount of material in it—cloth of gold inside and the finest silk outside. Here is the Last Supper embroidered in an arabesque—copied from da Vinci. What work. He might have painted it, and the colours will last better, have lasted better, than those in his masterpiece. Look at these paten covers—small, but each with its separate bouquet of flowers, fruits—and here is one with two birds. See how the breasts shimmer as they catch the light. These are unique—I have never seen anything like them. It is a privilege to touch them.'

'Let me see!' Princess Maria held out her small, plump white hand, and Emmanuel gave the beautiful things to her. Caroline turned to examine the cope, and as he threw back the folds, once again his hands touched hers. Once again their eyes met and he saw her lips move, forming soundlessly, one word: 'Wait.'

The princess rose ; she held two of the paten covers, and showed them to Emmanuel. 'I want those. . . . Oh, the price? Never mind, I want them! But this one is torn, see, a piece of the gold braid is loose. I shall want that repaired. Can you do it?'

'Certainly, Highness.' He examined the loose stitches. He could have sworn that they had not been torn when he packed the embroideries. He laid them on one side, and waited to hear her further orders.

'How still he stands!' Caroline thought. 'That is one of his greatest attractions—that quality of being still—of waiting.'

'And this, and this.' The little princess gabbled on. 'They must be sent home immediately. I may want others—later. These are sufficient for the moment. But the covers—those are what I like best. Please be careful with them.'

'Assuredly, Highness.'

Caroline, her hand to her lips, smiled behind it. 'Oh, Maria, Maria, if he weren't the exact opposite of Byron's heroes, he would be certain to see through you! You're very attractive, but you're not very clever, my dear.'

'Caroline, I must go! I am to meet Theodore in the Prater, and you know how angry he is if the horses are kept waiting. Shall I see you tomorrow? Well, send round a note when you are going to the opera—— No, not on a gala night! We'll make up a party of our own. That play of Stefan Gustave is—they say it is amusing.'

'Very, I believe. Herr Gollantz did the *décor*.'

'You did? How interesting. There, I must go, Caroline. Goodbye, Herr Gollantz. I shall come and see your beautiful things one day.'

'I shall be honoured, Highness.'

They left him, standing among his beautiful embroideries, in a billowing sea of colour, gold and silver. Mechanically he stooped and began to fold and lay carefully on a chair all the things which he had scattered for their inspection. Would she come back? She must—that was why she had whispered 'Wait'. What would she say to him? Did she realize that his heart was on fire? Did she understand that he was hungry for the sight and sound of her? The princess, pretty, exquisite, like a piece of Meissen china—and as uninteresting!

The door swung open. He turned, a piece of apple-green satin embroidered with silver laurel leaves in his hand, and faced her. Her lips parted in a smile, her eyes danced with amusement. The material slid from his hands and lay unheeded on the floor.

'Well?' Caroline said. 'Were you surprised that I sent for you?'

'I know what gratitude is for the first time in my life,' he said. 'I have never before had reason to be grateful to anyone.'

'How go the English lessons?' His calm made her feel like a schoolgirl.

'I have learnt the only verb that I need. It was ridiculously simple.'

'Do you want me to ask you which verb that is?'

'I can't believe that you don't know.'

She came farther into the room, and sat down near to where he stood. 'The princess says that she is certain you live a terrible life, gamble, and break women's hearts. Is that true?'

'I never had any real life until a week ago, when I was born in a café near the Stadt.'

She made a movement of impatience. 'Oh, you talk too easily, too glibly! You make everything seem so—so light.'

163

His face changed, he looked down at her gravely. 'Because it is all so serious, so important,' he said, 'I must make an effort to treat it lightly—in my words. That is the only way I can make it bearable.'

'You mean that—or are those only more words?'

'I mean that I worship you, that I would die for you ; or if you wished it, live for you. I am yours—entirely.'

With apparent inconsequence she said: 'Give me those paten covers. The ones the princess has bought.' He handed them to her, and she slipped her finger inside the folded silk of the lining ; from the second cover she drew out a small, impossibly fine handkerchief, edged with lace and, twisting it round, showed him the corner, where the letters M.D., intertwined and surmounted by a crown, were embroidered.

Emmanuel stared at it, then stretched out his hand and took it.

'I will send it back with the materials,' he said.

'You will do what she intends you to do,' Caroline returned. 'You will take it back yourself.'

'But—but, I don't think that—I mean, it is impossible. . . .'

For the first time, she laid her hand on his arm. 'Listen,' she said. 'I am a person of importance in Vienna. This life is like living in a house of glass. There is only one compensation, that everyone else lives in houses of the same material. I'm forced to safeguard myself.'

Somewhere in the depths of Emmanuel's consciousness something stirred, as if protesting. He felt a sudden sense of distaste, felt that a rough finger had swept over the bloom of his romance. Then, meeting her eyes, it left him and he felt wildly happy, expectant again.

'Maria Dietrich is married to a man old enough to be her father. She has done all that was expected of her, provided him with two sons, and she has learnt to hate him in the process. I don't blame her. He has never curtailed his own liberties, never denied himself anything that he wanted. So, if you wish to please me—if you wish to see me again—take back that handkerchief tomorrow and realize, for the moment at least, that the princess is a very lovely woman.'

'If I want to see you again!' he repeated. 'It is the only thing I do want, the only hope that life holds—to see you again.'

Caroline's hand remained on his arm. It was pleasant to listen to this young man, with his chivalry, his love of beauty, and his whole-hearted admiration. She realized how sick and tired she

164

was of Lukoes, with his heavy hands, his loud voice, and his utter insensibility. She had married him because she was tired of being poor, tired of living in a house where the rain came in through the broken roof, where the walls were spotted with mildew and where almost everything of value had been sold to pay the gambling debts of her father and her two brothers.

Stanislaus had seemed a way of escape. He was rich, he admired her, danced attendance upon her, paid her heavy and cumbrous compliments. When he asked her to marry him, she knew what was expected of her and accepted him. It was not until she had been married nearly a year that she saw him in one of his wild bouts of drunkenness, and listened to his screaming and howling. It was like living with a wild beast—while it lasted.

She had never been afraid. His noisy brutality, his alcoholic excesses had not made her miserable, they had merely made her contemptuous. True, her father drank port until he slid quietly and unobtrusively under the table, her brothers were beginning to grow heavy and florid with too much wine. Stanislaus was different. He drank with a sort of sulky determination, a brutal fixity of purpose—bottle after bottle. Not the smooth port which her father drank, but fiery spirits imported from Poland, drinks brewed by peasants in the hills, from gentian roots.

While these fits were on him he sat alone, and not even the commands of the Emperor could stop his drinking. For days it would last, and he would only emerge at intervals to yell like a lunatic, howl like a beast of prey, and curse like a soul in torment. Then followed illness, days when he wept and cried, when he shivered and trembled, when he retched and spewed, coughed and spat continually. When he refused to wash or shave, and lay tossing in a foul bed which he forbade his servants to touch. At last, white-faced and shaking, with his eyes sunk deep in his head, looking like pieces of raw meat, with his lips swollen and cracked, he would take up his life again. There was no sense of shame in him, rather a kind of dissolute pride that he could have drunk so much and lived. He might totter as he walked, but he swaggered more than he tottered.

Once when the butler told him that the cellar was almost emptied of spirits, he shouted with laughter, leaning back in his chair, his mouth open showing his strong yellow teeth. 'Empty, eh? My God, it takes a Polish nobleman to show these effete Austrians how to drink!'

She was weary of brutality, tired of strong red hands which

clutched and held her, sickened by his loud voice assuring her that she was the most attractive woman in Vienna, revolted by his perpetual hinted questions as to when she was going to give him a son.

'Do all English women breed slowly, Caroline? Don't their husbands get impatient? Like your damned heavy English horses, you're a long time getting into your stride.'

'You should have bought a brood mare,' she said. 'You don't understand women—you're incapable of it.'

He had hunched his broad shoulders and squinted evilly at her from his red-rimmed eyes. 'I'm capable of siring sons. Go back to Poland and have a look at the stock I've raised there! I could muster a regiment of my own sons. I started before I was fifteen.'

'How commendable!'

'Damned useful at all events.'

Now she sat in her drawing-room, watching Emmanuel Gollantz, conscious that she longed for romance, that she wanted tenderness and gentleness. She wanted just once more to hear a man speak softly of intimate, secret things. She wanted to know that he felt his heart beat more quickly for her presence. It was foolish, dangerous even—but she must keep her head. Other women had taken lovers; true, not handsome Jewish art dealers, but other races and other trades less reputable.

She was barely thirty, she was a passionate woman, and she had been married for five years. She had grown to hate Stanislaus, and yet, sooner or later, she knew that she would have to give him children. She was young, there was plenty of time. First, she would savour romance again, and then—she shrugged her shoulders—after that let Stanislaus have his children, if he hadn't killed himself by that time, or—her lips twisted—killed her in one of his ghastly rages.

She held out her hand, and when Emmanuel took it, drew him nearer to her. 'I trust you, Emmanuel Gollantz,' she said. 'I don't know how foolish or how wise I am being. Perhaps at the moment I don't care very much. Tell me that you love me.'

He slipped on to one knee before her. In any other young man the movement would have been slightly theatrical, even for Vienna in the 'sixties; for Emannuel it appeared perfectly natural and right.

He lifted her hand to his lips. 'I worship you. I have never loved any women except my mother and my beloved grandmother

until now. It is all new to me. You must make allowances for me
—only know that there is nothing, nothing in the whole world
I would not do for you.'

He met her eyes steadily. His whole face was transfigured, he
seemed to her like some young knight ready to fling his challenge
to the world.

She bent her head towards him. 'Kiss me . . .' and after a long
pause, 'Emmanuel.'

He caught his breath, it was as if a sob filled his throat. Then
he caught her face between his hands and drew her mouth down
to his. She felt his lips, young, ardent and cool against hers, and
compared them with those other lips which revolted her. He rose
and lifted her to her feet, catching her in his arms and holding
her close. He was no longer a young man, tentative, playing with
words and phrases, ready to fill whatever position she assigned to
him—he was strong, possessive, and demanding.

'Emmanuel, my dear—let me go.'

'No, not yet. I am hungry. I have been starving ever since I first
saw you. Again, my most wonderful, again.'

When he let her go, he stood before her, very pale, but smiling
a little, as if he had become possessed of some marvellous secret.
He looked older, even more certain of himself. In his attitude
there was something of the conqueror.

'You must send me away,' he said. 'It is impossible for me to
leave you unless you order me to go.'

She nodded, breathless, panting a little, her hand pressed to
her side.

'Yes, yes, you must go. Go quickly, Emmanuel.'

'And tomorrow?'

A smile flickered across her lips.' Tomorrow you will return
Maria Dietrich's handkerchief. Are you sure that I have no need
to be apprehensive?'

'Of many things perhaps—of Her Highness, never. And afterwards, when and where may I see you?'

'I have an old governess who lives in an apartment in a little
street called Ottakar Strasse—number eleven. She gives English
lessons. Will you call there at four tomorrow and ask if she will
take you as a pupil? Say that I have recommended you to go to
her.'

She reflected later that it was typical of him to ask no further
questions. He nodded gravely, then turned and began to pack his
embroideries into a neat parcel. When the footman entered in

answer to Caroline's ring, he saw the tall, elegant young Jew bending over her hand, saying: 'Again permit me to thank you for your gracious patronage. It is very valuable to me, and I am very grateful.'

3

I

MARIA DIETRICH awoke the following morning with a pleasant sense of expectancy. She had felt so when, as a child, she had awakened and remembered that it was her birthday. Lately there had been nothing new to look forward to. Theodore was dull, blinking at her through short-sighted eyes, with his little prim mouth pinched and thin. His one excitement was the discovery of new facts—it scarcely mattered what they were so long as they were facts. How thrilled he had been to discover, after long and extensive calculations, the exact number of buttons worn on the tunics of His Imperial Majesty's army. He knew the precise number of horse carriages in Vienna, the approximate number of currants used by all the pastry-cooks every day in the year. There was no end to his items of interest, and he would discuss them all day long.

She had her two children, both boys, one five and the other only two. They were dear little things, pretty, taking after her, not after Theodore. She had been expected to produce sons; she had done her duty, and she felt that now she had some right to expect a little amusement.

There had been several young men who had interested her, but her interest had either died or they had become tiresome. Young Guchowski had been handsome, had danced divinely, but his utter stupidity and conceit had bored her. Franz Mayerhausen had been so ugly that half his attraction had lain in his irregular features, but he had taken everything so seriously. He had actually expected her to leave Theodore, fling away her position and leave Vienna with him for some impossible castle in the depths of Bavaria. Max von Furstberg had amused her longer than any of them, until he had begun to write music and insisted on playing over endless piano concertos to her—such bad music too!

Then, yesterday, she had seen this young Jew. Caroline Lukoes might be superior about him, might smile that queer, twisted smile of hers and, raising her eyebrows, murmur that he was only a tradesman no matter how handsome he might be. While she bathed and dressed, Maria wondered when he had found her handkerchief, and if he had realized that it was, in effect, a card of invitation to one of the most magnificent houses in Vienna?

She drank her coffee and nibbled her fresh *brioche*, entered her carriage and drove in the Prater, bowing right and left like a queen. All the time she wondered if he would come, if possibly he was already at the house? She ordered the coachman to return quickly. The major-domo hurried forward. Prince Theodore had asked for her—he was leaving Vienna for a few days, in search of some information he needed for his newest pamphlet. He had left a letter for her, and his regrets that he could not delay his departure.

'There is a young man waiting, Highness. Emmanuel Gollantz, the son of the art dealer. He is in the little waiting-room. He refused to go without seeing Your Highness.'

'A young man?' Maria looked vague and uncertain. 'Gollantz? Ah, I remember, I bought some embroideries from him yesterday at the house of Baroness Lukoes. What does he want, Ferdinand? I will see him.'

Emmanuel had been waiting for some time. His patience was almost exhausted. He hated this rôle, found it undignified; he could only suppose that Caroline knew best. After all, who was he to understand the ins and outs of these curious people, who set such apparent store by convention and social opinion, and yet went to such lengths to flout both? His own race were supposed to be difficult, secretive, and yet they appeared simple in the extreme when compared with high-born Austrians.

He entered the room where the princess awaited him, half impatient, half amused. He came forward, a small, flat packet in his hand. Maria met his eyes frankly; her smile was delightful, almost friendly. Her key-note had always been a kind of childish disregard for social barriers.

'Herr Gollantz, how very prompt and kind. You have brought back the covers—mended?'

'It is nothing, Highness. A stitch here and there, five minutes perhaps.'

She opened the parcel and examined the contents with a great show of interest.

'Which of the two is the more valuable, Herr Gollantz?'

'To the ordinary dealer, Highness, this one with the clusters of roses. I have special knowledge and I found, yesterday, that the one with the birds embroidered on it was far more valuable.'

'Indeed! Why?'

'Not for itself, but for what it contained.'

'What it contained!' Her large blue eyes opened more widely than ever.

Emmanuel slipped his hand into an inner pocket and extracted a piece of old plum-coloured silk; this he unfolded, displaying the handkerchief.

'It's mine, surely!' Maria's astonishment was admirably done.

'I was afraid so.'

'Why afraid, Herr Gollantz?' Her voice had softened perceptibly.

'Because, Highness, I have a reputation which I dare not imperil. It is a reputation for honesty. I had no doubt that it was yours, the initials betrayed that fact. I had no option but to return it.'

She blushed, twisted the scrap of cambric in her fingers, and said, very low: 'Did you not want to return it?'

'I was faced with two evils, each holding a compensation—to be dishonest and keep what had once been yours, or to return your property and to see you again if only for a moment.' He shrugged his shoulders. 'Ah, well, Highness, perhaps you will at least remember me as an honest man!'

Maria turned away from him and walked over to one of the long windows which overlooked the formal Italian garden which stretched away from the back of the house.

Emmanuel, his lips twitching a little, followed her. He saw her dab her eyes with the little handkerchief, and came closer.

'Highness . . .' he said softly, 'you're not well.'

'I'm not happy,' she returned. 'I'm very unhappy indeed.'

Emmanuel, leaning forward, could find no trace of tears, no hint of unhappiness. She was young, exquisite, her cheeks had the bloom of perfect health—but it pleased her to imagine that she was unhappy.

' "What lost a world, and bade a hero fly?" ' he quoted. ' "The timid tear in Cleopatra's eye!" '

'Are you a hero?'

170

He made a little gesture of excuse. 'Highness, do I look like one?'

'Do you want to fly?'

'Only like the swallows—to avoid the winter and be ready to return in the spring once more.'

Maria sighed. 'You are too obscure. I am a simple person with simple ideas. But you interest me, Herr Gollantz. I care nothing for social distinctions.'

Emmanuel thought: 'Caroline would never have made that mistake!'

'I like people for what they are—you interested me when I saw you at Baroness Lukoes'. I love old things; china, lace, glass—er—carpets. I should like to come and see yours. Tomorrow morning?'

'I am at your service, Highness.'

'At eleven o'clock.'

'That will be wonderful—I mean, I shall have everything ready.'

'Then—*auf wiedersehen.*'

He bowed over her hand, lifted it to his lips and kissed it, then turned and walked quickly from the room. As he walked back to his father's house he smiled. What nonsense it all was! The silly, pretty little princess, who so obviously sought for a little amusement, who took nothing seriously, but who played an elaborate game. She would come to the galleries, she would buy lace and ivories, china and silks, because by doing so she could purchase amusement.

Then his smile died. His lips curved with faint disgust. How cheap this 'playing' was! How unworthy when compared with the real love which he felt for Caroline! It seemed almost disloyal to flirt—even if the other person fully recognized the fact—when his heart was in reality filled to overflowing with an emotion which was real, serious, and deep.

He entered his own home and walked into the long gallery. The moment he entered he was conscious of a sense of impending disaster. Simon Cohen seemed nervous, appeared to watch him with half-frightened eyes, and more than once opened his mouth as if to begin to speak, then closed it again without uttering a word.

'What's wrong, Simon?' Emmanuel asked. 'You're as jumpy as a cat.'

'Nothing, Emmanuel—that is—I mean, of course—what I

171

mean to say is that your father wishes to speak to you, in the salon.'

'Why so nervous?'

'I'm not nervous, Emmanuel—really—not in the least. I think you'd better go to your father.'

Hermann stood by the fireplace, his worn face wearing an expression of the deepest concern. Rachel sat near him, and it was evident to Emmanuel that she had been weeping bitterly; her eyes were red and her mouth still quivered.

'You wanted me, Father? Is anything the matter?'

Rachel buried her face in her hands and began to cry sgain.

Emmanuel thought: 'What a day of tears! First the princess, and now my poor mother!' He went to her and laid his hand on her shoulder. 'Mother, my dearest Mother, what is wrong?'

Hermann sighed. 'Emmanuel, something terrible has happened. I think it only right to tell you. Your mother will forgive me if I speak plainly before her. The maid—Gerta—is in trouble.'

'In trouble? What is the trouble? Someone ill?' He could not understand why Gerta's trouble should affect his mother so.

'Emmanuel,' Rachel cried, 'how can you speak like that! She's going to have a child. She admitted it to Rosa this morning. Gerta sleeps alone, and Augusta sleeps with Rosa. Gerta told Rosa when she went in to wake her this morning. Gerta was—was not well, and Rosa suspected the reason.'

Emmanuel stared at her. Instinctively he felt sorry for the girl and resolved to give her money and promise to help her. Stupid little thing. That was the result of bringing country girls into the town: they played the fool and got into trouble like this. Poor, silly, pink-faced Gerta!

'I'm sorry,' he said. 'I am sure that it has upset you, Mother. Don't be too disturbed. Perhaps the man will marry her; I'll see him if you like and find out what can be done. There, don't cry.'

Hermann cleared his throat. 'Emmanuel, before you say anything else—let me tell you. Gerta says that—you are the father of this child. . . . No, listen. She produced a handkerchief of yours from under her pillow while Rosa was talking to her. I am sure—quite sure—that you can clear yourself.'

'Me?' Emmanuel said. 'Me? The girl must be mad!'

'Is this your handkerchief?' Hermann held out a crumpled linen handkerchief.

'Certainly! My dear Father, neither the fact that my handkerchief was found under her pillow nor the girl's statement, affect

172

me in the least. The only thing that affects me is that you and my mother could believe that I—your son—could or would carry on an intrigue with a servant in my own home.' He shrugged his shoulders. 'Without being undutiful I must say I am disappointed in you both. Perhaps you will give me an hour to think this over. Please do me the favour of not discussing it further until I have decided what to do.'

Without another word he turned and left the room. Rachel began to cry again, while Hermann Gollantz, his face whiter than ever, repeated: 'I don't believe it ; I never did believe it!'

Emmanuel went back to the gallery and, going over to the desk where Simon Cohen always sat, pulled up a chair and began to talk to him.

'You heard, then, Simon?'

'I heard something, Emmanuel. I don't believe it.'

'Thank you. Oh, I'm not a saint, Simon. Only as it happens I don't care for fat, pink, Tirolean girls.' He smiled. 'It's not you, is it. Simon?'

'My dear Emmanuel—please!'

'No, no, that was only a joke—and a poor one. My father is the soul of virtue. There only remains one other male about the place—Jean Hirsch.'

'On whom,' Simon said eagerly, 'I should have thought suspicion would have rested immediately.'

'People always miss the obvious!' Emmanuel leaned back in his chair, crossed his legs, and laid the tips of his fingers together. 'I don't trust Herr Jean. His clothes are always too new, too expensive—and what bad taste! He is always able to afford the play, the opera, balls—someone told me that he gambles quite considerably. Where does the money come from, Simon?'

He was smiling again, his anger, his pain at the attitude of his father and mother were apparently forgotten.

Simon, watching him, thought what an easy-going fellow he looked, what a dandy in his beautifully cut clothes, with his tight shirt-cuffs, his gold links and his pearl scarf-pin! And yet—there was a line about the jaw, a certain turn of the firm lips which contradicted the smiling unconcern of his general expression. It struck Simon that he was glad not to be standing in the shoes of Herr Jean Hirsch.

Emmanuel nodded his handsome head, with its well-brushed, beautifully-cared-for black curls. 'Yes, Herr Jean gambles—well. so will I. Just once, and for fun. Is he in, do you know, Simon?'

173

'He never misses a meal. He ought to be here now . . . Listen. Yes, there he is in the corridor.'

Emmanuel sprang to his feet, whispering: 'Simon, stand by me!' Then dashed out into the corridor. He re-entered a moment later with a slightly sulky Jean.

'What the devil is the matter? Rushing out and making a mystery about wanting to speak to me.'

Emmanuel laid his finger on his lips. 'Hush, hush!' he entreated. 'It may be wiser if no one knows you are here. We've no time to lose. Listen—have you seen Boad this morning?'

'Boad—this morning? No. No. He only comes down to the shop twice a week.'

Again Emmanuel nodded, darting a look at Simon. 'Simon and I have been out together. We have both seen Boad. Jean—he's found out! Mind, he was very—what shall I say?—considerate about it. Only Simon and I know; we are the only two people who need know. Now—what are you going to do?'

Jean Hirsch's sallow face had changed to a dirty grey, his mouth hung a little open, his eyes seemed to quiver from Emmanuel to Simon.

'It—it wasn't so very much,' he quavered. 'Nothing at all really.'

'Yes, but you know what Boad is!'

'How in God's name did he find out? He hasn't looked at the books for weeks. I could have made it right by next month. Did he tell you how he found out?'

'That,' Emmanuel said gravely, 'I don't think I can tell you. The point is what are you going to do, Jean? Have you got the money?'

'No, I lost what I'd got ready to put back two nights ago. Emmanuel, help me! It's only a hundred and twenty gulden. Let me have it, I'll get back quickly and put it straight. I may get there before him. He always eats a big meal in the middle of the day, and then rests for a couple of hours.'

Emmanuel took out his pocket-book and opened it slowly. 'There's just one other thing,' he said. 'What are you going to do about Gerta?'

Jean's pasty face quivered. 'Have they found out? The damned little fool! How?'

'You're so careless,' Emmanuel said pleasantly. 'You left a handkerchief in her room last night, under her pillow. Stupid of you! My mother and father are terribly upset over it.'

Some of Jean's courage returned. His mouth closed, then looked sulky.

'Oh, well, that's nothing to do with me!'

The pocket-book was slipped back into Emmanuel's pocket. 'Neither has this business with Board anything to do with me,' he said gently. 'That's all right, Jean—go and get the money somewhere else, if you can.'

'What do you want me to do? Marry the damned girl? Not likely!'

'No, no! The girl's a fool, but she deserves a better fate than that. No, only admit that you have been visiting her at night. After all, I heard you demanding kisses from her in the corridor. You see, both Simon and I feel that suspicion might fall on either of us—and we neither of us like the rôle of Don Juan. Just admit to us that this particular fault is yours, and here you are—one hundred and twenty gulden, and I'll write you out an I O U.' He took a piece of paper, and wrote a few words on it quickly, handing it to Jean. 'Your name there, please.'

'This isn't an I O U. *I was in Gerta's room last night, and on several other nights.* That's not an I O U.'

'It's the only one I want,' Emmanuel assured him. 'Please sign it.'

'You know you can't claim the money back, don't you, if this is all you want? There! Now—let me have the money, and I'll put it back before Board sticks his horrible hooked nose into the books!'

The money was handed to him; the slip of paper went into Emmanuel's pocket; Jean turned to go. Emmanuel, with a gesture, stopped him.

'Oh, when you see Herr Board don't mention either Simon or me, will you? We have been out together—but not for months. We have seen Herr Board—but not for a year at least. In other words, we drew a bow at a venture, and it smote you under your fifth rib, cousin Jean. One thing more, when you go visiting, don't take my handkerchiefs, and if you do—don't leave them behind in future. I dislike carelessness of that kind.'

The youth stared from one to the other. His face was suffused, his eyes started with rage, words poured from his lips like a torrent; he looked as he stood there, in the doorway, like some devil. He cursed them both, but he reserved his deepest and most desperate curses for his cousin.

Emmanuel, his lip curling, shook with silent laughter.

'You fool!' he said. 'You utter fool! Get out, before I come and soil my hands by throwing you out. D'you think that I'm afraid of you? Do you think that you can hurt me? You poor, pitiful bit of ghetto dirt.'

II

His pride was desperately hurt. He returned to his father and mother, cold, aloof, and dignified. He handed the signed paper to his father, saying as he did so: 'There, that is Jean's word—possibly it may carry more weight than mine. I did not realize that my own was not sufficient for you both.'

Hermann, with his eyes full of tears, begged him to listen to explanations.

Emmanuel answered: 'There is only one explanation—that you did not trust me!'

Rachel cried, declaring that he was cruel, that their doubt had sprung from their anxiety.

'Have I ever caused you anxiety?' Emmanuel asked.

He could not know that Hermann's strength of will, his firmness of purpose, had been sapped and weakened by the life of perpetual concealment which he had lived, and under the strain of waiting week after week for some new demand which should be made on him. With the arrival of Jean, life had not become easier. The boy was for ever wanting this or that. He had been apprenticed to Boad, the carpet importer and dealer ; Boad knew more concerning carpets than any other man in Vienna, and he demanded a large premium. Ishmael wrote declaring that his son must have a chance to make good in the world, stating that his own hand-to-mouth existence sprang from the fact that he had never learnt any trade fully.

Hermann had paid, and now the boy was for ever needing new clothes, stating that he must have books on carpets and their manufacture, books which he kept at Boad's warehouse or shop so that, he stated, they were at his hand whenever he could snatch a moment for study. Now this new problem had arisen and the girl must be provided for.

Rachel sobbed: 'That wicked girl! To lie so. No wonder such a woman led Jean away. Poor boy, so young!'

For the first time Emmanuel flushed, and his eyes were angry. 'How old is the girl, Mother, pray? Only a child herself and

176

without the advantage of having education, travel, and good surroundings to widen her mind. I have been fortunate lately—one or two small investments of my own have done well. With your permission, I will see that the girl is sent somewhere where she will be well treated.'

'You will arrange it!' Rachel exclaimed.

'With your permission—or does the fact that I should wish to do so proclaim my guilt, Mother?'

'How can you be so cruel, Emmanuel?'

With the girl facing him, some of his certainty left him. He stammered a little, he found it difficult to use the right words; he was so anxious not to hurt her, wound her feelings, that he could scarcely make his meaning clear. She admitted that there was a young man in Tirol, a good fellow, who had wanted to marry her. She thought he might forgive her—especially if she had a little dowry. Until she could hear from him she would go to her cousins in the town; they kept a little baker's shop. Yes, they would be quite kind to her. She cried a little, and taking Emmanuel's hand kissed it. He seemed to her to be something not far removed from a god, kindly, gentle, and very wise. It never occurred to her that his age was the same as her own.

'Herr Emmanuel, I was wicked, I tried to blame you, I was—afraid!'

'Good-bye,' he said, disregarding her protestation. 'Go to your cousins at once, and when you hear from Hans, come and see me. I will arrange everything; you can trust me.'

'I do! Oh, Herr Gollantz, I do indeed! I shall never forget.'

Emmanuel, changing his clothes—for after the encounter with Jean he felt soiled and dingy—found that his pride still smarted. It was unbearable to him that his father and mother should have trusted him so little.

'To imagine that I could have been guilty of such a breach of good taste! Well, whatever qualms I may have had, that incident has dispelled them! I have played the industrious apprentice too long. I have become a pack horse; my mind has run always along the lines of work. Now, I might allow myself just a little—life.'

He tied his cravat with care, brushed the coat which he intended to wear, chose a handkerchief with attention, and adjusted his shirt-cuffs so that they displayed the exact amount necessary of their snowy surface. His boots glinted in the light. He passed a silk handkerchief round his hat, swung his cape of very fine black cloth round his shoulders, took his gold-mounted cane and, whistling a merry little tune, went out, turning his steps towards number eleven Ottakar Strasse.

The narrow, crowded streets had never seemed so full of life. The shop windows were filled with attractive wares. Each woman who passed appeared to Emmanuel Gollantz to be the incarnation of grace and charm. The men who walked slowly, sauntering along in the afternoon sunshine, were models of dignity and good breeding.

'There is indeed only one Vienna!' Emmanuel decided.

Number eleven was a small house with trim windows, each decorated with a box of bright flowers. It was undistinguished, spotlessly clean, and like a dozen other houses. He knocked, and the door was opened to him by an elderly woman, who wore a maidservant's uniform. Her thin, harsh face looked as if it had been cut roughly from a block of wood and left unfinished.

'Is your mistress at home?' Emmanuel asked.

'She's engaged at the moment, sir.'

He offered her his card. 'Perhaps you will give her this, and say that I have come to inquire about English lessons. I am sent here by the Baroness Lukoes.'

The wooden face showed some faint spark of animation. 'Oh, if you've come from Miss Caroline—wait a minute. Step inside, please.'

She spoke fluently enough, but her accent was atrocious. Emmanuel followed her into a narrow hall, where the furniture struck him as being quite foreign to Vienna. It had the appearance of having been torn up by its roots and transplanted. A faint smell of beeswax and turpentine hung on the air.

'Miss Brightwin will see you, sir.'

He followed her again, into a small room, which in its turn was filled with queer, heavy furniture, too big for it. A woman rose and came towards him. Tall, and not unlike her own maid, with a long, narrow face like a good-tempered horse, hair which was dragged back from a high, bumpy forehead, and kindly grey eyes which peered at him from behind strong, gold-rimmed glasses.

'Herr Gollantz? You were sent here by Baroness Lukoes, my maid tells me.'

'Yes, Fräulein.'

'Come and sit down. I am expecting the baroness any moment. Any friend of hers is welcome here. Ellen, bring tea, and make toast. You know how the baroness likes it. Now, Herr Gollantz, come and sit down.'

Emmanuel hesitated. A friend of Caroline's. . . . The position was a little difficult. Could he claim friendship? On the other hand it was impossible to explain that he loved her, that she filled his whole horizon. He smiled, and Marion Brightwin thought, as she watched him: 'What a delightful young man! If only Caro could have married someone like this, instead of that detestable Stanislaus!'

'I don't know that I can claim to be a friend,' Emmanuel said. 'The baroness has been very gracious to me, and I am very grateful to her. I am an antique dealer from whom she has bought a number of things.'

The grey eyes twinkled. 'Even antique dealers can sit down, Herr Gollantz. And, listen—here is the baroness—she shall decide what is your exact position in her scheme of things.'

He stood perfectly still, and the sudden change in his expression told Caroline's one-time governess all that she wanted to know. The door was flung open and Caroline entered.

'Marion, I know I'm late, don't be angry with me. I was detained. . . .' Then she saw Emmanuel's tall figure as he stood on the farther side of the fireplace. She dropped Miss Brightwin's hand, laughed suddenly, and said: 'Oh, you got here first. Marion, he wants to learn English. Have you begun your lesson?'

'I proposed to begin it with tea and buttered toast,' Marion Brightwin said. 'Herr Gollantz seemed to be in some doubt as to whether it was entirely permissible. He almost refuses to admit that he is a friend of yours.'

Caroline's laughing eyes met his. He thought that he had never seen her look so young, so vital, or so attractive. Her golden eyes were brighter than ever.

'Herr Gollantz is very stupid and Viennese,' she said. 'What does it matter? Here at Marion's house we're in England—no longer living in the shadow of sixteen quarterings! Now, for the rest of the time we are here, we speak English. You haven't said "How do you do" to me.'

Emmanuel bowed, her hand in his. ' 'Ow do you doo, plese?'

Miss Brightwin was at the door, calling some order to Ellen in the kitchen.

'Is that all the English you know?' Caroline whispered.

He shook his head. 'No—leesten—I loff you very march,' he whispered.

179

4

WEEKS passed, and Emmanuel Gollantz found that his devotion to Caroline Lukoes increased daily. He discovered that she was totally unlike the Jewish and Austrian women he had met ; her mind was more individual, her ideas were her own, not the well-worn beliefs of others. She had the courage of her opinions, and was interested in subjects other than the latest waltz, the latest scandal, and the latest rumour from the court.

Almost every day he visited the little house in the quiet street and talked in his halting English to the two women. Marion Brightwin might lack physical charm, but she possessed a fine intelligence, and when Emmanuel listened to her discussing literature, poetry, or English politics with her old pupil, he was filled with admiration.

That she liked him was evident from the warm welcome which she never failed to give him ; what puzzled him a little was how much she understood of his feelings for Caroline. He rarely saw the baroness alone for more than a few moments, for Marion Brightwin was the best of chaperones and did her duty admirably. The only time they were alone were the brief moments when Miss Brightwin went to bring out cake or biscuits from her store cupboard. Those moments were to Emmanuel what water might be to a man consumed with thirst. They were something too precious to be wasted by asking questions as to what Miss Brightwin knew or did not know.

'Caroline—how wonderful to be alone with you!'

His arms would be round her and he would whisper all the tender, intimate assurances of love which had been repressed for twenty-four hours.

'You still love me, Emmanuel?'

'Still? Always, for ever. I have only one regret—I never see you alone, Caroline. Why?'

'S-sh!' Her fingers would be laid lightly on his lips. 'Be patient ; only be patient, Emmanuel.'

It was a difficult life for a young man who was terribly in love, and Emmanuel Gollantz had reason to congratulate himself that he possessed self-control and restraint. He possessed also a sense of humour, and there were times when his lips curved into a smile as he remembered that he had spent two hours with the woman he loved and her late governess, and that the conversation had been concerning the relative values of Heine and Lord Byron.

He had been visited by the Princess Dietrich, who had spent long hours in his show-rooms, seated in a Louis XIV chair, her draperies carefully disposed round her, playing the part of a visiting queen. He watched her graceful movements and compared them with those of his mother's white Persian cat. He noticed the clear skin, the large blue eyes, and thought again that she was like some beautifully painted, but utterly conventional portrait by a French artist. He flattered her gracefully; he spent hours searching for the amusing trifles she liked—patch-boxes, old musical boxes, queer packs of playing-cards, counters of mother-of-pearl, elaborate chess-men of carved red and white ivory—these things amused and interested her. She cared for nothing which in order to be appreciated demanded real knowledge.

'I like pretty things,' she told him. 'I want to be amused. My life is so tragically dull in that great, dreary palace!' She would look at him and sigh. 'Oh, dear—and all I really want is happiness.'

Then one morning she confided in him that her husband bored her. She admitted that he was not unkind, 'And he is certainly not a wild beast like the man poor Caroline Lukoes married, but he is so dull! I know quite certainly that one day I shall fall in love, and then—I am afraid to think what might happen!'

Emmanuel listened, amused and able to estimate how much truth there was in her assertion. He thought that if any woman was capable of extracting amusement from life, that woman was certainly Maria Dietrich.

'Why do I talk in this way to you?' she demanded. 'I suppose it is because I feel you understand, I feel that you are my friend, and that I can trust you.' She sighed again and lowered her eyes suddenly.

'My grandmother used to say,' Emmanuel said, 'that no beautiful woman could ever afford to trust a man, no matter how trustworthy he appeared.'

'Oh—don't you want me to trust you?'

'I might be more flattered if you said that you dared not do so.'

She rose; the lace at her breast fluttered, her eyes were averted.

'I think—I think, perhaps, that you had better take me to my carriage.'

He offered her his arm and knew that as her fingers lay on his coat sleeve they tightened suddenly. He made no sign; it was a game, a game which no one understood better than Maria Dietrich. She meant nothing to him, and—in reality—he meant nothing to her. Emmanuel had no illusions. It amused her to pretend that she found him attractive, and she found it quite impossible to imagine that she did not make an irresistible appeal to him.

As she entered her carriage, she turned and whispered: 'These visits are growing too precious—that means they are dangerous!' She laughed softly. 'Or that you are.'

Emmanuel bowed: 'Whichever Your Highness pleases.'

He was thankful at this time that his life was filled with Caroline, for his home had ceased to have any attraction for him. It seemed that his mother was determined to atone to Jean for the temptation which had been thrown in his way by the unfortunate Gerta. She petted the youth, prepared the foods which he liked best, spent money on him, and generally encouraged him to think a great deal of himself. It appeared to Emmanuel that she gave all her affection to her brother's son and retained none for her own.

His father, who had suffered terribly after the scene when Emmanuel had vindicated himself, felt a sense of shame whenever he remembered the incident, but he was too weak, too lacking in determination to refer to it, talk it out, and try to begin again with a firmer basis in Emmanuel's affection. The fact that Emmanuel had loved him, had shown him tender consideration and now offered no more than cold politeness and grave attention, hurt him unbearably. He longed for the old pleasant affection, and yet lacked the strength of will to try to restore it. True, he made a few spasmodic efforts, always wanting in firmness, to get the relations between himself and Emmanuel on a better footing.

'I am going to the sale at Melchoirs this morning, Emmanuel. There are some interesting lots, I see, in the catalogue.'

'Indeed, Father? I hope you will be fortunate. Baron Voronich was asking for a silver epergne—perhaps if you see one you might remember.'

Hermann would hesitate, look at his handsome son a little wistfully.

'You—you wouldnt care to come with me, Emmanuel?'

'Certainly I will come, if you particularly wish it, Father.'

'No, no, not if you have other plans. I thought it might interest you.'

And the breach between them would grow a little wider. Emmanuel shrugging his shoulders, would decide that his father didn't really want him particularly ; if he had done he would have pressed his point. Hermann would sigh, and think regretfully of the days when Emmanuel accompanied him, and of what fun it had been to listen to his comments on the lots and the men who were bidding for them.

II

He found Miss Brightwin alone when he called on the afternoon of the day on which Maria Dietrich had visited him. He tried to hide his disappointment, tried to keep his eyes from the door every time it opened to admit Ellen with tea, cakes, or additional hot water, but he found it difficult.

'I don't think that Caroline will be here this afternoon, Mr. Gollantz.'

'No?' He made a great effort to keep his voice even. 'She's not ill?'

'Her husband is. . . . Oh, his own fault, but nevertheless, she feels that she must be at hand should she be needed. Poor Caro!'

Emmanuel threw up his head, as if he suddenly felt the need for air.

'It is unthinkable! Horrible! That she should be tied to that terrible man—not a man at all! Oh, everyone knows of his debaucheries ; it is common property.'

Marion Brightwin poured out the fragrant China tea with grave attention. Not until Emmanuel had taken his cup from her with a hand which shook slightly, did she speak.

'I have known Caro for a very long time, Herr Gollantz ; since she was eight years old. I think I know and understand her better than anyone. That is why—I am going to be quite frank with you —I have allowed you both to make my house a meeting-place. It is very dangerous. If the baron found out I should probably have to leave Vienna—he is very powerful. I am trusting—believing—that he will not find out. I am quite consciously using you to safeguard Caro. That is not a very commendable thing to do, Herr Gollantz, and you may dislike me intensely for it.'

'I don't think that I understand. . . .'

183

'Caro is past thirty. She is vital and very attractive. She hates her husband. She wants romance, kindness—love. He gives her none of these things. These years are the most difficult. Later, her vitality will diminish, she will find consolation in her books—perhaps in her children. Life will be easier for her. At the moment you supply what she needs most. I trust you as I would never trust some young Austrian officer, as I could never trust any of the men about the court. You're different. Oh, I admit that where Caro is concerned I am unscrupulous; she is the only person I have ever loved devotedly, she means everything to me. Now, tell me that you are indignant, that you consider me a scheming old harridan.'

Emmanuel sipped his tea, then set down the cup. 'No!' he said. 'You see, Mees Brightveen, I don't mind in the smallest. Eff it is true zat I haff—no, em—I em off use to Keroline—zen I em gretified—no, set-is-fied. I haff no ozzer veesh.'

'Suppose we speak in German! That shows a marked improvement, but your own language will be easier for you. Do you really mean that, or is it merely the romantic expression of a young man who fancies himself in love?'

He shrugged his shoulders. 'I am disappointed, Fräulein. I had believed you to be a woman of great intelligence. Do you think that a young man who imagines himself in love would come here day after day, and be satisfied with a love affair run on these— what shall I say?—distinctly formal lines?'

'Do you mean to tell me that you and Caro never see each other anywhere except here?'

'I do—assuredly.'

Her grey eyes watched him intently from behind their gold-rimmed glasses.

'My dear young man!' she exclaimed. 'I didn't know that. How both you and Caro must dislike me, and what a blind old bat I've been. You poor children!' She left her chair and came and stood beside him, her hand on his shoulder. 'Promise me that you'll not allow her to run into danger, Emmanuel,' she said. 'I may be a very wicked woman, but I can't deny her a little happiness. There will be so many years ahead of her when she won't have you— or me.'

'I shall always be there if she wants me.'

'It is only possible for poor and unimportant people to have the things they want most—need most,' Marion Brightwin said. 'You cannot incur debts without knowing that you will be pressed for payment one day. Caroline—at her father and mother's instigation—incurred a debt. She'll have to pay it, and it will be impossible for the Baroness Stanislaus Lukoes to have—everything she wants.'

'No, I understand. I find it very dreadful to think of that time.'

As he stood there, his handsome face very grave, his hands clenched in an agony of intensity, the door opened and Caroline entered. At the sound of her voice Emmanuel's face changed, and Marion Brightwin, watching him, thought that life was not going to be easy for Emmanuel Gollantz. He might not give his heart very often, but when he gave it he kept nothing back. His love was complete and entirely generous.

'Marion—Emmanuel—say that you're glad to see me! I couldn't face it any longer. All night long. Horrible, degrading, and oh, so nerve-racking. Verschagen has been and administered a drug to make him sleep.' She held out her hand to Emmanuel. 'And so I ran away to you and Marion and peace.'

Miss Brightwin pushed her gently into a chair. 'I'll go and make fresh tea—Ellen is out. Sit there and rest.'

Emmanuel knelt beside her, his arms round her. She let her head rest on his shoulder. 'Oh, Emmanuel, you smell so nice. What is it? Scent?'

He laughed softly. 'Eau de Cologne—I like it, it smells clean.'

'I don't feel that I shall ever be clean again,' Caroline said. 'My dear, why do we have to live like this? I want to see you every hour of the day, I want to dance with you, dine with you, I want you to take me to amusing restaurants——'

'And I want so much more than that! Oh, Caroline, I love you so. Kiss me, Caro—tell me that when you are here with me you can forget all the horrible things. Oh, that abominable man, how I hate him! How I wish that I could challenge him, kill him, and set you free! Why didn't I meet you before—years ago, when things were quite different?'

She held his face between her hands. 'Because years ago you would have been a small boy in a wide collar and short jacket, like the picture you showed me the other day. Remember that I am ten years older than you are, Emmanuel. Why, even now I sometimes wonder if—well, if it's not a pity for you to begin— like this.'

His tone was indignant. 'Caro—like this! This is almost perfect. How can you say such things?'

'I don't know. . . .' Her voice was more gentle than he had ever

185

heard it. 'You're so young, unspoilt, and you're learning in a school which will teach you to conceal, to pretend. An intrigue with a married woman many years your senior!'

'Years don't matter if we love each other,' Emmanuel protested.

'Years always matter terribly, my dearest,' she said.

With his arms round her Caroline knew that she felt her overwrought nerves relax, felt that the horrors which she had been forced to witness for the past days retreated into the background. Stanislaus, with his purple face, staring eyes, and slack, moist mouth had nothing in common with this young Jew, gentle, dignified, and kindly. They belonged to different worlds; they lived their lives by different codes. And yet—she almost smiled when she remembered that to Stanislaus young Emmanuel Gollantz was the member of a class which he held to be despicable. As a Jew he could never hope for admission to those sacred circles which opened their doors to Stanislaus Lukoes. That society might admit drunkards, libertines, loose-livers, and gamesters—but Jews were unthinkable.

Emmanuel was not even a Jewish financier; he was a tradesman pure and simple, a man who bought and sold, who treated his clients with the respect which their station demanded. His beauty, his education, his dignity all went for nothing.

Stanislaus might drink until he became lower than the beasts, but he remained a Polish baron of distinguished ancestry. Young Guchowski might boast—as he did among his brother officers—that he was in debt to every tradesman in Vienna, that he had never found a woman who retained any charm or mystery after one night had been spent in her company, but he considered himself the undoubted superior of all those men whose bills he obstinately refused to pay. Ugly Mayerhausen, who possessed the best figure of any officer in the Imperial Army, was so conceited and so unbearably self-centred that he bored one to extinction in five minutes, but because he and his forefathers had held the same patch of utterly unproductive forest land for five centuries he was accepted everywhere. Oh what a queer, muddle-headed world it was!

Emmanuel stood before her, talking in his soft, almost lisping Viennese, his face alight with happiness, his whole bearing that of a man who is finding life full of beauty. The thought struck her: 'How magnificent he would look in uniform! The white tunic, with its gold lace and scarlet sash. The long, narrow blue trousers strapped under the shining boots. What a joy to dance with him at one of the Imperial balls, instead of waltzing perpetually with young men who, while they might dance superbly, spoke in the mechanical *clichés* which the Emperor had made acceptable as conversation.'

'Emmanuel, can't you come to the ball next week? Masked—such fun!'

He smiled, he was too happy to allow anything to make him bitter.

'Have you forgotten my name?' he asked. 'Shall I repeat it for you?'

'Oh! It's so stupid! I want to see you there—in uniform—to dance with you, laugh with you, stand on one of the balconies and listen to a Strauss waltz. I want to clink glasses with you and watch the bubbles rise in that sickly sweet pink champagne whose only recommendation is that it is pretty!'

Marion Brightwin said with mock severity: 'Caro, you're talking like a sentimental schoolgirl!'

'I feel rather like one—a schoolgirl who must go back to school in a very few moments! Oh, Emmanuel, wouldn't it be fun?'

He smiled down at her, his smile touched with gravity. She felt that he had been right; the years did not matter—at that moment he was older than she was.

'Do you want it very much?' he asked.

'Terribly!'

'Then it is obvious that I must obey.'

Impulsively, Marion cried: 'Caro, don't allow him to do anything foolish. You mustn't risk a scandal, you know that! Emmanuel, don't be stupid.'

'I have been reminding you that I am a Jew,' he said. 'With the danger of seeming tedious, I must repeat it. Jews never take risks; didn't you know that? Baroness, I shall do my best to obey you in this—as in everything.'

Emmanuel went home after leaving Miss Brightwin's, his heart aflame. Caroline's wish that she might dance with him seemed to him an indication that she, like himself, longed for their relationship to be closer and more intimate. She was not content that their meetings should be restricted to afternoons spent with her governess, however understanding and kindly that lady might be. To dance with him—that in itself was nothing; it was the implication, the meaning which lay beneath.

187

He thought too—if only he could enter this particular ball, it might be possible to persuade Caroline to attend others. True, this was given by those who moved in the highest circles, given for their own associates, and the masking was merely to give an additional air of romance. This was no ordinary masked ball, to which students, nobility, even superior tradesmen might obtain entrance. This was a ball given by the Princess Battista, and a select—a very select—committee of ladies. The proceeds were destined for some worthy cause—to provide new clothes for the orphans of some asylum, or endow new wards in the hospital, perhaps. 'I have forgotten,' Emmanuel thought, 'and probably so have the entire committee!'

He arrived home to find Stephan Gustave waiting for him. Gustave was growing stouter, his face was rosier than ever, his clothes always appeared a little too tight for his corpulent figure. He was successful, and he was deeply in love with Minna Rosenfeldt, the soubrette, who sang his music so charmingly. Minna was not singing that evening; he had just sold a new opera, and the world was a fine place in which to live.

'And so, tonight,' Gustave cried, 'I make merry. My friends will come and drink to the success of my latest and finest work. All day I have been looking for you—for are not you my best and dearest friend?'

Later, Emmanuel found the rooms of his apartment in the Karntnerstrasse filled with well-dressed people. Everyone knew Gustave, and everyone liked him. Singers rubbed shoulders with young diplomats, actors talked with painters, journalists imparted their latest news to rising financiers, and here and there the brilliant uniforms of officers gave an additional sparkle to the crowd. The men came, but they left their women behind them when they mixed with the Bohemians.

Emmanuel, in his severe evening clothes of smooth fine cloth, with the high white cravat and frilled shirt which he still affected in defiance of fashion, his height, his good looks and his general appearance of dressing to suit himself and not to obey the dictates of other people, caused every woman and a good many men to turn their heads to watch him.

He was well known in Vienna, and was declared by the women of his own race to be the most handsome young man in the town. It was said that had he exerted himself there were many Gentile women of fashion who would have been willing to overlook his social status and his Jewish birth for the sake of his looks. He was something of a mystery, this young Emmanuel Gollantz, they decided. He talked with everyone, but singled out no woman in particular as the object of his attentions. His name was connected with no one ; rumour did not credit him with a trail of broken hearts, expensive mistresses, or immense gambling debts.

He had been responsible for the mounting and general *décor* of two of Gustave's most successful works ; he had been in and about the theatre, but he had never attempted to take any part in the life which went on there. Ladies of the chorus had not found him a suppliant for their favours. He had smiled, laughed congratulated them—and gone his way.

Minna Rosenfeldt said to Gustave: 'This young Emmanuel of yours is either a very great fool or a very wise fellow. I have not yet decided which.'

Emmanuel enjoyed the evening. He felt elated and confident. Caroline loved him ; she had been kind—and who knew what the future might hold! He even indulged in dreams, dreams which were so beautiful, so tender that the recollection of them made his lips curve into a smile.

Gustave's rooms were handsome and spacious, Gustave's food was excellent, and Gustave's wines were admirable—if just a little heady.

'Gustave has some queer friends!' Minna whispered to him behind her soft, fat hand. 'His latest addition to the collection is —what do you think?—an American. His name is Paul Minger. On his cards he has "Paul H. Minger". Look, there he is, yawning because he wants to go and play cards. It appears that Americans play cards all day long, and he has a new game called poker, which Gustave has learnt and likes so much already. I have learnt it also. I won a great deal last night. Jews are always good card players!'

Later, Emmanuel found himself standing by a table at which sat Gustave and the American, who spoke German with a queer, nasal inflection which Emmanuel found not unpleasant. It was, he thought, as if the language had been impregnated with vinegar. In addition there was Carl Osker, the tenor, and Lieutenant von Habenberg. The young soldier was dark, with curly hair. His face was pleasant and weak, but his hands betrayed him.

Emmanuel, watching them, thought : 'He is nervous, this man. His hands cannot keep quite still. He's a bad gambler—otherwise he would realize that the American has noticed his twitching fingers and read the sign correctly.'

The game progressed. Emmanuel's eyes followed the fall of

the cards and, while he refused to play, he derived some enjoyment from watching the others. Suddenly, a suspicion which had been growing in his mind became established. The American met his eyes across the table and, without moving a muscle of his face, dropped an eyelid. It was evident that he believed Emmanuel shared some secret with him.

The soldier was winning, and as each success was followed by another, so his stakes rose higher and higher. The amount of money on the table was considerable. The American's face was like a cold mask; neither Osker nor Gustave had noticed anything. At intervals Gustave exclaimed at his bad luck, or Osker declared that he was sick of losing every hand; otherwise the game progressed normally.

Emmanuel, standing with his shoulders against the mantelpiece, a cigar in his fingers, smoked and watched. The truth dawned upon him. He did not understand the finer points of the game, but he understood very clearly that the soldier was cheating his companions. In some way which Emmanuel could not fathom, he—provided that he dealt—possessed some knowledge of what cards they held. Only when he dealt the cards did his bets increase to a marked extent—and then he invariably won.

The Empire clock which stood on the mantelpiece behind Emmanuel's broad shoulders chimed two. The American finished the hand, paid, and rose.

'Well, I'm for home,' he said. 'Herr Gustave has work to do.'

The others stood up, pushing back their chairs. Osker admitted that it was time he went home, Gustave yawned frankly and talked of a heavy day tomorrow; the other guests had gone. Emmanuel, von Habenberg, and the American left the apartment together.

'Come back to Hôtel Sacher with me, boys, and have a last drink.'

Emmanuel hesitated. He was perfectly certain that the American had seen as much as he had; he was equally certain that he wished to speak of what he had noticed.

The soldier hesitated, then said: 'Well, why not? Perhaps we might have another little game of cards.'

'Well, we might do that,' the American drawled.

In his private sitting-room at the Hôtel Sacher, the American busied himself with producing bottles which he set before them.

'This, Mr. Gollantz, is real American whisky. I commend it to you.' He continued with a scarcely noticeable break: 'An' while

190

we drink it, you might tell me what we're going to do with this young gentleman here.'

Von Habenberg started, his hand closed tightly on the back of one of the gilt chairs, the knuckles showed bloodless. Emmanuel could not force himself to meet his eyes. He had no particular love for the army; he was not actually an Austrian, but he felt a sensation of horror that a stranger should be in a position to accuse one of the nobility of Vienna. Von Habenberg was young, scarcely more than a boy; Emmanuel knew him to be the son of dignified parents, people of integrity and great social standing. A breath of scandal such as this would end the boy's career, spell ruin, and probably break his parents' hearts.

The American had lost very little. Gustave and Osker were both rich men. No one was seriously affected. Emmanuel turned and forced himself to meet von Habenberg's eyes. They were staring into his, wide, frightened, beseeching. His forehead was damp, the dark curls clung to it, heavy with moisture. Emmanuel drew a deep breath.

'I am afraid, Mr. Minger, that I don't follow you.'

The American, his hands busy with bottles and glasses, looked up. 'What?' he exclaimed. 'I don't get you, Mr. Gollantz.'

'Then we are alike,' Emmanuel said, smiling, 'for I admit that I don't understand you. Possibly the lieutenant does?'

Von Habenberg licked his dry lips. 'I don't know what he means, I'm sure.'

'Say, what is this?' Minger asked. 'Is this some bluff? What are you trying to put over on me, you two? Mr. Gollantz, are you in this?'

'I am—in nothing,' Emmanuel protested. 'I have never met Herr Lieutenant before this evening. I can only repeat that I do not understand you. Is this my glass? Thank you.' He sipped the whisky and water which his host had poured out for him, finished it, and set down the glass. 'It's—interesting—a new experience for me.'

The tall, thin American smiled suddenly. 'One good turn deserves another, and as you've certainly given me a new experience this evening, take this as my contribution. What about these show-rooms of yours, Mr. Gollantz. I'd like to run around to-morrow and take a look at them, if I may?'

'And now,' Emmanuel turned to von Habenberg, 'if you are ready, we won't keep Mr. Minger out of his bed any longer.'

5

I

DURING their walk from the Hôtel Sacher to the Bargerspital,
von Habenberg did not speak, except to ask: 'Where are we
going?'

Emmanuel replied: 'To my home. It is not very far, Herr
Lieutenant.'

They paced on silently and their footsteps rang out clearly in
the still night air. Von Habenberg's mind was in a turmoil. What
was this young Jew going to demand? It was obvious that he was
playing a hand on his own, that he had no wish to include Minger
in his plans. Money, the young soldier decided—that was going
to be the price of silence. He remembered the stories which he had
heard, of men like himself, heavily in debt, goaded almost to madness by the importunities of their creditors, who had been unable
to resist temptation. Gollantz, standing behind him as he dealt,
had seen what had happened, and now intended to make the best
and most material use of his knowledge.

Money—von Habenberg shivered and drew his cloak closer
round his shoulders. The thought chilled him, and yet he knew
that in this case it must be found, or that he must face utter and
entire disgrace. Some huge sum demanded by this cool young
Jew, raised—heaven only knew how—and then at intervals further demands, every one of which would have to be paid.

He watched Emmanuel, who paced beside him, and wondered
if it would be possible to pick a quarrel with the fellow, to challenge him, and end the whole matter once and for all. Rapiers, a
pistol, and the thing would be over in a few moments—it seemed
improbable that a Jew tradesman would know much about the
science of arms! Von Habenberg frowned. Impossible ; that road
was closed. How could he challenge this man who belonged to a
different order, a different nationality?

What a fool he had been! What a mess to have landed into.
How could he have believed that cheating at cards would be the
solution of his problems? He had been mad. First the girl at
the opera, a dancer with a face like a flower and the acquisitive
mentality of a jackdaw! Clothes, jewels, a carriage, servants, and

an elegant apartment. Racing debts, cards, speculations which had been so successful at first, and which lately had never brought anything but additional debts! How often had his father warned him never to allow himself to 'get into the hands of the Jews'! Yet here he was being marched along at the order of one of them, so that he might have terms dictated to him.

'If only I had sufficient courage,' he thought, 'I should blow my brains out and end it all. That might be the cleanest way out, a bullet—extinction. Oh, God, why didn't I exercise a little will-power? Why didn't I look ahead, and realize that a day of reckoning must come, inevitably, sooner or later? It's horrible—horrible.'

Emmanuel halted suddenly, at the entrance to a huge court-yard.

'My home is in here, Herr Lieutenant, please follow me.' He crossed the courtyard, and opened a heavy door which gave on to a wide hall filled with beautiful old furniture. Von Habenberg, despite his misery, could not help noticing the subdued splendour of the place. Emmanuel turned, and the light from an old oil lamp which had once illuminated some Turkish mosque shone down on his face. He was smiling.

'Would you mind coming to my own room? It is rather apart from the rest of the house and we shall not disturb my father and mother. Along here.'

The room which they entered was half bedroom, half study. There was a great French bed with olive-green brocade hangings, looped with old gold cords, covered with a magnificent piece of embroidery. In the window stood a writing-desk, inlaid with tortoise-shell, with graceful silver handles. There were many shelves holding books in rare bindings ; there was a dressing-table, covered with toilet articles mounted in silver ; a huge wardrobe occupied one side of the room, its polished wood catching the light, gleaming warm and smooth. The room was splendid, it was even luxurious, but there was a restraint about its furnishing which was very attractive, and prevented it being merely the room of an idle and comfort-loving young man. It was, in addition, the room of a student and a man of taste.

Emmanuel pointed to a chair.

'Will you let me offer you a glass of brandy?' he asked. 'I can recommend it—it belonged to my grandfather.'

Von Habenberg's face was suddenly convulsed with rage. 'For God's sake don't torture me!' he exclaimed. 'Have you brought me here to play with me? Tell me why you behaved as you did before Minger, and what you are going to demand from me? I can't bear this suspense—this play-acting.'

Emmanuel stared at him for a moment, then swung off his cloak and threw it over the back of a Louis XVI chair. 'Why I behaved as I did?' he said gently. 'I wonder if I can tell you, Herr Lieutenant, and not make myself appear to be a rank sentimentalist? Sit down, I beg of you, and let me give you something to drink. Don't be apprehensive.'

He spoke so simply that von Habenberg sank into the chair and accepted the big goblet, at the bottom of which reposed the golden liquid which was nearly a hundred years old.

Emmanuel, a goblet in his own hand, stood with one foot on the fender of hand-worked steel, and began to speak very softly.

'It is a little difficult to explain,' he said. 'I shall ask you to be patient with me. It was through no particular desire to help you; it was a more personal matter. I am not an Austrian, I am a Jew —my grandfather was Dutch, my grandmother Italian. On him and on her be peace! I have lived in Wien all my life. I have been —except for one or two periods—very happy. Through your class my father and I have made a very adequate living. We are grateful.

'Minger—who, I am sure, is an estimable person—is an American. He will take back his opinions and impressions to his own country, he will argue from the particular to the general. Frankly, Herr Lieutenant, I did not feel it incumbent upon me to join hands with a man of another race, to—please forgive me—dishonour the country which is mine by adoption. Your father has been instrumental in advancing many reforms which have benefited us all. He is a representative of the best of Viennese society.' His lips curved suddenly, as if he remembered something very beautiful. 'I have a particular reason for wishing to protect the honour of that exalted class to which you belong, because of the regard I feel for one of its members. There, I have told you my reasons—not really altruistic, you see.'

Von Habenberg stared at him, incredulous and frowning. It was coming. 'Not altruistic'—that was the beginning. After all his fine phrases and his wonderful air of frankness, the fellow was going to state his demands. Well, let him! There was always a pistol, and it would be over quickly.

'Yes, and now?' von Habenberg demanded.

194

'And now, I am going to venture to make conditions,' Emmanuel said very quietly.

'Ah! I expected this! Go on, please.'

The young soldier rose and stood, tense and white-faced, before Emmanuel. They were of an equal height and there was little difference in their ages.

Emmanuel sipped his brandy and set down the goblet. The smile had died, and suddenly the face had hardened, grown cold. When he spoke, his voice was like a wind blowing off the Alps— von Habenberg felt the chill which it carried.

'I understand. I am sorry to have kept you waiting. My demand can be stated very briefly. You will never play cards again in Vienna or any other place in Austria, Lieutenant von Habenberg. That is my demand.'

'And what else?' The words came from dry lips. 'Go on, state the material demands.'

'If I did not realize that you were suffering under considerable strain,' Emmanuel said, 'I should waste the remainder of this excellent brandy by flinging it in your face. How dare you? Let me come with you, and show you the door into the courtyard, Lieutenant. There is no more to be said, except to wish you— good morning.'

Von Habenberg's eyes stared at Emmanuel's controlled face. He blinked them stupidly, like a man who enters a brilliantly lighted room from outer darkness. His lips moved soundlessly, his mouth twitched, his eyes were suddenly childishly bewildered, even pathetic.

'You mean—you can't mean that all you demand—is that I shan't play cards again! It's impossible—I—don't believe it. You're trying to trick me. For the love of God and His Blessed Mother, don't torture me! It's—cruel—I can't bear it! Don't you see that you can break my whole life?'

The tears which he had struggled to keep back overcame him and, covering his face with his hands, he sank back into the chair, sobbing wildly. He was no longer an officer in the Imperial Army, he was only Max von Habenberg, twenty-one, very miserable and terribly frightened.

Emmanuel watched him for a moment, then laid his hand on the boy's shoulder.

'Please don't! I beg of you, don't distress yourself so. I have told you everything, I swear it. I am keeping nothing back. I am not a money-lender, I am a man who, like yourself, wants to be happy. There, lift your head, let me hear you agree to what I ask, and—it is all forgotten! I am a very simple person, and I stated my condition quite simply, that is all.'

The shaking hands were lowered and a tear-stained face was raised, while the still confused dark eyes met his. 'I can't believe it—it seems impossible. Why should you do this for me?'

'I don't, I have told you that I don't. I do it for the'—he laughed softly—'the high world of Vienna, into which I shall never enter.'

'Oh God!' A sob caught his throat again. 'I've been so wretched. I'm head over ears in debt ; the money-lenders are at my heels day in, day out. I'm afraid to tell my father—I owe so much. I've been half frantic. Tonight I knew that Gustave and Osker knew scarcely anything of the game. I did. I met some Americans last winter. They taught me. I tried'—even now he found the word difficult to enunciate—'cheating then. It was so simple. Tonight I thought no one noticed, I imagined that the American had too much wine inside him to be very quick.'

'If you had tasted his whisky, you would have realized how little effect Gustave's champagne would have upon him,' Emmanuel said.

'I didn't know anything. I only knew that I was tired of being pressed for payment, that I was desperate. When he turned round and spoke to you in Sacher's, I thought that I should die of fear. I wanted to die. Gollantz, I don't know you, I had never met you until tonight. I have no words. Whatever I can say seems so poor and mean after what you have done. I swear that I will never play again.'

'Remember, it will be difficult,' Emmanuel said. 'Men will ask why, women will try to persuade you. It will need courage.'

'I tell you, I swear it. If you ever hear that I have played cards for money again, then I give you full leave to denounce me, and I swear that I will not defend myself.' He looked round the room, 'Have you a Testament here, so that I may take an oath for you?'

'I regret—I have no Testament. You forget we are Jews. Would the Talmud satisfy you?' Emmanuel smiled.

'I don't care what it is! I don't care what you are—Jews, Turks, Greeks, Lutherans—I only know that you'—his face flushed, he looked very young indeed—'you seem like the dearest, wisest brother to me.'

'I don't want an oath—your word is an oath. Now it only remains for both of us to forget what has happened. It is over! Indeed, I begin to wonder if it ever happened, Lieutenant.'

196

A cloud passed over the other's face; some of the brightness left it.

'But tomorrow, if Minger comes to see you. . . . When he asks you—what will you say? You'll have to offer something—won't you?'

'I shall assuredly not offer him this brandy,' Emmanuel said; 'and let me give you a little more. It is so good. I shall offer him a decoction of Alpine roots, very raw and fiery. He will appreciate it. I shall probably sell him a picture, possibly two, and some candlesticks. Oh yes, certainly some candlesticks! I think that will be all.'

'But,' von Habenberg came near, and laid his hand on Emmanuel's arm, 'if he mentions me, if he asks if you saw—what happened? What then?'

'Then, oh, well . . .' Emmanuel shrugged his shoulders as if so remote a possibility were not worth consideration. 'If he is so foolish, I shall remind him that I owe a certain duty to my friends —if that won't offend you—and suggest that if his eyes really deceived him to such an extent, I must offer him my services with a pistol—the day after tomorrow, to improve them. You see, he is only a tradesman—like myself, and he could have no possible excuse for not meeting me. But, believe me, it won't happen! I think you may safely disregard that possibility. There is only one thing. I do recommend you to tell your father of your debts. Oh, don't think that I am preaching, I am talking business. I know the preposterous percentages these people demand, I know that you will never get away from them unless you make a supreme effort. After all, the Imperial Army is an expensive profession; everyone knows that.'

Max von Habenberg nodded. His courage was returning, and he no longer felt hopeless and desperate. He loved his father, and knew that though he might have to face a short, sharp scene, it would pass and be forgotten.

'You're right. I will.' He held out his hand. 'If you care to take it I shall be very proud. I wish'—he flushed and looked very boyish—'I do so sincerely wish that there was something I could do to show my gratitude to you. Think—isn't there anything?'

Emmanuel did not reply for a moment, but stood frowning, pinching his lower lip between his finger and thumb. A moment later his face cleared, and he smiled at von Habenberg. 'I wonder . . .' he murmured. 'It seems fantastic, but it might be worth trying. Do you dance?' he asked abruptly.

'I hate it! I have to attend state balls and stupidities of that kind, but I dislike it—always have done.'

'Ah! Then I shall not be depriving you. I, on the other hand, like dancing tremendously. I want very much to attend the masquerade—I think you might be able to help me.'

'You want an invitation?' Von Habenberg was distressed. Here was a man who had done him a great service, who had shown him exquisite courtesy and genuine kindness, but who was asking the impossible. How could he go to the Chamberlain and ask for an invitation for Emmanuel Gollantz, the Jew art dealer—however handsome, however charming he might be! Yet to refuse might be to hurt this splendid fellow terribly. It was almost as if Emmanuel had demanded an insult. Von Habenberg's face lost its look of alertness, and appeared suddenly uncertain and miserable.

Emmanuel noticed the change of expression. 'I am afraid that you do not quite understand me,' he said. 'I am not asking that you should try to obtain a card for me—through the official channels. I am asking you to join me in a sort of minor conspiracy. Let me use yours.'

'Mine?' The young man's face cleared. He was sufficiently young to regard any escapade in the light of an adventure; he cared nothing for the stiff conventionality of the court, and to circumvent it in any way appealed to his sense of fun. 'You mean that—wearing a mask—you'd go—as me!' He laughed. 'Herr Gollantz, isn't there a romance behind this?'

'It is possible.'

'I was certain of it! Now, we must think. We are of a height—both dark. You would have to remain carefully masked, remember. I dare not risk either of us being discovered. . . . I have it! On the night of the ball I shall come here to visit you. You will admit me to this room, where you will put on my mask and uniform. As you leave—leaving here as me, you understand—I shall say in a loud voice, "Many thanks, Herr Gollantz," and you will reply that you hope I shall enjoy the ball, and declare that you are going to shut yourself in this room and read quietly for the rest of the evening. I will remain here until you return, when you will let me out unobserved. That will meet the case I think! I have a brain which lends itself to strategy.'

Emmanuel walked to the end of the road where his father's house was situated, then stopped a carriage which was plying for hire, and drove to the great hall where the masked ball was to be held. The fact that the driver, with his forefinger lifted to his shining hat, replied in answer to the order: 'Yes, Herr Lieutenant!' gave him courage. He entered, holding his head high, his face covered by his black silk mask.

The great room was lit entirely by candles; hundreds and hundreds of them burnt in the great candelabra and in the sconces on the brocade-covered walls. He was early, for the ball did not begin until nine and it needed several minutes to that hour. Folding his arms, Emmanuel leant against the wall, near the door, his eyes watching the men and women who entered. He was both pleased and slightly amused to find that he experienced no sense of discomfort or embarrassment in wearing the magnificent uniform which belonged to von Habenberg. It fitted perfectly, and Emmanuel's little smile might have deepened had he known that the lieutenant was reputed to have the best figure in the Imperial Army.

Men and women were beginning to arrive; Emmanuel felt a thrill of pleasure at the sudden increase of colour in the great room. There were splashes of old rose, a delicious shade of faded blue moiré; he noticed the new shade of which Caroline had spoken—Teba, and decided that he didn't think much of it. The horrible crinoline had vanished, killed by the Empress of Austria and the Empress Eugénie. How much more lovely women looked, he thought, with dresses which allowed their own graceful lines to be seen, without the distorting effect of hoops and wire frames.

A stir at the farther end of the room and Johann Strauss entered with his orchestra. Emmanuel lifted his hand, then dropped it, amused at his own reaction to force of habit. Johann could certainly not see him, and if he did the mask concealed his features. He was conscious that his excitement was growing, that his heart was beating a little faster, and that he was silently rehearsing what he should say to Caroline.

He recognized many of the guests as they entered—many of them were his clients—and once again he felt a spasm of amusement. What if someone should ask him: 'Pray tell me who is the elderly man in the green uniform?'

'His name, General, is Kilspuel. He collects china under the guidance of Emmanuel Gollantz, for his own taste is deplorable.' Or again: 'Do you know the lady in the dress of lemon-yellow silk trimmed with feathers?' 'That is Baroness Sonnenburg, whose passion is old French books, rare—and as improper as possible. She asserts that she collects them for the love of the fine old paper and printing, but what she really enjoys are the salacious wood-cuts.'

There was old Prince Dietrich, and with him Maria, a vision in blue with silver fringe. Both were masked, but Emmanuel recognized Maria's quick, almost birdlike movements. Instinctively he snapped his fingers in sudden annoyance. Maria! He had forgotten her! His mind had held only thoughts of Caroline. He noticed the popular and talented Mathilde Wildauer, and his thoughts went back to that evening not very long ago, when he had heard her in that popular opera, *The Merry Wives of Windsor*. How good she had been, how he had laughed, how splendidly Schmid had sung and acted. Then—and had anyone watched Emmanuel intently, they might have seen that his pale face flushed suddenly—Baron Stanislaus Lukoes entered with Caroline.

He caught his breath as he watched her. How graceful she was, how animated, without ever losing either her charm or her dignity. She wore a dress of old rose, with long, silken fringe of a darker shade. Her hair was elaborate, with one curl which fell on to her white shoulder. The mask which she wore, Emmanuel thought, only served to accentuate the beauty of her skin and the dazzling brightness of her eyes.

As he watched her, he felt a sensation which was almost pain. He loved her so much, he wanted to walk over to her, catch her in his arms and defy the whole world to take her from him. His eyes devoured her, eager and intent. She turned, and he knew that she had seen him. She had seen through the disguise of the mask, she had recognized him in spite of his borrowed uniform. Her lips parted in a smile—that wide, generous smile that he loved—it was as if she sent a wordless message to where he stood.

'They may talk and write of the pleasure of loving,' Emmanuel thought. 'What fools they are. Love must always bring with it pain, uncertainty, resentment that time cannot stand still!'

He forced his eyes away from where Caroline stood. It was

dangerous to watch her for too long; he felt that he would betray himself, that it was utterly impossible that no one should notice his intent gaze and draw their own conclusions. With a sense of gratitude he heard the first notes of Strauss's latest waltz, and noticed the sudden ripple of expectancy among the company.

Now! His hour had begun! He must be careful, he must run no risks either for Caro or for himself. He watched Lukoes step forward, take her in his arms and begin to dance. How purple his face was, how shapeless he was growing. As they passed, Emmanuel's eyes met Caroline's for a second, and he noticed the beads of sweat which stood on Lukoes's forehead.

'He won't dance very much!' Emmanuel thought. 'Half a dozen turns will be too much for him.'

The waltz ended. Lukoes escorted his wife back to her seat, then, bending over her, appeared to make his excuses. He straightened his huge, ungainly figure and walked away. Emmanuel squared his shoulders and crossed the ball-room. A second later he was bowing before her.

'Will the gracious lady do me the great honour?'

The dancing eyes met his. 'Do I know you, Lieutenant?'

'Assuredly, Baroness. And my uniform is an introduction in itself.'

She handed him her programme with its little pencil hanging by a silk cord. 'I hope that you dance well.'

'I shall do my best.' He was scribbling a queer little cabalistic sign on her card. 'How generous are you prepared to be, Baroness Lukoes?'

'Moderately.' He handed back the card. 'Five, Lieutenant? Too many!'

He glanced towards the orchestra. 'The first is beginning.' He held out his hand. She rose and they moved forward. Emmanuel did not speak for some moments; his heart seemed as if it would suffocate him, he felt suddenly weak, almost lightheaded. Her face was so close to him; with the smallest movement he could have laid his cheek against hers. He could feel her breath soft on his neck, the scent which she used reached his nostrils.

'Caro—my wonderful, wonderful Caro!' he whispered.

'How did you get here?'

'I will tell you tomorrow. Now I cannot talk, I can only think.'

'Dear Emmanuel. . . .'

Later, she said: 'Maria is here. Be wise, and dance with her. If you dance only with me, people will notice it. Besides—Maria will take your presence here entirely to herself, and'—she laughed softly—'it is safer that she should.'

'I only wish to obey you.'

He stood before the princess, his heels together, bowing from the waist. Maria smiled, made some conventional remark about the floor and the orchestra, then handed him her programme.

'You are . . . you are . . .' She laughed. 'I've forgotten your name, Lieutenant.'

Emmanuel slipped his fingers inside his tunic where the card which had admitted him lay folded. He opened it and held it out for her inspection.

'Lieutenant von Habenberg,' she read. 'Of course. . . . But, I thought . . .'

'The next dance but one, may I have that?' Emmanuel asked.

Maria nodded, smiling, but her smile was puzzled. As they danced, her blue eyes met his.

'Your name is—von Habenberg?' she said.

'My real name is—Your Highness's Devoted Servant.'

He felt her draw her breath sharply. 'Emmanuel Gollantz! What are you doing here? Why have you come here?'

'I am dancing with Your Highness, I have come here to dance with Your Highness. Could I have better reasons? I cannot imagine what they could be.'

'My dear!' she whispered, satisfied and entranced. 'How daring, how dangerous! What if they found out?'

'I should explain that I am a haunted man, I should tell them what haunts me—and they would be filled with sympathy for me.'

'What haunts you?'

'The Vision of Perfection,' Emmanuel whispered back.

Caroline said, as they stood together in one of the little ante-rooms, looking out over the quiet square: 'Maria will be confident that you have come here to see her. She will hint to me of a romantic attachment when we meet.' She paused, laid her hand on his arm, and said: 'Tell me, tell me that you did not come here, take this risk, to dance with Maria Dietrich.'

He said: 'Caro, how can you ask such questions? There is no one, never will be anyone but you.'

'You're happy, content?'

Emmanuel turned suddenly and caught her in his arms, pressing his lips to her white shoulder. 'No, no!' he said urgently.

'Neither! This is not enough. I want so much more. Caro—beloved—I want you, I want long hours with you. You and I alone. I know you so well—and I know you so little. These hours, half-hours, they are like offering delightful sweets to a man who is dying of hunger. We were made for each other, darling.'

She lay in his arms, unprotesting, her eyes half closed, her lips parted.

'Listen, Emmanuel!' she whispered. 'Stanislaus is going away. Soon. The doctors advise a cure, a complete change. He will go to Aix, I think. Then . . . Oh, my dear, Tirol is so beautiful. A country for lovers.'

'A country for us, Caro. You promise—you won't be afraid?'

'With you! How could I be?'

'I shall see you tomorrow——'

'Yes—tomorrow. No, today, Emmanuel. It is long past midnight.'

In the card-room, where Baron Stanislaus Lukoes played whist for twenty gulden points and two hundred gulden on the rubber, with three other gentlemen of his own rank and character, a sudden quarrel began. Lukoes, his mind inflamed with perpetual drinking, stated that his partner played like a pickpocket. He added, in a voice which was like the bellowing of a wounded bull: 'Let me tell you that you have virtually robbed me of five thousand gulden this evening! If you aspire to play with gentlemen, you might at least learn to play like one!'

His partner rose ; he was tall and thin, with the heavy jowl of the Hapsburgs, and possessing their belief that the Almighty created the world and all that moved therein for their especial benefit. He glared, stammered, and finally hectored.

Lukoes howled insults, stated that he cared nothing for the bastards of any family, Imperial or not. 'In Poland, I'd hand you over to my servants, they'd deal with you!' The tumult grew, it was impossible to quieten either of them.

'My friends will wait on you tomorrow, Baron Stanislaus Lukoes!'

Lukoes staggered into a chair, his legs spread wide, his head thrown back, shouting with laughter. 'Polish noblemen don't fight with any except their equals. . . .'

The tall, thin, heavy-jawed man walked to the door. 'It would seem that it would be impossible to arrange duels with—pigs! For that reason there must be very little dueling in Poland!' He turned. 'All the same, my friends will wait on you.'

Lukoes yelled after his retreating figure: 'Let 'em! Come with
'em, and I'll teach you all how to play whist like gentlemen!
Damn you and your Imperial blood!'

6

I

EMMANUEL lifted his face so that he might feel the soft whispering wind which heralded the dawn. He knew that he was intoxi-
cated with love. He knew that, at that moment, nothing was too
dangerous, nothing too fantastic for him to attempt and accom-
plish. He was, at that hour, a super-man. As he walked, he rejoiced
in the easy movement of his limbs, in the knowledge that his body
was firm, supple, and in splendid training. It was good to feel the
play of his muscles when he moved his shoulders under the stiff
uniform tunic. He took a conscious pride in his body and its
beauty, a pride which had nothing in common with conceit, but
which was the outcome of an appreciation of perfect physical
fitness and a real love of beauty.

Caro had said that tomorrow—today—she would talk to him,
tell him of her plans so that they might snatch a few days from
the restraint in which they lived. Emmanuel's mind flew forward,
his imagination rushed on to the hour when his hopes might become realities. He pictured some little country inn, quiet, clean,
and homely. A red-faced landlord, with his fair-haired wife greeting them at the door. A supper eaten by a crackling fire of pine-
wood and fir cones, with candles burning on the table. Simple,
well-cooked country food, and perhaps a bottle of unexpectedly
good wine. Caro, laughing at him across the table, her lips parted,
her eyes dancing. How plainly he could see her!

White, scrubbed stairs, which creaked a little; a door swinging
open ; a room with wide windows which looked over to the snow-
topped mountains. His own voice saying to the landlord: 'Good
night—sleep well.' The door closing, and Caro in his arms! Darkness, soft, kind darkness, with one star glimmering and glinting
in at them through the window like a friendly eye.

He sighed, and knew that his whole body was shaken with

love for her. Tomorrow—the day after—and then, perhaps his dreams might come true. He would be so tender, he would take such care of her, make her smile, laugh—at his foolishness. He would watch her throw back her head and listen to her peals of laughter echoing through the tall trees as they walked together on a carpet of pine needles. They would forget that Stanislaus Lukoes existed; they would only remember that they were together, content because they knew the perfect fulfilment of love.

Mechanically, without lifting his head, he turned into the courtyard of his father's house and crossed the wide paved space. His foot was on the lowest step which led to the big door of the house, when he raised his eyes and realized that someone was trying to open the door. Someone who fumbled and rattled with a key, who swayed a little, and muttered under his breath. His cousin Jean Hirsch had returned from some late party, more than a little drunk. Emmanuel halted, and swiftly flung his long military cloak round him, concealing the splendid uniform; with a lightning movement he replaced his mask, and stood like a panther waiting to spring. He dared not give Jean the opportunity to betray him! Discovery might affect not only himself, but Max von Habenberg. The repercussion might even touch Caro!

Jean turned, still swinging a little on his heels. 'Warrer devil . . .!'

Emmanuel sprang forward. In a second the vast cloak was flung round Jean's unsteady form, over his head, and Jean himself was lifted bodily in his cousin's arms. His voice, muffled and indignant, was smothered in the enveloping folds of heavy cloth, and easily and rapidly Emmanuel carried him to the little lodge where all day the porter sat. The key was in the door; he withdrew it, and deposited Jean inside. Then, with one movement he snatched off the cloak and shut the door, turning the key as he did so. With the cloak flung over his arm, he walked back to the house, opened the door and let himself in.

Max von Habenberg, clad in a magnificent dressing-gown of purple silk, an almost empty bottle of wine and a box of cigars at his elbow, rose from the huge arm-chair as Emmanuel entered his room. He stared at the tall, splendidly proportioned figure, at the pale handsome face, with its small dark moustache, fine eyes and general air of distinction. The thought flashed through his mind: 'What a soldier he would have made! There isn't a man in the Guards to touch him. He looks like a prince. Compared

205

with this man Rudolph would seem like a peasant!'

'Hello, Gollantz!' he said, trying to smooth his tumbled hair as he spoke. 'How went the romance?'

Emmanuel's fingers were already busy with straps, frogs, and buttons. He smiled. 'I have only to thank my benefactor—and I do, sincerely.'

'Everything went well?'

'Perfectly.' The tunic was flung aside and he stood, in his fine cambric shirt and the tight military breeches, looking taller and more graceful than ever. 'Johann excelled himself, the floor was divine, the supper superb——'

Von Habenberg said: 'And—she?'

'Was herself—perfection perfected.'

As Emmanuel divested himself of the rest of the uniform and whilst von Habenberg dressed, they did not speak. Only when the soldier stood stiff and military in his uniform did their eyes meet again.

'I wonder who she is, Gollantz?' von Habenberg said softly.

'The only woman in the world.'

'We have all said that some time or another.'

'In this case I happen to speak the truth.'

'Some day perhaps I shall know—then'—his face lost its look of gaiety and he faced Emmanuel, serious and sincere—'I shall tell her that you are a prince among men, and one I am proud to call my friend. I have talked with my father ; he was very angry, he stormed—but the storm passed and the sun broke through again. He promised to forget my foolishness. He will! I shall never forget—never!' His eyes were suddenly filled with tears, his lips trembled.

Emmanuel laid his hand on von Habenberg's shoulder. 'Please!' he exclaimed. 'You make me ashamed because you rate so small a thing so highly. Come, let me take you to the door, I have a duty to perform.' His lips smiled again as, in a whisper, while they traversed the long corridor, he confided to von Habenberg the incident of Jean. The young soldier leant against the door, helpless with laughter. Emmanuel reflected that he was a typical son of his race—able to submerge everything in laughter. How pleasant his laughter was too! Laughing, he pushed him aside, swung open the big door and stood, his head bent to catch a possible sound.

'Listen,' he said. 'There! My cousin is protesting.'

He turned the key of the little lodge, flung open the door, exclaiming: 'Who is there? Come out instantly!'

Jean emerged, ruffled and furious.

Emmanuel, simulating astonishment, said: 'Jean! What is this? Have we all gone mad?'

'Mad—no!' Jean stuttered in his fury. 'I arrived home some hours ago to find a masked man trying to enter the house. I ordered him to be off, said that I should send for the police. Without a moment's warning he lifted me in his arms, pushed a gag into my mouth, and half pushed, half carried me here, swearing that if I made a sound he would stick a knife in my ribs. He went through my pockets, carried off my wallet which contained not only my own money but a considerable amount belonging to my firm, and slamming the door—left me.'

Emmanuel's face was a mask. 'The lieutenant'—he bowed to von Habenberg—'was passing. He heard your cries, and very generously went out of his way to call me.'

'I was on my way back from the masked ball,' von Habenberg interposed. 'Tell us,' he asked anxiously, 'what sort of a man was this robber?'

'What sort of a man, Herr Lieutenant?' Jean said eagerly. 'A huge brute with a heavy moustache, a brutal black-jowled creature, a typical cut-throat, speaking a hideous dialect which I could scarcely understand. Oh, an unmistakable ruffian.'

'A terrible experience! You would recognize this ruffian if you saw him again?'

'Assuredly—can you doubt it, Herr Lieutenant?'

Emmanuel, appearing very tall in his long purple dressing-gown, stood with his arms folded, looking down at his cousin. His expression was inscrutable, his lips seemed to von Habenberg to have become thinner, his mouth strangely hard.

'The door is open, Jean,' he said. 'I should get to bed, I think. I will see the lieutenant to the gate and close it. Good night.'

Jean was obsequious. 'Good night, Herr Lieutenant; a thousand thanks. I am more than grateful. But for you I might have been left there all night. I am your grateful servant, Lieutenant von Habenberg. I shall remember the illustrious name. Again, my thanks—my sincere thanks.'

As they walked to the big gates of the courtyard, von Habenberg glanced at Emmanuel's grave face. 'What is it?' he asked. 'It was great fun, but you look as if you had witnessed a tragedy, Gollantz, my friend.'

'I have,' Emmanuel returned, his eyes sombre. 'That lying little thief is a Jew—as I am. Did you hear? He will turn this incident to account to extract money from my father. He will state that he was robbed of his money, of his firm's money. My father will pay what he asks, for my father is the most honest man in Vienna—in the world, I think. Von Habenberg, please remember that this cousin of mine is the greatest burden laid on my race—the Jew who spends his time dragging his people's reputation in the dirt. How angry it makes me! How heartsick! These are the people who give the Christians the right to sneer at us, to stigmatize us as money-grubbers, swindlers and thieves!'

Von Habenberg laid his hand on Emmanuel's arm. 'My dear friend, don't take it so to heart. Who could ever think these things of you? No one who retained the smallest degree of sanity. That shaking little creature, what does he matter? Nothing.'

'By those Jews we are judged,' Emmanuel said gravely. 'Good morning—and again, my thanks.'

'I shall see you again—soon? Oh, we must meet again. I can't lose my friend whom I have just found.'

The obvious affection in his voice reached Emmanuel and soothed his frayed nerves; his stern face relaxed. 'I hope so—yes, we must meet.'

II

'After you had left,' Caro said; 'I don't know how it began. Some quarrel in the card-room. He offered to fight Stanislaus; Stanislaus insulted him further, they said. The Emperor heard of it and forbade the fight. Stanislaus is furious and is ordered to the palace this afternoon. I don't know what the result will be.'

'What result can there be?' Emmanuel asked. 'Either they will fight or the Emperor will forbid it. Nothing else can happen.' He caught her hand in his and said with sudden intensity: 'Nothing else can happen. Can it, Caro?'

'I don't know.' She spoke slowly. 'I don't know. They're so strange. They do things which are so unexpected and—violent. I don't understand them.'

'No, no.' His voice was very tender. 'No, Caro. You're tired, you danced too long last night. That makes you apprehensive and worried over trifles. Let us forget it, and tell me your plans—our plans.'

He tried very hard to make her smile, but it seemed as though a cloud had passed over the face of their sun, blotting out the brightness and warmth. For a few minutes Emmanuel could catch and hold her attention, make her smile, and talk of the little inn he knew which lay hidden among pine trees, where the food was simple and honest, and the wine good and of a fine flavour. Then, he would feel that she had slipped away from him again, he would know that her eyes were for ever turning towards the window, as if she feared the approach of some disaster.

He told her of his cousin, of the incident of the supposed robber, told his story with wit and a wealth of comedy, and though Caro smiled, even laughed, he still felt that he could not hold her complete attention.

Marion Brightwin joined them, poured out tea, and smiled at Emmanuel over a plate of buttered toast. She asked him questions, made little jokes at his expense, told him that he was growing too romantic and that he spent too much time and thought over his toilet.

Caro listened, scarcely speaking, her face grave, her eyes for ever turning away from them to the window.

'This is the third new waistcoat I have seen you wear in the last month,' Marion Brightwin said, 'and heaven only knows how many more you have at home! No wonder that your English progresses so slowly, your mind is occupied with new——'

Caro's voice cut her sentence short. 'There!' she exclaimed suddenly. 'I knew it would come. Marion, there is one of my husband's footmen at the door!'

Miss Brightwin started to her feet, and as she did so they heard the harsh knocking on the door.

Emmanuel moved a little nearer to Caro. 'Did you expect him?' he asked.

She shrugged her shoulders. 'Sooner or later—I knew that he would find out. How like Stanislaus to send a servant!'

Her hands were perfectly steady as she took the letter from the maid who brought it into the room ; her face was quite calm as she read it, turning back the page as if to make certain that she had read it correctly. The letter seemed to Emmanuel to be terribly—almost unbearably long.

'Tell the man to wait,' Caro said. 'I will send out a reply.' As the door closed behind the servant, she turned to Emmanuel, twisting the letter in her fingers.

'Stanislaus knows,' she said. 'I always felt that he knew. I have seen him watching me, smiling, so often lately. As if he had some delightful secret. That is so like Stanislaus. He loves waiting—and pouncing.'

'Yes, yes,' Emmanuel said. 'But what does he say? What is he going to do? What does he wish you to do?'

Marion Brightwin wrung her hands, her voice shook.

Emmanuel, hearing the tremor, thought: 'She is older than she looks. I always thought so. Poor lady, she is afraid—the fear that old age has of uncertainty.'

'He is leaving Vienna,' Caro said, turning back to the letter. 'He has seen the Emperor; he is very angry with Stanislaus and tells him that Vienna will be more pleasant without him. He says, —she read from the sheet in her hands.

'I am sorry to interrupt your lessons, or instruction in any subject, but it is unavoidable. We leave Vienna tonight for Poland. If the Hapsburgs are done with me, well, I am done with them. I beg that you will not make any scenes. I have been very patient, very tolerant. You must have believed me to be a great fool, and that annoys me a little. Your young Jew may be clever, he may have looks, manners and all the things which I have discarded long ago, but I am your husband and I want you with me. If he has been your lover, I cannot pretend that it matters very much to me. What does matter is that this silly, schoolgirlish intrigue must end now. The journey to Poland is exceedingly dull, and you play piquet remarkably well. Say your farewells and return home immediately. Tell him that your duties as Baroness Stanislaus Lukoes, and your duties as the wife of Stanislaus Lukoes, demand your immediate attention. I have been both patient and and tolerant—in future I shall be neither. S.L.'

She folded the letter and stood watching Emmanuel gravely.

He shivered suddenly, then said: 'But you won't go back, Caro? This is our opportunity. We must take it.'

'How?'

'I will go back quickly to my father. He will let me have sufficient money to get us out of Austria. We will go to Italy—I have relatives there who will help me. I shall work for you. I shall see that you are safe, loved—happy.'

'And poor?'

He made a little movement as if begging her forgiveness. 'Perhaps, for a time. Not for very long, I promise you. There! I won't waste time. I will go at once. My father will understand; he will only want our happiness.'

She shook her head. 'No, Emmanuel, no. We can't do that. I must go back immediately.'

'To him—you will go with him to Poland? Caro!'

'Yes, I shall go with him.'

'But—but . . .' He stammered a little in his inability to understand. 'But you hate him—you have said so. Then why even think of going back?'

She met his eyes steadily. Her ugly, intelligent face was white; only her eyes seemed to become intensified in colour.

'I am going back because I could never face being poor again. I married Stanislaus because I feared and hated poverty, and that is why I shall go back to him now. Oh, Emmanuel,' she cried passionately, 'don't look at me like that! You don't understand, you've never been poor. I have! You've never known what it was to be denied all the—silly, little, unimportant extravagances that make life tolerable! I suppose I'm small and petty and mean, but I've become used to being Baroness Lukoes—I couldn't face being nobody. I couldn't face being sneered at, being ostracized —it would kill me. I do hate him, but I have sufficient money to buy drugs which make me able to disregard him—books, clothes, jewels. I can amuse myself—because I have money. Comfort, luxury, can make most things bearable, Emmanuel.'

'Without love?'

'Love dies on a cold hearthstone.'

'You will be alone in a strange land. You will not even have friends round you—away in Poland.'

'Money will buy most things, even friends. Stanislaus is restless; he will want to travel—Paris, Rome—anywhere except Vienna.'

'I thought—I believed'—for the first time his voice shook a little—'that you loved me.'

'I did—I do—I think that I always shall. Emmanuel, don't make it too hard for me. Don't make me do something we might both regret all our lives—when it was too late. I tell you'—she beat her hands together in desperation—'I can't face poverty! It would blot out all our love, it would spoil everything. I should grow hard and bitter; you would be hampered and forced to work too hard. There would be no time left to remember that we loved each other. Oh, Emmanuel—try to understand.'

She turned to Marion Brightwin. 'Marion, make him understand!'

'My dear—it's so difficult. I cannot say what——'

Emmanuel said: 'I do understand. Honour, love, happiness, content, may all go ; they count for nothing when they are weighed in the balance against money. They are imaginary things ; money is real, concrete, solid. And so what I have given you goes for nothing. Devotion—oh God, I have given you that so wholeheartedly! There is nothing I would not have done, nothing I could not have done for you and because of you. Each day has only mattered for the hour I might spend with you. You have been the sun, the moon, the stars—you have been my world and . . .' He stopped suddenly, and as he closed his lips Caro saw how bloodless they had become. 'I beg your pardon,' he said. 'I was allowing myself to become melodramatic. May I take a message to your husband's servant?'

'Emmanuel, don't let us part like this . . .'

'Then how should we part?' he asked, coldly and furiously. 'What do you suggest ? Would you give me your kisses to remember you by? I don't want to remember you! Would you like us to hold each other's hands, look into each other's eyes? To what purpose? Should we arrange that one day, if this and this and that happen, we will meet in Paris or London or Berlin? Would you like me to beg that I may write to you once a year—and send you a red rose to show that I still love you? No, these things are delightful for the theatre ; they don't belong to life.'

Miss Brightwin, speaking nervously and with a certain trepidation, said: 'To some of us those—softer things—are life, Emmanuel.'

He stared at her as if he had never seen her before, and did not understand why she should address him.

'Perhaps you are right,' he said. 'I thought so once. I see now that I was wrong. Foolishly, romantically wrong.'

Caroline stood watching him ; her face was pale but quite composed. Only her restless hands, with the fine long fingers twisting, betrayed her. Her lips were firm, set tightly and resolutely. It seemed that having declared her intention, having admitted her fear of poverty, she had ceased to have any interest in Emmanuel Gollantz. She watched him as she might have watched an actor playing his part on the stage—with detached and impersonal interest.

'Marion dear, I must go,' she said. 'I will write to you from

Kalkratz. You must come and stay with me, you'll be interested. Good-bye, my dear, you've been very good to me always.'

The elderly governess was crying now, the tears falling on to her folded hands. Caro came over to her, taking her hands.

'Don't cry, Marion. I shall be quite safe. I shall look forward to your coming.' Then, after a little pause: 'Marion, say that you understand, say that you don't think too harshly of me.'

'I have never been able to think harshly of you, Caro. Good-bye, and God bless you. Yes, I will come to you—I couldn't bear to be separated from you for long, you know that.'

Emmanuel was at the door, standing stiffly upright, his hand on the white china knob. As she reached him, Caroline Lukoes stopped, their eyes met.

'You will need a carriage. The man came on foot. Shall I tell him to call one?'

'If you please.'

He opened the door and spoke to the waiting servant. 'Call a carriage for the baroness, please. Be quick, she is waiting.'

'Immediately, sir.'

He returned and closed the door. 'He will get one at once.'

'Emmanuel, must we say good-bye—like this?'

'I wish you a very pleasant journey, Baroness.'

'That is all you have to say to me?'

He bowed. 'It is all that I *need* to say.'

'Shall I write to you?'

'Baroness, you have been very kind to me; I am deeply indebted to you for many things. May I beg you will add to all your kindnesses, to all the things which you have done for me— and not write to me? I shall be even more deeply in your debt— without letters.'

She held out her hand impulsively. 'Emmanuel—I have loved you!'

He disregarded her hand, bowed again, saying: 'I have always been your very obedient servant, Baroness. Ah, there is the carriage.'

He swung open the door, and walked with her to the hired carriage which stood waiting. Very gravely and with great courtesy he handed her into it and stood, his heels together, bowing from the waist.

'Good-bye . . .'

'Good-bye, and a safe journey, Baroness.'

III

White-faced, he stood before his father some hours later. Hermann, glancing up from the catalogue which he was studying, said:

'Ah, Emmanuel.' Then with sudden anxiety: 'Emmanuel, you are not well! What is the matter—is anything wrong?'

'I have been very unhappy, Father.' Then the well-cut lips curved into a smile which held nothing but bitterness. 'I invested everything I had, and lost! No, no, don't be anxious, I am not speaking of material things. I am only trying to explain why—perhaps—I looked ill. It is over, all over. I don't want sympathy. I only tell you this to show you that I am grateful for your love ; it is only because of that love that I can come and speak to you now. Father, please give me a great deal of work to do. For the next weeks I want to be very fully occupied.'

Hermann closed the catalogue, then said gently: 'Poor boy! A woman?'

'I have thought of her as—the woman.'

'Yes, yes. And now it is over? Is she still in Vienna?' Then, with that quick sensitiveness which was typical of him, Hermann added: 'I ask only because I thought you might like to go away.'

'No, she is doing that. She leaves Vienna tonight with her husband.'

'You have done nothing dishonourable, Emmanuel?'

Emmanuel shrugged his broad shoulders. 'No, Father—not for lack of intention, but for lack of opportunity. Oh, I know that you have rigid ideas to what is right and what is wrong. I was too deeply in love to care. I don't say this to excuse myself in your eyes ; I am trying to be honest.'

For the first time Hermann Gollantz smiled. This handsome son of his, for all his sophistication, was very young. 'I respect you for your honesty, Emmanuel. But, nevertheless, I shall breathe more easily for what you have just told me. You are very young, very handsome ; you have great attraction for women. Those things are wonderful assets, but they must be used as servants, never allowed to become masters. What I mean is that you must never rely on them, you must rate them at their proper value. There must be integrity in love as in a well-conducted business. Roguery is roguery wherever one finds it. . . . No, no'—holding up his fine, white hand—'I don't say—I don't suggest that my son is or could be a rogue ; what I do beg is that he will always allow me to be as proud of him as I am at this moment.'

He held out his hand ; Emmanuel took it, and for a moment they stood looking into each other's eyes. Hermann's were very tender, very compassionate. The hardness faded from Emmanuel's face, every line softened, the lips quivered suddenly, and the eyes which looked into Hermann's were filled with tears. The self-assurance vanished. He stood there, a young man, very unhappy, desperately hurt.

'Poor Emmanuel,' Hermann whispered.

'It seems that this is the end of everything for me, Father.'

'I understand. When I was your age I went through just such a disappointment. For a time it made me hard, unkind. You must recover more easily. I could not face watching you suffer, my son. Still less could I bear to think that you were—with splendid courage—hiding your suffering from me.'

'No, no—only just at first—it is unbearable.'

'Perhaps'—rather wistfully—'it is just a little easier because you have shared it with me?'

Emmanuel nodded. 'Yes, you're right, Father. We won't speak of this again, only you will know and understand. It was not just a—a—romantic interlude ; it was real. It's over, and'—with a great effort to regain his control—'now will you show me the catalogue, and tell me what you think of buying tomorrow? It ought to be interesting ; someone told me that there was a letter written by Elizabeth of England. That might be amusing.'

Hermann flicked over the pages of the book, pausing with uplifted pencil to consider the various lots.

'I don't think that letters—even from Elizabeth of England—have much real or permanent value, Emmanuel. A passing interest—that's all.'

'Perhaps you are right,' Emmanuel agreed, then added with greater conviction: 'I am sure that you are right. There is a First Empire dinner-service, I am told, decorated with . . .' And once again the two heads, one black and the other white, bent over the pages. The House of Gollantz was at work again.

7

DURING the weeks that followed, Emmanuel was conscious for the first time of the wonderful kindliness and understanding which his father possessed. He had always loved both his parents, though it must be admitted that he was far too intelligent not to recognize the fact that his mother was a rather foolish and ultra-sentimental woman, but he had never until now understood the full beauty of his father's nature. On those days when his heart still smarted and stung, when he felt that life was empty and knew that his thoughts turned constantly to Caro, trying to follow her journey in imagination, his father's love and consideration did much to soothe his pain. To nerves which quivered Hermann's quiet, beautifully modulated voice acted like a salve ; to a mind tortured by imagination Hermann's cultured outlook, his knowledge and appreciation of beauty offered distraction.

The recollection of that one incident when Emmanuel felt his father had treated him unfairly was wiped out by these new evidences of love and understanding, and father and son were in closer accord than they had ever been before. Simon Cohen, who loved them both, watched, grew a little sentimental and moist about the eyes as he realized the affection which seemed to grow daily in strength.

Emmanuel suffered, and suffered deeply. He had loved Caroline very dearly, he had found in her all that appealed to him most in women. She had been gay, intelligent, witty, and possessed of great tolerance He had learnt much from her, his manners had acquired greater ease, and his capacity for self-expression had grown. He was no longer afraid to voice his opinions in the romantic, rather colourful style which seemed in such perfect accord with his appearance. He had been a handsome, intelligent youth when he met Caroline Lukoes ; he was a man possessing great charm when she left him.

For several weeks he found it impossible to visit the little house where Marion Brightwin lived. He longed to go back there, but each time he contemplated doing so he seemed to react that last interview between himself and Caro, and knew that he was afraid to awaken too many memories by returning. Then, one morning, he found a letter from the elderly governess, such a letter as a mother might have written to a dearly loved son. She begged him to go and see her. *For* [she wrote] *you are not only my promising pupil, but you are my friend.*

Making a great effort, he called at the little house and tried to assume an air of unconcern. It was terribly difficult, and he knew that his voice sounded hard and lifeless, realized that his hands were shaking. Marion Brightwin talked, so it seemed, of everything and everyone except Caroline, and he was grateful.

'Tea, let us have some tea, Emmanuel!' she said, and added quickly: 'And English tea-cakes. I wonder if you will like them.'

At that moment he felt that he loved her, because she had not suggested 'hot buttered toast'.

When he left, he held her hand, giving his small, ceremonious bow. 'I am so very happy to be back,' he said in English. 'I hef meesed you ver-ry mooch, Mees Br-rightween.'

'It was time you came back, Emmanuel,' she said, almost primly. 'Your English is quite deplorable—the accent, well it is that of a foreigner. And that'—she smiled—'is the most terrible thing that a teacher of English can say to a pupil.'

That evening he sat with von Habenberg in the 'Spiel', while Strauss, who had come on there from the 'Two Doves', played his latest waltz. Von Habenberg loved the 'Spiel', despite its reputation, far better than the more aristocratic 'Zogernitz'. Emmanuel tolerated the place, was amused by the people he saw there, but in his heart he had long ago determined that one day he would make the 'Zogernitz' his usual haunt.

'You are better, Gollantz,' von Habenberg said suddenly, as he watched Emmanuel's face, alight and full of amused interest. 'I have been very unhappy for you.'

The laughter died from Emmanuel's eyes. 'Yes, I am better. It was kind of you to say nothing. It is over—I am content again.'

'I would rather hear you say that you were happy. Content is a pale thing ; happiness is colourful.'

Emmanuel shook his head. 'But content is safer. The higher you climb the farther you can fall ; content is nearer the earth.' Then, as if resolutely pushing his dark thoughts away, he added: 'But today I have fallen in love—no, no, don't look so interested ; don't ask what she is like, for I cannot tell you. I believe she is depicted as a lady in a helmet, with a trident, and her name is— Br-ritannia. I have fallen in love with the English nation.'

'My dear Emmanuel, is this madness or minor treason?'

'Neither! I have realized that we—I am speaking now as an Austrian—are nearer to them than to any other nation. We ought to be allies. We could sweep the world. You see, we are both very old, very aristocratic, and very certain of ourselves. The French' —he shrugged his shoulders—'are commercial, and they have chopped and changed, they have become busy and—middle-class. The Germans are heavy and so full of themselves; they eat too much, and drink too much beer. They are so insular. Spain—dead people, allowing their mentalities to get as out of date as their manufactures. Italy—I am partly Italian—they are too young, and their youth makes them just a little unreliable. They will always be young, just as their country is always young in spite of its age. But the English—how admirable. One day I think that I must go and live in England.'

'But what is all this? Tell me what brings you to these conclusions.'

'I cannot tell you the whole story, because it is not all of it my story. The facts, which made me realize how admirable, how courteous, how superb they are—well, one of them offered me a cake called "tea", when she might have offered me buttered toast. Then, when she might have been sympathetic, she contented herself with correcting my English accent.'

'And for that you have fallen in love with her and her nation! I should not be so content myself if I visited a lady and she offered me only cake and corrections.'

'She is over fifty,' Emmanuel said. 'She is utterly without any figure, she wears a small grey moustache, and her feet are tremendous. Nevertheless, she is English and wonderful.'

Max von Habenberg threw back his head and laughed. 'Try them *en masse,* and see how you would like them. My uncle was at Saint James's for two years. He says that the coolness of their climate is only equalled by the coldness of their women.'

Emmanuel sipped his coffee, then sat twisting the stem of his glass of cognac in his fingers. 'Yes, one day I will see them and know them—*en masse.* I believe that I should be happy working in England.'

II

That night he arrived home to find his father and mother still up and talking. His mother was flushed and a little excited; Hermann looked paler than usual, and seemed nervous. As Emmanuel entered, Rachel Gollantz looked up from the embroidery at which she was working and exclaimed as she flung the piece of material away from her:

'Ah, here is Emmanuel! Now I can tell the whole story over again! I have twisted all my silks in my excitement. Emmanuel, listen! Tomorrow your Uncle Ishmael returns to Vienna—returns a rich man. He will stay here until he finds a suitable house—did I say a house?—a mansion. Is not this great news? And did I not always maintain that your uncle would make money, a great deal of money? Of course I did!'

Emmanuel stood silent, his face flushing suddenly. To him the news came bringing a sense of dismay. He had no belief in the fortune which Ishmael Hirsch was supposed to have amassed. Even if he were rich at the moment, Emmanuel felt certain the money would not last long. He had not realized how deep was his dislike and distrust of his mother's brother, how relieved he had been as the months had lengthened into years, and Ishmael had remained away from Vienna. He looked towards his father, and in his anxious eyes and twitching lips saw his own apprehension reflected.

'Aren't you pleased?' Rachel asked sharply.

'No, Mother, not very—I say that, even at the risk of hurting you.'

'And you do hurt me!' she returned quickly. 'You hurt me deeply. Your father, ever since the news came, has been twisting his lips, frowning, and answering me in the fewest possible words. Have you no warmth of heart, both of you?'

'My father has the warmest, kindest heart in the world,' Emmanuel answered. 'No one could doubt it—but perhaps he has grown to like living tranquilly, and the thought of two additional people in his house disturbs him.'

His mother rose, her ample bosom heaved, her still beautiful dark eyes flashed. 'It is useless to excuse your father, Emmanuel. I can see it all—I understand that my brother is not welcome here. Very well, I shall explain to him that he must find his mansion as quickly as possible. I hope that will satisfy you both.'

She flounced from the room, closing the door behind her. Hermann sighed and sat silent, his head resting on his hand. Emmanuel stood watching him gravely, wondering if now his father would confide in him. Hermann lifted his head and smiled at his son.

'I am afraid that we have hurt her, poor little Mother. It is only natural that she is glad to see her brother again.' He sighed. 'After all, Ishmael may have altered for the better.'

'For him to alter for the worse would be impossible.'

'One must make allowances, one must be charitable.'

Emmanuel's fingers closed suddenly. 'Charitable!' he exclaimed. 'I wonder how far one must carry that charity? Must it be extended until it becomes material as well as spiritual, Father?'

He watched his father closely, saw the pale, sensitive face flush, and thought: 'Now he will tell me, now he will admit what Ishmael Hirsch has cost him! Once he admits everything, then we can fight together against this scamp of an uncle of mine!' But the flush died, and when he spoke, Hermann's voice was as gentle as ever.

'That is an interesting point, Emmanuel. Duties to Jews—even to such *link* Jews as myself, are their privileges, and charity—whether visiting the afflicted, which is the spiritual type, or offering, in all humility, help to the *schnorrer*, which is the material type—is one of those privileges. It would be difficult to say where . . .'

Emmanuel walked over to the bookcase and with great unconcern began to look for a volume. He was suddenly angry; he felt that his father was concealing something from him, and that the delightful friendship of the last weeks was being destroyed. This was what Ishmael Hirsch could do, even before he entered the house—he could make a barrier between his father and himself.

'Thank you, Father,' Emmanuel said coldly. 'I am not interested in these verbal hair splittings. I, like you, am *link*. I leave them to the Rabbis. Talmudic discussions interest them, they weary me. Good night.'

Two days later Ishmael Hirsch and his wife arrived. When Emmanuel entered the dining-room that evening his nostrils were assailed by the smell of roast goose, and the table bore evidences of his mother's industry during the day.

'The return of the wanderer,' Emmanuel thought. 'A feast is made.' His uncle was standing near the fire-place, and he held out his hands in a slightly overdone welcome to his nephew. Emmanuel noticed that his hands were fat, white, and that he wore a number of large rings. He had grown very stout, and his waisted frock-coat of fine, black cloth served to accentuate the bulkiness of his body. His face was florid, and yet unhealthily flabby, the cheeks seemed to have dropped and sagged downwards towards the points of his high linen collar. His hair was brushed forward over the ears, and his full, loose-lipped mouth was partially covered with a straggling grey moustache. His wife, who had grown almost as stout as her husband, sat perched on one of the small gilt chairs, and to Emmanuel it seemed that her flesh descended in huge billows.

His uncle cried loudly: 'Here is my favourite nephew! The elegant Emmanuel! Well, well, how aristocratic he has become. I am certain that all the girls in Vienna sigh after him. Am I not right, Emmanuel?'

'How are you, Uncle Ishmael?' Emmanuel offered his hand, and evaded the overwhelming embrace which he felt threatened him.

'No longer Ishmael, my boy! I realized before it was too late that such a name was a drawback to me in my financial activities. I had no wish that men should say: "Ah, Ishmael Hirsch, his hand is against every man and every man's hand is against him!" Such a name was a hindrance. I am Justus Hirsch. A noble name, I think—no?'

'Very impressive.' Emmanuel bowed to his aunt, asking: 'And my cousin?'

Hirsch lifted his hands in admiration at the very mention of his daughter's name. 'Married—very quietly—a month ago. Married to a French nobleman of splendid family, with the magnificent name of Cariadies.'

Emmanuel's eyebrows were raised. 'French? I have known people who came from the Levant bear similar names.'

Hirsch shot him a look of annoyance, but his smile never faded.

'It is possible; nevertheless my son-in-law is French. Count Phillipe Cariadies.'

During dinner both Hirsch and his wife ate enormously. Emmanuel, watching them, reflected that time had not improved their table manners, and more than once he felt a feeling of revulsion at these two gross people who seemed determined to eat until they could eat no more.

The meal ended and Rachel Gollantz and her sister-in-law left the three men to drink their wine alone. Hirsch, his frock-coat unbuttoned, displaying his elaborate tartan velvet waistcoat, the three last buttons of which he unfastened, allowing his frilled shirt to protrude, stuck his thumbs in the arm-holes of his waistcoat and prepared to talk. Hermann Gollantz played nervously with his wineglass, while Emmanuel sat stiffly upright, his handsome face a mask.

'Well, and how are things with you, Hermann?' Hirsch asked.

'Quite reasonably good,' Gollantz replied. 'We have not set the Danube alight, but we have held our own against newcomers.'

'That is not enough!' Hirsch said, with vigour. 'What is needed in these days is courage, ability to make the best of opportunity. That way lies the money! I have never neglected an opportunity, I tell you.'

'An opportunity to do—what? Emannuel asked smoothly.

'To make money!'

'How?' The tone was so insolent that Hermann ceased twisting his wineglass in his fingers and, lifting his head, stared at his son. The younger man's face was expressionless.

'How? You ask how? By work, by being always ready to jump in——'

'Irrespective of how much dirt clung to your feet?'

Hirsch's florid face turned a deeper purple, his small, bright eyes bulged, his wide mouth fell open, slack and foolish. He glared at his nephew in silence for a moment, then turned to Hermann.

'Tell me, is this how your son speaks to his guests?'

Emmanuel leaned forward. 'Not *my* guests, only my father's relations by marriage. One chooses one's guests—one's relations write and announce their arrival.'

'This is intolerable!'

For the first time Emmanuel smiled. 'I agree—quite intolerable.'

'I have never been so insulted——'

'Possibly. Some people lack courage, others are too indifferent.'

Hirsch turned again to Hermann. 'Will you allow this to continue in your own house? Will you allow this whipper-snapper to insult his mother's only brother?'

Hermann stammered ; his face was pale, his expression worried. 'Perhaps Emmanel has spoken too harshly, perhaps——'

Emmanuel lifted his hand. 'Father, with all respect to you, will you allow me to speak? I am protecting you, because it is evident to me that you cannot protect yourself. For two years we have housed this man's son ; he has lied to you, to me, to my mother. He has cheated, and because to have exposed him would have involved others I have said nothing. Now, as your partner, Father, I take a stand. This house is our place of business, and as such must retain its character. That character will be jeopardized by the presence of this—Mr. Justus Hirsch. For one night we are bound to extend hospitality, but I am sure that Mr. Justus Hirsch will see that it is necessary to find his suitable mansion—or an equally suitable hotel—tomorrow.' He turned to his uncle, still smiling, still completely master of himself. 'I am sure that you grasp my meaning.'

'I shall never enter this house again!'

'That *was* my meaning,' Emmanuel said. 'I congratulate you on your perspicacity.' He reached forward and addressed himself to his father. 'Do you mind if I have another glass of cognac? How excellent it is, and how additionally enjoyable in these really big glasses.'

Hermann did not reply. He sat there glancing from his son to his brother-in-law, nervous and apprehensive. He had been tolerant for so long that Emmanuel's high-handed attitude half frightened him. He had worked so hard to conceal from his wife the true character of his brother-in-law, that now the dread of Rachel discovering the truth filled him with anxiety. For years he had replied to all the demands which Hirsch made upon him, without declaring the truth to a living soul. He had successfully kept his private account books and ledgers hidden from his son. Emmanuel had never known the immense sums which had been sent to Ishmael Hirsch, and now Hermann trembled lest his son should realize how much of his fortune, that fortune which was one day to be Emmanuel's, had been dissipated. True, the House of Gollantz occupied a position of distinction in Vienna; Hermann Gollantz was—on paper—a rich and successful man; but Vienna knew no more than Emmanuel, no more than Rachel Gollantz or Simon Cohen, the vast sums which had been asked for and given to this fat, gross fellow, who called himself Justus Hirsch.

Hermann Gollantz, honest and hardworking, sensitive and essentially kindly, understood as he sat at the head of his table that evening, that he would have been wiser to have trusted his son, and to have risked shattering the ideal to which his wife clung. Mentally he reckoned the sums which he had paid over to Hirsch in the past years. Ten thousand gulden here, packets of notes issued by the Austro-Hungarian bank, drafts on Paris banking-houses—they had all disappeared into the capacious maw of Justus Hirsch; and Hermann, remembering all those demands, counting up all those huge sums, turned his eyes towards Emmanuel, wistful and unhappy.

223

'It has been—almost—blackmail,' he mused wretchedly. 'Once I had paid, once Hirsch knew that I had paid in order to prevent Rachel from being worried, there was no reason why I should not pay again. Jean has been the same. He has sufficient wit to know that I could not bear to worry Emmanuel. He has made me pay—blackmailed me. Oh, it's too late now to tell Emmanuel the truth. Maybe Ishmael has made money, maybe he is as rich as he says, and maybe he will not make further demands. Perhaps he will be sufficiently angry after what Emmanuel has said to stay away. Then Rachel will wonder why; she will ask questions. . . .' With the nervous irritation of weak men, Hermann thought: 'It might have been better if he had stayed in Paris, and made his demands from there. Then no one—except we—need have known!'

Emmanuel was sipping his brandy with appreciation; Hirsch sat huddled in his chair, purple-faced, breathing noisily, and much occupied with a toothpick. Finally he hoisted himself out of his chair and addressed himself to Hermann.

'I have been insulted this evening, and I shall not forget it. Had your son been other than my sister's child I would have horsewhipped him. As he is—who he is—it is impossible.' He turned to Emmanuel. 'What have you to say to that?'

Emmanuel looked up, smiling. 'Nothing, except that you amuse me.'

'Had I been younger I should not have amused you so much!'

'No, I admit that I find some consolation in the fact that you are growing old.'

With some difficulty his uncle buttoned his splendid waistcoat.

'My wife and I will leave here tomorrow. I shall go direct to my room. Please send my son Jean to me when he returns. I shall have difficulty in restraining him from demanding satisfaction from you, Emmanuel bar Hermann.'

'I think not—you see I know Jean quite well—too well.' Emmanuel rose, opened the door, and held it wide to allow his uncle to pass out. Closing it, he returned to his seat and faced his father.

'How tiresome that vulgar man is! Might I open the window a little?'

'The window? Certainly, yes, certainly. Emmanuel, I don't know what to say. I don't approve. You have broken one of the most sacred of laws—that of hospitality.'

'There are times, Father,' Emmanuel said, with a slightly over-done suavity, 'when even the most sacred laws must be broken.

224

May I recall to your mind the incident when Moses found it necessary to break the whole Ten Commandments. I am sure that you will excuse me, I have an appointment.'

Hermann felt the tears rush to his eyes. He loved his son, and it had made him very happy that during the past weeks a firm friendship had existed between them. Emmanuel had laughed with him, together they had studied catalogues, visited sales, discussed schemes of decoration. Now, with the advent of Hirsch it seemed that Emmanuel had grown cold and aloof again. He held out his hand, and in a voice which shook with emotion, cried:

'Emmanuel, don't let this man come between us. You are all I have in the world. You are the person for whom I work; my plans are all laid for you and your ultimate benefit. The last weeks have been so happy for me. I have enjoyed—everything. I admit that it seemed terrible to speak as you did, to a guest. Perhaps I am wrong. Tomorrow he will go, and everything will be well again.'

Emmanuel turned back from the door and came back to where his father sat. His lips were tender, his eyes very kind. He took his father's hand and, lifting it, laid it against his cheek. For a moment he did not speak, then said gently:

'I am grateful to you, my Father. I have it in my heart to forgive my uncle everything, because—through him—I have this beautiful moment with you. May I be forgiven if I speak plainly now— as a man to his great friend? I have a great deal of sentiment, but I have no sentimentality. Because Hirsch is my uncle, the brother of my mother, he is no less objectionable. You will—you have— made excuses for him because he happened to be born my mother's brother. Had he been born the brother of Charles, the wood-worker, you would have disliked him as cordially as I do. It is possible that you do dislike him as much, but you make excuses for him, you treat him leniently, you allow him to worry you, and permit his son to rob you—because of an accident of birth. Do not think that I am trying to probe and pry, but I beg that you will not cripple yourself because of this man, through a mistaken idea of duty. That is all, and now we are back where we were at first—the best friends in the world!'

Hermann's face was alight, and Emmanuel, watching him, thought what a delightful man his father was. So distinguished with his white hair, his fine eyes, and beautiful teeth. He seemed to have thrown off years, and when he rose to his feet, facing his son, Emmanuel noticed how firmly he threw back his shoulders, and heard with pleasure the firm ring in his voice.

'You are right, Emmanuel, and I am grateful! The man is horrible, and it is an affliction for your dear mother to have such a brother. I admit that there have been times when I have been foolish, sentimental, but they are over.' As he spoke, Emmanuel heard with dismay the faint touch of bravado in the words, heard that the firmness had changed to forced intensity. 'He goes tomorrow, and I shall make it quite clear that he must expect neither help nor introductions from me! You were right—a little ruthless, perhaps, but right, indubitably. Good night, and enjoy yourself, my dear, dear son.'

'He means it all,' Emmanuel thought, as he walked rapidly towards 'The Two Doves', where he was to meet von Habenberg. 'And yet—oh, how lacking in trust I am! But I wonder what will happen when Hirsch has been in Vienna a month and spent most of his money? Poor Father, so admirable, so clever, and so much too kindly. I wonder where I got my hard streak from? Not from him, that's certain.'

8

I

HIRSCH departed, taking Jean with him, and the House of Gollantz settled down again into its ordinary, dignified routine. True, Rachel hinted from time to time that Justus was doing wonderful things with the house which he had taken, that Henrietta shopped only in the most expensive establishments, and that Jean was on the point of contracting a brilliant marriage. Emmanuel and his father listened with the courtesy which was characteristic of them, but they made few comments, and gradually Rachel kept silent regarding her brother and his family.

Justus appeared one morning in the gallery and announced that he wished his 'great salon' to be decorated by the firm of Gollantz. No expense was to be spared, and he wished it to be a replica of one of the great salons in the Imperial Palace.

'I regret,' Emmanuel said, 'that we have no means of viewing the salon in the Imperial Palace.'

Hirsch flung back his head, displaying a set of broken and discoloured teeth. 'Clever, very clever! You see, nephew Emmanuel, I am not a man to harbour a grievance. You insulted me, but I have forgotten and forgiven. I appreciate your wit, your smartness. Do the room according to your own taste; the world knows how good it is.'

Simon Cohen, twisting his mouth as if he had tasted something unpleasant, said to Emmanuel later: 'Make some terrible scheme and take no trouble over it, Emmanuel.'

'Impossible, Simon. For my own credit, whatever I do must be good.'

'Let us use cheap paint, inferior gilt—he will never pay—never.'

'Again, impossible. He would tell everyone; it would damage our reputation. No, whatever we do must be good. Make him pay a deposit, Simon, it's all we shall ever get.'

The deposit was paid readily enough, the salon was decorated with taste and distinction, and the remainder of the bill was never paid.

'The old brute is clever,' Simon whispered. 'Tell me who else in Vienna can get a salon decorated by the House of Gollantz for six hundred gulden—mirrors along each wall, too!'

Emmanuel shrugged his shoulders. 'It is done. Let's forget it, I am going to read English with my teacher. A book by a lady called Mees Austeen. Charming and, oh, so proper!'

His old longing for Caroline had died, or, more correctly, he had drilled himself into never allowing his thoughts to dwell upon her. At first it had been not only difficult but unbearably painful, and he had known nights when he had paced his room, racked with longing, miserable and hopeless. Now, he had his thoughts under control, and even his visits to Marion Brightwin had ceased to cause him heart-aches. He accepted them at their face value. Where previously they had been hours of complete happiness, times to which he looked forward with longing, and looked back on with delirious joy, they were now delightful interludes when he read the English he was growing to love, and listened to the even and cultured tones of a woman he both liked and respected.

'I have an application for lessons from a new pupil, Emmanuel,' Miss Brightwin told him one afternoon. 'A most distinguished lady—no less a person than Princess Dietrich.'

'Princess Dietrich?' he repeated, and suddenly the thought came to him that he had not seen her since the night of the court

Ball, when he had held Caroline in his arms for the last time. The memory came, bringing a stab of pain with it. Caro had gone, he neither knew nor dared to ask where. She had chosen her course, and after his one outburst he had accepted it. Caro belonged to the past ; whatever scars had been the result of wounds inflicted by her, they were nothing more than reminders of what had once been. Emmanuel was young ; youth renews itself, and the future was his. Sitting there, in the rather prim little room with its trim antimacassars, Berlin wool mats, and terrible walnut atrocities known as 'what-nots', crowded with ornaments which possessed neither intrinsic value nor beauty, Emmanuel was conscious of a sense of expectancy at the mention of Maria Dietrich's name. He had no illusions ; he knew that she had liked him because he appealed to some rather immature romanticism in her. He knew that she was a woman without real intellect, though possessed of a certain intelligence, but he was sufficiently young to be flattered —almost against his will—at the realization that Princess Dietrich had remembered that he took English lessons, and that she had taken sufficient trouble to discover where those lessons were given. She wanted to see him again, she still felt that romantic urge towards him!

Then, as he sat there by the polished grate, where the copper kettle sang on the little hob, a flood of memories swept over him. In this room, under these same circumstances, he had sat and talked with Caro. At that moment he felt that a vision of her appeared to him. A vision so clear, so vivid, that only with difficulty could he restrain himself from crying out with the pain of it.

He could see her fine, narrow hands, her ugly, distinctive face, her beautiful slim shape ; he could hear her voice saying : 'Emmanuel, how ridiculous you are, darling.' Caro—his Caro—had chosen to leave him because she could not face even moderate poverty! She had left him for that gross, half-bestial Lukoes! Caro belonged to the past. . . .

Yet, as her remembrance remained with him, he felt his anger and resentment flare again. Caroline Lukoes had flung him aside, Maria Dietrich still retained a wish to meet him again. He was young, handsome, terribly sensitive to slights and imagined rebuffs, and the thought that the wife of Theodore Dietrich—herself lovely, attractive, sought after—wished to continue their mild flirtation, flattered him, acted as balm to his sore heart. Caro had been everything to him. Only now, by the strength of his feelings when he allowed himself to look back, did Emmanuel Gollantz realize all she had meant to him, or how much her loss had wounded him.

He turned to Miss Brightwin, smiling. 'Most distinguished! I know the princess a little. Perhaps you will be so kind as to allow me to meet her again?'

Marion Brightwin, astonished at herself, and thinking: 'Really, how dreadfully continental I am growing!' said: 'Emmanuel, I believe that you feel sentimental about the princess.'

'Half Vienna does, dear mees.'

Then she remembered that she taught English to supplement a very small income, remembered that in order to be acceptable to the Viennese aristocracy her house must remain beyond reproach. True, with Caro she had permitted herself to run risks—that was because Caro had begged and persuaded, and she had never been able to refuse Caro anything. It must never happen again. On that she must be quite firm.

'I hope,' and her lips twisted primly as she spoke, 'that you have no—er—ulterior motive in asking to meet the princess, Emmanuel.' She blushed, thinking that she had possibly been indelicate. After all, the princess was married!

'Dear mees, none. Only that from time to time her Highness has been charming to me ; she is very beautiful, and'—he laughed —'it is always pleasant to meet attractive people.'

'Very well.' She smiled back at him. Really he was delightful. 'I will see what can be done. The princess will come for her first lesson the day after tomorrow.'

'My own lesson is the day after tomorrow,' Emmanuel said.

'Hers is at four, yours at half past four. Suppose that you came in at twenty minutes past and Annie will bring in your name. That will give the princess an opportunity to ask for you to be admitted or not—as she pleases.' Marion Brightwin always regarded her tact as one of her most valuable gifts.

He came, conscious that he was pleasurably excited. He had dressed with his usual care, and although his violently patterned trousers, short sack coat with its preposterous slit at the back, and narrow necktie over which his fine linen collar was folded, made him feel slightly ridiculous, he remembered that these clothes were the latest and most correct style. Before he left home he entered the long gallery where Simon was working. The little man looked up and blinked at him through his strong, gold-rimmed glasses.

'Emmanuel!' he exclaimed. 'What clothes are these?'

'The very latest, my dear Simon. I came to show you, to listen to your approbation. Look at the hat!' He exhibited the small, hard, round hat with pride.

'Shall I hurt you if I say that they almost—what is the word? —distress me, Emmanuel? In the frock-coat, the tall hat, carefully tied cravat and strapped trousers, there was dignity. This—is ugly, undignified. It is surely'—Cohen sighed—'a sign of the times.'

'Perhaps!' Emmanuel spoke lightly. 'Still, one had better be dead than wear a last year's hat. Good-bye, Simon.'

As he walked towards Marion Brightwin's little house he smiled. Of course his clothes were preposterous, almost ridiculous. But so many things were both. It was incredible that he should be walking now, swinging his gold-headed cane, smiling and taking off his little pudding-basin of a hat in greeting to his acquaintances, as if he had not a care in the world.

'They say that every man is two distinct personalities,' Emmanuel mused. 'How stupid! I am half a dozen people. I am my father's partner, rather worried because he went off this morning to some mysterious appointment, and returned silent, pale, and unwilling to say where he had been. Later, when I suggested that we might have the galleries redecorated in a new scheme which I had worked out, he hesitated, and finally said that he did not think we could afford it. I understood that he had been to see my Uncle Hirsch!

'I am also a good salesman. This morning Countess Batthyani bought the Ninon fan and pomander. Why? They were terribly expensive, I had no right to have bought them. True, the price she paid gave me only a bare profit, but, then, I paid too much in the first place. Ivory, chicken-skin, a little paint, and gold leaf. But she bought them because I happen to know a good deal concerning Madame Ninon, and I have learnt how to tell my stories. Stories which when I read them amused me, stories which when I retail them—amuse the countess. That fan, that pomander will always recall those half-cynical, half-romantic stories to her. So —she paid!

'Then I am a stupid, flattered fool. Dressing himself up in new clothes to go and meet a pretty woman who bores me to ex-- tinction after half an hour. But that silly, conceited side of me is flattered that Maria Dietrich has not forgotten me! There still remains what is perhaps the real Emmanuel Gollantz. Someone who still dare not think of Caro, because Caro still has the power to hurt—perhaps will always have that power. And under all and over all is my pride. Pride in my house, in my work, in my race, and in myself! How can I ever understand myself, when I have to admit that I am four, five, six—a dozen people—some of whom I despise and some for whom'—his smile deepened—'I feel something like warm affection?'

He arrived, and was admitted. Maria Dietrich, wearing the latest creation of the great Worth, a wide, graceful, puffed skirt, introduced to meet the demands of Princess Pauline Metternich, who had declared war on the crinoline, offered her hand, over which Emmanuel bowed. Their eyes met, and he felt a thrill of pleasure at her fair beauty.

'I am so glad to meet you again, Mr. Gollantz.'

'I am honoured, Highness.'

'This lady,' she inclined her head towards Miss Brightwin, 'has kindly consented to teach me—to try to teach me—to speak English.'

Marion Brightwin fluttered a little. 'Your Highness will make very good progress. I am sure of it.'

It was obvious to Emmanuel that Maria was determined to show herself at her most charming. She chattered gaily of Paris, from where she had recently returned ; she told stories of Princess Metternich, of the beautiful Empress, and of the gaiety of the court. Marion listened entranced, her eyes resting on the small, white, ever-moving hands, on the magnificent clothes, and the splendid jewellery of her latest pupil. Emmanuel listened, amused and half-contemptuous. He knew that Maria was determined to attract him, realized that she was doing her best to appear not only amusing, but as a patron of the arts.

'The crinoline is dead—I for one attended the funeral with satisfaction, a satisfaction which sprang from my hatred of anything so lacking in aesthetic beauty. . . . Winterhalter is charming, and when one has said that, one has said all that it is possible to say. . . . Paris is delightful, but her chief delights are those of the past. . . .' And so on ; her small and rather ineffective epigrams were scattered right and left.

Emmanuel thought: 'How she talks, and how little she says! But, how pretty she is!'

She went on to speak of the Austrian Court, guardedly at first, and gradually with greater freedom. She mentioned the Emperor, and shrugged her graceful shoulders over the rigidity of the life at court. She turned the conversation to the Empress, and declared that she was 'wise as a woman, but foolish as an Empress'.

'How is that, Highness?' Emmanuel asked.

'She loves freedom,' Maria replied, meeting his eyes and keeping her own almost disconcertingly steady. 'That is right for a woman. Women must be as free to love—when they do love—as the stronger sex. But if one wishes for freedom, one must not marry an Emperor. That is folly. To be an Empress and free—how impossibly difficult.'

'You think, then, that women must be free—when they find love?'

'When they find love, it is death not to follow where love leads.' Her gravity was tremendous, her voice carried with it an artificial sincerity which was almost convincing. Once again Emmanuel knew that his thoughts went back to Caro. How often had they talked of love, and yet never with this pomposity, this tremendous portentousness. This was a game and Maria was overplaying her part a little. His cynical amusement deepened.

The little clock on the mantelpiece struck five. Maria started up and gave a little scream.

'Five o'clock, and I am still here! Miss Brightveen, what must you think of me? And Mr. Gollantz, what will happen to your English lesson?'

'Believe me, you have given me a dozen lessons in this last half hour, Highness. I have learnt so much concerning the great world.'

'He has learnt to flatter, has he not?' Maria asked Miss Brightwin ; then, with a gesture which was patently pathetic in its helplessness, she asked: 'How can I get back to my home? Is it possible to get a carriage? I dismissed my coachman when I arrived. I did not know how long I should be here.'

'I am the best lackey in Vienna,' Emmanuel assured her, and went out, to return a few minutes later with a hired carriage.

'You will come back when you have seen the princess to her carriage, and have your lesson?' Miss Brightwin asked.

Emmanuel shook his head. 'It is impossible. I have to get back to meet an important client.'

Maria, with perfect unconcern, asked if she might drive him to his house, the carriage would pass the gates. 'I have robbed you of your lesson, I must make reparation.'

In the carriage Emmanuel sat silent, his hands folded on the gold head of his cane. Maria leant back in her corner, sighing from time to time.

'Emmanuel,' she said at last, 'you have changed.'

He turned and smiled at her. 'Never in—important things; only in superficial ones.'

She sighed again. 'I have missed you.'

'Even in Paris?'

'Do places matter?'

'Don't they? He stretched out his hand and laid it on hers. 'How small your hand is.'

He sat watching her, and thought how pleasant it was to be driving with a pretty woman again. How attractive women were, with their soft, scented hair, their delightfully smooth, small hands. Her voice was pleasing when she did not talk too fast and let it reach too high a key. She was the product of all that was expensive and artificial, but he disliked neither evidences of wealth, nor artificiality.

'It is wonderful to be with you again—Highness.'

'Maria,' she whispered. 'To you, Emmanuel—only Maria.'

Again a silence. The pressure of his hand on hers increased. She said with apparent irrelevance: 'Theodore is away—he has gone to Egypt or Syria or some other place where it is hot and sandy.'

'You are alone?'

'I have been—terribly lonely. Tonight I wish to go to the "Two Doves" to hear Strauss play his new waltz. I am going with Charlotte Grunner and her husband, Rudi. She is the sister of Max von Habenberg.'

'How astonishing! I was planning to go to the "Two Doves" to meet von Habenberg. He is my friend. I am very fond of him.'

'Then you will join us?'

Emmanuel twisted round so that he faced her; his lips were twisted half whimsically, half cynically. 'What—meet you in public, with the Grunners? What will Vienna say?'

Maria raised her eyebrows. Her manner was autocratic. 'Did you not listen when I spoke of the rights of personal freedom? If you are the friend of Max von Habenberg, can you not be—my friend as well?'

'And if I assure you that to be—your friend would be intolerable to me, what then?'

'My reply might surprise you. . . .'

He laughed. 'But I dislike surprises. I would prefer—naturally —a reply which gratified me. If that were impossible, I would rather have disappointment than—a surprise. I like to know where I stand.'

'I should hope never to disappoint you, Emmanuel.'

Emmanuel lifted her hand to his lips and kissed it.

II

The month which followed seemed to Emmanuel to resemble a play in which he and Maria were the chief characters. There were moments when he longed to tell the whole story to Gustave, offering it to him as the plot for a new comedy. He felt certain that in her heart of hearts Maria loved him no more than he loved her, and was equally conscious that a strong physical attraction existed between them, that they admired each other and found each other vastly amusing.

Whatever else Emmanuel Gollantz might be, he was a Jew first and foremost, and it was one of the characteristics of his race which made him enjoy being seen with a woman who was not only beautiful, but who held a great place in Viennese society. It amused him to know that their discretion was so elaborate that it was patent to everyone. When they met, for example, at the 'Two Doves', or at the 'Green Gate', their greeting was so casual, their manner towards each other so studiously aloof, that anyone with the poorest intelligence must have wondered how they could meet so often at either place and still remain so indifferent to each other. It amused him, too, to know that Vienna watched them and wondered, speculated and talked.

As he entered the 'Spiel' one evening, the proprietor, the stout Scharzer, came forward bowing. Scharzer exuded the joy of living, a joy which not all the cares and worries of a large and fashionable restaurant could diminish.

'Good evening, Herr Gollantz!'

Emmanuel swung his wide, black cloak from his shoulders and handed it to an attendant. 'Good evening, Herr Scharzer. Your restaurant is full—as always.'

Scharzer's smile widened, and into his eyes crept an expression which was at once friendly and approving. He liked handsome young men to patronize his restaurant.

'Her Highness is here, Herr Gollantz.'

Emmanuel's face became cold, his voice icy, when he spoke.

'I congratulate you, but which Highness?'

'Princess Maria Dietrich, Herr Gollantz.'

'Really! The "Spiel" increases in popularity. Tell me, is Herr Gustave here yet?'

Scharzer, scarlet in the face, realized that he had made a mistake.

'I—I could not say. I don't—don't think that I have seen—Herr Gustave.'

'Please find me a table, and when he arrives tell him where I am sitting. Here? Very good. Let the waiter bring me the wine list.'

He sat down, ordered his wine, then leaned back in his chair, surveying the restaurant with a slight air of boredom. His quick eyes found Maria, seated with Countess Grunner. He rose and bowed, then walked over to where they sat and begged that he might pay his respects. This done he returned to his own table, where he sat for the rest of the evening alone, for the probable arrival of Gustave had existed only in Emmanuel's imagination.

Later, Scharzer came to him, bowing, trying to atone for his lack of tact. Emmanuel talked, smiled, and accepted the unspoken apology. Scharzer never made the same mistake again.

So they continued to meet at the 'Spiel', which, despite the statements that it was not possessed of the most immaculate reputation, was amusing and cheerful—at the 'Two Doves', the café which was the headquarters of Johannes Strauss and his magnificent orchestra, and at the smaller 'Green Gate'. They drank coffee together at Dommayer's, and even sat together at the aristocratic 'Zogernitz' where all Vienna could see them.

Theodore was away in the wilds of the desert, Maria was bored to extinction, and Emmanuel liked to spend his time with a pretty woman. The weeks passed pleasantly, and gradually he knew that she was becoming a habit and part of his daily life. The Emperor had never liked old Prince Theodore, the Empress rarely troubled her beautiful head over the morals of the court, and Maria had long ago declared that she cared nothing for the rules and regulations upon which the Hapsburgs relied too much.

Max von Habenberg only once ventured to speak to Emmanuel concerning his association with Maria. They were walking back from the opera one evening, and von Habenberg recalled various looks and whispers which had reached him when Emmanuel visited Maria's box during the interval.

'Emmanuel,' he began with a certain hesitation, 'I feel that I ought to tell you what I heard and noticed this evening.'

'Ought?' Emmanuel's voice was suddenly sharp. 'What you heard and noticed?' Then the old smoothness returned, only his fingers closed a little more tightly on his friend's arm. 'I have always thought—referring to what we have seen and heard this evening—that *Stradella* had been given too often. That it had lost some of its freshness. It may have done for us, but how admirable the Hoffmann's performance was tonight, it might——'

'I was not thinking of the performance, Emmanuel.'

'No? Let me advise you, Max, to think of nothing else, it is so much wiser. As I was saying, it might have been the first time she had played her part. Quite admirable!'

'You mean that you do not wish . . .'

The grip of Emmanuel's fingers ceased, his touch became almost affectionate. 'I mean that I do not wish to discuss anything which might damage our friendship. I feel that Erl and Meyerhofer are just a little too robust ; because they are playing bandits that is no excuse for roaring like lions. Don't you agree?'

Old Marcus Breal heard the stories which circulated concerning the good-looking, arrogant young Jew and Princess Dietrich. He smoothed his chin, frowned, and asked Emmanuel to dine. As they left the dining-room, both content after a magnificent dinner and admirable wine, Breal tried to open the subject.

'I hear your name mentioned in quite a number of conversations, Emmanuel. It would appear that you move in exalted circles these days.'

'Indeed?' The tone was full of amused surprise, then suddenly Breal felt Emmanuel's hand under his elbow, and heard him say quickly: 'Be careful, please, Herr Breal.'

'What is it? Why did you do that?' Breal asked.

'I was afraid for a moment that you were going to make a false step,' Emmanuel explained, then added: 'Your polished floors are beautiful, but just a little dangerous.'

Breal stopped dead, stared at him, then laughed. 'I see!' he said.

'I am delighted,' Emmanuel returned, and the incident closed.

9

BEING the lover of Maria Dietrich, Emmanuel reflected, sometimes was a little wearing. She was like a kitten, charming, attractive and amusing, but at any moment her claws might shoot out,
and scratches, which although not dangerous were certainly painful, might be inflicted. She was jealous, and possessed an ability
for making scenes. Emmanuel often thought that she enjoyed
making them, that it gave her definite satisfaction to begin with
tender reproaches, proceed to slightly tearful statements that
he had ceased to love her, and pass on to the next stage, which was
to work herself into a state of weeping hysteria.

She liked to spend her time between Vienna and Paris, and it
was after one of these visits that she attacked Emmanuel.

'. . . and told me that you were behind the scenes every evening
while I was away.'

'That is not quite true. I was behind the scenes only four times.'

'And why must you go behind at all?'

'I went on business——'

'Always on business?'

'No'—very coolly—'only the first time. After that for my own
pleasure. The same reason that took you to Paris.'

She flounced away from him, wresting herself from the arm
which he had thrown round her, her lovely face furious with
temper.

'And your pleasure was to stand and talk all the evening with
the Hettner!'

'Not all the evening,' he corrected. 'She is playing an important
part, and is on the stage most of the time.'

'But whilst she was not on the stage?'

'I was talking to her.'

So it would continue, until Maria burst into hysterical tears,
and Emmanuel—who knew that he feared women's tears more
than anything else in the world—would take her in his arms and
swear that only she mattered, that the Hettner was plain and only

amused him because he was lonely without his beautiful Maria. While he whispered to her, as he felt her lovely body relax in his arms and her lips warm on his cheek, he would wonder where it was all going to end, and what would happen if by some strange chance Caro ever came back to Vienna.

It was a relief to escape to the plain little apartment near the theatre where Theodora Hettner lived, to climb the long, steep stairs, and sit on one of her big shabby chairs, while she played to him. She was a friend of Gustave's; she was clever, young, and beautiful in a queer, fierce fashion which had nothing in common with Maria's pink-and-white loveliness. She liked Emmanuel Gollantz but never loved him, and once when he hinted that she was occupying a large part of his thoughts, she exclaimed with some irritation: 'For God's sake, don't spoil it all! I shan't have time to think about love for another six years at least. I am much too busy.'

'Have I mentioned the word "love"?' he asked. 'I only suggested that I might like you too much for my own peace of mind.'

'I know! And having hinted that, you will begin to watch me, to see if I show signs of falling in love with you. When you discover that I am doing nothing of the kind, you will be hurt, annoyed, offended'

Half piqued, half hurt, he would fling out of her room and return to Maria, lashing himself into a state of sentimental tenderness towards her, wanting her physical presence, her touch, her embraces—until she lost her temper again.

The truth was that he longed for love and could not find it. He might be self-sufficient, he might and did swagger through the streets of Vienna, conscious—and not displeased—that every woman's eyes followed him, but he knew that neither Maria nor Theodora could give him the love for which he craved. He knew that as the days passed his heart continued to ache for Caro, and that whereas Maria had acted as a drug when they met again, now she had become merely an irritant, and a slightly boring habit.

'Women are always asking questions about you,' von Habenberg said.

'Women?' Emmanuel repeated. 'What women are these? The women who dare not get to know me and ask those questions for themselves, eh?'

'Oh, come.' Max could never bear to remember that Emman-

uel was debarred from the houses where he himself was welcomed. 'Not all of them. Princess Maria, my sister——'

'And who else?'

'Lots of them.'

'No, Max—no others. Your sister likes me because I am your
friend ; Princess Maria—has always been very charming to me ;
but there are no others.'

'But, good heavens, you don't care, do you?'

'Ah, that is another matter. One half of me laughs, the other—
oh, Max, I am a sensitive fool. Much too proud, and much too
easily hurt.'

Things were becoming difficult between himself and his father.
He knew that somewhere, somehow, money was leaking out of
the business at a far greater rate than it was pouring in. He knew
that Hirsch made constant demands on his father, knew that
Jean came in and out, that he was closeted with Rachel Gollantz
and emerged smiling and content. Hirsch himself rarely came to
the house, and when he did, Emmanuel found a certain cold
pleasure in acting the part of creditor.

Hirsch, gross, badly and horribly over-dressed, would enter the
gallery, and whilst Emmanuel disposed of a client, wander round,
noisily picking his teeth. The client disposed of, he would come
forward with a great show of cordiality.

'Your dear father—is he here?'

'I regret, he is away this morning. But'—and Emmanuel would
hesitate—'if you came to pay the small outstanding amount, the
eight hundred gulden which has been owing—— Simon, how
long has the account of Herr Hirsch been outstanding? Nearly
a year? Thank you. . . . Nearly a year—I shall be pleased to give
you a receipt.'

Hirsch, puffing and blowing, his face purple, would bluster.

'Not paid yet? Surely it was paid weeks, months ago! I gave the
money to my secretary, or to Jean—I forget which. I shall see to
it.'

'A thousand thanks, I am most grateful. May I escort you to
your carriage, Herr Justus Hirsch?'

Those incidents made him smile, amused him. True, the amusement was slightly bitter, but it was diverting to watch Hirsch's
discomfiture. The last occasion was not even bitterly amusing,
it was almost tragic. It began when Hermann entered the gallery
to find Emmanuel, his face full of interest and pleasure, arranging

239

a dinner service on one of the tables. Hermann stopped, picked up a plate and examined it carefully.

'Sèvres?'

Emmanuel, holding a magnificent tureen in his hands, turned and smiled. 'Sèvres, indeed!' he said. 'The royal period, the soft paste, and hand decorated, signed by the artists. See the pale blue mark, the beautiful twist with the letter A in the centre. Who knows, this may have been ordered by the Pompadour herself. A find, eh, Father?'

'When did you buy this?'

'Yesterday. I said nothing, I wanted it as a surprise for you.'

'And the price?'

Emmanuel drew a deep breath. 'I admit that it seems a great deal, but it is worth three times what I paid. Six thousand gulden.'

It struck him that his father's face looked suddenly grey, but he supposed it was some trick of light from the long window. He turned back to the china and continued setting it out with loving care.

'Is it bought for a customer?' Hermann asked, his voice not quite steady.

'Not actually. But we shan't have it very long. Be certain of that.'

'Listen to me, Emmanuel!' Hermann's voice was harsh, and had Emmanuel heard anything but the harshness he would have known that it was the voice of a man whose nerves are strained to snapping point. 'Listen to me. I will not allow you to spend money in this reckless fashion. It is insupportable that you should go and buy a Sèvres dinner service without even asking my permission to do so. Last week it was four hundred gulden for an English Queen Anne cabinet——'

'Which I sold for five hundred!'

'No matter! I am master here. I will not be disregarded in this fashion; it is intolerable. Please remember that in future. This china here—it must be returned. I won't pay for it!'

'Father! I don't understand you! Send it back? Impossible!'

Hermann's face was white and twitching. Emmanuel, equally pale, faced him. Never in his life had he heard his father speak so to him. He was dismayed, distressed, unable to understand what had happened.

'I tell you it shall go back. By tomorrow it must be out of here. Six thousand gulden . . . do you think that I am made of money?'

'I shall sell it for eight thousand!'

'But when, when, when? Can I afford to have six thousand gulden lying idle? No, you know very well that I can't. I have great expenses—this house, your mother's allowance, Simon, your salary, your bills which have to be paid . . .'

'I understand, Father.' Emmanuel spoke very quietly. 'Please say no more. From now I shall work on commission only; you shall have no more bills. I am sorry that I have been extravagant. As for the dinner service, it will be sold by this evening. I shall hand you the money, and'—he paused, then continued—'ask you to return to me five per cent on the two thousand gulden profit.'

Hermann made a rather ghastly attempt to recover himself.

'No, no, Emmanuel. I don't want you to work in that way. Take your salary as usual, you're worth every penny of it.'

Emmanuel's hands were busy with the china, his eyes were averted.

'Thank you, Father. To work on commission only will remind me that I must not take too much upon myself. Believe me, I shall not make this mistake again. Please let us say no more about it.'

An hour later Emmanuel, looking immensely tall and elegant in his long, tightly fitting frock coat, immaculate linen, cravat and gloves, presented himself at the great house where Max von Habenberg lived. He had never called there before, refusing all his friend's invitations.

'You are my friend, Max, but you must not expect your friends to accept me.'

Von Habenberg had flushed, scowled, and muttered that it would give him the greatest pleasure to deal with anyone who refused to accept Emmanuel.

'I believe you, fire-eater that you are!' Emmanuel said, laughing. 'But I am thinking of my own pleasure in this case. I should hate to watch you defending—my position. No, it is better as it is.'

Now he presented himself at the door, gave his card to the footman who opened it, and stated that he wished to see the lieutenant. A few moments later Max von Habenberg came hurrying through the great hall, his hands outstretched in welcome.

'This is splendid! I have wished for this visit so long. Come into my sitting-room.' Then, to the footman, 'Bring coffee—or wine. Will you have wine, my dear Emmanuel?'

'Neither, thank you.' He paused, and Max noticed how pale he was. 'I am here,' he said slowly and with careful distinctness, 'on a matter of business. Did you not notice that I sent in my business card?'

'Card! I only looked to see your name. What is all this about? You are making game of me. Come and sit down, you look pale.'

Seated in his friend's room, Emmanuel told the story of the Sèvres dinner service. 'It is magnificent, but my father has been—I think, just a little unreasonable. I have declared that I will sell the service, and so I have come to know if you will tell me of anyone you think might require such a service. I do not as a rule hawk my wares round Vienna, but this is a rather special occasion. So I came to ask of you—your help.'

'But I am delighted. Tell me the price.'

'Eight thousand gulden.' He smiled and added: 'You see, it is a very beautiful service, a royal service, Max.'

Max von Habenberg's face flushed. 'This is terrible. I spoke so glibly, and now I have to admit that it is nearly the end of the month, and as usual I am impoverished! Oh, that little Carlotta, and she does love flowers so, and loves jewels still more! But here is an opportunity. I have long wanted you to meet my father—he is at home now. He has heard of you from me—I am always talking about you—and he will be so happy to meet you. He knows that you were—very kind to me when I was in a great difficulty.'

Emmanuel shook his head. 'Max, I won't pester him to buy something he doesn't want because of a purely imaginary kindness he believes I once did you. That's virtually asking him for eight thousand gulden. I can't do it. Think, do you not know of someone who would buy such a thing?'

'At least let us go and ask him if he can help us. He may know of someone.'

Half unwillingly Emmanuel consented. Together they stood before Baron von Habenberg, stout, white-haired, with bright blue eyes which, under all their sternness, were kindly. Max introduced his friend, and continued to embark on a panegyric of Emmanuel's good qualities. Emmanuel, distressed and embarrassed, held up his hand in protest.

'Max—please!'

'Herr Gollantz is right,' the baron said. 'Max, you talk too much. I have always said so. Herr Gollantz, be seated. I have wanted to meet you for a considerable time. For two reasons: first because I heard on all sides that you are a man of taste, and when I wished to have some of the rooms here re-decorated, my mind turned to you. I mentioned the matter to my son; he begged me not to send for you. He said—— No, Max, hold your tongue, I shall speak!—that to do so would be to make your first entrance into my house as other than a guest. I saw the justice of what he said, and because'—the sudden smile was like a burst of sunshine over a winter landscape—'I wished very much to have you here as my guest, I gave the decorating to another firm.

'The second,' he stretched out his hand and laid it on his son's arm, 'I do not need to enter into now. You know it, Max, and I know it. Now we will drink some wine, to celebrate your first visit to my house and hope that it is the first of many. Max, go and order wine—tell Hartmann that I wish for a bottle of the wine marked "59".' As the door closed behind Max, the baron said to Emmanuel: 'And now tell my why you came here today, after having refused all my son's invitations?'

Briefly, coldly, Emmanuel told his story. His tone was so impersonal that it was bordering on the offensive; it was as if he scorned himself for having introduced business into his friend's house. The baron listened, with pursed lips, his bushy brows drawn close, his fingers drumming on the top of his desk.

'I believe that you dislike your reason for coming here,' he said.

For the first time Emmanuel's voice held a personal note. 'I do—intensely.'

'Is this service, then, not worth the money you ask for it?'

It amused the old man to see how Emmanuel's handsome head was flung up at the implied challenge. 'Certainly it is. If I waited I might get nine thousand. It is perfect.'

'Then it is an opportunity? Literally, an investment?'

'Without a doubt. I have never seen such a service; it is magnificent.'

'Then why deny your friends the chance to make an investment, to acquire something that is admirable?'

'Because one does not pester one's friends to buy!' He was indignant, half afraid that the baron was trying to put him at his ease with a flood of sophistry.

'Pester! Who used that expression? Not I! Come, come, Gollantz, you are a young man, you should have more modern ideas. Everyone has something to sell; always there are people who wish to buy. How do you suppose my friends obtain positions for their sons? They come to me; they say: "Baron, you have influence. . . " "Baron, you have the ear of So-and-so, will you be so good. . . ." Later, when I have done what they asked, they remind me that I once admired this picture, liked that wine, stated that I enjoyed shooting antelope, was pleased to bet on horse races, indulged in speculations—when they were safe. They beg me to accept the picture; they send me a case of old wine, invitations to shoot; they draw me on one side and whisper that this or that is certain to make money.

'What is that but buying and selling? Next time I buy one of those dubious old masters, what shall I do? I shall say: "Oh, Max, ask your young friend to come and take wine with us tomorrow." You will come—at least I hope that you will come—and I shall turn the conversation to art. I shall point to the Velasquez of my great-grandfather, and you will say it is beautiful. Gradually I shall work to my new find. I shall state that it is, without question, a valuable old master. You will wag your head, cock your eye, and ask if you may examine it. I shall express my pleasure, and reiterate that it is a magnificent picture. You will look, touch, stand back and look again, and—deliver judgment. The picture is not good. "I doubt," you will say, "if it is worth three hundred gulden." I shall have obtained a specialist's opinion for the cost of a glass of wine!

'Poof, my dear young man, we live in a commercial age, however we may pretend to despise commerce. Many of us are rich, but no man is so rich that he does not like to be richer. My son-in-law, Rudi Grunner, is so rich—on paper—that he has never enough small change to pay his dinner bill at a restaurant. Max is supposed to be rich, so am I. But—money is worth less than it used to be. Get rid of these magnificent ideas; they do you credit, and put no money in your bank.' He paused, took out an immense Russian leather cigar-case, extracted one and lit it with care. 'Now, I am not going to buy your Sèvres service!'

'With all respect, Baron, might I remind you that I have not asked you to do so?'

The baron threw back his head and gave a sudden yelp of delight.

'There you go again! I have told you not to be so proud! I am going to sell it for you. My wife will buy it—she really is quite a wealthy woman!—and give it as a marriage present to the

244

daughter of Princess Hohenstein. Such a plain girl, with the most beautiful little feet! I want the history of the service written out. Put in a great deal about Pompadour—women like that sort of thing! Now, I shall write an order for my bank to pay you eight thousand gulden.' He wrote out the order and signed it in his small, cramped handwriting, then pushed the slip of paper over to Emmanuel.

'But,' Emmanuel objected, 'you have not seen the service! It may not be all that I have said.'

'Still this pride! I have seen you, that is enough. Here is Max with the wine. Now—the business is over, Max, and for the rest of his life Gollantz is going to value my pictures for nothing—except a glass of wine taken with you and me——'

'And my mother,' Max added.

'Assuredly with your mother as well. Now, Gollantz, drink that and tell me if it is good, then I will tell you its history.'

11

Emmanuel returned home, the order on the bank in his pocket. He felt warmed, stabilized, happy. They had been so friendly, so utterly without rigidity, it had been like talking to friends he had known all his life. The baron had shown him pictures, teased him when he gave his opinion on them and sworn that he was trying to belittle his possessions. The baroness had looked up from her embroidery and said: 'So this is the mysterious Herr Gollantz that Max talks of so much! Why didn't you come to see us before?' And Max had glowed with pride and pleasure each time his friend said anything which flattered the baroness or called forth the approbation of the baron. He had sold his service, he could hand the money to his father and all would be well. In his happiness he had forgotten the difficult little scene which had taken place before he left home that evening.

The house was dark except for one light burning in the gallery. Emmanuel hesitated at the door, thinking that someone had left the light burning. The sound of voices reached him—two voices one loud and angry, the other quiet and nervous. His father and his Uncle Hirsch were talking in the gallery. As he opened the door, their words were distinct.

'I tell you, Hermann, I must have the money. Without it I am ruined, and in that ruin you and your precious house will be buried.'

'And I tell you,' his father's quick, nervous voice replied, 'that it is impossible. I can do no more. I must think of my son's future. Of my own business. That is the best I can do—that is the last krone I can give you.'

'Damnation! Ten thousand gulden when I need five times that amount——'

Emmanuel closed the door behind him and walked forward so that he stood within the little ring of light. Hermann lifted his head and showed a face so distraught, so wretched that Emmanuel could have cried with pity. Hirsch swung his huge bulk round in his chair and stared, his loose mouth a little open.

'What you need and what you will get,' Emmanuel said, 'are not at all the same thing. My father is tired. He and I still have business to discuss. Please go.'

'Your opinion was not asked!' Hirsch shouted. 'Speak when you are asked to, not before. I have come here to talk important business with your father.'

The light from the shaded lamp fell on the three faces, throwing them up into high relief. Hermann, leaning heavily against the wide table, his sensitive face anxious and distressed. He looked like a man grown old before his time, trying to shoulder burdens too heavy for his strength. Hirsch, gross, purple-faced, with slack lips and pouched, red-rimmed eyes, the picture of a man who had abused every gift, tasted too heavily of every sensation and had become bankrupt in honour. Thirdly, Emmanuel, with his youth, his beauty, and his intolerance of all that was second-rate. Baron von Habenberg had told him that he must not be proud, that he lived in a commercial age. He glanced at Hirsch. This was what lack of pride produced; this was the type of creature which belonged to an age when money was the primary force in men's lives!

'Father, this is your house. I ask your permission to send this man away for good. Tell him that we—you and I—are done with him and his children, that we have tolerated him too long.'

Hermann lifted his heavy, tired eyes. When he spoke, Emmanuel thought that he had never listened to a voice so drained of all strength.

'It—is—very difficult,' he said. 'Your dear mother's brother——'

246

Emmanuel snapped his fingers impatiently. 'Then, for tonight at least, make him go away. I have a great deal to say to you, Father. I realize many things. Are we to sacrifice everything, the whole future of our work, our business, to keep this man?'

With an obvious effort, Hermann nodded, saying: 'Yes, go now. I am very tired. Tomorrow I will come and talk to you. Emmanuel is right.'

The huge, bulky fellow seemed to crumple like a pricked bladder. His great flabby face quivered, his large, puffy hands trembled. 'But the money you promised me! I tell you without at least ten thousand gulden by tomorrow morning, I am ruined! Not only am I ruined, but——'

Emmanuel stepped forward, he took from his waistcoat pocket the order for eight thousand gulden and, unfolding it, gave it to his father.

Speaking to Hirsch he said: 'Do you think that we keep thousands of gulden in the house, waiting for you to come and demand it? If my father chooses, take this—you can cash it tomorrow—and go! My father will speak with you tomorrow.' Leaning down he spoke very softly, 'Go, I tell you, or I shall forget that you are an old man and throw you out.'

Hermann pushed the bank order across the table. Hirsch clutched it, and rising, stumbled towards the door without looking again in the direction of his nephew. Hermann dropped his head in his arms and began to sob weakly, as if he had been an overtired child. Emmanuel sprang to his side, laid his arm round his shoulders, and spoke to him tenderly and with the deepest affection.

Hirsch made his way down the wide corridor and fumbled with the handle of the huge door. As it swung open he found a man standing on the topmost step, holding a note in his hand.

'Herr Emmanuel Gollantz?'

Hirsch hesitated for a moment, then said: 'I am Herr Gollantz. I was about to lock the door.' He took the note, twisted it in his thick fingers. 'Who is this from?'

'I cannot tell you. It was given to me by a man in black and claret livery. He told me to give it into the hands of Herr Gollantz. He gave me two gulden and said that you would double that amount.'

Hirsch dipped his fingers into his pocket and extracted the money.

'There, be off, and hold your tongue.'

The man turned, ran down the steps, and was lost in the darkness. Hirsch turned the envelope in his fingers, feeling the thickness of the paper, noting the absence of any device on the flap. He licked his lips—it might be that something useful had fallen into his hands. By God, he'd use it!

Down the corridor he heard the quick steps of Emmanuel, and heard his voice demanding, as he might have spoken to some beggar, Hirsch thought: 'What are you doing there? Did I hear you speaking to someone?'

'No, no one. Damn you, Emmanuel bar Hermann, may not an old man rest for a moment before he goes out into the night?'

'Not here! I have told you to go!'

The heavy door swung to, banging behind him. Ishmael Hirsch made his way down the steps, muttering in his anger, with the letter still clutched in his hand.

10

I

EMMANUEL returned to the long gallery and found his father leaning back in his big carved chair, his eyes closed, his white hands resting on the arms of the chair as if the exertion of the past hour had been too much for him. Emmanuel drew up a velvet-covered stool, and sat down very near to his father. He looked at the pale, tired face, noted the absence of strength, the expression of utter weariness, with tenderness and pity.

'Father,' he said gently. 'Father, I am sorry that I was so hasty this evening over the Sèvres. You were right, of course ; I had no business to have bought it. Only it seemed an opportunity, and'—he laughed—'I kept my word and sold it, didn't I?'

Hermann opened his eyes and smiled at his son. 'My dear Emmanuel, my beloved son. You are too generous. I was nervous, worried, and allowed both those things to affect my behaviour to you. It shall never happen again. I have not treated you quite fairly ; I want to make reparation if I can now though the time is late. Will you please listen to me?'

'Not tonight, Father. You are too tired. Tomorrow will be time enough.'

'No, no.' Hermann's voice was almost fearful. 'Tomorrow will not be time enough. Now, Emmanuel, now, you must listen to me.'

'Very well.'

Slowly and with considerable effort Hermann Gollantz told his son of the drain which Hirsch had been on his resources. He quoted instance after instance where he had been crippled in business, limited in activity through the demands which Hirsch had made upon him.

'In Vienna, in Berlin, in Paris—no matter where he has been, he has never ceased to apply to me for help. His children have been ill, his wife needed an expensive holiday, his business would fail without additional capital. Always somthing.'

'And you,' Emmanuel said softly, 'have always listened to his requests.'

Hermann nodded. 'Yes, because I felt that he was my responsibility. He is your mother's only brother ; she loves him, is proud of him, she still believes in him. I could not bear to hurt her— my wife. The knowledge of what he is would hurt her terribly. More, I have always held that it was my duty to do whatever was possible to keep a name so closely connected with my own clean and free from reproach. I could not allow men in this city, Viennese, to look at Hirsch and say: "There goes the brother-in-law of Hermann Gollantz, a bankrupt, a debtor, a swindling thief—in effect, if not in actuality". You see, Emmanuel, I am very proud, I have always been proud. To me this feeling is stronger than all others.

'Perhaps in this case, in the case of Ishmael Hirsch, I am being punished for my pride. I have known that I was called "the only honest dealer in Austria". I have felt proud when I remembered that saying. Having determined to protect your mother from anything which might hurt her, wound her, I could not turn back. So my burden has grown heavier and heavier until he has almost crushed me. That is my punishment.'

'If it is a punishment, then it has ended tonight. Hirsch shall never come into this house again! I swear that!'

Hermann turned and laid his hand on Emmanuel's arm. 'Gently, gently. I admit that he is detestable, but he grows old, and—life is not easy for old people, my son. The unscrupulous young man who tricks, who lies, who virtually robs his friends—one can say hard things of him. But the old man who does not know how to be honest, who regards trickery as part of his stock-in-trade, who has forgotten that it was once difficult to ask for money, whose sense of shame is lost—isn't he to be pitied? Hasn't he lost everything that might make life worth living?'

'I don't know. Perhaps it is difficult for me to see through your eyes. I see only that you have been imposed upon, robbed. You can't expect me to have much pity in my heart for my uncle, Father.'

Hermann, leaning back in his chair again, his eyes closed, spoke slowly and very softly. Emmanuel wondered for a moment if he were ill and wandering in his speech, but the words were clear enough. He sat forward, his elbows on his knees, listening.

'There are a great many advantages possessed by our race,' Hermann said, 'and one of them is that the rest of humanity have formed such an entirely erroneous conception of us. We are credited with being meek, with assuming a humility which has almost become part of us. We are supposed to love money above all things, to be hard and revengeful. In short, we are acclaimed as the supreme actors of the world, and into our most simple acts or statements the rest of the world reads something which is deep and considered.

'We are not meek, we resent injury, we hate being imposed upon, and most of all we hate those cheap sneers which are directed against us because of our race. But we are neither hard nor revengeful. We know the values of material things—we have been forced to learn them in a hard school, but revenge——' He opened his eyes and smiled his particularly beautiful and kindly smile. 'We are usually much too busy to spend—to waste—time on petty revenge. I always laugh when I read *The Merchant of Venice* and wonder what will be the opinion of the playgoing world when some actor dares to play Shylock as a gentleman and not as a greasy old money-lender! Perhaps you may live to see it. I envy you!

'One day, Emmanuel, you will have a certain heritage. How much, how little, I cannot tell you. The world moves very quickly in these days. But whatever it is, remember, and I say this seriously, that the most important part of that heritage is your Jewish blood. It is at once a tremendous advantage and a handicap. It gives you many things, but it gives you that same over-whelming, almost senseless pride which I have always possessed. Accept the pride of race which is yours by inheritance from your father and your grandfather, who was artistic adviser to the Emperor Napoleon, the Great Napoleon—but never permit it to force you into unworthiness. We all like money, for in the world today money means power. We love power! But even money can cost too much ; even power can be bought too dearly. So many of our race fall into that error. They can value every-thing at its proper cost except—money. That, they buy in mar-kets which are too dear, and the price is paid not only by them, but by every member of the race to which they belong.

'You see, an honest Jew is accepted, but not acclaimed. A dis-honest Jew is acclaimed as such by everyone. One honest Jew remains one honest Jew, one dishonest Jew is hailed as a type of his race.' He sat upright, his eyes suddenly bright with excite-ment. 'Listen, Emmanuel, for this is something you must re-member always. We are a scattered people, we are sheep without a shepherd, we come from all corners of the earth, we are denied rights and privileges because we are not, politically, a nation. Yet we are judged as a nation by the rest of the world, and the judg-ment passed on us, as a whole, is the lowest judgment passed on one of us as an individual.

'A merchant trades with some poverty-stricken Hebrew in the wilds of Poland, Russia, or Eastern Germany, some poor, half-educated peasant, who has learnt his code of morals as a parrot might learn snatches of conversation—mechanically. His very poverty, his very ignorance, have made him cunning, deceitful, dishonest. His trickery, his unfair dealing, his lack of truth are discovered, and that merchant goes through life believing that in his discovery of that wretched peasant he has discovered the truth concerning the whole of the Jewish race. One Viennese meets Ishmael Hirsch, and by Hirsch he judges all of us, for-getting that there is—I am afraid that I sound conceited, but no matter, we are speaking together in confidence—such a man as Hermann Gollantz. But'—his lips twisted suddenly—'in meeting me, he will not forget my brother-in-law!

'So remember, and I charge you most seriously never to for-get this, that in your hands may lie men's opinion of your whole race. Never, I beg you, Emmanuel, do anything to lower that race in the opinion of the world. That pride is justifiable, that pride is honourable. For ten just men the Cities might have been spared—it may be that through ten just men the reputation of your race will depend. See to it, Emmanuel bar Hermann, that you are one of those just men.'

He ceased speaking, and passed his hand before his eyes, sighing. 'I am very tired,' he said. 'It is late. I am very glad to have talked this way to you, Emmanuel. You have been very patient with me.'

'I am glad that you have wished to speak to me, Father. I am grateful. You will let me help you more, stand at your side. I have been selfish. Oh, I have worked hard enough, because work interests me, amuses me. I have not always been very tolerant. I have been impatient. Headstrong! Please forgive me—for everything.'

With his hand on Emmanuel's arm, Hermann walked to his own room. It seemed to Emmanuel that he leant heavily on him, and that once he caught his breath quickly. He was tired out—tomorrow he must rest.

'Good night, Father. Sleep well.'

'Good night, my son.' Hermann took Emmanuel's face between his hands and kissed him on both cheeks. 'I am very proud of you, Emmanuel.'

II

It seemed to Emmanuel that he had only just fallen asleep, when he heard a sudden hammering on his door and a voice calling to him.

'Herr Emmanuel, Herr Emmanuel, come at once, come at once!'

He was out of bed, wrapping himself in his purple silk dressing-gown in a moment. Flinging open the door, he found one of the maid-servants, weeping and wringing her hands.

'Oh, the poor master, the poor master—come quickly.'

In his mother's bedroom lights were burning. His mother, her hair hanging loose on her shoulders, stood rocking herself to and fro beside the great carved bed on which Emmanuel had been born. The wailing cry which issued from her lips told Emmanuel everything; this was the wailing of bereaved women as old as the Jewish race itself.

252

He came closer to the bed. His father lay there; his fine, sensitive face seemed to be carved in ivory. Emmanuel, stooping down, felt for his heart, tried to discover that the pulse in his wrist still beat.

'This is now he was lying when I woke!' Rachel sobbed. 'Always I wake early, and make him his first cup of coffee myself. I thought that he was still asleep. I carried it to him, touched his shoulder, and said: "Hermann, here is your coffee. It is half past seven." I have said that for twenty years! He did not move—— Oh, God of my Fathers, let me die with him!'

Very tenderly Emmanuel led her from the room and tried to soothe her.

He himself was overcome with misery. He had loved his father, and he felt that the tragedy was intensified because only last night they had come to an understanding, and had resolved to rely more upon each other. Mechanically he attended to the matters which touched upon his father's death and burial.

Simon Cohen, making no attempt to conceal his tears, was distraught and confused. To him, Hermann Gollantz had been everything, the very centre of the universe, and with his death Cohen's small world was shattered. Emmanuel, grave, controlled, gave orders, issued instructions, answered messages, and granted interviews. Marcus Breal came to him, wise, saying little, offering no spoken word of sympathy, but by his very calmness soothing and comforting. Max von Habenberg, disconcerted by the presence of death, came bringing messages and offers of help from his father and mother, stammering out his own words of sympathy. Later in the day, Ishmael Hirsch, with his wife and son, called at the house. Emmanuel refused to see them.

'If my mother wishes to see her brother—and it is only natural that she should,' he told Simon, 'take them to her. For myself, I will not meet any of them again. I do not know them any longer.'

That evening Rachel sent for her son. Her still pretty, round face was swollen and disfigured, her eyes red with weeping. She looked pathetic and helpless. Ever since her marriage she had relied on Hermann for everything, and now without him, lacking his care and attention, she felt lost and abandoned.

'Emmanuel, where have you been all day?' There was reproach in her tone.

Emmanuel sat down near her, and took her plump, soft hand in his. 'There has been a great deal to do, Mama.'

253

'Could Simon not help you?' The reproach had changed to a certain querulousness. 'Simon knows all about everything. Your beloved father trusted him implicitly.'

'Simon has been working hard all day. It is pitiful to watch him.'

She wiped her eyes on a scrap of a lace handkerchief. 'Oh, I don't doubt it. But what do any of you understand of my loss, which is so much greater than anyone else's? I am bereft of everything. I do not know how I can live without him.'

Emmanuel listened, and offered what comfort he could, whilst she continued to talk of his father and her own terrible loss. He wondered if it relieved her overcharged heart to repeat over and over again how much she had loved her husband, that she would live for the rest of her life inconsolable and wretched. She talked so much, it seemed that she was suddenly endowed with special strength, that she found it possible to reiterate everything so often. Her words became to Emmanuel meaningless, he had been working very hard all day, he had slept very little, and his heart was heavy at the loss of the father he had loved so much. He sat there, holding his mother's hand, allowing his own thoughts to occupy him, while his mother's flood of words poured over him, only half heard, half comprehended.

Later, she insisted that she would attend the funeral. Her friends, her sister-in-law, Simon Cohen, all protested that it was unheard of, that women did not go to funerals. Rachel, with a new strange dignity, replied: 'What do I care for custom? It is sufficient that I go. Other women may do as they please.' They came to Emmanuel and begged him to dissuade her. He shook his head.

'It is my mother's affair. Why should she not go if she wishes? If to bury her dead will soothe her pain, then of course she must go.'

So Rachel Gollantz walked in the procession, leaning on the arm of her tall son, and when people whispered, Emmanuel silenced them with his cold eyes. The Jewish cemetery was very cold, the wind swept over it, ruffling the clothes of the mourners, chilling the hands of the men who held the ropes which were to lower Hermann's coffin. Emmanuel saw no one, his eyes were fixed on the plain casket which held his father's body; he heard only his mother's convulsive sobbing, felt only the pressure of her fingers on his arm.

As they drove home she shivered, and he heard that her teeth chattered. He helped her out of the carriage, and she almost fell into his arms. Simon and he helped her up the steps, and as they entered the house she slipped, and, before they could catch her, lay at their feet. All that night her heavy, dragging breathing could be heard through the house. She lay in the huge bed, her pretty face distorted and suffused.

The doctor talked wisely to Emmanuel of strain, over-excitement, and shock. 'She has a great deal of blood; she is a very heavy woman, your mother.'

'But she is not old.'

The doctor shrugged his shoulders. 'Age has not a great deal to do with these things. It is due to the pressure of the blood, to the arteries, to the brain, to a hundred things. We must hope for the best.'

On the third day she had not regained consciousness. The doctor came, stared down at her, and shook his head.

'The breathing is not so difficult, not so noisy,' Emmanuel whispered, trying to force the doctor to give him some measure of hope.

'Because she is weaker. I do not think she will regain consciousness. Are her family here?'

'Her brother is here. He is the only relation living in Vienna.'

'Perhaps it would be well to send for him to see her alive.'

Emmanuel turned to Simon who stood at his side. 'Go and bring Hirsch.'

But Ishmael Hirsch would not come. Death frightened him, and he sat huddled in an arm-chair by the crackling wood fire. He shook, his great bulk quivered, he begged Simon to bring him a little brandy to restore him.

Emmanuel stood by the bed. The room was very quiet, he could barely hear his mother breathing. In the darkness a nurse moved about, arranging basins, bottles, the paraphernalia of the sick-room. The lamp threw monstrous shadows along the walls, the fire leapt suddenly, and filled the room with unexpected light. His mother stirred. Emmanuel bent over her, his white face very tender.

'Mama, Mama,' he whispered, 'speak to me.'

The eyes opened, her face seemed to have regained its beauty, the mouth was no longer distorted. She smiled up at him.

'Hermann, beloved. . . .' Then the heavy lids were lowered again, and she had passed.

Hirsch sipped his brandy. What admirable brandy Hermann kept—no, not Hermann. Hermann no longer kept anything. Everything belonged to that puppy Emmanuel. His fat fingers groped about in his waistcoat pocket for a folded piece of paper ; the knowledge that it lay there gave him satisfaction. Princess Maria Dietrich indeed! He would show his nephew how badly it paid to make an enemy of Ishmael—or, rather, Justus—Hirsch.

The door swung open and Emmanuel entered. He looked taller than ever in his deep mourning, his black cravat swathed up so high that nothing but a narrow rim of white linen collar was visible. His face seemed to shine in the half-light of the room ; it was ghastly, but quite composed.

'My mother is dead.' His voice was toneless, colourless.

Hirsch scrambled to his feet. 'Rachel dead! My sister—why was I not sent for? How dared you keep me from her?'

'You were sent for. Simon Cohen came to bring you to her. You preferred to stay here, sipping brandy.' He paused, then continued: 'Now, please go.'

'Go! Without seeing my sister?'

'The women are with her. If you care to wait a little you may see her, then go ; and remember that from now I do not know you.'

Ishmael's heavy, flabby face twisted suddenly ; he looked grotesque in his unusual sincerity. His bloodshot eyes were swimming with tears, his loose mouth trembled ; when he spoke his voice was high and quavering. 'I never thought that Rachel was so ill,' he said. 'I didn't think that she was going to die, I thought that you were trying to frighten me.'

The cold, impassive face of Emmanuel did not change, the dark eyes watched him without the faintest hint of regret. For the first time Ishmael realized that affected though he might be, dandy though he undoubtedly was, Emmanuel Gollantz possessed a strength and fixity of purpose which made him a better friend than an enemy.

'Emmanuel,' Hirsch held out his hands towards his nephew, 'let us forget what is over. I have been to blame. Now, in this time of trouble, can't we join hands, and from this night help

256

each other? I beg you from the bottom of my heart, forgive me and be my friend.'

Emmanuel stared at him, his lips compressed. It was as if he had not heard, or, rather, as if he had not allowed himself to hear what was said to him. The firm chin was lifted a little higher, the eyes were colder than ever.

'Ask Simon to find out if the women have finished. See your sister—and go.'

'That is your last word?'

'My last word, Ishmael Hirsch.'

The door closed. Emmanuel's self-control left him. He sank into a chair, buried his face in his hands, and cried bitterly. He was conscious of his own loneliness, conscious of the temptation it had been to accept Ishmael's offer of friendship—not because he either liked or trusted the man, but because he was the only one of his own blood left.

So, Simon Cohen found him half an hour later, when he crept into the room. He stood, pinching his lower lip between his thumb and finger, his eyes shining behind their thick glasses. Very softly he came forward and laid his hand on Emmanuel's shoulder.

'Emmanuel, Emmanuel,' he whispered. 'Come now, you must not cry so.'

The dark head was lifted, and Emmanuel looked up at the kindly little man he had known all his life. There was nothing left of the handsome young Jew who trod the streets of Vienna as if they belonged to him, who swung his cloak as bravely as an officer of the Imperial Army, who held his head so high, and stared so intolerantly at the society of Vienna.

'I know, Simon,' he said, his voice still thickened with his grief, 'I know, it's only that I realize how terribly alone I am, and how many mistakes I have made. Mistakes that now I cannot ask forgiveness for.'

'Your father—on him be peace—was very wise,' Simon ventured.

'Oh, my father! He and I understood each other very well; we talked so long the last night he was alive. He loved me, and knew that I loved him. I am unhappy about my mother, my pretty, gay mother.'

Simon drew up a chair and sat down. He was very tired; it seemed that with the passing of Hermann Gollantz he had grown old and weary. No one would ever understand what Hermann

257

had been to him. He had saved him from moral disaster, he had trusted him, taken his advice, and been his friend.

Little Simon Cohen, small, unattractive, with his weak eyes and undistinguished face, had lived for Hermann Gollantz. He sighed, as if he tried to lift the heavy weight which lay on his heart. He must try to help Emmanuel, for Emmanuel was Hermann's son, all that was left to remind him of the man he had almost worshipped.

'I know, I understand,' Simon said. 'You began to—live apart from her after there was a little disturbance about Jean? Yes? You could not understand why she forgave Jean, took him back, loved him and excused him. No? Let me tell you, please. Rachel Gollantz was not very clever, but she was all—maternal. She longed to cook for people, wait on people, be a mother to them. Now, see what happens. Your father—beloved man—was engrossed in business; his tastes were so simple that he almost resented that she should make wonderful dishes for him. If her face was flushed, after cooking, he would look up and say: "Rachel, Rachel, my dear, why will you weary yourself to cook things for me? I am happy only with bread and a little cheese and fruit." You—you are so strong, so well able to take care of yourself, so old for your years. She could not pet you, call you "darling" and "my baby". So she turned in her desperation to Jean. Jean accepted all that she could offer him—love, consideration, motherly love, kind words—he was the only outlet which she had. When one must offer gifts or die, in the spirit, Emmanuel, one does not stop to consider the worthiness of the recipient of the gifts. Do you perhaps understand better now?'

Emmanuel nodded. 'Yes, thank you, Simon. It is going to be very lonely for me. Until now I have always had my father, or my mother in a lesser degree, to stand between me and the world. Whatever waves broke over me the shock was made less because my father always tried to allow them to break over him first. He tempered the winds which touched me, he sheltered me from storms and tempests—he and you, Simon. Now I am the Head of the House and I feel that, at first, the burden is too heavy for me. You will help me, Simon? You will stay here with me, and be to me what you have been to my father?'

For the first time Cohen averted his eyes. He twisted his fingers and traced the elaborate pattern of the carpet with the toe of his boot. . . .

'Things may not be quite the same, Emmanuel,' he said slowly. 'The business will go on!'

'I think that it is too late to talk any longer,' Simon said. 'It is very late. It will be well for you to rest a little. Tomorrow will be a long and difficult day. Let us say good night.'

BOOK FOUR

1

I

MARCUS BREAL settled himself in his huge leather chair and then leant forward and rearranged the papers which lay on his wide desk. Emmanuel lounged in a chair opposite, his long legs crossed, his face betraying a certain expectancy. His father and mother had been dead over a month—he was waiting to hear the exact state of his own finances.

'I have been through everything, Emmanuel,' Breal said. 'I am prepared to give you the facts and figures relating to the business.'

'I am waiting.'

Again Breal shuffled his papers, Emmanuel's lips curved suddenly. Men called Marcus Breal a clever lawyer, he reflected, and yet here he was giving himself away by his obvious unwillingness to state his case. Poor Marcus, he was too tender-hearted. Could he not realize that this was purely business and not a personal matter at all?

'Come, Uncle Marcus,' Emmanuel said, 'let me hear the worst. Don't be afraid. I shan't burst into tears.'

Breal, heavy featured, with a thick beard already iron-grey, with great pouches under his bright, intelligent eyes, and the forehead of a thinker, ran his fingers through his thick, curling hair.

'You won't weep, eh? Believe me, Emmanuel, I could have it in my heart to weep bitterly. When I think of the cleverness, the integrity, the essential nobility of my poor friend, Hermann Gollantz—it is terrible to me.'

'Then there is—nothing?' Emmanuel's voice was still even.

His question seemed to inspire Breal with courage. He touched a pile of papers with his finger-tips contemptuously. 'Investments —rubbish. Property—so heavily mortgaged as to be worthless. Balance at the bank—*sheidermunze*—pennies, that is all! I cannot tell you how terrible it is to me to have to tell you this. Both you and I know where the money has gone.' He raised his hands above his head and shook his clenched fists. 'Oh, that *gonoph*! How I should like to have him here to——'

'Exactly,' Emmanuel agreed. 'That, however, would not bring back the money my father gave him. Then, there is nothing?'

'Except the stock in the galleries.'

'That will have to be sold to pay debts outstanding, wages, and so forth. I have valued it—or, rather, undervalued it, because that is safer, at . . .' He paused and frowned. 'Pah, I can never get used to these talers and krones—my father always worked in gulden—let me see—eight thousand taler. A little more, or a little less. Of that I owe six hundred taler to my tailor. Oh, I admit that I have been extravagant, but I shall need no new clothes for years and years. Debts—what do you reckon them at? Three thousand? Yes, not more, I think. That leaves four thousand for Simon Cohen, and four hundred to keep me.' He smiled. 'So it all works out very well indeed.'

'Four thousand for Cohen!' Breal ejaculated. 'You are serious?'

'Entirely serious.' His tone was so assured that Breal said no more. He knew these Gollantz men, they were always so suave when they were most determined. 'And you propose to live on four hundred taler?'

'Only for a short time. I shall make more. I shall make a great deal more. My father—on him be peace—was not only a dealer, he was a collector. That collection will form the nucleus of my business. The rest—I carry my stock-in-trade under my hat! The collection is small, but there are some exquisite things. I have been through them and they have astonished me. Canton enamel —you know it? What colouring and what finish. Some of it almost, one might say, a fairy story in paint. There is some Yung-lo —I dared scarcely touch it, for fear my hands might crush it to pieces—that is Ming, Marcus Breal, the early Ming. How I wish these confounded Chinamen did not reproduce old china so well. It does add to one's difficulties! Some Rouen, with the tangled fleur-de-lis—that is pottery, interesting only for its age. A small— very small—Boucher, rather improper and altogether entrancing. Four Tanagra figures—and how I dislike them except for their value! A Virgin and Child by d'Evreux, and furniture which is delightful. Carpets—not many but admirable. A few ivories—Gothic and rather charming. But there is——'

He broke off suddenly and laughed. 'Poor Uncle Marcus, how I must bore you. You know what I am, once I begin to talk about old things, I go on for a year and never tire, only tire my listeners. No, I am a fortunate fellow and you must not worry about me.'

'Four hundred taler is not much,' Breal grumbled.

'I agree that it is less than four thousand, but it is more than forty!'

'You have always lived well, not to say luxuriously.'

'I shall continue to live well, possibly luxuriously.'

'Let me invest some money in whatever venture you have in mind?'

For the first time, Emmanuel's face lost its smile. He rose and came over to where Marcus Breal sat, with his great shoulders humped, his heavy, clever face wrinkled with anxiety.

'Dear Uncle Marcus,' Emmanuel said, with real feeling. 'There are no words to thank you. How well I know that half-defiant, half-angry tone of yours. You always adopt it when you intend to be generous in your most princely fashion. I know that I can ask for any amount when you speak as if you would grudge me a single taler! No, I shall do very well, but I am going to ask a favour, a great favour. Simon Cohen will be without work. He grows old, he is lost and heartbroken without my parents. Can you offer him work? Something which will not be too hard, which will not worry him to death, and yet will not allow him to feel that you have manufactured a position for him? You will? I am very grateful. Now, I must go. I have an appointment.'

Breal moved impatiently. 'But what are you going to do? You have told me nothing. I want to know—I have a right to know.'

'You shall,' Emmanuel assured him. 'Only at the moment I scarcely know myself. It is simmering in my brain. When the plan is cooked, it shall be laid before you. Until then, my kindest of friends, good-bye.'

II

Once the door of Marcus Breal's house had closed behind him, some of his lightness died. Emmanuel's face lost its smile and he strode along, his expression serious, his brows drawn together in a frown of concentration. Four hundred taler—for Simon must have sufficient to keep him in reasonable comfort, despite the fact that he protested he had saved enough to live on. Emmanuel had replied that what he had saved was no concern of the House of Gollantz. 'I insist that you accept a small—an almost insultingly small, gift on your retirement, Simon.'

Four hundred taler! And to that he might add his father's small but exquisite collection. As he walked he glanced right and left, wondering how many people recognized him, wondering with a sort of horror if they knew his position, and possibly pitied him. He shivered. Pity was something which he could not face with equanimity. That was why he must leave Vienna and begin elsewhere. To remain in Vienna, to move to a small house, where his clients might come because they remembered what the House of Gollantz had once been and wished to help him, was not to be contemplated. To know that his clothes became shabby, out of date, that his boots would have to be mended, perhaps patched. No, Vienna was impossible. To know that people saw him, and whispered behind their hands to each other: 'There goes Emmanuel Gollantz. Poor fellow; once he was the best-dressed man in Vienna; now he has fallen on evil days, and his clothes, though well kept, are shabby. How sorry I am for him!'

He sighed. 'No, there is only one Imperial city, that is Wien! But my beautiful Wien, you are a city for the gay, the rich, the secure. You have no place for the man who must have his boots patched and his clothes turned. I must go somewhere less lovely.'

As he passed a café he heard the sound of the orchestra playing one of the latest waltzes. He stopped for a moment and listened. To him Vienna would always move, and live, and laugh, to the time of a waltz. No wonder the Viennese loved their Strauss, loved their 'Blue Danube' and their 'Wine, Women, and Song'. Strauss was the high priest of the social religion. His baton beat out the motif which echoed the heart and spirit of the place. 'But,' Emmanuel reflected, 'lovely as you are, beloved as you will always be, you are no place in which to live seriously. No place in which to fight for a living—as I must fight from now on.'

He had turned into a long avenue, where stood the great houses of the rich aristocrats. Maria had been very sweet to him since the death of his father and mother, she had sympathized charmingly, she had even shed a few tears at the thought of Emmanuel's grief. It had been a relief to turn to her when the day was over and he was tired to death with business discussions and the thousand and one affairs which had occupied him since his parents' death.

He had been visited by those of his relations who could spare the time to travel to Vienna—Jaffes, Salamans, and the rest; rich, generous, almost overpowering people who offered him help, and seemed to long to take his business into their own large, capable, and be-ringed hands. After these people—and Emmanuel loved them all, though he found them a little exhausting —the quiet of Maria's boudoir, her charming voice and still more charming appearance, had done much to soothe his overwrought nerves. He did not love her, he had never loved her, but she was delightful.

He approached the great house, preparing, as he always did, his small, set speech. 'Kindly inform Her Highness that Emmanuel Gollantz has called with the designs she ordered,' or, 'Tell Her Highness that I have brought the figures she wished for.' Tradesman he might be, but no servant had ever dared to show by word, look, or even inflection that he regarded him as such. They might reply: 'Her Highness will see you,' but it was said as they might have spoken to one of the Royal Archdukes.

'Her Highness will . . .' The footman was saying, when a small, thin figure crossed the great pillared and gilded entrance-hall. A figure which was clothed in rusty black cloth, an old-fashioned coat with narrow sleeves, and a collar that was too high for present fashion. The parchment-coloured face, wrinkled and dried, quivered slightly. The man stopped and stared at Emmanuel. Then turning to the footman he demanded: 'Who is this?'

The footman opened his mouth as if to speak, shut it again, and fumbled with the tassels of his shoulder cord.

Emmanuel stepped forward. 'My name is Gollantz,' he said. 'I represent a firm of antique dealers, decorators, and designers. I have the honour to be employed by Her Highness.'

'Antique dealers—decorators—designers, heh?' The thin face twitched, whether with annoyance or satisfaction, Emmanuel could not decide. For one moment his heart had beaten more heavily as he recognized Theodore Dietrich, but now it had steadied again. He could hold his own if he kept cool.

'Yes, Highness.'

The wrinkled lids lifted. They were like the lids over a lizard's eyes, Emmanuel thought. Indeed the man himself was not unlike

265

one, quick, with darting eyes, dried up, generally unattractive.

'Ah, you know me? Come into my library. I should like to ask your opinion on—er—on some writings. Manuscript—yes, manuscript.'

He followed the prince into a room so large that the farther end seemed to be lost in obscurity. The prince went immediately to a desk which stood in the middle of the room, and upon which a lamp was burning. He unlocked a drawer and produced a letter, which he laid on the desk.

'I want to know what you think of this.'

Emmanuel stepped forward, bent down, and examined the sheet. The writing was Maria's; the paper was that upon which she always wrote to him. The letter was one which he had never seen.

Why have you not come here today? (the letter ran). *I have waited for hours. You have changed. I cannot understand it. I await you. M.*

He heard the quick, nervous breathing of the prince, and, looking up, met his eyes, dark and restless.

'You know the writing?' he asked.

'Certainly, Highness.'

'The envelope is addressed to you—Herr Emmanuel Gollantz. You understand what it means?'

'Certainly, Highness. The princess was very angry with me.'

'Because you had not called to see her, to carry on an intrigue.'

Emmanuel stepped back as if he had been struck. 'Highness! What are you saying? You are pleased to joke with me. Angry—because I had not brought the patterns.'

'Patterns? What patterns?'

'Of brocade, Highness. I was ordered to bring them, for Her Highness's boudoir. I admit that I was to blame. I was occupied; my workmen were giving trouble; I had to attend a sale. You see, Highness'—with great frankness—'I deal not only in antiques, but in modern furniture. I heard that one, Franz Müller, was selling up his house. He has had trouble with his daughter-in-law, and wants to leave here and live in Bavaria. As a matter of fact, Müller is not an Austrian at all, at least not a Viennese. He is a good fellow, and I have known him for years——'

Theodore Dietrich drummed impatiently on the desk with his

finger-tips. 'Don't bother me about your precious Müller! Get on, explain this letter.'

Emmanuel stopped, stared at him, his mouth a little open.

'The fellow may be good-looking but he's a half-wit!' Dietrich thought.

'But I am trying to explain it, Highness. It was this furniture of Müller's that I had gone——'

'Death and damnation! I don't want to hear about the furniture. Tell me what does this—*I have waited for hours. You have changed* mean?'

'The princess expected me, I didn't come. I—I suppose that I have changed, Highness. I was very anxious to do the room for Her Highness, I tried very hard to get all the patterns she wished to see. But—but—it's difficult to explain—I mean, perhaps Your Highness . . .' He was in such evident distress that Dietrich said more kindly:

'Yes, go on. Say whatever you wish, whatever is true.'

'Highness, I was trying to do my best ; I do with all my clients, but—forgive me—Her Highness is so exacting. Perhaps I have not come as often or as immediately as I might have done, for that reason. I know that I should have done, but'—he drew himself up and assumed a slight air of pride—'I am a good workman, I know my job, and—well, I don't like to be ordered about too much. Oh, I'm not trying to excuse myself, I admit that I have been wrong, but Her Highness is a difficult person for whom to work.'

Theodore Dietrich listened, his chin in his hands. He summed the fellow up correctly, he felt. Clever—to a point, cultivated—to a point, good-looking and probably badly spoilt. Not used to being ordered about and having his suggestions pulled to bits. He was right, Maria could be difficult. As for the note, the young man's obvious frankness was proof that it had meant nothing. Maria had waited, allowed herself to fly into a temper and sent off the note. Curious that she should sign it with one initial only, but she did queer things when she was annoyed. Probably assuming Imperial rank in her own mind!

Dietrich nodded. 'Yes—Her Highness is highly nervous, very energetic, she likes matters carried through quickly ; and I know what you Viennese workmen are, you like to take your own time.'

Emmanuel's lids were lowered: he answered in a voice which

was almost sulky: 'I shall never decorate another room for Her Highness.'

'Rubbish! You can't afford to refuse custom in that way! You must learn to accept what your employers offer. People in the position of Her Highness have many things to occupy their minds. They can't be expected to enjoy being kept waiting by tradesmen. You see that?'

'Yes, Highness.' The voice was still muffled and sulky.

'Good! Now,' the prince continued, 'you seem a hard-working, honest young man. I am going to confide in you that you have an enemy. This note was handed to me by a young man—dark, thin, with a sallow complexion. I admit that he made such a story out of it that I was deceived concerning its true meaning. I tell you, in confidence, that he demanded money for this letter and I—oh, I am ashamed of myself, I say that frankly—paid him a certain sum for it. That young man obviously has a grudge against you. Do you know who I mean?'

For the first time the pale face before him flushed, and when the eyes met his, their expression startled Dietrich. Somehow those eyes were not in keeping with the character of a hardworking young tradesman. They were arrogant, fierce, and scornful.

'I know the person. I am deeply grateful to you, Highness.'

'I have told you that in confidence. I can rely on you not to—to have an open, a public, quarrel with this young man?'

Once again the dark eyes met his. They seemed to hold an expression of resentment, as if this tall young man felt himself insulted. Dietrich frowned. Queer, five minutes ago he had imagined that he spoke with a half-wit; now it seemed that his social peer rebuked him!

'Highness, I only quarrel with my equals. Again, I thank you.'

'Certainly—that is, yes.' He was worried; this tall fellow disturbed him. 'I mean that it is never good to quarrel. Then—that is all. You will, I am sure, treat this interview as confidential.'

Confound the man, he had not meant to speak to him in those terms. He was talking as if they were equals. He ought to have said: 'And see that you keep your mouth shut about what I have said.' What had come over him? He had actually admitted that he was ashamed of himself. The fellow was strange, he stood so still, was so much master of himself, and yet—five minutes ago he had mumbled about 'Müller's' furniture!

Emmanuel gave his little ceremonious bow. 'Assuredly, Highness.'

'You are not to repeat anything that I have said. I forbid it.'
That was the way to talk to him. He stood there bowing like some
archduke. As if he conferred a favour by bowing.

'I have entirely forgotten what Your Highness said.' His hand
went to his pocket. 'And now, Highness, if I might be permitted
to see the princess, so that I may submit some figures to her, and
offer her particulars concerning some ivories—I shall be infinitely
obliged.'

The prince blinked his short-sighted eyes, eyes which had
grown a little dim through poring over ancient manuscripts and
deciphering old and worn inscriptions. He looked at Emmanuel,
who stood smiling a little, holding a little packet of papers in his
hand.

'Yes, yes, if she will see you, if she is not occupied. Go along
and see her.' He paused, blinked his eyes again, then said: 'You
might come and see me again. I might—we might do some business. I mean—I cannot say—you may have things to sell which
might interest me—old manuscripts or Greek pottery.' He
glanced round the room where they stood. 'You might redecorate
this room, or some other room for me, hey?'

The smile deepened. It was a very pleasant smile. The prince
thought that it seemed to lighten the rather gloomy room. A son
with such a smile would be delightful. Vaguely he hoped his own
sons might one day smile as did this strange young man.

'I deeply regret, Highness, that I shall be leaving Vienna very
soon.'

'Leaving! I thought you had a shop here in Vienna?'

'I am closing it. My father and mother are dead; there is
nothing to keep me here. I shall go to . . .' He hesitated, for indeed he had no very clear idea where he was going; then his eye
fell on an old map which hung on the wall opposite, his face
cleared of its momentary expression of speculation and he continued: 'I shall go to London.' He lifted his hand and pointed to
the map of England. 'There! That is where I go to make my
fortune, Highness.'

'Oh . . .' The prince's voice trailed off into silence. He was un-
reasonably disappointed. He wished Gollantz might have stayed
in Vienna. 'I see. I hope that you will be fortunate. Very fortunate.'

'That is very kind of you. And now, will you excuse me, I am
afraid that we are keeping Her Highness waiting. Good-bye,
Highness, and many thanks.'

Dietrich nodded. 'Good-bye—yes, don't keep Maria waiting. Again, I wish you good fortune.'

Emmanuel left him. The old, dried-up aristocrat sat down at his desk, his weak eyes staring at nothing in particular. He still thought that he could hear the vibrations of that strong young voice. A strange young man but likeable, there was no mistake about that. What was he? A Jew—but not in the least like those Jews who came to sell him Greek vases and old carpets. More like the young men on the Egyptian frescoes, on the vases, on the walls of the temples he had so lately visited. Dietrich rose and walked to where he could see the map of England more clearly. He peered at the word 'London', nodding his head.

'That's where he is going, eh? One might visit London some day. There are Roman remains there—yes. A strange young man—but delightful.'

III

Maria rose and came towards him, her hands outstretched. Her charming face was flushed. Emmanuel, catching her hands in his, reflected that someone had been having a difficult time with Princess Maria.

'Emmanuel, where have you been? I have been so furious with Charles, the blockhead, to allow Theodore to take you to his room. What did he say? What does he know, suspect? Tell me, I am half-mad with anxiety.'

He lifted her hands to his lips and kissed them. 'The prince had found—how it does not matter—a letter of yours. No, no, I was able to explain it all. You must remember that you are very angry with me, because I had not brought the patterns you wanted. Terribly, dreadfully angry.'

'A letter! Theodore found a letter! My God, we are ruined.'

'No, no.' He soothed her, speaking as he might have spoken to a frightened child. Not once did he hint that she might have known better than to send letters by a footman who was not trustworthy, who gave them with a few gulden to any loafer, so that he might go off and dance at some servants' ball. Carefully he told her of the interview, of what he had said, and of the result. She listened, the anxious expression fading from her face. Finally she smiled.

'My dearest, how clever you are. And what an old fool Theodore is. Then all is well, and we can be happy together again—oh, I am so glad.'

Emmanuel, watching her, seemed to have a vision of an old man, wearing an old-fashioned coat, because no one cared whether he had new clothes or continued to wear those which he had worn for years. An old man, alone with his books, maps, parchments, and notes, short-sighted and only half understanding the world in which he lived. Feeling that he ought to be jealous of his wife, zealous for her honour, and yet not really having any part in her life. Making an attempt to bluster and shout, and lacking both strength and conviction to continue to do either. Ending the scene by wishing a young man he did not know, a social inferior, good fortune. Somehow, Emmanuel Gollantz at that moment felt more tenderness towards Theodore Dietrich than he had ever felt towards his beautiful wife.

'My dear, I have come to say good-bye to you. I am going away.' Briefly he told her of his plans.

She turned, flung her arms round his neck. 'Emmanuel, you are not going to leave me! I can't bear it. I shall leave Theodore and enter a convent. This is my punishment for having loved you. You shan't go. Why do you wish to go? Is it money? I will give you more than you need. Oh, Emmanuel, I can never let you go. It's impossible. You are my life, we belong to each other. I forbid you to go.'

She wept. Emmanuel tried to comfort her. She accused him of having tired of her; in the next breath she lauded him as a devoted knight who was leaving Vienna for her sake, because he was afraid that his presence might compromise her. Then, he was avaricious, trying to make a fortune in another country; and immediately afterwards she reproached him for his pride in not accepting the income she offered him. He loved her too well; he loved her too little. She had given him too much and wearied him; she had not given him enough and had disheartened him. He was magnificently unselfish; he was the most self-centred of men. She would never look at another man; she would console herself immediately.

Emmanuel listened, his face impassive, controlled. When he spoke, his voice was very gentle, his words tender and kind.

'You have broken my heart,' she protested.

'Maria, dear, beautiful Maria, your heart is not broken. We have been very happy; this has been a beautiful interlude. I am grateful to you. I shall always be grateful.'

271

'You are saying good-bye!' She stamped her foot. 'I hope that you may marry an Englishwoman; they are like ice, and their noses have drops on the end in winter. Go, I never wish to see you again.'

He went.

She walked to her mirror and powdered her delicate nose. After all, he had been dreadfully serious lately, always thinking, for ever absorbed in his wretched business. Handsome, dancing divinely, and always beautifully respectful, but . . .

It might be amusing to talk to her good-looking, worldly, spiritual adviser concerning the possibility of entering a convent. For a time. How Vienna would chatter. Strauss might write a waltz and call it 'Convent Dreams'. She would certainly return from the seclusion of the convent to dance to it. How well Emmanuel had danced. She sighed deeply. He and Max von Habenberg—though Max always protested that he hated dancing. He had danced with her two nights before and seemed to enjoy it. How good-looking he was, and amusing. Always laughing at everything. So splendid he looked in his uniform.

'I wonder,' she said to her reflection in the mirror, 'what he meant exactly when he said last night that Emmanuel had so much that he lacked? That, though he might be von Habenberg, he was poor in all those things in which Emmanuel was rich . . .' Again she sighed. 'Poor, dear Emmanuel, I shall always know that he was the real love of my life. I will make Max talk of him a great deal—he is so charming when he is enthusiastic over Emmanuel. Dear Max. . . .'

2

I

As HE walked away from the palace of Prince Dietrich, Emmanuel reflected that leave-takings were wearing things. Apt to flay the nerves and stimulate the emotions, and once one's emotions got out of hand, they ran away with one, distorted one's values so that it was almost impossible to judge if they were real or false. Did he really feel tender when he thought of old Dietrich, or was it only that his old clothes, so badly brushed, the front of his coat all spattered with snuff, seemed tragic to a young man who believed that clothes were of tremendous importance?

What was it his father had said? That old age was pitiful, and demanded tenderness. Perhaps his father was right and Theodore Dietrich was pathetic. For the moment a sense of acute distaste swept over him. Why had he ever embarked on a love affair with Maria? It had been a piece of stupidity from start to finish. They had never loved; they had amused each other, flattered each other—lied to each other!

'Pah!' Emmanuel swung his cane irritably. 'It has all been a very second-rate business, and I ought to be ashamed of myself! What made me drift into it all? Loneliness. A wish to have a pretty woman for a companion. We gave each other nothing. And we both knew it.' He paused, for he was not far from the theatre. 'I will go and see Theodora Hettner. She always acts on me like a tonic. I will say another of these horrible farewells.'

He mounted the narrow wooden stairs which led to her little apartment. As he knocked on the shabby door, he heard her voice—she was evidently rehearsing some speech. Emmanuel smiled, reflecting that she would not be best pleased at the interruption.

The door swung open. Thea stood there, frowning.

'Oh, Emmanuel!' Then less sharply: 'What brings you here?'

'I have come to disturb you for the last time,' he said. 'I have come to say good-bye to you.'

As he looked at her handsome pale face, with the great burning eyes, noted the full red mouth and the clear skin, he wondered if he did not perhaps love Thea Hettner. She was so intelligent, so vital. What would she say if he asked her to marry him and come to England?

'Good-bye?' she repeated. 'Why, are you going away?'

He nodded. 'Yes, to London.' Then, with a hint of tenderness in his voice: 'Won't you let me come in—for the last time, Thea?'

'Why, of course. I'm very busy. For the first time Gustave has given me a decent part to play. He has written a serious play, almost a tragedy. I am to play the lead. It's a great opportunity for me, Emmanuel.'

He followed her into the apartment, saying: 'And you are working very hard? Well, I have known you quite a long time, Thea dear, and this is the first time I have ever disturbed you.'

She had picked up the manuscript of the play and was turning over the pages. Mechanically she said: 'What is the first time?'

273

'That I have ever wanted to—disturb you. I should like to feel that you are a little disturbed because I go away so soon.'

She nodded, her eyes still turning to the script of the play. 'Oh yes, I am, of course. I am very sorry. You're going to London, are you? They say that there is splendid acting there. Who is the man who plays Lear so wonderfully? Phelps? You must go and see him, write and tell me about him.'

'In the intervals of trying to make a living, I shall be delighted to play the part of dramatic critic, Thea.'

She looked up. 'Dear God, you're hurt. Don't be so stupid, my dear. Of course I'm sorry you are going, but I'm absorbed, filled with my own worries. There isn't any room left for anything or anyone else at the moment.' Her fingers were turning the pages again. 'Listen—how would you say this line—"It matters nothing to me—why should it? Once the very thought would have filled me with delight. That I can no longer . . ." and the rest of the speech I can manage. Would you say—"It matters nothing to *me*," or, "It matters *nothing* to me"?'

He frowned. ' "Nothing"—it's a bigger word. More important.'

'I believe you're right, though the reason you give is wrong.'

He went towards her and caught her hand in his. 'Thea, wouldn't you like to come to London and'—he laughed softly— 'hear this actor Phelps for yourself?'

'No!' she said. 'It's impossible ; we begin rehearsals tomorrow and produce in three weeks' time. Thank you just the same, Emmanuel dear.'

With sudden irritation he flung her hand away. 'You'll make a splendid tragic actress! You have no sense of humour. There, I won't keep you. Incidentally, I have been asking you to marry me.'

For the first time he felt that he held her attention.

'You were? I never heard you. How nice of you, Emmanuel, but I couldn't—I have my work, you see. Good-bye, and I hope you make a great success.'

'Good-bye, Thea, and you *will* make a great success! There, was I right to put the accent on the word—"will?" No, I'm joking. Good-bye.'

He walked away, his hands clasped behind him. Queer how just for one moment he had felt that he wanted to take her with him to England. Now the emotion had passed, and he thought of her as an attractive woman with no sense of humour.

He was superintending packing. This case was to go to the sale-rooms, that one contained goods which he had sold privately, that picture and this china were to accompany him to England. Marcus Breal, ungainly and grave, visited the galleries for the last time and bought generously. The small, colourless figure of Prince Theodore Dietrich moved through the rooms, peering at this and that, asking prices, making notes, and finally carrying away with him a tremendous amount of stuff. Baron von Haben-berg with his fabulously rich wife came, spent money, and wished Emmanuel good luck. Gustave, his pockets full of authors' fees and royalties, came bewailing the fact that Emmanuel could be so foolish as to leave Vienna. Strauss rushed in between two re-hearsals and selected and paid for all the delightful little silver boxes he could cram into his pockets. Artists from the opera, actors and actresses from the theatre came, wasted a great deal of time, and spent a great deal of money. The galleries hummed with activity.

At last everyone was gone. The galleries were stripped ; they were almost empty. Packing cases replaced the cabinets ; folded pieces of sackcloth had taken the place of exquisite carpets and rugs ; the china, glass, the gold and silver, the bits of enamel, had disappeared.

Emmanuel sank down on a case, his hands in his pockets, and sighed. 'My house is left unto me desolate,' he said ; then, turning to Simon: 'Let us eat, drink, and be merry. Franz, go and tell Anna to bring a great deal of hot coffee and some sandwiches—*pâté* for preference. Sit down, Simon, and rest.'

Simon sat down. 'It is very sad—all this, Emmanuel.'

'Depressing, perhaps ; nothing more, except that I hate leav-ing you.'

'I have been here so long. My whole life seems to have been lived in these rooms.'

'You will be happy with Uncle Marcus, Simon. The work will interest you. I shall come over to see you—perhaps very soon.'

'I hope so. I love you very dearly, you are like my own son.' He broke off suddenly—habit was too much for Simon Cohen, his eyes noticed everything. 'That mirror—why was it not packed?'

'Franz will pack it later. It needed a special case. Oh, Simon, let's forget business for an hour.'

'Business,' cried a gay voice at the door. 'Who is talking business? I forbid it. Emmanuel, find me a drink. You have to drink my health and wish luck to my adventure.'

Emmanuel started to his feet. 'Max—and in full military splendour. Where have you been, what is the meaning of this?'

Von Habenberg entered, flung himself down on a packing-case, his sword clattering. Simon watched him with open admiration. He was so young, so vivid, so handsome. He always had a joke on his lips, his eyes danced, his love for Emmanuel was so frank.

'I told you that I could not face Vienna without you. I have embarked on a great adventure. I am going with the Archduke Maximilian to Mexico.'

Emmanuel frowned, Simon wrinkled his brows.

'To Mexico?' Emmanuel said.

'With the Archduke Maximilian?' Simon muttered.

Max nodded. 'He signed the Act of Renunciation this morning. He is to be made Emperor of Mexico. I am going with them as his aide. What an adventure! An honour too, as the Emperor pointed out to me when he gave me the appointment.'

Emmanuel listened, his face suddenly grave. When he spoke, his voice sounded deeper than usual. 'But, Max, what will America say to the establishment of a monarchy in Mexico?'

'Oh, the Union won't object, they'll favour it.'

'Yes, yes,' impatiently, 'but if in this war, the North—with Lincoln—win, what then?'

'Then Austria and France will arrange something.'

'Something.' The impatience was growing in his voice. 'But, what, Max, what? Men, ammunition, can't be transported in five minutes from here to Mexico. Max—don't go. Leave it; stay here. You love Vienna; it's your home, it holds your people. Don't go.'

'Emmanuel, why this tragic tone? I have agreed to go for four years. Then I return on long leave to Europe—six months or more. It's an adventure. . . . Oh, wine! That's splendid! Let's drink—come, Simon, join us! Now, Emmanuel, to my future with the new Emperor!'

He swung his glass high, leapt to his feet. There was a sound of splintering glass. Max turned in dismay; he had driven his foot through the gilt-framed mirror with its Imperial eagle hovering above it.

'Emmanuel! How could I have been so careless! I am so sorry

—and a mirror too. Let's hope that it doesn't mean bad luck for me, eh?'

Emmanuel, biting his lips, answered almost too quickly, with almost too great a demonstration of heartiness: 'My dear Max, that's nothing. I never liked the thing, a bad period. I owe you a debt for having destroyed it. Bad luck—what rubbish! You and I surely don't credit those old wives' tales, do we? Franz, sweep up this glass quickly. Now, Max—the toasts. Here's to the new Empire, its new Emperor, and someone who matters far more than either—Max von Habenberg.'

Only when Max had left them, did Simon notice how silent he was and, watching him, felt that his eyes were shadowed. Emmanuel went about his work in silence, his face heavy with anxiety, as if he already saw the firing party standing in the early morning sun of Mexico. It was as if the shadow which was to fall on Maximilian and his court had touched Emmanuel Gollantz as he moved through those long, empty rooms.

He tried to shake off his depression. 'He will be back in four years. He will come and see me in London. How splendid to meet again. What tales he will have to tell me. He is right. It is a great adventure.'

Three years later, in London, he was to read the news from Queretaro, and remember his depression and the shadow which had seemed to fall on him.

That evening he went to see Marion Brightwin for the last time. He found the neat little house in disorder ; ornaments were gone, the white antimacassars had disappeared, the flower-vases were empty, and when she entered, Marion Brightwin was flushed and confused.

'Emmanuel—I hoped that you would come.'

'Dear Mees, you sent asking me to com'.'

'I thought that perhaps you might not have time.'

He laughed. 'Alvays ven a beautiful vife——'

In spite of her confusion she remembered to correct him: 'Lady, not wife, Emmanuel. I have told you that so often.'

'Yes, yes—a beautiful lady sent for me, it is necessary zat I com'.'

'I am going away too, you see. Almost immediately. In a few days.'

'You are leaving Vienna? This is impossible, surely.'

'No, I am going.' She pointed to a chair. 'Sit down. Let me tell you. I am taking everything with me. I shall not come back here.

277

Vienna can hold nothing for me—with the two people I love best gone. You are one of those people, Emmanuel my dear.'

He looked at her plain, elderly face, and thought how kind she had always been. He remembered those dreadful days when he had hungered for Caro; that was when Marion Brightwin had tried to comfort him, that was when she had not offered him—buttered toast, and in consequence he had loved her and felt that he admired the race from which she came.

'You mak' me verry prroud,' he said.

'Oh no.' Her face was pink with excitement and worry. 'Listen, let me explain. I am going to live in—Poland.'

She heard Emmanuel catch his breath. 'Yes? In Poland?' he repeated. 'I see.'

'Caro wants me, and I have never refused to go to her when she asked me. I never shall. She is lonely. Stanislaus is wild, he drinks more than ever. He is terribly jealous of her—in his strange way I think he loves her. I leave tomorrow.'

'I see. Countess Lukoes will be ver' heppy, I think, yes?'

There was a long silence. Emmanuel stared at the white, scrubbed boards from which the carpet with its pink roses and green leaves had been taken. Marion twisted her thin, rheumatic fingers; her lips moved as if she silently rehearsed a speech.

'Emmanuel,' she said at last, 'you leave Vienna in a few days' time. I am going to tell you something—a secret. Lukoes has been ordered to Vienna; he has been offered a place in the suite of the new Emperor, to go to Mexico. He has refused it. The Emperor himself tried to persuade him, so did Maximilian. He laughed at them both, said that he had no wish to take service under a tin-pot Emperor in a tin-pot Empire.'

Emmanuel sprang to his feet. 'Why do you tell me this? What do I care for Lukoes? Not'ing, less than not'ing. I will not hear.'

'You will hear,' Marion said with quiet dignity, 'because Lukoes is not alone in Vienna. Caro is with him. She wishes to see you.'

He flung back his head and laughed, then said, reverting to his own language: 'She wishes to see me. How amusing! Why, I wonder? To see if I am still young and romantic, to see if she still retains the power to hurt me?. Thank you, Mees Brightwin, my answer is "No". I am not even flattered that the countess should remember me.'

'You will read her letter to you,' Marion said gently. 'I think then that your answer may be different. Remember, Emmanuel,

278

that Caro is exiled in a strange land. Even the proudest of us can afford to be pitiful.'

He moistened his lips. When he spoke his voice was harsh. 'Please let me see this letter.'

He carried it to the window, and stood there reading it by the light of the dying day. His hands shook, he seemed to Marion to take a very long time to read the few lines which the letter contained.

We are both leaving Vienna very soon. Will you come and see me here? Don't be afraid, I am not going to make a scene—I know how you hate them. I have something to say to you, it is important. (Then, as if she had written the words as an afterthought): *To me, at least.*

He folded the letter and slipped it into his pocket, then turned. 'You always like her to have her own way in everything, don't you? You wish me to go?'

'I think—I think that it would be kind. She has been—she is— very unhappy and lonely.'

'I have been both,' Emmanuel said. 'Very well, I will go.'

'If you will go to the palace at eight o'clock,' Marion said, speaking rather breathlessly, 'I shall be there. I will admit you and take you to her. Emmanuel, don't be hard—it's so easy to be hard.'

'Hard! Dear Mees, if I am hard, it is because I have cultivated hardness as a means of self-preservation.' His lips smiled, but the smile did not touch his eyes. 'I was not very happy after she went away, you know. I have had to learn a great many things.'

As he walked towards the palace of Stanislaus Lukoes that evening, Emmanuel frowned, his mind in a turmoil. He wanted to see Caro again—he dreaded meeting her. He longed to beg her to let them resume their old relationship—he hoped that he could assume a tone and air so light that she might believe he cared for her no longer. He swung mentally from one side to the other. More than once he decided to send word that he could not come. Even when he reached the palace he hesitated, undecided as to which course he should take. Then, with a sudden impulsive movement, he ran up the steps which led to the house.

He asked for Miss Brightwin and, a moment later, Marion entered the hall and greeted him. 'If you will come to my room, Mr. Gollantz, we can have the lesson there.'

Emmanuel knew that his heart was beating very fast, knew that he was excited and not completely master of himself. To see Caro again—it was reviving emotions which he had believed dead. He had thought that he had banished all thoughts of her and closed the door of his heart on her memory for ever. Now, he realized that all his old longing for her had returned, and that his breath came more quickly at the thought of standing face to face with her once more.

Marion stopped outside one of the doors on the first floor, she glanced up and down the long corridor, then tapped. 'Caro,' she said softly.

The door opened, and Emmanuel saw Caroline Lukoes again. She held out her hands. 'Emmanuel, it is kind of you to come here.'

He said nothing, only stood looking at her as if he had been hungry for a sight of her.

The door closed. Marion Brightwin had left them alone.

Emmanuel's mind was working terribly quickly.

'This emotion which I am feeling now,' he thought, 'has nothing to do with the love I once felt. That is over. I watched it die. Caro began to kill it, and I gave it the *coup de grâce*. This is only a pale, bloodless ghost struggling to assert itself. She is attractive to me ; in my memory she will always live as the most attractive woman I have ever known ; but though my heart is beating like a sledge hammer, though my breath comes quickly, and my hands are not quite steady—I am still master of myself. This is not love. It is memory stirring, it is romance, it is sentimentality, it is a dozen things ; but not one of them is love.'

'You sent for me,' Emmanuel said. 'Will you tell me why?'

'I heard that you were leaving Vienna,' she said. 'I came here with Stanislaus ; the Emperor sent for him, he wished him to go to Mexico. You see, Stanislaus is half Austrian. He refused to go. He is only remaining here long enough to put his property in the market, and take away whatever he values—pictures, china, and so forth.'

Emmanuel nodded. 'So I heard from Mees Brightwin. But why did you wish to see me?'

Her eyes were very steady as they met his. To Emmanuel there was something in her gaze which contained a queer masculine frankness.

'You may think me a fool,' she said. 'You may think that it was a very insufficient reason. I wanted to say that I was sorry that I had ever caused you unhappiness, and to—take away with me the knowledge that you forgave me.'

'And that was all?' His eyes had lost their gravity. With the sensation of meeting a friend after long separation, Emmanuel watched her face change. This was the Caro he had known, the Caro who laughed. As long as they had laughed together, they had been happy; only when they had allowed themselves to grow serious, heavy with apprehension, had they suffered.

She laughed suddenly. 'Not quite.' Then gravely: 'I don't want to hurt you, Emmanuel.'

'But you won't. I swear that you won't.'

'I wonder if that means that—I cannot hurt you any longer?'

'It may be, Caro. That ought to please you——'

'I don't know.' She pursed her lips. 'No woman really likes to know that she had lost her power.'

'There was sufficient left to bring me here! Now, why did you want to see me?' He lifted one of her hands and kissed it. 'Oh, Caro, it is such great fun to see you again. I am really so happy.'

'You didn't kiss my hand like a lover,' she said, as if the realization startled her. 'You kissed it like—like——'

'Like your devoted friend.'

'Ah!' The exclamation was half amusement, half relief. 'You feel that, too. That was why—or partly why—I wanted to see you. For my own sake. I wanted to know if I still loved you.'

'You never did love me.' He still smiled.

'I think I did—I think you loved me. Didn't you?'

'At least we both—thought—that we did.' He began to walk swiftly up and down the room, speaking as he did so. 'I believe that we were both right. I didn't think so at the time. No one ever believes that the other person is right, at the time. I was right to ask you to leave everything; you were right to refuse to do so. We were both in love with the superficialities of each other, we were not in accord over the fundamentals. Now . . .' He stopped in his walk, stood before her again, laughing. 'Oh I wish that I wasn't going away, so that we might see each other every day, and talk and laugh.'

'Then we might fall in love again.'

'I don't believe that one ever does—with the same person.'

'You're not unhappy to be leaving Vienna?'

'I wasn't. I am now, when I remember that Vienna holds you.'

'Did Maria Dietrich teach you to pay compliments?'

His smile widened. 'Caro, that's not fair! And you're going

281

back to Poland, and taking Mees Brightwin with you?'

She began to tell him about her life. It seemed that she was not unhappy; because she had learnt to 'close her eyes' she saw only what pleased her. Stanislaus liked to travel, and in the capitals of Europe he had his friends, she had hers.

'I am so much stronger than he is,' Caro said. 'I realized that when I began to dictate to him, to state my terms, to declare how I intended to live. Once I asserted myself, once I determined never to fear him, life became bearable. Oh, I had been a weak, frightened fool too long. When he is sober, when he behaves decently, then we are friends—not great friends, but able to be civil to each other. When he is drunk—I don't allow myself even to think of him. It works quite well. Occasionally—I tell you this as a compliment to you—he refers to you, generally when he is drinking. He still regards you as a rival.'

'Shall I meet him and assure him that his fears are groundless?'

'No, no!' She laughed. 'I find the shadow of Emmanuel Gollantz so useful at times. Please allow me to let him still think that you are always waiting with horses ready to carry me away, if I send to you.'

'Take care that you don't send for me. The shadow would materialize. I should certainly come very quickly.'

'I believe you are ready to fall in love with me again.'

'But of course! Can you doubt it? Whenever you wish——'

The door was flung open. Marion Brightwin, white-faced and shaking, stammered: 'Caro—Emmanuel—he is here! Stanislaus is coming up the stairs now. He is asking for you, Caro . . . oh, my dear. . . .'

Emmanuel was at the window; he stepped out on to the balcony and looked down, then returned. 'Not too far,' he said. 'Caro, forgive this unceremonious leave-taking. My name—as a threat—is always at your disposal. Dear Mees, good-bye. Caro—it's been so charming to see you again. My dear—be happy.'

He was on the balcony, Caro standing beside him. 'A garden?' he queried. 'I can find a gate? Yes? Good-bye again.'

'Emmanuel, it's too high. It's dangerous.'

'Dangerous! Nothing of the kind. Watch.'

His hands caught the rail, his body vaulted over, and he dropped down into the darkness. Caro, leaning over, heard a smothered exclamation, saw a dark shape cross the garden, and stepped back into the room as Stanislaus Lukoes entered.

3

EMMANUEL leant back in his corner of the jolting railway carriage. He was very tired, his arm still gave him considerable pain, and his nerves were raw as a result of taking his leave of little Simon Cohen. He had had enough of farewells, he reflected. Never again would he allow himself to be dragged into such a whirlpool of emotion. Maria, Thea, Marion Brightwin, and Caro —he smiled when he remembered Caro. What a woman!

His hand went to his injured shoulder, and he reflected that if Paris had been worth a Mass to Henry of Navarre, then certainly Caroline Lukoes was well worth a dislocated collar-bone to Emmanuel Gollantz. Indeed, he read something like a fortunate augury into his accident. He was not the first man to begin a new and successful venture with a fall! He remembered that his last glimpse of Caro's face had been when he looked back for a second over his shoulder, as he slipped away through the darkness, to find the wooden gate which would admit him to the wide, quiet street.

Caro had not flayed her nerves, had not racked his emotions. Caro had been herself, amusing, provocative, and utterly delightful.

'We neither of us love the other any longer—perhaps we never did—I don't know,' he reflected. 'I only know that we both like each other more now than we have ever done.'

There had been his last interview with Marcus Breal. Uncle Marcus who sat in his great, splendidly decorated room with that huge desk, his heavy figure slouched in a vast chair, his white waistcoat protruding. His eyes under their heavy, wrinkled lids had been inquisitive.

'So you are going to England? Why are you going there, pray?'

Emmanuel felt that he had made his explanation both amusing and sound. He had stated that he had seen pictures of the interiors of English homes. Their ugliness appalled him. It was obvious that sooner or later there must be a revulsion of feeling against such horrors. He felt that these strange English would begin to invest money in objects of beauty, that they would demand decoration which was delightful to the eye. 'That is where I shall step in,' Emmanuel explained.

Breal had nodded, and after a moment's hesitation had offered him, instead, a place in his banking business. Emmanuel had thanked him, but protested that he felt not the slightest interest in banking. Breal had then offered him money to establish his business on a firm footing. Again Emmanuel thanked him and declined, as he had already declined similiar offers of help from von Habenberg, his son, Gustave, and Prince Dietrich.

'My business will be run on unique lines. Lines in which I believe. Other people might protest and have the right to protest, that I endangered their money and what little I have of my own.'

'Take the money,' Breal grumbled. 'I don't care how you use it.'

'But I should feel that you might care, and what would be worse, that I ought to care. It would hamper me,' Emmanuel said.

The big, ungainly figure before him stirred. Breal produced a great bunch of keys, dragging them up from the depths of some pocket at the end of a long gold chain. He unlocked a drawer in the desk, and produced a packet of letters, yellow with age. These he pushed across the table to Emmanuel.

'Those letters were given to me by your father—may my end be like his—they were given to him by Fernando Meldola of Paris. Letters of introduction to important dealers in London. Your father never used them; you might care to do so. The men you will meet, without doubt, will be the sons of those men to whom they were written, as you are the son of the man for whom they were written. So the world moves on, eh?'

Emmanuel weighed the packet in his hand. They were links with the past, written by a man who had seen, perhaps spoken with the first Napoleon. Time was really a thing of very little account.

Breal began to speak heavily and yet with a certain caustic inflection in his rumbling voice.

'I am going to give you a piece of advice—as you won't take money. The Englishman is a strange creature. In his heart—oh yes, they have hearts and remarkably warm ones—he always retains a dislike and a fear of the Jew. You see, Jews remember, Englishmen forget. They forget that their God was a Jew, and when that unpleasant thought comes into their minds, they pray —with sincerity—that at His next coming He will have the good taste to come as an Englishman. But'—he held up a large, pale

hand—'if they dislike Jews, there is something else they dislike
even more. They despise the Jew who is ashamed of being a Jew
and tries to pretend that he is a Gentile.

'The other day an English lord came to do business with me.
He said: "Be Gad!"—they all say "Be Gad!"—he said: "You're a
Jew, Breal, but, damn me, if I wouldn't rather do business with
you than with half a dozen Englishmen I could name." He went
on: "I always say that when a Jew deals straight, when he's
honest, he's the honestest man alive!" Now that is sheer rubbish.
An honest man is an honest man, no more and no less whatever
may be his race. But once get an Englishman to believe in a Jew—
and they aren't fools, oh, dear me, no!—and he'll trust you with
every penny in the Bank of England. They may fear you, they
may even dislike you, but once they trust you—you're a made
man.'

'I shall remember, Uncle Marcus.'

'I shall keep my eyes open on your behalf. I have some knowledge of pictures, works of art, brocades, and so forth. If I find
anything worth buying I will get it for you. I shall charge you
only a nominal commission for buying.' The dark eyes were suddenly very bright. 'Shall we say only fifteen per cent?'

Emmanuel's expression changed. He was no longer an elegant
young man taking leave of a man who had known him all his life.

'Fifteen per cent! Uncle Marcus, how amusing you are. I never
pay more than ten.'

Breal shrugged his massive shoulders. 'Well, ten then.'

Emmanuel laughed. 'No, no. I pay ten for goods bought on my
instructions, goods which I know and have valued myself. You
will be buying on a purely speculative basis. You will not have
your finger on the pulse of the English taste—even after I have
begun its education. You will not be able to judge what is sought
after and what is to be avoided. I offer you my thanks, but five per
cent is as much as I could allow myself to pay.'

'Five! It would not pay for my time wasted in sale-rooms!'

'And yet you told me that you would—as a special favour—
allow me four and a half per cent on any money I placed in your
bank.'

'You talk like a fool. There. Have it your own way, five per
cent.' They had said good-bye and Emmanuel had been touched
at the unwonted warmth of the old man's parting. He left the
banker's house content that in Marcus Breal he possessed a good
friend.

Little Simon Cohen had been a different matter. He had taken Emmanuel's face in his hands, and with tears streaming down his face had blessed him. He had spoken of Hermann and Rachel with the deepest affection, and had protested that without Emmanuel his life was virtually over.

'No, Simon, no. You will come to England one day, perhaps. I shall come to Vienna again. You must not take this parting so hardly.'

'In your father—on him be peace—I found brother, father, and patron—in your mother the kindest of friends, a sister, and a benefactress. In you, Emmanuel bar Hermann, I found a son. I am losing everything. All my life I shall go heavily. The God of your Fathers be with you now and always. I shall never cease to pray for you and your happiness.'

Recalling his words, Emmanuel reflected that Breal would have said 'pray for your success'.

'Happiness,' he thought, 'I know very little about it. I have known it and always it was followed by disaster, or what I believed to be disaster at the time. I have never known a long period of uninterrupted happiness. Perhaps I shall find it in England. I was happy with my brother; I was happy with my father at intervals, with Caro for a time. But whenever I have said, "Now I am consciously happy, now I am fortunate, now I am grasping my dearest desires, disaster has fallen on me." Perhaps I am not to be happy. What is it that Gustave says?—to be fortunate at cards is to be unfortunate in love. It may be that I may gain success and never find happiness, who knows?'

He stood up at the window and watched the towers and spires, the bridges and the silver ribbon of river which went to make up Vienna disappearing from sight. The thought of all that he was leaving filled him with a sense of loss. There was only one Imperial city—Wien. He had known her and loved her so long, he had understood her moods, he had grown used to living his life to the music of the waltz. All the beauty of women, the splendour of uniforms, the brilliance of the opera and the magnificence of the theatre had been part of his life. The life of the cafés, the 'Spiel' in the Leopoldstadt, the gaiety of the 'Two Doves', the laughter which rang at the 'Green Gate', the aristocratic air of the 'Zogernitz', and the crowded tables at Dommayer's had each filled some part of every twenty-four hours.

At night, men and women would glance round the 'Spiel' wondering what had happened to Emmanuel Gollantz. Strauss,

286

lifting his baton as his musicians prepared to play a new waltz, might turn his eyes towards the table where Emmanuel had sat, and remember that he was no longer part of the clientèle of the 'Two Doves'. Gustave would recall, when his latest play was staged, how Emmanuel had stood at his side and advised this or that. Even Thea might think of him when she wondered which was the better word to stress.

'It is all changing,' Emmanuel thought, turning from the window, his eyes suddenly misty. 'Mees Brightwin's kind, ugly little house stands empty ; Caro leaves to bury herself in Poland ; Max —my dear Max—goes to a new world, with a new Emperor ; the galleries which were once filled with beauty stand empty, and—I am going to England.'

He moved impatiently. What was wrong with him? He was allowing himself to grow sentimental, mawkish, and regretful. If the galleries were closed it was because that was what he had chosen to do. Max had elected to set out for a new world, he had done the same. Life was his, to live—to make the best of.

As he sat back in his corner, his chin on his hand, his handsome face grave and thoughtful, he realized that until now he had never stood quite alone. There had been his father, his mother, and Simon ; after his father had died, there still remained Simon and Marcus Breal. To either of these men he had been able to turn for advice or help.

He had worked hard, worked well ; he had no sense of false modesty concerning his ability. He had made money for his father's business, and he would make money for his own in the future. But there was a difference. In the future, if he failed to justify his position, then he must face ruin. In the past, whether he effected a sale or not, his home, his food, his comfort were all assured. There had never been the slightest hint of urgency in the business of Hermann Gollantz. Sales were conducted with dignity. They took time ; there was no sense of rush, haste, or anxiety. If a thing was not sold today, then in all probability it would be sold tomorrow ; if not tomorrow—well, there was plenty of time.

Now he stood alone ; he was entering a new life in a country where he was an alien, where he had no friends—for letters of introduction might mean civil acquaintances, but friends came only with time. He had very little money, his stock was beautiful but it was not large, and he had no knowledge of the conditions under which he must begin to work.

287

True, Breal, von Habenberg, and Prince Dietrich had offered him money. Gustave had wished to press a bundle of notes into his hand, Max had begged him to take with him various pictures, collections of glass and china, old lace and brocades which had been left to him by his aunt, Princess Hohenbach. Emmanuel had refused. His pride had made it impossible for him to accept these things. The fact that they were offered impulsively, kindly, and generously delighted him, but did not alter the fact that his face flamed suddenly when he listened to the offers of financial help. To each of his friends he had answered in the same strain.

'I thank you from the bottom of my heart. Never were there such friends, never was a man so fortunate as I to possess such friends. I shall never, never forget, and whenever I am lonely, sad, disheartened, I shall remember these evidences of your kindness, and my loneliness, my sadness, and my lack of heart will vanish. But—I cannot accept.'

He sighed. 'Today I have to face the fact that I have grown up. It may be that in Wien we are all too young, just a little irresponsible. I have laughed a great deal; even when I was sad, the sound of the general laughter reached my heart. The most serious business in Wien is the business of enjoying oneself. That is terribly important. In that the whole population are astonishingly successful. Now—I must laugh less; my chief aim must be to make money, to be a financial success. I think'—he smiled— 'that I shall suffer at first from growing pains.'

II

He thought London the most gloomy place he had ever seen. He stood in the dim station, surrounded by his boxes, bags, holdalls, and cases and stared round him in dismay. It was barely four o'clock, the date was early in March, and the whole place seemed wrapped in night. A porter surveyed the mountain of luggage, scratched his head, and asked:

'Wanter fly?'

Emmanuel tore his dismayed gaze from the station and its gloom, and stared. 'I vant to fly? Is it thet you are ver' funny?'

The man grinned suddenly. 'Nah. I fought you was a furriner w'en I fust see'd yer. A keb, eh?' He raised his voice. To Emmanuel it seemed that the fellow believed him to be deaf. 'A keb? Ter drive ter a 'otel?'

288

'Yes, if you please.'

'Won't all go on one keb—too much.'

'Then,' with magnificent dignity, 'it will go on two kebs.'

So the Head of the House of Gollantz made his first entry into the English capital, driving in a four-wheeler which smelt deplorably of damp straw, which rattled and bumped, while he leant back, his fine cambric handkerchief held to his nose; he tried to see the outline of any building which should resemble either St. Paul's or Westminster Abbey, the only London buildings he had seen in pictures.

Marcus Breal had given him the address of an hotel off the Strand, where he himself had stayed twenty years before. Emmanuel had imagined himself arriving at an hotel resembling Sacher's, only more distinguished. He almost died of chagrin and disappointment when the cab drew up at a slightly dingy, flat-fronted place, the wall of which bore the name, in tarnished gold letters: Millet's Hotel, Commercial and Family.

He stood, conscious that he was very tired and that his shoulder ached badly, and watched the luggage taken through the gloomy portals of Millet's Hotel. A red-haired fellow, wearing a waistcoat with black sleeves, ran about shouting orders. He turned to Emmanuel and said:

'Traveller, sir?'

'Yes,' Emmanuel returned pleasantly. 'I am from Vienna.'

'Cases to the stock-room, sir?'

Stock-room! What in heaven's name was a stock-room? He frowned and said: 'Eet is not possible that I understand.'

The man with the sleeved waistcoat shouted to some assistant: 'No, not to the stock-room. Gen'leman's a foreigner. Shove 'em in the passage.'

The two cab-drivers, with purple faces, hoarse voices, which suggested frequent visits to four-ale bars, stood before him, their hands outstretched.

Emmanuel queried: 'Please, 'ow mooch?'

The more fiery-faced appeared to struggle with a mental calculation.

'Oughter be a quid apiece wiv all that luggage. Call it fifteen bob apiece. That 'urt yer, Cap'n?'

Emmanuel looked up from the purse which he had opened. 'Bob?' he repeated, then: 'Ah, vait, I hev heard it! Von sheeling— a bob?' Then, touching his shoulder, he smiled. 'Hurt me? Thenk you, not verry mooch. Eet is not'ing really.'

He walked up to his room, still smiling. These people were at least kindly. It was pleasant that a cab-driver should ask after his shoulder. His smile died as he entered the room. It was stuffy, dark, and lacking all those things which he had grown to believe were essential to comfort. The bed was of wood, but it looked terribly hard. The curtains at the windows were of coarse and not too clean lace, the mirror on the dressing-table was flecked and spotted with brown marks. The carpet was very thin, lacking any pattern, the fire-place was stuffed with white paper, there was one gas-jet only, and the two pictures on the walls made him shiver. His mind fled back to Sacher's—its dignity, its elegance, its comfort.

He tried to conceal his disappointment. What could Uncle Marcus have been thinking of? He would assuredly die of depression here.

'I need hot water, please,' he said. 'A verry grreat deal of hot water. Also some verry hot, strrong coffee. And,' he glanced at the unfriendly grate, 'please to hev a fire litted et once.'

The boots leant forward, his hand to his ear. 'Did you say—fire, sir?'

'Indeed, yes. Immediately.'

'Don't often have gen'lemen arsks for fires, sir. I don't think theer's been a fire in that grate fur twenty years.'

'No, the lest time was no doubt ven Herr Marcus Breal of Vienna stayed here. Let us brreak the rrule, und hev one et once.'

As the man was closing the door, Emmanuel called: 'Leesten. Not coffee, but tea—und buttered toast!'

Later, he wrote a letter to Max. He said: *I am in a city of night. There is a great deal of noise, but no comfort. The tea and the toast are worth coming to London to experience.*

In spite of his determination, his spirits sank lower and lower, and it was not until he began to dress that evening that he felt them return. He stood before his foggy, insufficient looking-glass, and repeated to himself that he had come to conquer London. His reflection gave him confidence; he looked every inch a conqueror.

His black suit was exquisitely cut, his linen, his cravat, his jewellery were all admirable. His pale skin made his hair and small, carefully trimmed moustache look unbelievably dark, and the sweep of dark hair over his forehead gave him that touch of romance which had caused the hearts of the ladies of Vienna to flutter when he entered a café. He took his gold-headed cane and descended the gloomy staircase, conscious that the addition of the black sling in which his arm still rested added to, rather than detracted from, his appearance.

The boots, an aged waiter, and a buxom young woman watched his descent. The young woman sighed gustily. 'Proper masher, ain't he?' she said.

The waiter turned a jaundiced eye upon her. 'Masher!' he said with some scorn. 'I know what 'e is—'e's a refugee—aristocrat refugee.'

'And what might 'e be seekin' refuge from?' the boots demanded.

'That's arskin'. 'Ow should I know?'

The boots snorted. 'Refugee! Refugee—nothink!' Then catching Emmanuel's eye he sprang forward. 'Yes, sir?'

'Kindly dirrect me to zee first t'eatre.'

'First? Mean the best, sir? The best—well, the Lane takes a bit o' beatin'. Drury Lane, sir. Fust night ternight. Phelps in *The School for Scandal.*'

Emmanuel smiled. Here was an omen. Thea had told him to go and see this actor, and he would go. 'Call me a cab ; tell him to drrive to R-romano's. Go to this t'eatre and buy a stall for me. Brring it to me at R-romano's. Esk for Herr—thet is Mr. Emmanuel Gollantz.'

He swung his wide cloak round his shoulders, glanced at his pale-lavender kid gloves as if he feared that they might have become soiled on the journey from his bedroom, sent a smile flying round the admiring little group, and passed out of the hall.

The waiter turned to the buxom young woman. 'What did I tell you? I was right. Only a aristocrat can give 'is orders like that an' get away with it. Mister! . . . I lay any money he's a Archduke in 'is own country.'

III

Within a month he had established himself. What little money he had was safe in the Bank of England, his beautiful brocades, ivories, pictures, carpets, and furniture shown to the best possible advantage in the house which he had taken on Campden Hill. He had rejected the idea of a shop as unsuitable to the type of business which he intended to do. People must see his goods in their proper surroundings ; he must have rooms, and later, galleries.

Shops were for tradesmen. Emmanuel Gollantz was a specialist.

He visited those dealers to whom he had letters of introduction. His manners were so charming, he treated his seniors with such deference, and yet spoke with such authority, that he gained both respect and good feeling.

Old Gelbe in St. James's was so taken with the good-looking young man that he offered to take him into partnership along with his stock. Marchant visited him at Campden Hill and offered to buy the whole stock, or to sell it on commission while Emmanuel travelled Europe for new treasures.

Emmanuel listened to both offers, bowed from the waist, and declined. He had not come to England to be absorbed into the business of other men, he had come to found a business of his own.

Fat Moses Abrahams came puffing and blowing, with his elegant son, who aped the English and already talked of changing his name to Marcus Arbuthnot. The old man stuttered and stammered in his broken English, while his son hummed and hawed and tried to patronize the young man from Vienna. Augustus Morris visited his show-rooms; Emmanuel liked the dark-skinned young Jew, who spoke like a costermonger from the East End and yet possessed a knowledge which was almost uncanny. Last of all came Samuel Lane, with his fat son Jacob. Lane held Emmanuel's hands and wept, because he remembered not only Fernando Meldola, but also Abraham Gollantz and Emmanuel's own father.

'Now dey're all tead,' he sobbed. 'To rememper dot makes me t'ink vot an olt men I pecom'. Oi, oi—I doan't lest so much longer, I doan't t'ink. Poor ole Samuel Lane. Lane ain't my right name, neider. I vos porn Levi!'

His son, peering here and there, cried suddenly: 'Fadder, see here! It's a Bellini, unless I'm very much mistaken.'

'You are mistaken,' Emmanuel said gently. 'It is a Verrocia.'

Old Lane's tears dried immediately. He held his sides and rocked with laughter. 'Dere, Jacob! Vot did I tell you of dis Gollantz! You are cleffer, but he is clefferer, so!'

Later, he asked Emmanuel how long he had been in England and how much he had sold. Emmanuel replied that he had been in England for six weeks and that he had sold nothing.

Lane's hands went up in horror. 'My poor poy! Vot ken ve do to help?'

Young Jacob, watching, felt that despite his father's three

score years and ten, he was younger than the young Jew who addressed him.

'Nothing, except give me your friendship and good wishes,' Emmanuel said. 'I ken vait mit patience and serenity. For,' he smiled, 'in my heart of hearts, dere is a leetle belief dot Fate, Destiny, God—call it vot you veel—is on der side of der Children of Israel.'

Old Lane departed wagging his head, declaring that the young man was not only clever but wise, not only intelligent but *froom*. He sent people to him, he gave him introductions, and Emmanuel soon found that though his business was negligible, his list of acquaintances grew rapidly.

The Leons—brother and sister—remembered his father years ago. The Bernsteins welcomed him, and wondered if he might not prove a very suitable husband for Miriam. The Lewis's, whose only child, Adah, was sallow and delicate, sighed with pleasure when Emmanuel bowed over her hand and inquired after her health. The rich Salamons told each other in the privacy of their huge overfurnished bedroom, that even if Gollantz was poor, Esther had enough for both of them. While the Davises, whose daughter Elizabeth was small, and really very attractive, decided that they need seek no further for a bridegroom for her.

Emmanuel himself had no thoughts concerning a possible marriage. He was far too proud to contemplate marriage with a woman richer than himself, and far too ambitious to be willing to become absorbed in any woman until his business was firmly founded. He smiled on them all, he was charming to them all, but he singled out none of them for special attention, unless it was Rachel Leon, who corrected his English and taught him how to tie a cravat like an Englishman.

4

FOR three years Emmanuel Gollantz lived in the house on Cap-
den Hill surrounded by his antiques, to which he added from
time to time. His business was growing rapidly ; he himself dated
its obvious growth from the day he met Sir Walter Heriot in
Hammet's Sale Rooms in April, 1866.

The morning was sunny, and Emmanuel whistled as he dressed.
It always excited him to visit sale-rooms, to him they were verit-
able gold mines ; he might find a valuable nugget, he might come
away with nothing. He had devloped a love and understanding
of woods, and it added to his amusement to watch the faces of
other dealers when he turned from the obviously valuable
articles and bought half a dozen badly broken chairs, an old table,
or a battered wardrobe.

'I hev brrougrt you more vood, Mason,' Emmanuel would say
to his carpenter, a small undersized fellow who always had shav-
ings adhering to his clothes. 'Not, you veel unterstend for now.
Deese arre vot ve name infested kepital.'

Mason, scratching his sandy head, would reply: 'Just so, sir.
But what am I ter do wiv it all?'

'Brreak it up. Store it avay. Von day ve shell be gled of it.'

'Mind yer, 'e's rite,' Mason confided to his henchman, Wil-
lows. 'It almost mikes me blush w'en 'e comes 'ome wiv a lot o'
junk an' broke bits of furniture. Ondly w'en 'e explained—light
dawned, as yer mite say. Mark my words, Willers, one day we'll
be glad an' thankful fur this stuff.'

The porters in Hammet's had grown to know Emmanuel Gollantz. They called him the 'furin swell', and liked to make him
talk to them in his queer, clipped English. They admired his
clothes, and on this particular morning, when he strolled into the
dingy rooms, they nudged one another delightedly. 'Got 'isself
up proper terday, an' no error.' Emmanuel presented a noticeable
figure in his tight, brown frock coat, brown-and-white checked
trousers, patent leather boots which caught the rare sunlight and
gleamed. His cravat was of brown satin, fastened with two scarf
pins connected by a thin gold chain. All these were English

enough, but his broad-brimmed hat added a hint of eccentricity to his appearance.

Walter Heriot, with his brick-red face, tight mouth, and bright blue eyes, stared at him. 'Feller ought to look ridiculous with that damned hat! Queer that he doesn't. Looks right somehow.' He held a catalogue in his mahogany-coloured hands and marked various lots with a stump of lead pencil. Emmanuel, standing near him, noticed that one of the pencil marks was beside 'Lot 137. Four occasional chairs. Queen Anne. Original needlework seats'.

Emmanuel grimaced. He had seen those chairs. He had looked at them once and turned away, convinced again that the English knew nothing about old furniture. Original indeed! The impertinence of these people! The thin man with the catalogue looked up and caught Emmanuel's eye. The blue eyes danced and the thin, wide mouth twisted. It was as if he said: 'Watch me. I'm a knowing one!'

The auctioneer's voice boomed suddenly. 'Four Queen Anne occasional chairs. Original needlework seats. Unique—quite unique. What shall I say, gentlemen, for these very fine, very remarkable chairs?'

Somewhere, someone said: 'Fiver ver lot!' and there came a smothered giggle from a group of Jews. Emmanuel's face was like a mask. His eyes were fixed on the red-faced man, who stiffened suddenly, evidently preparing to bid. Once again Emmanuel caught his eye, raised his finger and whispered: 'No!'

The blue eyes lost their twinkle, the man edged a little nearer. 'What?'

'No,' Emmanuel whispered again. 'They are no good. Leave t'em alone, if you please.'

'Good Gad!' The words came like a small explosion. 'Can you show me better ones?'

'Infinitely much better. Please follow me.'

With that he turned and walked from the sale-rooms. Walter Heriot, in recounting the story years afterwards to his grand-daughter Angela, said: 'Never looked back. Never doubted that I should follow him. That's what he's done all his life. Typical of him. I shall never know why I went after him. C'n see him now with that big soft hat, and the best-fitting coat I ever saw in m'life. That's how I met Emmanuel Gollantz!'

On the steps, Heriot burst into a flood of questions, never waiting for replies.

'What made y' stop me? Think I shall have lost 'em? 'Stonishing thing to do, just as the bidding started. Damme, I shall be annoyed if I've lost 'em, eh?'

Emmanuel smiled. He felt tolerantly amused. The man was obviously a fool; he might realize that no one but an expert would have dared to stop him buying those preposterous chairs.

'You did not need to hev followed me,' he said.

'Damme, I don't quite know why I did,' Heriot returned. 'Except'—he hesitated, then continued—'except that somehow I liked the look of you.'

Emmanuel bowed. 'I, also, if it might be said, liked the appearance of you very well. T'ose chairs are bad chairs. Maybe the smallest piece of the vood is Qveen Enne. They are vot are called—rrestorated chairs.'

The other man stiffened again, his face assumed a deeper, richer shade. 'God! I've got it! You're a dealer. Got chairs of your own to sell, I'll be bound.'

Emmanuel drew himself up and stared at the man, his face cold, his expression that of a man who sees something which disgusts him. That cold stare shook Walter Heriot badly.

'I rregret,' Emmanuel said. 'I spoke as von chentleman to another. I find my mistake a little late. I haf no Qveen Enne chairs, und I vish you a pleasant goot morning.'

With that he lifted his broad-brimmed hat, turned on his heel, and walked away towards the Strand. Heriot stared after him, his eyes starting, his mouth a little open. Then, cramming his catalogue into his pocket, he made after him as quickly as his bow legs would carry him.

'Here—I say,' he called. 'Hey! Don't go off like that.'

Emmanuel stopped, turned and stared at the scarlet-faced little man as if he had never seen him before.

Heriot continued to splutter out remarks. 'Here,' he said again. 'Half a minute. How was I to know that you weren't a tout—oh, damn, I ought to have known, I suppose. Made a damn' fool of myself. Look here—offer my apology. Shan't make the mistake again. Here's my card—again, accept m' apology.'

Emmanuel took the card, read the words engraved upon it. 'Sir Walter Heriot', and in the corner the mystic word: 'White's'. Then Heriot was talking again, asking if he'd take wine at 'The Roman's'. Again he was referring to his error. 'Let's forget my damn' silly mistake, shall we?'

'I hev entirely forgotten what occurred,' Emmanuel said. 'May

I, in rreturn, offer my card, und giff my name. I am Emmanuel Gollantz, late off Vienna, und now of dis city.'

'And—now don't fly out again, I mean keep your hair on—you are a dealer in antiques?'

'Indeed, yes, und in tecoration, und golt und silfer—yes.'

'Have you got some good chairs?'

'I hef told you, Sir 'Eriot, no. I hev seen them in Carter's of Pond Street. Perfect! He esks a hundred and fifty for four.'

'Carter don't employ you?'

Emmanuel, amused and smiling, shook his head.

'But,' Heriot continued, 'you'll want commission or whatever you call it?'

'Thet hed not occurred to me. You see, I did not meet you in business. I permitted myself to speak mit you. I vatched you. I t'ought, dot is a man vot likes rreal t'ings. O'der t'ings, he can't digest t'em. T'ere, Sir Heriot, you hev my explaining and apology.'

'Very handsomely said! Be Gad! And now we might have a look at these chairs, and afterwards will you do me the honour of lunching with me. And, by-the-by, call me Sir Walter, or just Heriot, not Sir Heriot, will yer?'

A few days later Heriot came to Campden Hill. He confided that he was about to be married to the most beautiful girl in England, and that he wished the house to which he would take her to be as beautiful as possible. Money did not matter, he'd pay whatever Emmanuel asked. The house was in Grosvenor Square; Emmanuel could do what he liked with it.

'Don't often have ideas,' Heriot added. 'Had one this morning. You want a sign. They all do. Here's the model for it.' He took Emmanuel's card from his pocket. 'Bigger, of course, but like that.'

Later he told his friends that he had found an honest Jew. 'And when a Jew is honest,' he added, 'damme, if he isn't the honestest fellow on earth. This chap—Gollantz—is as handsome as a picture, straight as a bit of string, and proud as Lucifer. And, b'Gad, he's got a manner that 'ud carry him anywhere. It's going to carry him as far as my dining-table, and into m' wife's drawing-room at all events.'

Outside Heriot's mansion in Grosvenor Square, among the ladders and scaffolding, was displayed a particularly neat board, fashioned like a giant's visiting-card, upon which was inscribed: 'Gollantz, Decorations and Furnishings. 92 Campden Hill.'

II

Walter Heriot brought others. He dragged all his family and
relations to Campden Hill, until the place seemed to swarm with
Wilmots, Drews, Harringays, and Busfords. Tall women in well-
made country clothes, with voices grown loud through living in
the hunting-field and talking with the wind in their teeth, moved
through the rooms ; elderly men in tweeds came asking for 'something suitable for a weddin' present. Third cousin. One of the
Gloucestershire lot'. Heriot brought his brother-in-law, William
Drew, a tall thin fellow with a long upper lip, who watched Emmanuel as if he expected him to try to sell him a fake if he wasn't
careful, and who, before he left, said in his precise lawyer's voice:
'Many thanks, Mr. Gollantz, I am very greatly obliged to you. If
you'll dine with us, my wife will write and suggest an evening.'

Heriot rubbed his hands over every sale, standing before the
big Adam mantelpiece which Emmanuel had picked up for a
song, swaying backwards and forwards on his toes.

'Business not too bad, eh? The English contingent came up to
the scratch very nicely, eh?'

'Indeed, yes. And how charming they are, t'ese people. Every
day my edmiration for your rrace grows.' Then, laying his hand
on Heriot's shoulder, he added: 'How gled I em thet ve hed that
—rrow—on the steps of 'Ammet's, my dear frriend.'

Despite his acquaintances, despite the fact that every month
his profits increased, Emmanuel was conscious of a certain loneliness. These people liked him, he was welcomed by both Jews
and Gentiles—and he never realized how these somewhat conventional English people flew in the face of all their social laws
by inviting him to their houses—but he remained very much
alone. True, his manners were charming, his conversation was
reasonably amusing, and his appearance was beyond reproach.
Women smiled on him, men liked him, but he was conscious that
he longed for a more intimate relationship. His love affairs had
been tinged with romance, even his lighter relationships had been
colourful, and he missed both romance and colour.

He loved women ; all his life he had admired them, talked to
them, and made easy love to them. Much of his love-making
had been nothing more than verbal, but he had enjoyed paying
compliments, had liked sending flowers and notes to the object

of his momentary devotion. The fact that both he and the woman lacked serious feeling had not detracted from his pleasure.

These Englishwomen, even the English Jewesses, were so friendly, so cool to Emmanuel their attitude seemed almost boyish in its lack of emotion. They talked to him, they played to him, they sang to him ; when the occasion demanded it, they wrote notes to him, but it was all done so frankly and openly. Their nice eyes met his without a trace of embarrassment, their hands touched his so honestly that it was impossible to increase the pressure of his own fingers.

'You are all so frriendly,' he said to Rachel Leon one evening.

'You don't want us to be—unfriendly, Emmanuel, surely?'

'No, no.' He hesitated. 'But you never indulge in—rromantic intrigues?'

'I don't know. I suppose some women do. An intrigue of any sort would worry me to death. Sighs, notes, meetings, artificial heartaches. No, I don't think you'll find much of that sort of thing in England.'

'Artificial, perhaps,' he admitted. 'I see nothing objectionable in the artificial—if it is vell done. I feel so often dot ven I talk mit Eengleesh ladies—vimmen, I beg your pardon—dot I talk mit verry nice young poys! To—philander—ven both know dot it is philandering, is like dancing down a pat'vay of prrimrroses. Delightful!'

Rachel, handsome, clever, and already growing much too stout, because she preferred poring over books to taking exercise, made a movement of impatience. 'Pah! Sometimes you annoy me, Emmanuel. Dwelling on these small, unimportant, trivial things.'

His air of amusement died suddenly. He nodded gravely, and she thought how handsome he was, and wondered if he would ever love her as she loved him. She wished that women had the freedom she so longed for, and that she might tell him all that he meant to her.

'Rachel, my dear frriend,' he said, 'life is made up of leetle t'ings. Everyt'ing which hes heppened to me dot hes been important has sprung from leetle t'ings. I came to England because I loved the English. Vot made me love them? Von day an English lady offered me the tea-cake instead of—buttered toast. Vhy do I tecorate der house of all der Trews und 'Eriots und Veelmots. Because Valter und I hed a qvarrel over some faked chairs? Von day I shall merry, and love my vife beyond all t'ings. Believe me, it vill all begin mit leetle t'ings.'

He saw love as something of wondrous beauty, something which he had glimpsed once and once only, something which had faded and died the day Caro chose Stanislaus when she might have chosen Emmanuel Gollantz. The memory had ceased to give him pain ; all that he felt was regret that love tarried so long, that the best years of his life were passing and were spent alone.

Gradually he came to immerse himself more and more in his work, because whilst lacking love, he was still conscious that he longed for the intimate society of women. He grew to be a little afraid of the dark-eyed daughters of his Jewish friends, of the blue-eyed daughters of his Gentile acquaintances. The fear grew, and became a real and vital thing.

'I will not go so often to their houses,' Emmanuel decided. 'I like them so much, I admire them so whole-heartedly that one day my liking, my admiration, and my longing for love will betray me. I shall rush headlong into some marriage which will hold nothing more than those things, respect and—safety. Rachel is right—Rachel is so often right. To philander is unworthy, it is like conducting serious business matters with imitation money. Not very bad, if both of you agree that you do not object to imitation money, but stupid, foolish to say the least of it.'

So he refused invitations, and even when he accepted them shunned the women he liked and admired. Men said that he was a serious fellow, and women wondered if he had suffered some reverse in a love affair.

'You are the only woman he really talks to, Rachel,' Mrs. Davis, who fancied that her pretty daughter Elizabeth looked kindly on Emmanuel, said with some sharpness.

'Talks to me, yes,' Rachel answered. 'That is because he likes me so much that he will never want to marry me. I hold no romance for Emmanuel. He is the incurable romantic.'

It was in early March that Lady Heriot brought the Countess of Crawley with her to Campden Hill. The Countess was like an illustration from a Book of Beauty, fair-haired, blue-eyed, with a skin like the petals of a magnolia flower. Her husband, Herbert Sholto Ulric Brassington, fifth Earl of Crawley, was sixty and looked more ; Alice was twenty-six and looked less. He was unpleasant to the sight, to the ear, and his affection for strong waters made him equally unpleasant to the sense of smell. She had married him because she longed to be Countess of Crawley, and her dislike and repulsion had grown daily.

Emmanuel met them, gave them his whole and undivided attention, discovered that Alice Crawley really understood beautiful embroidery and loved exquisite needlework.

Maude Heriot lisped: 'Alith—Lady Crawley ith tho clever about thethe old things.'

Emmanuel replied that he would do his best to interest Lady Crawley, and prepared to turn out his chests, drawers, and cupboards. Alice Crawley, watching him, decided that he was like 'Ernest Maltravers' and hoped he was wicked. She was very bored with Crawley.

Their fingers touched as they examined an old cope, Alice blushed, and Emmanuel felt his good resolutions shake. How soft her fingers were, and how admirably her dress—all ruched and flounced—of stiff, pale-blue silk, became her. Undeniably stupid —but utterly charming.

'I shall come again, Mr. Gollantz.'

'I shall scour London to find t'ings vich veel interest your ladyship.'

She came very often. Emmanuel kept his word, and parcels of dim old silk, fragile lace, and embroidery stiff with gold thread, passed from Campden Hill to Portman Square. Alice returned what she did not want, and explained her likes and dislikes in notes written in her elegant Italian hand. She spoke and wrote German fluently, and Emmanuel replied in that language. The affair was one after his own heart, light, not particularly serious, played with heads rather than hearts—or so he believed.

Then—someone suspected, someone whispered to Crawley, and not Alice but her lord drove to Campden Hill one morning, to find Emmanuel Gollantz sipping coffee and delicately spreading a fresh roll with honey. Crawley, scarcely sober after the previous night's potations, looked more unpleasant than usual. Emmanuel rose and offered his visitor coffee. Crawley shuddered visibly. Emmanuel protested that his housekeeper made the only perfect coffee in London.

Crawley lost his head a little. He blurted out what he suspected, what—for it was obvious that he loved his wife—he feared. Emmanuel raised his eyebrows, shrugged his shoulders and expressed careful surprise that his lordship should listen to servants' gossip.

'If it's moonshine, why does she cry half the night?'

'Your lordship can answer thet qvestion better than I.'

'She refuses food——'

'These delicate creatures have variable appetites.'

The light tone stung the peer. He forgot that he was speaking to a tradesman, a fellow he had boasted that he would horsewhip when he met him. Emmanuel towered above him, for Crawley was the smallest peer in England.

'Her door is closed against me!' he shouted. 'Damme, she refuses me entrance to her room! I'm her husband, I have my rights——'

Emmanuel, watching him, thought: 'My poor Alice,' and felt almost tenderly towards her.

'It's pretty obvious to me that she's in love with another man, and that man is——'

For the first time Emmanuel moved. He held up his hand enjoining silence. 'My lord, please—I must refuse to listen. I suggest that if, as you say, her ladyship closes her door against you, that she is merely proving vat I have always believed, what I have gathered in my business dealings with her—that she is a woman of fastidious taste.'

Crawley spat into a fine cambric handkerchief. 'Damned offensive! Blasted Jew furniture-dealer! I'll have you hounded out of town.'

Suddenly Herbert Crawley experienced that strange sensation which had once been felt by Theodore Dietrich, by Max von Habenberg, and by Walter Heriot—the queer feeling that he was the inferior of this tall young Jew with the cold eyes.

'The offence, my lord,' Emmanuel said smoothly, 'lies with you. You enter my house, invade my privacy, and offend my sight, my hearing, and my sense of smell—I detest brandy at ten in the morning! Your vife is my esteemed patron, I am her sincere admirer. I always admire people whose knowledge of sixteenth century needlework is—profound.'

'They tell me that she is discussed in the clubs——'

'She is a very beautiful woman——'

Crawley caught his arm: Emmanuel drew back, he disliked being touched. 'No, don't pull away.' The man was almost whimpering. 'Tell me, give me your oath that my wife has never been unfaithful to me—with you.'

Emmanuel was brushing his sleeve where the other's hand had rested. He did not look up for a moment; when he did it was to meet Crawley's red-rimmed eyes very steadily.

'Lord Crawley, I am ashamed for you,' he said gravely.

The drink-sodden face puckered, the man looked like a frightened child. 'My God, I didn't mean to say that. I apologise,

302

Mr. Gollantz. I tell you I'm half crazy for her. I love her f.
tically.'

'Then go and apologise to her ladyship.' Then, more kindly
'For your prrivate ear—I am to be married in less than a month.
Lord Crawley, may I vish you a very good morning?'

Later that evening a lady in a hired carriage drove to Campden
Hill. Emmanuel received her; she wept and he comforted her.

'He said,' she sobbed, 'that you were going to be married in a
month.'

'I am.'

'To whom?'

'That I cannot tell you. I do not know. I shall be merried in
a month's time, thet is all I know.'

She stared at him, her blue eyes wide and startled. 'Heartless!
I think that you wish me to break my heart.'

He lifted her hand to his lips. 'No, only to safeguard you from
evil tongues. I can only do this by—offering you so small a
sacrifice.'

'But we have done nothing—wrong!'

He looked at her, his handsome face grave and very kindly.
For the first time he felt that he did not want to lose her. She
was right. It had all been innocent enough—a few letters, flowers,
whispered talks, one or two kisses. How pretty she was, and how
horrible to think that she was yoked to a drunken brute like
Crawley.

'No, nothing,' he said. 'But you are a beautiful voman, I am
young. I have been playing with fire. It may be thet I am a
coward, and thet now I run away for fear of suffering pain.'

Her tears dried, she twisted in her chair. 'I don't believe that
you ever loved me; you are glad that this has happened.'

He thought: 'In one moment she will begin to talk like Maria,
and I shall hate her.' Aloud he said: 'You know only too vell thet
is not true.'

As he put her into her carriage, bent over her hand for the
last time, he sighed. It was a relief that it was over. As he turned
back to the house he murmured: 'The last time I will ever write
letters. I have been a fool—an unworthy fool. Rachel is right.
Romance is too fine a name for it. Never again! I will marry and
settle down.'

During the next forty-eight hours Emmanuel gave the matter
of his marriage careful consideration. He was already on the
way to becoming a rich man. He had no particular wish to marry,

his sense of chivalry, his wish to safeguard Alice Crawley had
ade him make the promise, and he was determined to keep it.
t was the least he could do to atone for the mistake he had made.
He knew, too, that it would mean safety. He knew his own weakness, realized his romantic love for women, and beautiful women
in particular. Marriage would mean safety not only for Alice,
but for himself. He had dreamed of a perfect marriage—one in
which passion, devotion, admiration, and romance should all
play their part. That must go. He would marry some delightful
girl, he would make her a good husband, a faithful husband. His
lovely tender dreams must go.

'I told Rachel,' he thought, 'that my life has always hinged
and turned on small things. Here is another proof—a lofe affair
which held nothing more serious than some stupid letters and a
few kisses, is small enough. As for my lord of Crawley—he cannot be more than five feet two!'

5

HE REVIEWED the various young women he knew calmly and
dispassionately. It was typical of the man that he was able to
realize, without any conceit, that there existed several personable
girls who would be more than willing to cast in their lot with his
own. They had shown him that they liked him ; they had done
more—they had demonstrated plainly that he attracted them,
and Emmanuel Gollantz would have despised himself, and have
deplored a false modesty which blinded him to this fact.

He knew that he liked several of them, and at the moment love
did not play any part in his plans. He believed that he could
make some woman happy. He was prepared to work hard, to be
generous, and rigidly faithful. He would make what was tech-
nically known as a good husband. In addition, he would be keeping his promise to Lord Crawley, and making atonement for his
folly with regard to Crawley's wife.

His lips twisted suddenly, as he reflected that he was paying
a considerable price for Alice Crawley's smiles, three-cornered
notes, and those kisses which had meant so little. Then he looked

the facts more squarely in the face, and admitted—since honesty was part of the man—that he was not contemplating marriage solely from a sense of chivalry towards Alice.

'I am too romantic, I am too susceptible to beauty, I allow myself to embark on these affairs too light-heartedly. If I were merely a cold-blooded rake, it would matter less. I should take what pleasures offered, and when they ceased to be pleasures and become obligations, I should throw them off—and forget. I begin lightly, and gradually allow myself to sentimentalize over women. Max once said—dear Max!—that love was a kind of fever, that with it went an increase in temperature. His temperature went down easily. Mine rises as time goes on. That is really a hopeful sign. I may not love anyone at the moment, but it is possible that after marriage, with knowledge, with companionship, love will come.'

He rose from his great carved chair and began to pace the room restlessly. 'What nonsense!' he thought. 'How can love come slowly; how can it creep in like the tide when, if it is real, it catches and sweeps one along like a torrent. I am becoming a sophist! Let me at least be honest with myself. I had hoped one day to find someone who would be to me what Caro was in those few first days—those days when life was wonderful, when every colour was intensified, when every hour spent with her flew past like a moment, and every hour passed without her dragged itself out into a year. When to think of her made my heart beat more quickly, when to catch sight of her as she passed in her carriage made me shake like a man with ague. When Johann's waltzes were poor, pale, colourless things compared with her voice.

'She was ugly—my Caro—but her ugliness was more charming than the beauty of other women. That passed—we ended it all, laughing, while I climbed over her balcony. I had always dreamed of a love which should remain perfect, romantic, and yet faultlessly real. Well, I shall never find it now. I have myself and my own weakness to blame.' He sighed. 'Still, it must be possible to live quite happily outside the gates of Paradise!'

He returned to his chair, and unfolded the fringed napkin which lay beside his breakfast plate. He poured out his coffee—the only perfect coffee in London—and felt a thrill of pleasure at the gloss on the tall Dresden coffee-pot, and the smaller, covered milk jug. His rolls were hot and crisp, the butter was hard and its colour pleased him. Very delicately he split the crescents of bread, and leant forward to lift the cover from the little jar of

305

honey. Again he sighed, this time with satisfaction. China, shining silver, golden honey and yellow butter, white crisp bread—all these might be small things, but they added materially to the pleasures of life.

As he sipped his coffee he reviewed the women he knew. There was Rachel Leon. How clever she was—perhaps too clever. Her ideas were so advanced ; she thought that women had a right to be doctors, lawyers, and so on. She even talked of the time when they should sit in Parliament. Why did they want to sit in Parliament, he wondered, when there were so many other more pleasant places! How queer women were! No, Rachel was too clever. She laughed at him, mocked his small dignities. There had been times when Rachel annoyed him seriously. In addition, she was allowing herself to get much too fat.

Miriam Bernstein. He shook his head. Too pious, too *froom*. Her life was spent observing fasts and feasts, she worried over small ceremonies. Emmanuel was proud of his race, he accepted its moral laws with an easy tolerance. He went to *shule* twice a year, he kept *Yom Kippur*, and only a few weeks ago he had sent money to Vienna for prayers to be said for his uncle Ishmael Hirsch. At the same time he had written stating that he never wished to communicate with any of the family again, and that should they write to him their letters would be returned unanswered.

No, Miriam Bernstein ought to marry a rab. Religion, carried to excess, made women tedious. It affected their complexions, he shouldn't wonder. Look at Adah Lewis. There was a nice kind woman, intelligent, and not weighed down by religion, but she was dreadfully sallow. Her teeth were not good, and he fancied that her ankles were thick. No, emphatically not Adah Lewis.

He pushed away his plate, took out his cigar-case and selected a cigar with care. The decision was more difficult than he had anticipated. True, there were Drews, and Wilmots—but in his heart there existed a doubt as to whether those families would welcome a Jew into their circle. Gwendoline Drew was a handsome girl, so was her sister, but he doubted if they would accept a Jew, and an Austrian Jew at that.

Again he turned back to the women of his own race—Cohens, Levis, and Salamons. None of them attracted him. They giggled, they were too elaborate as to clothes, their taste in jewellery was bad. . . .Then his face cleared. He paused, his coffee-cup half-way to his lips. How stupid he had been! He had forgotten the most charming of them all—little Elizabeth Davis, the daughter of Reuben Davis, the notary. His smile deepened as he made a mental picture of her. Small, with smooth dark hair parted in the middle and drawn down on either side of her heart-shaped face. Her eyes, liquid, gentle, and yet full of intelligence. He doubted if she was intellectual—but did he really want to marry an intellectual woman! Elizabeth liked his antiques, admired his pictures—though he doubted if she really cared much for them, suspecting that she preferred the Landseer and those crowded pictures by Frith.

The Davis's were sufficiently wealthy to have given Elizabeth a good education. She played the piano and sang a little, in a small bird-like voice. As Emmanuel thought of her, he was conscious that his heart became almost tender towards little Elizabeth. When could he see her?

He consulted his engagement-book—everything was happening for the best. He was to dine with her family in their big house at Westbourne Terrace that very evening. He would ask Elizabeth to marry him as soon as he had mentioned his ambition to her father. In a month she would be Mrs. Emmanuel Gollantz—he would have kept his word, he would have married a charming, attractive girl, and he would have safeguarded himself against his own too romantic proclivities.

That night he dressed with more than his usual care. More than once he sighed as he dressed, and then rebuked himself for sighing. How very foolish he was—still hankering after romance, passion, instead of realizing that warm affection and mutual respect would probably wear better and last longer. He eyed his severe breastplate of stiff white linen with disfavour, and thought with regret of his frilled shirts. He disliked the cut of his waistcoat—these English tailors cut them too high—and what an idiotic habit it was to 'stuff a handkerchief into the top of the waistcoat, with a rigid fold displayed. The coat was not sufficiently waisted, it lacked elegance. 'Some day, when I can afford to be considered eccentric, I will go back to my own style of dressing.'

He looked at his reflection and sighed again. 'Some day' . . . It sounded so long, so endless, that it depressed him. His mind went back to his splendid grandmother Miriam, with her eccentricity, her wit, and her massive beauty. He thought with tenderness of his father and mother—how kind his father had been, how good, how honest in all his dealings. How attractive his mother had looked; he could recall so plainly how her curls had swung and twisted when she talked excitedly. Maria, her queer, dried-up husband. Caro—at that moment he regretted Caro with an intensity which was almost painful. Gustave, Strauss, and Max, his dear, dear Max, who had given his life in defending the ruler of that 'tin-pot Empire'. These people belonged to his life in Vienna, that beloved town where men could laugh at serious things, and be immensely serious over trifles. Life flowed past quickly smoothly, easily in Wien.

He picked up a white gardenia, and placed it in the lapel of his coat, leaning forward again to peer into the glass to make sure that the flower was perfectly fresh, that it had not begun to turn brown at the edges. He sprayed his hair and small side whiskers with eau-de-Cologne, picked up a pair of new, white-kid gloves with one button, and sighed again. Life moved to a slower tempo in England. The very fact that cafés were unknown argued a radical difference in the temperament of the two nationalities.

He hesitated for a moment when it came to selecting a hat. There was his new opera hat, which collapsed when pressed against the bosom, the latest style. Emmanuel picked it up and twisted it in his sensitive hands, then put it aside. He might not be able to afford to be eccentric, but he would stick to his broad-brimmed hat! The last little bit of Vienna! His hat and wide, black cloak.

His housekeeper met him in the hall, and stared at him in admiration.

'Master, you look like a bridegroom.'

Emmanuel raised his hands. 'S-sh! The truth is sometimes hidden in a jest. Wish me *Mazal Tov*!'

In the road he picked up a hansom, and sat with his arms folded on the apron, dreaming and still a little sad. This was the end of a period of his life; after tonight everything would be just a little different. Firmly he meditated upon Elizabeth and her admirable qualities. Her musical ability, her excellent housekeeping, her kindness and gentleness, her essential goodness of heart. Again he sighed. He was going to be serious, successful, and sensible. He would have preferred to be gay, romantic, and just a little foolish.

He entered the room where the guests were assembled, where Miriam Davis stood, with Elizabeth beside her, beneath a great cut-glass chandelier. He lifted Miriam's hand to his lips, then turned to her daughter and repeated the gesture. He met her dark

eyes, saw that her lips were parted in a smile, and wished that ⌐
heart might have beaten just a shade more quickly at the sight o
her. It was perfectly steady.

Rachel Leon nodded and smiled to him. He joined her.

'You look like some young man in a Disraeli novel,' she said.
'All perfection and carefully trained personality. I am certain
that no one has ever dared to call you "Manny", have they?'

'My dear Rachel!' His eyebrows were raised. 'Never!'

Reuben Davis bustling about, shook Emmanuel's hand. 'How
are you? Pusiness goot, ches?'

Emmanuel thought: 'Why can't he speak German to me, when
his English is so deplorable?' He said: 'I should like very much
to hev a little word with you, later, if you permit.'

Mrs. Davis, with Elizabeth, joined them. 'So late we are!' she
grumbled. 'It is all because of the countess.'

'Who is this?' Emmanuel asked. 'What countess will this be?'

'She is Papa's countess,' Elizabeth said, speaking very fast, her
cheeks flushed a little. 'She is a client of Uncle Walter's in Paris.
She has come over to discuss the sale of some property with Papa.
She has brought boxes and boxes of clothes. Her boxes are all
very, very large, and her clothes are very beautiful. She is——'

Her father checked her. 'Elizabeth, vot a chen you make offer
anyt'ing. It's not'ing at all, dis countess. She is the vidow of Count
Leone Lara of Perus, Valter's important client. Not'ing, not'ing
at all, only a foreign title. Not der same as an English Countess.
No, I should say not. Qvite different!'

'But,' said Hermann Leon in his gentle voice, 'how infinitely
more romantic.'

'Pooh! Dese foreign titles—two for a penny.'

'Good value for the money then.'

Emmanuel nodded. He thought poorly of Reuben Davis, with
his scorn of titles. He knew that Reuben was delighted in his heart
that the two Leons, the rich Salamons and their daughter, Emmanuel Gollantz, and even young Bernstein—who stated that he
was going to change his name to Burns—should witness his
triumph. Reuben Davis, whose father had been Aron Diveker, a
poor notary in an obscure Polish town, loved a title, and his
scorn was just a little overdone. 'Inartistic,' Emmanuel thought.

He was watching Elizabeth, who was talking almost feverishly
to young Bernstein. Emmanuel disliked the fellow, thought him
vulgar and generally unpleasant, but something in Elizabeth's
face disturbed him. Could it be that he was too late? Could it be

309

at she had already promised herself to this tall, fair young Jew, who made no attempt to conceal his dislike of his own race. He saw her mother touch her arm, watched her turn away from Bernstein, and make her way towards him.

'Mama is so sorry that we should be delayed in this way, Emmanuel.'

He smiled. 'I shall not regret the delay if you will stay and talk to me.'

'But you must be growing so hungry!'

'Some things are so delightful that they make one forget hunger.'

She laughed softly. He had pleased her, but her eyes still followed Bernstein. Emmanuel began to feel that he detested the man!

'You must not laugh, Elizabeth,' he said. 'I am speaking seriously to you. You look very charming tonight. Particularly charming.'

'Do I? I'm glad of that.'

'But you're too serious—even though you laugh at me. Why are you so—so detached?'

She turned to him suddenly, impulsively. 'Emmanuel, it is so difficult. I am not very happy, I am disturbed. Please forgive me. It will pass and—oh, there is the countess at last.'

There was a little stir near the door; Isaac the butler muttered something inaudible. A woman entered, and caught Miriam Davis's hands in her own. Emmanuel could hear her protesting, in a warm, husky voice, that she was terribly ashamed.

'My maid, poor, half-witted thing, demented after the Channel crossing, mislaid all my chemises. They have only just been found. I contemplated coming down without one, but there remained the problem of what to wear instead. Not that its absence would have been apparent, but the moral effect—on me—might have been disastrous.'

Miriam Davis was obviously shocked. Reuben's face was scarlet. Young Bernstein stretched his thick neck in his high collar and coughed. Both the Salamons were examining an Empire clock with overdone attention. Little Elizabeth whispered: 'Oh! How could she!' Emmanuel felt a sudden spasm of irritation shake him. He turned, caught Rachel Leon's eyes and laughed outright. The countess swung away from Mrs. Davis and faced him.

This time he had no doubt as to the steadiness of his heart. It had not only fluttered, it seemed to him to stop beating for some seconds. He felt breathless, as if he had been submerged by a great wave which swept over him. Her long, narrow eyes danced as they met his, the pencilled eyebrows, arched so perfectly above the eyes, were slightly mocking. Her mouth was wide, generous and full lipped, the parted scarlet lips showing very white, strong teeth. Her nose was short and broad at the nostrils. Her ash-blonde hair was curled in little ringlets all over her small head. She stared at Emmanuel, surprised, amused, and arrogant.

'You agree that it was a catastrophe?'

He bowed. 'On such apparent trifles the fate of empires rest.'

'I assure you that it was found—they were all found.'

'The world has ceased to shake.'

Then Reuben bustled forward, offered his arm to the countess, and they went in to dinner. Emmanuel found himself on her left, with Elizabeth on his right. He tried to talk to Elizabeth, tried to remember that this evening was important, because he was going to ask her to marry him. He almost laughed aloud. How utterly ridiculous! He was going to marry the woman with the husky voice, the queer long eyes who talked in public of her lost chemises. While he listened to Elizabeth's long story of some play which she had seen, he heard, in reality, nothing but the husky voice on his left. When at last Elizabeth turned to speak to Horace Bernstein, Emmanuel, with his eyes on his plate, felt that he might listen to that voice in peace.

'Are you very stupid or only hungry?' the soft voice demanded suddenly.

'Certainly not very hungry, I hope not very stupid, but I am terr-ribly rromantic.'

'Do you find romance on your plate then? That is where your eyes have been for the last five minutes.'

'No, I kept them there so that I might listen more intently.'

'To what, please?'

He lifted his eyes and met hers, still dancing with amusement. 'I might dare to tell you, if I was not quite certain that you know.'

She laughed. 'I should not have blamed you. What good food this is. The French understand the art of cooking, the Jews the art of eating.'

'You are a Jewess?'

'Oh yes.'

She turned back to Reuben Davis, and Emmanuel began to talk to Elizabeth again. She thought that she had never known

311

him so gay, so amusing. She wondered if Papa and Mama were right, if he really wanted to marry her as they said they suspected that he did? She wished they would leave her alone, to marry Horace Bernstein, who was not so handsome, but so much more human. Still—Horace was not looked on with favour, and if she must marry Emmanuel Gollantz, he would certainly make a very handsome husband.

Emmanuel thought: 'How I am talking and talking! I am excited. I have come to life. I have wanted romance, and here it is! I shall live it for the rest of my life. It will be exciting, exhilarating. There will be cool shades, hot plains, mountains which one will scale with difficulty; there will be storms, tempests, and long stretches of sheer, quiet beauty. I want to stand up now, take her hand, and tell them all that we are going to be married. I wonder if she has realized it too? I wonder if she is glad, as I am? Perhaps she has been searching, seeking love, and here it is in Reuben Davis's dining-room. I am glad that I decorated and furnished it —the whole house is my work. I am satisfied that our love should be born in a beautiful place. Red velvet and modern gilt might have killed it. Poof! What am I saying? Nothing could kill it. It is too real, too vital.'

Later, the countess wandered round the big room with her host, speaking to his guests, smiling, and laughing softly. Only when she reached the brocade-covered sofa where Emmanuel stood beside Rachel Leon, did she take the seat which he offered her.

'Ah! That is very pleasant, Mr. Davis, I must not keep you from your charming friends. I will stay here and talk for a little to Miss Leon. She will forgive me if I am dull. I am just a little tired after my journey.'

Emmanuel stood before her, making his stiff little bow when he addressed her. Rachel Leon thought that she had never seen him so attractive, never seen him look so handsome. Even his queer, stilted English seemed to hold a fascination. He listened with great gravity while the countess told him that her great wish was to see London.

'I wish to see this city above all things,' she said. The Tower, the Houses of Parliament, Westminster Abbey, even Madame Tussaud's Waxwork Exhibition in Baker Street were things she wished to see. It appeared that she had a passion for English history, and, 'these things are part of it. Mr. Davis tells me that he knows nothing of them. I must find an escort.'

Rachel pointed to Emmanuel. 'Here is the man. No English-man knows more of the famous places of London than he does. Why, he even knows his way to the British Museum and the National Gallery.'

'It might bore him,' the countess said. 'He looks as if he might be bored very easily.'

Emmanuel protested that nothing could give him so much pleasure as to escort her wherever she wished. He did not state that the Houses of Parliament were no more to him than a Gothic outline against the sky, that the Tower was something of which he had heard but never seen, and that the National Gallery and the British Museum were merely places which were useful for reference in his business.

'Tomorrow morning will suit you, Mr. Gollantz?'

'Admirably. Shall I call for you at eleven? And if I might suggest that we lunched somewhere, then we could continue our explorations during the afternoon without interruption.'

He was conscious that the Davises watched him with cold eyes, that young Bernstein wondered what he was going to try to sell the Frenchwoman, and that Hermann Leon's eyes twinkled. He cared nothing; he remained unmoved, smiling, and cool.

Later he drove Hermann and Rachel home to their tall house in Bloomsbury. As he left them, he held Rachel's hand, saying: 'Dear Rachel, perhaps you recall an old paste r-ring which you gr-reatly admired the other day at my gallery. It will be sent to you in the morning, with my love. Tell me, before I go, hev either of you a book on the Tower of London? Also vat is the Tower of London, and how does one r-reach it?'

Hermann said: 'I have no book, and neither will you need one. There are picturesque guides who will tell you everything—leave it to them. Any hackney driver knows the way, and will take you there. As for what it is—it is a state prison of great antiquity.'

'Dear God!' Emmanuel said piously. 'Why should von vish to visit a prison? Still—again, I thank you both.'

Rachel caught his sleeve as he turned away.

'Emmanuel, my dear,' she whispered. 'Walk, don't slide.'

He laughed softly. 'Too late, Rachel. I hev fallen already.' He dismissed his cab and walked home through the quiet streets. He felt utterly content. He had no fears that Juliana Lara might refuse him when the time came. He had known, when their eyes first met, that she was his destiny.

'To think,' he mused, 'that only this evening I sighed for ro-

313

mance, looked back upon Wien with regret! And all the time she was here, in London, in the house of Reuben Davis—trying to find her chemise! I wonder if she had been in time, and I had been a little late, how things might have turned out? Oh, they would have been exactly the same. This is too big, too stupendous to be affected by small things. This is reality, and from tonight I begin to live.'

He had reached Campden Hill, and realized that he was terribly tired. He opened the door and said softly: 'I must find another house. Juliana cannot live so far out of the West End.' Then closing the door behind him he turned off the light and walked up the wide old stairs, swinging his broad-brimmed hat in his hand.

6

THREE days later, Juliana Lara visited the house on Campden Hill. She was escorted by Mrs. Davis, who disliked old furniture and works of art, and who almost immediately sought out Emmanuel's German housekeeper to obtain a recipe for pickling herrings, leaving them alone together.

Emmanuel showed Juliana his treasures. She was interested, she was very intelligent. Twice she opposed his opinion, and each time he was forced to admit that she was right. His admiration grew with every tick of the English grandfather clock which stood in the corner of the long room.

Juliana examined a case of miniatures. 'How pretty they are. This—who is this? Lola Montez? Where did you get that?'

'It belonged, I believe, to my father. He bought it in Paris. I am very fond of it.'

She turned it over in her hand. 'Lola Montez,' she repeated. 'But see, there is another name written on the back—the ink is too faded to read it. I wonder what it means?' But her curiosity was not very deep, and she turned to others. 'Ah! Ninon l' Enclos. The most beautiful woman in the world—for ever the most lovely.'

314

'This time,' he said, smiling, 'I shall hold to it that you are wrong.'

'Authorities hold that she was.'

'I am an authority, I disagree. Their knowledge was limited.'

'So is yours——'

'Was,' Emmanuel corrected, 'until three days ago.'

She frowned. 'I hate flattery.'

He made a little impulsive movement towards her. 'Oh, but so do I. If what I try to say sounds like flettery, it is because I speak so badly. My heart wishes to say such beautiful t'ings, such—tr-rue t'ings. And instead I speak like a shopman, or an ector. For the first time in my life I wish that I was a poet.'

She sat down in the big, dark oak chair with its faded red velvet cushion from which long tassels hung, her hands on the arms looking strangely white against the old wood. Emmanuel stood before her. His arrogance, his assurance had left him. He might have been some subject standing before a great queen who granted him an audience.

'Emmanuel Gollantz,' Juliana said gently, 'I know what you are trying to say; I should be a fool to pretend that I did not know. You want to ask me to marry you——'

'I want first to tell you that I love you,' he said.

'Tell me,' she went on, ignoring his interruption, 'do you think that I could make you happy?'

'I only know that I cannot be happy without you. Surely the more important question is, could I make you happy?' Emmanuel said.

Juliana frowned. 'I have no illusions about the ability of anyone to make me happy. I doubt if any of us can make another person happy, though it may help materially if they believe that we can. We make ourselves happy. You believe that you cannot be happy without me. You love me—yes, I believe you do. Now let me speak quite frankly—I don't love you. I love no one except Juliana Lara. You attract me, you are very handsome, and I abhor ugly men. You are romantic—I like romance. I like to be made to feel that I am the personification of all that goes to make it. You are a Jew. But'—she held up her hand—'you are an Austrian Jew, I am a French one. Your French—and, thank God, I have only heard you try to speak it once—is deplorable. I am a countess, my family are aristocrats. I married an aristocrat, and you are a merchant. Now, what have you to say?'

'I am glad that you find me handsome, that you love romance,

315

for to me you are romance. I thought that I hed lost it, until that wonderful evening when I met you. French'—he shrugged his shoulders—'I vill begin to learn to speak it in a vay which will please you at vonce. Now, let me tell you somet'ing which escapes you. Love has a language of its own ; like music, it is internetional. I did not hope that you could love me—though I hope that you may do so one day.'

Juliana drummed with her finger-tips on the arm of her chair.

'And the rest? I don't know that I like you to be so humble. I admire arrogance. I thought that to be called a—merchant might have stung you into something like annoyance.'

'I admit that to hear you say that astonished me,' he said gravely. 'I have alvays held, alvays known, that every Jew is an aristocrat. If he falls short of the ideals and the behaviour of one, it is due to himself. Base Jews are base because they hev adopted a set of false values. Oh no, your title, your position, do not frighten me at all.'

She laughed. 'That is better. I understand that high-handed assumption better than humility. Go on, Emmanuel, give me some good reasons why I should marry you. It may be that I am only waiting to be convinced.'

The light in the long room was growing a little dim ; through the farther window the sky could be seen, already tinged with the scarlet and orange of an angry sunset. Here and there a slanting finger of light touched an ornament, the gilt frame of a picture, or the sheen on a piece of polished furniture. Emmanuel, tall and slim, stood there among the beautiful things which he had collected and allowed his eyes to wander from Juliana's vivid face to the things which he loved. Then, smiling a little, he turned back to her.

'Look,' he said, 'all these things belong to the past ; you belong to the present and you are my future. That is how my life has been. In it there are a grreat many t'ings, some good, some in-different, a few—I regrret—which were cheap and poor. All those t'ings belong to what is past, and yet they hev all gone to make up the Emmanuel Gollantz who is here before you now.

'I have bought and sold, I hev studied fine woods, I know a grreat deal about polishing furniture, restoring it, and even making it. But the most important t'ing is thet I have learnt to recognize beauty and to love it passionately. That is the one t'ing about me which maybe is vorth while—that is what I can offer

316

you now. Perhaps t'ose t'ings which were mean and paltry have slipped avay, I vill hope so.

'It was strange that just before you came into Reuben's drawing-room and into my life, I hed been trying to rearrange my life, because I felt that I was allowing myself to—this is a difficult vord—schlip. I was, I t'ink, losing some of my pride, accepting t'ings which were small and cheap, because that was the easy vay to take against somet'ing that I dread—loneliness. But, what I vish to say is this—I hed begun to rearrange my life before you came, it was as if I had already begun to sweep, to clean, to throw out small, unvorthy t'ings—t'ough I did not know for vhy.'

'I see,' she nodded. 'I wonder if you really had a premonition that I was coming. How strange if you had.'

'No, not that you were coming,' he said quickly. 'I must not pretend. I had almost plenned to esk another person to marry me. But that was the effect, not the cause.'

'Did you love her?'

He laughed. 'Not a leetle bit, but I would hev been a good husband.'

'Have you loved many women, Emmanuel?' Her tone was so intimate that he felt encouraged, as if she had assured him that his case was not hopeless.

'I once only t'ought that I loved someone. No, I am wrong, I did love her very dearly, with all my heart—as much of it as was awake in that day. I found out after a time that we hed both forgotten that we hed ever loved. We said good-bye, laughing a grreat deal.'

'Have you ever been very unhappy?'

He clenched his hands suddenly, and for a moment he did not reply. When he spoke his voice seemed to have taken on a deeper tone.

'T'ree times,' he said. 'Vonce when I saw my father lying dead. But he hed lived his life—it was terrible to lose him, but not terribly sed. Many years ago vhen I lost my brother, who was young and heppy and had a rright to live ; and again two years ago——' He shivered suddenly. 'Oh, that was abominable. That was my friend, Max von Habenberg, a very lovely young man, who was murdered through the wickedness of two old men.' He made a gesture as if he would push away the thoughts which crowded in on his mind. 'If you will not mind, we will not speak of t'ese t'ings. Please let me rreturn to what is uppermost in my mind. Look!' With a movement as if he swept all the contents of his gallery together, he went on: 'All my life I hev collected beautiful t'ings—it is unbearable that I should lose the only perfect thing that the whole world holds. Please marry me—marry me soon—I am a verry impatient man.'

She smiled, showing her strong white teeth. 'I am not easy, Gollantz. I demand a lover, not only a husband. Can you be both? Can you go on being my lover after you have become used to being my husband? I am older than you. Reuben told me how old you were. I have lived in a world where I had attention, admiration, adulation. Can you give me those things. Not the heavy, sickly attention that a German pays to his wife in public and forgets in private. Not the easy, proprietory attitude of the Frenchman, who keeps a mistress round the corner and accepts his wife's lover as his own best friend; and certainly not the stolid, respectable affection which Englishmen give to their wives. I shall not promise to be eternally faithful to you—I don't know. I know nothing with any certainty except that I will not, now or at any time, endure boredom. Will you promise never, never to bore me, never to allow me to be bored?'

'I am a man very much in love,' Emmanuel said, 'therefore I will promise anyt'ing; but what is more important, I shall try every day to keep my promise. Now, please may I have my answer, I am so impatient.'

She did not reply, but smiled and, turning, bent her attention upon the pretty things which lay on the table near her. She picked up several, handing them to Emmanuel, saying: 'I will have that,' and, 'I think that I will take this.' He fell into her mood, accepting what she gave to him, answering: 'Yes, that is Louis XIV,' or, 'This is from Vienna.' Only his face, suddenly white and a little drawn, betrayed him.

Juliana was still selecting the things which pleased her when Mrs. Davis entered.

'Have I kept you? I hope not. But it was so interesting. I wished to ask so many questions. Juliana, I hope that you have not been weary of waiting for me.'

Juliana Lara laid her hand on her friend's arm.

'Weary! I have been interested. So interested that I have persuaded myself that I wish to live among these beautiful things all my life.'

Miriam Davis laughed. Emmanuel's hand, resting on the back of a chair closed suddenly, the knuckles showing white.

'How amusing you are, Juliana!'

'No, no, I am serious. Emmanuel is making me a partner in the House of Gollantz. We are engaged to be married.'

'But when . . .' Mrs. Davis gasped.

Emmanuel stepped forward. His face had lost its expression of anxiety, he smiled easily. 'Next week we shall be married,' he said. 'Tomorrow we shall search for a suitable house to place the most beautiful thing the House of Gollantz is ever likely to possess.'

As Miriam Davis, half thrilled, half annoyed, swept down the steps to the waiting carriage, Emmanuel in the darkness of the hall caught Juliana in his arms.

'Oh, my beloved, my Rose of Sharon,' he whispered, 'I will take so much care of you always.'

Then, taking her hand in his, he led her down the steps and opened the door of the carriage. For a second he pressed his lips to the hand he held, then stood back, making his little ceremonious bow as the carriage drove away.

If you have enjoyed this book and would like to receive
details of other Piatkus publications please write to

Judy Piatkus (Publishers) Limited
Loughton
Essex